TOMINDA ADKINS
VESSEL
BOOK I • THE ADVENT

Year of the Tiger Press
Seattle, WA

Vessel, Book I: the Advent is a work of fiction. Names, places, and incidents either are products of the author's imagination or are used fictitiously. All trademarks used without permission in accordance with United States fair use and copyright laws. Characters and concepts are the property of the author.

Published by Year of the Tiger Press

Copyright © 2011 by Tominda Adkins. All rights reserved. No part of this publication may be reproduced or transmitted in any form or by any means, electronic or mechanical, including photocopy, recording, or any information storage and retrieval systems, without permission in writing from the publisher. Published in the United States by Year of the Tiger Press, Seattle, WA. Manufactured in the United States.

www.yearofthetigerpress.com
www.readvessel.com

ISBN 978-0-9830550-0-6

LCCN 2010938303

Typeset in Adobe Calson Pro
Book design and illustrations by Year of the Tiger Press
Edited by Beau Prichard

For Lindsey and Ashton.

"Let's get this road on the show already!"
—*Jesse Cannon, c. 2008*

VESSEL
THE ADVENT

ADVENT

Ghi cannot breathe.

It is his primary concern. He's been in a state like this before, or so he's been told. But this time around, he's thinking that his luck won't be so good.

Ghi is splayed out on the frozen concrete floor of a warehouse basement, not far from a flooding elevator shaft. Water pounds down from the level above, and fire roars in the stairwell. There is blood between his teeth. He is asking his limbs to move, but they are asking him for oxygen first.

And he can't give it. He can't pull any air in. It is wet and sticky where the air is supposed to be. The blood is gliding up his throat and filling his nostrils. He can feel it sloshing in his lungs, in all kinds of places it doesn't belong. There are broken ribs in there, he realizes. A bunch of them in a row, snapped clean and folded in neatly, like the frame of a parasail or the legs of a drawn-up, dead spider.

The Hollow moves closer and kicks him sharply in that spot, laughing into echoes. Ghi sees stars. He doesn't see his life flash by, and that's a real shame. He tries to validate the situation, tunneling back to the accessible parts of life. Thinks about how less than a month ago, his only duties were dry cleaning and bill paying. Water the plants. Doctor visits. Those kinds of things.

He wants to understand. He wants to jump back thousands of years to the unseen corner of creation where this supposedly all started, to make a connection, but he can't. It's all been so quick. So nonsensical. He doesn't know how he and the others ended up here. He can't make it fit.

Why us? is all he comes up with.

Ghi is supposed to be a hero. He is supposed to have something smart-ass or moving to say, or some ironic reflection on his mind as he dies. But let's face it: if he could breathe right now he would be screaming and begging for mercy.

PART I

CHAPTER 1

My name is Jordan Murphy, and I'm the fastest one-armed bartender in the world.

Or I used to be. These days, you won't catch me behind a bar. And the bar I used to work in, you couldn't find it if you tried. It wasn't on some busy street, with bold strangers stumbling in every night or polite regulars eventually working up the courage to ask what had happened to me. You couldn't slip in from a downpour, or run in with your wedding dress on and mascara-black tears in your eyes, sit down, and expect to hear how I lost my arm, like the beginning of some tired old movie.

I wouldn't have told you, anyway. Not there. Not over a couple of shots.

It's not that kind of story.

Telling it this way is easier. Writing it down, I mean. Everything I saw with my own eyes, and everything I was told about the rest—it takes a hell of a lot of time to get it all straight. It takes even more time to work up the energy to start. And god knows that these past couple of years, I've had more than enough time on my hand.

(*Hand.* Get it?)

Whatever. It's not like anyone else is going to tell you about it. And why am I? Hell if I know. Maybe I'm just bored. Maybe I'm bitter. Maybe I just feel like you *should* hear it, like there isn't any point to it all without your awareness of what happened, and your gratitude that it *did* happen. That could be it.

And one more thing: this isn't a story about my arm. We'll get to that part, sure. But trust me, a few missing pounds of bone and meat is totally beside the point, considering what I'm about to tell you. This story is about the air you're breathing, and the light of day you take for granted every morning. In this story, it's *your* life that's on the line, same as mine. The Vessel knew that from the very beginning. I only know it because I was stuck in the back seat for the entire ride. No one ever had to tell me about it, or ask me what I believed. I was there. I had to believe. There wasn't a choice.

Honestly, I guess that's why I'm telling it. And I guess that's really all I'm asking in return.

Just believe.

Exactly twenty days before Ghi found himself smashed to pieces on a filthy basement floor, he existed in two places at one moment in time: both in the Boston dry cleaners shop where he worked, and on the star-shaped platform surrounding the Statue of Liberty, which was inside the sudden epiphany of Corin Charles Livingston III, who happened to be breakfasting somewhere in Australia at the time.

That might actually qualify as three places. But no one's counting.

It's important to note that Corin didn't know he was thinking about Ghi. Not then. He simply could not have known, even though the dream which shocked him with sudden recall that morning was not a new one. Even though it had always played out the same, with him ascending the wide steps to the statue platform alone on a gray, frigid day. Even though Ghi and the others were always at the top, waiting for him.

He didn't know he was thinking about Ghi because he had never met Ghi. Even if he had, even if he had been familiar with Ghi's shrugged stance and his twisting, ink-black hair, Corin wouldn't have had enough time to recognize him in the dream. Because always, the moment he dream-jogged to the top of the dream steps and saw those dream strangers, the dream changed.

It changed to water.

A torrent would always replace the statue and the strangers, instantaneous and violent. It rushed to immerse him, filled his stomach, pounded into his ears. It drummed away in so many pitches that it sounded like frenzied singing, like a liquid opera reacting to a bomb threat. The feeling was fleeting and primal and terrific, both panic and pleasure in one single moment. Always just one moment.

And then he would be awake in his bed, or sometimes on the plane or in the hotel suite, heaving for air and feeling confusedly foreign among the crisp, dry sheets. Why should the sheets be anything but dry? Why were his ears ringing? And how had that pillow wound up against the far wall?

He was never sure when they'd started, these dreams. For such a long time, they simply dissolved into the subconscious murk, side-by-side with other dreams. Dreams of his mother, of Bangladesh, of walking into his old prep school totally naked. The usual. He would just catch his breath there in bed, wiping sweat and hair off his freckled forehead, and marvel at the implications. *Stress*, he would say to himself. *All this stress. I really ought to get myself to Barcelona for a week. Christ.* And all would be forgotten.

But that shiny morning in the Sydney Hilton, just as Corin was spreading jam on his toast, the dream from the night before ran—screaming and guns blazing—into the quiet saloon of his thoughts, thoughts which had been minding their own business and reviewing the day's upcoming conference schedule.

The dream butted aside the noon executive meeting, body-slammed the budget committee conference, and physically disrupted the routine of his butter knife. By the time a full coat of jam had been laid, the dream and all its clones had hijacked Corin's total attention. And so in the time he would have normally used to scan the *Wall Street Journal*, he stared at the tablecloth instead, chewing toast, straining to remember all of the dreams, or at least one of them, from start to finish.

Rushed and only fleetingly interested, he keyed the scant details—the statue, the waiting strangers, the water—into his trusty Sabre smartphone and then moved on to arrange the report materials. Cryptic, recurring dreams would simply have to wait. It was his last conference day on the coast, every hour of it packed, and he would be damned if it didn't end with a lengthy evening of surfing to cure all his troubles.

To be sure, Corin got everything he wanted that day (which is no surprise, really—he was the type of person who usually got what he wanted). Oh yes, he got that five-figure annual donation secured for his partners in Burma. He got the finest snapper sashimi he'd ever tasted and vintage cabernet. And he got his evening of memorably splendid surfing.

That night, however, the four people on the platform got faces.

The rushing water came too late. Corin had time to look, to see who was waiting for him, before the waves took him under, and from the moment he awoke, he couldn't get those blasted faces out of his head.

Faces. All the way to the airport in the morning, all the way through the flight, Corin felt fizzy and out of sorts. He questioned the sashimi and suspected the wine, but they were not to blame. It was those four faces which kept bubbling up to the surface of his thoughts, demanding to be noticed and named.

These were not people he knew or people he recognized—minus one queer exception. With a sense of horrified reluctance, he confirmed beyond a doubt that one of the figures was Russian-born pop sensation Jesse Cannon.

Which was not at all helpful. Unsettling, but not helpful.

The thought that he was dreaming over and over again about some airheaded celebrity was just as troubling as trying to determine the identities of the other three. They weren't public figures or forgotten business contacts or anyone else he could imagine slipping from his subconscious to his dreams. And yet there they were, familiar in a way that was downright *weird*, borderline spectral.

Luckily, Corin was not a man of superstition. If he had been, the presence of Lady Liberty would have been just as alarming as the familiar strangers and the famous pianist. Because the next flight on Corin's agenda, less than three weeks away, was taking him to his eighth consecutive New York City Marathon.

If that particular connection did cross his fevered mind that day, then he didn't give it much thought. Again, Corin was not a man of superstition, not at all. He was a man of logic and deduction. Which is why in the weeks to come he avoided most sushi, all Australian wines, and any music made by Jesse Cannon.

@

Also on that day, Stella Rosin was entering what could have been any Luna Latum facility on the planet, flanked at all times by two silent escorts, who were touching her elbows lightly. She was being guided this way because she could see nothing.

She had seen nothing, in fact, since she'd left her flat in Zurich six hours prior, not even the escorts who had rang her doorbell. Over her eyes and the crown of her head she wore a smoothly carved mask of black ebony. The eyes of the mask were timeless and empty, neither inattentive nor concerned, the eyes of a Renaissance sculpture. Their contours shielded comfortably over her own closed eyelids, keeping her in total darkness.

The mask had been worn since the moment the escorts had arrived for her, had been worn down to the waiting car, through the private air terminal, on the chartered flight and during the ride to the Luna Latum's largest complex, where she now walked steadily and observantly despite the handicap, her well-carried bones tingling.

Stella Rosin was used to this sort of thing.

She was also used to the slight hiccups in bystander conversation as she passed through the corridors. This did not irritate her, nor did it arouse in her any secret pleasure or sense of smug occupational specialness. Had there been a time when such feelings rose up in her? Had she been young and a little bit zealous once; had all the hush-hush ever made her just slightly giddy? Just slightly? Maybe?

I doubt it very much.

If Stella Rosin ever derived any excitement from her unique duties, then she expressed it only amongst her colleagues. Stella Rosin was a hunter, and I'm not talking about your typical gap-tooth, trigger-happy buck hunter, either. I'm talking about Luna Latum hunters. They're a whole different breed: precise, alert, unpredictable, and in my opinion, chilly as Otter-Pops.

And the thing they hunt? You're not ready for that yet.

Moving on.

The Luna Latum, in its purest definition, is merely a collection of secrets. Secrets that are handled carefully among its delicate web of members, and handled most carefully among its hunters. Strict limits have always been in place regarding what and whom hunters are allowed to see. Or hear. Or know.

Hence, the fancy ebony blindfold. Affectionately referred to as blinders, these ornaments symbolically shield the hunters from classified information. The blinder's primary purpose, however, is something else entirely. Something far more imperative to the life span of a hunter than mere decorum or organizational security. And what might that something be?

You're not ready for that yet, either.

My point is that there was no mistaking what Stella Rosin was, not in those lush, stuffy corridors. And so it's only natural that as she was guided along, blinded and thus distinctly marked, people watched with intense curiosity. They continued watching even as the clicking of her shoes on marble hushed on carpet. And when two enormous wooden doors closed behind her and they could no longer watch, their eyes shifted, their toes lingered, and their ears strained from out in the wings. Some of these people knew nothing about what was going on beyond those doors, while others may have had a faint clue of the details. Secrets, within more secrets. Such is the nature of the Luna Latum.

One thing was clear to all of them, however, something which would have been obvious to any Luna Latum employee present, down to the lowliest janitor.

Allow me to summarize in universal terms:

When a hunter is personally admitted to a meeting of the Consulate, it means that the shit is moving dangerously close to the fan.

Perhaps thousands of miles away, perhaps only twenty, Whitney Leroy Jackson watched himself jog through the park in front of the Statue of Liberty. He was almost to the top of the platform, almost ready for the usual avalanche of fluid sand, when the pealing of bells tore the sky in half, eroding all of this from mind and memory.

He shot up in bed and immediately got another shock—he hit his face on the ceiling.

"Every time!" he shouted, grabbing his smarting nose. "Every goddamn time!"

No one paid him any attention. It was still dark, maybe four or five in the morning, and everybody else was already up, rushing through the room. He jumped down off the bunk like the rest of them, got his bearings, moved into the line, slid down the pole.

Finding his spot on the wall, he jumped into his overalls and boots, got into his coat, all while focusing on what the chief was shouting. The fog of sleep was completely gone, the feeling had returned to his nose, and his blood was really flowing. Fire at the Filbert Penitentiary. He pulled his gloves on and climbed into the driver's seat.

You just can't beat this job, he thought. *You just can't beat it.*

The fire had started while the inmate Su Kim Khan was asleep and dreaming.

CHAPTER 2

And where was I on that day? I was sitting in the kitchen of a South Beach condo, writing my two weeks' notice, while the regrettably familiar sounds of Jesse Cannon's carnal deeds shook down from the second floor.

That's right. Jesse Cannon.

Yes. The Russian Opera darling turned Broadway sensation turned Hollywood explosion, Jesse Cannon. That one. Exotic accent. Golden throat. Irresistible lips. Zero discretion. A total vacuum.

Don't get me wrong. By the standards that be, Jesse Cannon was an absolutely mesmerizing singer, a groundbreaking pianist, a schooled dancer, and lord knows the man could entertain. A true artist in every sense. I hadn't been impressed so far by the feature film acting, but hey, I'm no critic. Just a personal assistant.

And I was fed up.

The way I see it, I had squandered nearly five golden years of my precious young life taking care of this tart. Most other women my age would've sacrificed a kidney—maybe both—to have my job. I spent practically every minute of every day with a two-time *People's* "Sexiest Man Alive". I have rubbed his shoulders. I have rubbed his feet. I have mixed thousands of drinks and walked many miles looking for the correct bottled water, to deliver the dry cleaning, to find misplaced designer sunglasses. I have cleaned up after exotic pets. I've fought off sharp-nailed groupies. I've been his unwilling partner in white water rafting, in bikram yoga, in strange diets, in rock climbing, in bungee jumping, and some things I have forced myself to forget. I've nursed him through every illness, enabled every bad habit, and coached him through every break down, freak out, bad trip, and conniption fit since day one.

And yes. I have seen him naked. Please stop asking.

It was just before sunrise when I pulled the notice from the grip of my portable inkjet printer, eager to sign and date it. The noises from upstairs were beginning to transition from thuds and screams to footsteps and conversation. Which meant it was time to call a cab. I paced around for a few minutes and then started chopping papayas. I knew what I was doing.

The cab arrived just as the sun was starting to peek out of the sea, casting its glinting, orange light across the water and into the floor-to-ceiling picture windows, which bore many interesting smudge marks from the night before. I grabbed a grapefruit from the stainless steel fridge, and my phone rang.

It was Jesse's agent, Margot. The bitch. She *would* call from Tokyo, knowing it was six in the morning here. I wedged the phone against my shoulder and started to answer her questions, how the tour was going, if Jesse had signed the most recent contracts she'd emailed, whether we'd seen the new cologne ad or not, because apparently it had sparked some kind of Catholic outrage.

I interjected a "yep" whenever necessary and peeled grapefruit while pretending to write down details for February's Japan performances (a few months away still, and I had the dates memorized already). With my free ear, I could hear the sounds of two very satisfied fans coming down the stairs, a pair of stragglers from the night's impromptu after-party. They stopped in the entryway and looked at me expectantly, like they always do, and I paused Margot with a sigh to address them. These two were fairly typical: well-proportioned, trim and fit, highly attractive, both sharing that aura of quiet giddiness that often envelops people in the aftermath of a world-famous fuck. Flat abs, bronzed skin (waxed, for certain), and big, beautiful doe eyes. Brazilian maybe? Jesse does love his Latin men.

You heard right, ladies. Now don't go barking up the wrong tree.

I wearily gestured to the waiting cab below, and the pair saw themselves out with polite smiles, leaving me to squint against the blazing Florida sunrise. Without wasting a movement, I tossed a chili pepper into the blender and topped everything with a shot of vodka and generous shakes of ginger. Upstairs, I could hear a perfect opera aria being belted out over the roaring of the shower. Almost time. I rushed Margot off the phone and turned blender on full steam.

My timing was such that, when Jesse Cannon came down minutes later, wearing only jeans and his most effective hangover sunglasses, and moving somewhat sluggishly, I was pouring his usual "Hair of the Greyhound Post-Coitus Julius" into a chilled glass, complete with a lemon gumdrop on top.

I was awesome at my job.

Jesse perked up considerably the moment he saw it, making with the jazz hands and shouting one biblical exaltation or another in a grating falsetto. I did not consider this an unusual greeting.

"Morning," I mumbled, subtly sliding my two weeks' notice off the counter. I felt suddenly anxious about Jesse's obliviousness to my decision. Maybe I should have announced it more gradually? Or waited until the end of the tour? No, I told myself. No way. Today was the day, come hell or high water. Finding the best moment would call for prudence and tact, but I would not allow myself to turn back.

Jesse slid up behind me, squeezed me with a passing one-armed hug, and took the glass from the counter.

"Oh, these nights, Jordan," he moaned. Perfect pitch, that moan. "I can't keep this up, I have to sleep. You see how I'm starting to look old?" He thrust his chin upwards and threw a swallow of the drink between pouting lips.

I shrugged. "Your sins will find you out."

Jesse swiveled to face me with a wicked smile. "Thank god, they always do," he purred, then began humming "Night Fever" and bumping me vigorously with his overworked hips.

Before you get the wrong idea, this was a fairly typical way for Jesse to interact with me. With anyone, really, but I had long since become immune. And that, honestly, was the problem: the immunity. When it feels normal to be harmlessly dry-humped in the morning by an outrageously famous person, then it is simply time to move on.

I swatted him off and paced around the counter, folding and unfolding the paper in my hands, my resolve strengthened, but my nerves unwilling. Prudence, I reminded myself. Jesse went right on strutting around the general area of the kitchen, chattering between gulps, undaunted. "Was that Margot on the phone? Do we know anything yet about Chicago or what? Oh my god, that one guy had the *fugliest* tattoo I have ever seen on his—"

Fuck prudence. There was never going to be a proper moment.

"Jesse," I held a hand up. "I have something to tell you first."

"But listen, *listen*," he insisted, "it was a—"

I stopped him again, waving the sheet of paper. "I have to *give* you something."

"Oh?"

I handed it across the counter, and Jesse contemplated it over the tilt of the glass as he drank, removing the sunglasses. I could tell he wasn't really reading it word for word, because nothing was registering on his face.

"What's this?" he finally said.

"It's a two weeks' notice."

"What's a two weeks' notice? Do we have any straws?"

Sometimes I don't know if it's just the Russian, like maybe there are phrases he hasn't come across yet, or if it's just the dumb.

"It's me letting you know that I'm only working for you for two more weeks."

It took a minute. Then he cocked his head and looked at me, like the lovable animal set free at the end of a Disney movie, not quite getting it. It was evident that by the end of this, I would be the little girl forced to shout and throw sticks at him before riding away in Pa's truck, leaving him alone in the wild.

"Please don't be upset," I groaned pleadingly. I would have to be more blunt, more firm. Not to be cruel, but to make it easy. There's no dancing around an issue with Jesse Cannon, or he will be moonwalking to another subject in no time.

I took a deep breath and stuck to my guns. "I've been looking at other options."

"What? Jordan! Why?" He put the glass down to imply how alarmed he was and made a good show of it, letting his dimpled jaw slack just slightly.

"It's just too much, Jesse." I was doing my best to sound innocent, earnest. "I have a degree for god's sake. I should be, I don't know, settling down a little, kicking back, doing my own thing, you know?"

"I don't understand."

I really wanted to bypass specific reasons, all those examples which came to mind. Like the time I ran almost the entire length of the Macy's Thanksgiving Day Parade for a particular scarf, or the time I had to break into a Malibu beach mansion to retrieve the headline-worthy sex tapes being wagered as blackmail. Or how about the time he broke *my* glasses on the red carpet at the Grammys?

Need motivation to switch to contacts? Try having Steven Tyler escort you out of the men's room. That's all I'm saying.

Anyway, it seemed that examples were necessary. I started mild:

"I haven't had a vacation in two years, Jesse."

"Oh, what are you talking about?" he smirked dismissively, hopping backwards with effortless grace to sit on the counter. "Weren't we just in Maui for two weeks, hmm?"

"That was *not* a vacation!" I jabbed a finger towards him. "I spent the first three nights running to buy condoms and holding your head over the toilet. The only time I even *saw* the ocean was when you demanded genuine kelp for some recipe, and I stepped on an urchin and got an infection." Kicking off a flip-flop, I lifted my right foot up as far as I could without falling over. "Remember *that* part of the vacation?"

"Oh. Yeah." Looking at the scarred sole of my foot took him back. He squinted. "Yeah, that was *gross*."

"Jesse!"

"Like, super just . . . nasty."

"Jesse!"

"Ew! Put it away already!" He fake retched and distracted himself again with the drink, stretching against the counter in a feline way. "So what time is my tour bus getting here? Do we have time for shiatsu? Go check online and see if there's anyplace open this early."

He popped the dissolving yellow gumdrop upwards into the air, where it followed a perfect trajectory back down into his waiting mouth. When he saw that I was still standing there, arms crossed and glaring, he looked genuinely surprised, truly confused.

"Go on. Go, go," he shooed.

Unbelievable, right?

I snatched the paper out of his hand and waved it at him furiously.

"Oh, enough of that." He guided my raised arm down and smiled entreatingly. "Come on! Take your mind off it. Shiatsu! Mimosas! Let's do something for *you*, then! New jeans? You could use new jeans."

"We are going to talk about this. Now."

"Jordan, honey. Look at these things." He ignored me, indicating my perfectly attractive, comfortable jeans. Dropping down to his knees, he spun me around by the waist. "Look at this ass! Look at it! You are not glorifying that ass. You need to glorify it. Glorify. The. Ass. Get our stuff. Let's go."

"You get away from my ass!" I whirled around and glared down at him. "Jesse, I'm serious about this."

"Then what do you want?" he put his hands out, lost, still on his knees.

"I don't want anything. I don't want jeans. I don't want a vacation. I want to quit. That's it."

"Just ask, girl." He wasn't hearing me. "Whatever makes you stay, it's yours."

I stared at him, my jaw set. Now I have seen the worst of this man, the very worst of him. But I can't go any farther without putting a word in for his beauty.

It has powers.

Even as hung over and exhausted from meaningless group sex as he was at the moment, he looked alarmingly . . . perfected. The good people at *Vogue* never had to airbrush a thing. His hair was that honest blonde color, and it fell in an absurdly attractive mess nearly to his shoulders. His eyes were a dark honey brown, and—trust me, I know—they can make you do just about anything. Same applies to the dimples. His face was like something from a fantasy; flawless, tanned, elegant, and peculiarly feminine. And his body was a drag queen's dream—long, poised, smooth and taut, refined in every way. Jesse Cannon was a twenty-six year old masterpiece.

Thank god I lost any shred of sexual desire I had for him around the time he explained his annual colonic to me.

And so now this gorgeous man was kneeling before me, begging me to stay, offering anything I desired. Lucky me, right?

"Jesse . . . ," I groaned and sat down at the counter, "I don't *want* anything. I just can't work for you forever, that's all. So please just don't take it so personally, okay?"

Jesse didn't say anything right away. He just sat down on the barstool next to me and scooted over, put his head on my shoulder. Golden hair tumbled into my line of sight. I was too tired, too defeated, to move out of the way.

"But whatever would I do without you?" he said softly.

Probably drown in the shower, I thought, but I kept that to myself and let everything lay for the moment, at least verbally. But in two weeks, I told myself, I was out of there, no matter what. My signature said so.

Side by side, we watched the sun and the ocean do their dazzling thing.

"Jordan, I *need* you."

I rolled my eyes. "Now you tell me . . ."

"I do. I really think that I'm starting to lose it. And I need you. I can *talk* to you."

That little disclosure caught me way off guard, to be honest. Jesse didn't say things like that, not unless tequila was involved. My nose wrinkled, but I kept my mouth shut and my eyes on the ocean for a minute, not letting him trick me into promises. It was hurricane season, but the water looked so still and clear. A clean, flat horizon. I could almost taste it.

"What do you mean, lose it?" I finally had to ask.

Jesse eased off my shoulder and shook his head. He swirled the remnants in his glass and shrugged, a poor attempt at nonchalance.

"I keep having these dreams," he said.

If I only knew, I would've run like hell.

CHAPTER 3

Corin Charles Livingston III had never been much of a runner. He really didn't consider himself much of an athlete altogether. Running the New York City Marathon was just something to do, same as hiking the Appalachian Trail or walking the length of the Great Wall of China. Or surfing Waikiki, or climbing Kilimanjaro. Having done all of these things, it's safe to say that Corin was in darn good shape for someone who didn't call himself an athlete.

At twenty-seven, Corin had the time and money to do these things because he was all alone on a small branch of a very rich, very English family tree. Blue blood and old money ran through this tree. And every day it was filtering in more money from a massive stock portfolio and some very prosperous business ventures.

And the green grass grew all around, all around, and the green grass grew all around.

Like I mentioned before, Corin was the type who usually got what he wanted, mostly because he could afford to do as he liked. But before you go and label him some kind of indulgent aristocrat, give him a chance. The Livingston family business wasn't centered around retaining wealth so much as appropriating it. All because Corin's father—happily married, bereaved of his only sibling, childless at forty-five (and presumably sterile)—had made a midlife career of steering family wealth into third world philanthropist organizations. Corin Three came into this global equation very late—scandalously late, when his parents were both at the cusp of senior citizenship. Luckily for the Livingston beneficiaries, however, he turned out to be a compassionate, gracious, and well-traveled little protege. Instead of blazing through the post-graduate school haze of sports cars and plastic girlfriends expected of his wealth bracket, he'd spent most of his twenties substituting for his aging father in board meetings all over the world and securing grants for various foundations.

That's not to say he escaped a monied existence. Corin attended expensive institutions of private education and encountered equally as many cocktail parties as ashrams. He dressed smartly, possessed a taste for top shelf bourbon, and spoke with a genuine Oxbridge accent (the kind that reeks of caviar and riding breeches). But he was not a lavish spender. He wasn't some socialite prick, either. Actually, amid the boardroom-to-bushland lifestyle he maintained, there were only three decadent luxuries he consistently afforded himself: first-class flying, good liquor, and as many adventures as he could pencil in.

The New York City Marathon was one adventure he pointedly never missed. He always looked forward to the thrill of being among so many other people, all falling in and out of stride with one another towards their singular, frantic goal. The city air was salty and damp that time of year, and during the 26 mile run it poured in, lungful after lungful, a cold, gritty cleansing. Corin considered it his annual American baptism.

The New York itinerary was never without its workload, of course. A tight schedule of meetings sandwiched the marathon, and there were the usual companies to charm, executive officers to wine and dine—all of them American, none of them easy to sway. So in the two weeks following the Australian tour, there was no shortage of work to keep him occupied. Annual data to peruse and statements to arrange, all in accordance with Corin senior, who was insufferably stubborn and—at eighty-one—also insufferably deaf.

Yet Corin was more grateful than ever for the distraction. After his return to the family estate in North Devon, the dreams had only grown more vivid, more nagging and, to put it in a word, *urgent*. It was all he could do to brush the images from his mind each morning and keep himself busy with work and reading material at all hours. He could manage, he told himself. He would decompress after New York, take that trip to Barcelona. A vacation. He would be fine. Just fine.

Then came his transatlantic flight to New York. And there was nothing fine about that.

Corin *loved* flying. Always. Despite his active nature, he loved the feeling of transit, the respite between two different chapters of action. He loved the cushy seats and the chilled chardonnay. He adored the stewardesses and their perfect lipstick. He reveled in the tiny earphones wrapped in plastic and the *ding!* of the seatbelt sign. But that single flight to New York robbed him entirely of all of these skyward joys.

It started out over the Atlantic as a headache. Just a headache, a sort of heavy feeling. Without warning, this headache became outright nausea, a weighty, sick, prickling that circulated to the tips of his toes. No amount of Tums or time spent hovering over the little metal air john led to any relief. He didn't need to throw up. That wasn't the problem. He knew what the problem was, just as certainly as he knew he should check into Manhattan's finest workaholic rehab center upon arrival.

The problem was the water.

H2O. Miles of it. Miles wide. Miles deep. The blasted Atlantic was what pinned him down to his luxury recliner chair, and he knew it. It tugged at the pit of his stomach, pulled him down with what felt like twice the normal force of gravity. Waves of heat frothed under his skin, moving in sync with the undulations of the blue horizon. Those same motions continued to play across his sight even when he closed his eyes. He could almost hear the *sound* of it.

In a sort of fumbling panic, he yanked down the window shade and shunned the sight of the ocean. A stewardess, noting his obvious discomfort (and his appealing, boyish freckles, no doubt) offered up an airsick bag, which he politely declined. Never once had he been sick on a plane, and he wasn't about to start hurling into a little bag in front of God and everybody. No way.

In classic quiet desperation, he popped a few more Tums, leaned back, and looked to the small screen before him for salvation. The first in-flight movie was about to begin. If he couldn't sleep this ghastly feeling off, he thought, he could at least try to distract himself with some genuine American drivel.

Unless of course, the drivel starred an unwanted guest from his own troubled mind. The movie was none other than Jesse Cannon's latest release, a nautical World War II musical.

"Oh, Christ."

Corin immediately flagged down the eager stewardess, ordered a Glenlivet on the rocks, and asked for the day's *New York Times*, even though he'd already read it and pitched it back at Heathrow. For the unbearable hours that ensued, he kept his eyes off the screen, his ears plugged with swing music, and his throat wet with a responsibly paced yet ample amount of scotch.

Ages later, having gotten slightly more drunk than he'd intended and not feeling well by any means, he saw the lights blink on and heard the instructions start. Corin opened his window shutter to the sight of the Eastern shore, expecting to feel as the Puritans felt when they'd finished their own voyage, wretched but unspeakably glad. Instead, as his plane tipped towards JFK International Airport, with all of New York spread out below him—including Liberty herself—he felt only the electric chill of something like dread.

Ghiyath Ayman never quite understood that as a single male in his mid-twenties, he was not supposed to be watching soap operas when he was alone. Or at any other time, really. But that's precisely what Ghi himself—genuinely without shame—told me he was doing that first afternoon of November.

Like Corin, Ghi found himself holed up in a hotel room somewhere in Manhattan, feeling anxious and increasingly awful. Ghi was not in New York for business or pleasure, however. Ghi was in New York against his better judgement and, quite frankly, against his will.

If it were up to Ghi, he would have been in a nice, quiet place on the edge of familiar Dubai, not in big, gruesome, epileptic New York City. To Ghi, New York was terrifying, more terrifying than Boston, even. And although Ghi had found nearly every life change within the past five years to be increasingly more terrifying, this time he knew for sure: New York meant trouble.

But it was not up to Ghi. Nothing ever was. This fact was as natural to him as walking, as breathing, as laying on the big green office couch in Boston, where he had told Dr. Avery every last recollectable detail about his dreams and begged to be left out of the convention. Ghi kept no secrets from Dr. Avery. He *trusted* Dr. Avery.

And yet here he was anyway, on the eleventh floor of the Times Square Wellington, in the suite he and Dr. Avery were sharing for the week: betrayed, door bolted, shades drawn, soap opera on.

The doctor was out. On the grainy screen, a pregnant woman lay in a hospital room, comatose, while two dashing men debated heatedly from either side of her, arguing about which of them was the father of her unborn child.

Ghi stared at the TV with mild interest, reclining awkwardly on the short hotel couch, his legs draped over the armrest. He felt completely on edge, as if someone would burst through the door or window at any second and prove to everyone, by means of violence, that he should never have gone to New York.

"Ghi, there's nothing to worry about. It's just a coincidence."

That's what Dr. Avery kept saying, back in Boston, when the convention was still a matter of debate. Ghi recalled all his own hopeless protesting, and knew that he'd given in too easily. He rolled over onto his back and tossed a couch pillow from one hand to another, working hard to remember, replaying the argument in his mind.

"You've never been to New York. You were never in America until you came to see me. We're certain of that, aren't we?"

Dr. Avery liked to ask questions like that to sound reassuring. Most of the time, it just made Ghi feel like a moron.

The shapes of the hotel room blurred and shifted, until they lined up with the shapes of Dr. Avery's office. He had to fight, just for a moment, to remember where he was.

"It could be a collection of memories, easily, but the Statue of Liberty may be sort of . . . superimposed. Some sort of pop culture addition that your mind is manifesting in place of something it can't remember."

The pillow dropped to the carpet. Above it, the ceiling's patterns started floating off in two different directions. These frequent optical and motor lapses never helped matters. Ghi strained his eyes, forcing them to refocus, until both the ceiling and his memory were correct again.

This was where he had given in, he remembered. The creak of Dr. Avery's chair had indicated that he was about to say something in his resolved, sympathetic voice. *Ghi, I really feel . . .*

"Ghi, I really feel that this will be to your benefit. A lot of my colleagues are very interested in you, and maybe they can help you in ways I haven't thought of. And if it makes you feel any better, we won't be anywhere near Liberty Island."

It didn't make Ghi feel better.

"Susan knows the truth," one of the soap stars snarled through his perfect white teeth. "You just wait, you son of a bitch! You just wait!"

Ghi shuffled into the kitchen for something to calm what was becoming a nervous stomach. The clock on the microwave told him that it was four-o-clock, which meant that Dr. Avery would be back soon to take him to the second evening of the convention. The second evening of sitting on an auditorium stage under hot lights in front of fast-talking physicians.

Fantastic.

Ghi breathed deeply. He opened the freezer, where a lone can of Dr. Pepper was waiting for him. It didn't occur to him that the can was slightly misshapen, or that by putting it in the freezer he had created a frozen time bomb of frothy sugar. He just liked the stuff *cold*. Any other man in his mid twenties, unless he had grown up in a remote Amazon village, or unless he was just plain stupid, would know better. Ghi hadn't grown up in a remote Amazon village. And he wasn't stupid, either.

He just wasn't normal.

He wrenched at the icy metal tab, digging a finger into it. The tab bulged but did not budge. A feminine cry startled him, and he returned to the TV to see that Susan had come out of her coma.

Ghi stood there and watched Susan with rapt attention. She was sitting straight up, hair perfect, eyelashes long and pretty, staring at the two men who stood at her bedside. They asked her if she was alright, asked her for the truth, whatever it was. But Susan just stared. She didn't remember the truth. She didn't remember who these men were. She didn't even remember that she was Susan anymore.

Poor, poor Susan.

Ghi made a sour face and pried at the Dr. Pepper again. The tab finally lifted and frozen carbonated slush spilled down the sides of the can, down into the sleeves of all his layered sweaters. Ghi cursed and retreated to the kitchen before any of it could drip down to the carpet.

"You're a fireman, Mr. Jackson?"

"Yep."

"And so what exactly were you doing when you first noticed the suspect?"

"Getting something out of the vending machine."

The deputy took a moment to shuffle papers, papers that were not even related to the case at hand. He could not think of a counter question to that.

"I'm the driver," Jackson explained, fidgeting in the rolling chair and drumming a finger against the empty Gatorade bottle in his hands. "The fire was pretty minimal. So I was just sort of killing time."

The deputy bobbed his head vaguely, diagonally, so that he was neither shaking it nor nodding. "And what did you see then, from the vending machine?"

Jackson frowned. He had definitely gone over this already with at least two other officers. Why did these people write anything down if they were just going to ask again?

"I saw him coming down—"

"Who?"

"I saw *this guy*," Jackson, with clear exasperation, prodded a finger at the mug shot lying in front of him. "Coming down the fence on the south side of the prison yard."

"The outside of the fence?"

For crying out loud. Jackson flopped back in the chair and looked around at the people coming and going within the crowded police station. He wondered how many other convicts were running loose, and how long they'd be out there, since these guys took so damn long asking inane questions like this.

"No, *inside* the fence," he answered, with an obvious tone of sarcasm.

Not obvious enough, apparently. Or perhaps too thick. The deputy looked up from his notes, blank and disapproving.

"Outside," Jackson sighed. "He was coming down the outside of the outermost fence."

"And that's when you pursued the suspect on foot?"

"Yep."

"And you did not alert anyone else?"

"Nope. Just ran."

"How far would you say he ran before your encounter?"

Jackson shrugged. "'Bout a half mile or more? He took off down into the valley, followed the creek north, away from the highway."

He stared at the convict's photo on the cluttered desk as he spoke, replaying the whole thing in his mind. The sheer height of the guy, the way he ran, so fast and deliberate even in the dark, hurling himself through branches and shrubs like they didn't even exist. Until that rotting stump tripped him up. That was when Jackson had done what seemed most sensible to him in the moment: he'd tackled the guy.

That was also where Jackson's report got a little skewed. There were some things he had not mentioned to any of the officers, things he couldn't quite figure out himself. The strange, blackout impulse that had made him run in the first place, for instance. And the switchblade. He hadn't said a single word about the switchblade.

He'd heard it before he'd seen it, the metallic click and the little *whoosh* sound of sliced air. The guy twisted beneath him after they'd hit the snowy ground, got onto his back somehow and swung an arm out. Jackson dodged, fast but not fast enough, and the blade cut clean from the stubbled flesh under his nose to the broad side of his cheek. Could have been worse, he knew; it could have been his eye or his throat. Instead, he'd grown one half of a bright red, instant mustache.

They were both on their feet in the next instant, poised, frozen, staring into the dark at one another, the convict with his knife held at a threatening level, Jackson with his hands out, waiting to defend himself. The blood on his skin had felt hot as bath water in contrast to the freezing air. He remembered that vividly.

Neither of them moved for ten excruciatingly long seconds, during which the following thoughts occurred to Jackson, in this order:

Ouuch-Shit! Son of a bitch! Ouch!

How the hell do you get a switchblade in prison?

Hey. I know this guy.

It was dark, but Jackson was absolutely certain. He had seen that face before. Many times. Countless times.

The convict, it seemed, was having a similar revelation of recognition. Or, much less likely, a change of heart. The goliath figure straightened up suddenly, pocketed the switchblade, and without so much as a look over his shoulder, jumped across the creek and ran hard into the woods.

Jackson hadn't followed. He'd just stood there on the bank, smearing blood off his face with his hands, listening to the sound of slapping branches fade into the howling wind. "That's right, you run!" he'd shouted. "Cut my face, big mistake! Goddamn Commie!"

Jackson swiveled impatiently in the rolling chair, watching the hypnotic patterns of snow falling outside the police station window. It was eight in the morning now, but all was as dark and gray as dusk outside. The deputy had interrupted his own questions to take a call, but when he noticed a string of headlights entering the lot outside, he immediately flagged down a passing officer and handed the phone over to her.

"Those'll be the feds," he said to Jackson, gesturing at the window and standing up. "They're going to want to get a report from you, too."

"Are you kidding me?" Jackson turned back towards the desk, slapped his hands down on his knees, his wide green eyes wider than ever. "Look, man, I'm still on call for the next forty-eight hours and this blizzard's just getting started. They're going to need seven of me today."

The deputy shrugged unsympathetically.

Jackson shook his head and looked through the haze of snow again at the advancing figures, tall and shapeless in their black overcoats. He sighed resignedly.

"So this Kin Su guy—"

"Su Kim Khan."

"Right. So he's a pretty big deal, huh?"

The deputy's eyebrows lifted. It was the first actual expression Jackson had seen him make.

"Oh. He's a very big deal."

The officer who'd taken the phone leaned through the door again. "They said the snow's covered everything by now, wind's too high, dogs are no good." She looked to Jackson. "Which way did you say he ran from the site?"

Jackson opened his mouth, but didn't speak immediately. He wasn't thinking about the answer. He *knew* the answer. Across the creek and into the woods, due east. That was the answer.

He was thinking instead about that face, the face from the snowy darkness, the face from all those dreams. He didn't understand, but he knew somehow that this was right.

"West," he said. "He ran west, up the side of the mountain."

Satisfied, the officer disappeared again. The deputy excused himself to greet the agents in the lobby. Jackson watched them all through the shuttered office glass, rubbing at the flesh above his upper lip for the hundredth time that morning.

Nothing was there. Not so much as a scratch.

CHAPTER 4

On November 1st, one night after the Nashville show, the tour schedule called for another night in town. Not for a second sold-out concert, but for a party. A birthday party, if I remember correctly, for the fragrancier who'd produced the "Confession" cologne Jesse had recently modeled for. It was your typical black-tie affair. Private, no red carpet, easy and predictable.

The usual routine. I shadowed Jesse closely, usually for the first hour or so, wearing whatever cocktail dress he'd coaxed me into. It was my job during this time to record any phone numbers or invitations he received, remind him of names he'd forgotten, detect any previous one-night stands in the room (and remind him of how they'd gone), take candid photos, and order the drinks. It was a triathlon in heels.

This particular party was proving nothing more than average. A spacious loft rented out for the evening and decorated to the hilt. House music with the occasional country number thrown in for local kicks. Big names in fragrance and cosmetics, a couple of designers, some Nashville elite, and a sprinkling of celebrities. Jesse mingled, floated, kissed, and pinched, while I tagged along, doing my time. After a cherry cosmo and a peppermint manhattan, he drifted off into the deepest part of the crowd, and it eagerly consumed him.

That was my freedom cue. I took a seat at the bar, which, customarily, was the final destination for assistants, chauffeurs, stylists, and other accessory people. Rather than feign interest, we tended to drink ourselves through the remainder of these events while our employers fawned over one another. It's a survival technique.

On this particular night, I clearly remember drinking and flirting with someone's bodyguard. I don't remember what he looked like or anything, only that his name was Charles. Or maybe Christopher. Whatever. I was distracted—I had four days left to go as a contracted employee of Jesse Cannon.

I'll admit now that I was a little conflicted. Instead of thinking about any immediate plans—what to do next, where to move, where to vacation—my mind was chronically preoccupied with the way Jesse had been acting. That pissed me off to no end, but there was no way to ignore the changes. Ever since he'd let on about the dreams, I'd been picking up on things. He seemed to have less energy before every show. His eyes needed more moisturizer in the mornings. He wasn't sleeping; I could tell. He was taking on less sex to compensate, but it wasn't working. Most disturbingly, he seemed almost contemplative and silent at times. That was something entirely new altogether.

I'd decided that plain old exhaustion, poor habits, and age were probably starting to catch up with him, and that the dreams were just part of it. He only explained them to me one time, and I never gave them much thought afterwards. It wasn't unusual, after all, for Jesse Cannon to be dreaming about attractive young men.

He was looking much better at the party, I reassured myself from the bar. He was in high form, hogging the floor and commanding the mood effortlessly, and of course those people out there were just eating it up. This was the only side of Jesse that still impressed me after five years, the one talent of his that always held me in a kind of trance. It's easy to assume that around someone of Jesse's caliber, anyone else would unconsciously start feeling smaller, uglier, troll-like even. But that was never the case with him. I can't explain it, but being around Jesse Cannon always seemed to make people feel *more* beautiful, more graceful, more sexy, more happy. It's this natural phenomenon that he just sort of carried, and he controlled it somehow without even trying.

It was as if he had some sort of atmosphere quota to fill. He just couldn't stand it unless everyone in sight of him was having a good time. The more people present, the greater the challenge became, the higher his spirits got, the harder he worked to spread himself around. He was fearless. He left no person outside his circle of excitement, or for that matter, too far from his hips.

Speaking of which, he was positively ravaging the fragrance mogul's wife out there while I waited for his watermelon martini. I couldn't help but smile. He was dancing up behind her, singing close to her ear in a dramatically sultry way for the benefit of onlookers. She was laughing helplessly, and I believe she was wearing his tie. Everyone around them was going nuts.

"Watermelon martini. Two sugar cubes."

I took my eyes off the dance floor, turning to the bar to test the drink. I always did that. If it was crap, I sent it back. No one gets a poor drink past me. I'm Jordan Murphy. I know my beverages.

A little heavy on the sugar, but acceptable. I had just deemed this when I heard the commotion. No screams. Just that unsettling ripple of gasps that you get when something happens in front of a crowd. Praying that Jesse hadn't dropped the birthday boy's wife, I turned to see everyone staring towards the middle of the dance floor, at the ground. But I couldn't see Jesse anywhere.

I couldn't see him because he was the one on the ground.

If I was at all tipsy, then I sobered up at record speed. With watermelon martini all down the front of my dress, I charged towards the middle of the floor, clawing my way through all those size zero bimbos and pushing them back to get to Jesse. The seconds seemed to stretch indefinitely while I took stock of the situation. He was face down, out cold, breathing deep and steady. People were arguing about what had happened. The general consensus was that he'd just stopped moving and fallen over. He hadn't tripped or been pushed, just passed out on the spot. Bam. Fainted.

"Give him some air," I kept telling them. "Has anybody called an ambulance?" I raced to think of what could be wrong with him. Meds? Anemia? Is this a seizure? I slapped at the sides of his face. The bodyguard I'd been flirting with dumped a glass of water on him. No response. I noticed that his eyes were swiveling back and forth beneath their lids, a motion that continued rapidly, to my complete horror, even after I gently pulled one of them open.

Jesse was the lucky one.

Su Kim Khan passed out in the middle of a Missouri train yard during a blizzard.

Whitney Jackson passed out behind the wheel of a fire truck during that same blizzard.

Corin Livingston III passed out on a Manhattan side street. Strangers helped him, of course, but not before his wallet and shoes and other things had been taken.

Ghiyath Ayman passed out under the hot lights of an auditorium stage in front of fifty or more of the nation's leading neurologists.

When Ghi came to his senses again, he was not alone. Several of the specialists from the convention were herding around his semiprivate room, looking through his MRI and CAT scans, babbling in various languages, transfixed, fascinated.

They were looking inside his head.

There was an awful chemical taste in his mouth. Something was wrong with his sight. Light from every available source rushed for his eyes, splintering around the room in billions of individual trajectories. This reminded him where he and his mind had just been, and his heart spasmed violently.

He searched the faces, but Dr. Avery wasn't one of them. The other doctors noticed him at once and stage-rushed his bedside, wasting no time with the questions. Panicking, he pretended to be too confused to answer any of them, which wasn't far from the truth, and this bought him a few minutes of not having to say a word.

When Dr. Avery finally appeared and politely ushered the medical mob out of the room, Ghi wasn't sure whether to be relieved or terrified. The doctor's familiar face looked suspicious and grave as he rolled a chair to the bedside, holding the most recent cranial scans. Ghi held his breath and waited, careful not to be the first to speak. He could not dismiss the ridiculous notion that, simply by examining the translucent images of his brain, Dr. Avery would be able to see what he'd dreamed.

Or been told. Or whatever. It hadn't been like a dream at all.

"How do you feel?" Dr. Avery asked, sounding weary but sincere.

Ghi really hadn't had time to assess that himself. "I feel okay," he said, without conviction. "What happened?"

"Well now, that's what we're trying to figure out," Dr. Avery adjusted his glasses, kept looking at the scans. "You resisted consciousness for nearly eighteen hours, and we couldn't determine why." He was shaking his head, rambling his review. "All your vitals were fine, your tests came out normal, and you have no history of this as far as we can tell. And here's the really interesting part."

He held a scan up, and the light scrambled off its flimsy surface with every undulation it made. Ghi peered through this distracting luminous tangle and saw what he'd seen countless times before: a cross section of his own brain. He was pretty sick of seeing his brain. He was pretty sick of everyone else wanting to see it, too.

He couldn't help but notice, however, that his brain looked much more interesting in this scan than it ever had before.

"I've never seen anything like this," Dr. Avery said. He sounded nervous, incredulous to the point of actual frustration, and it sent a numb chill down Ghi's neck.

"Don't be alarmed, Ghi, but while you were unconscious, your brain activity was ... abnormal, to say the least. It was through the roof. What really concerns me, though, is that most of the activity was occurring in areas that people—well, most organisms, as far as I'm aware—never use. Areas that we *can't* use."

Ghi listened with an increasingly sick feeling in his stomach. He looked at the scans, trying to make a connection, but the new patterns meant nothing to him.

"Do you remember anything? Any strange dreams or sensations?"

Ghi stayed very still before choosing his words.

"No. Nothing."

"Are you sure?"

"Yes. Nothing at all."

Dr. Avery sighed and stood up. "Alright, I'm going to go arrange another CAT scan immediately. See what's happening up there now," he gestured at Ghi's disaster of black curls. "If you're in the clear, we'll get back up to Boston and start some more testing. Sound good?"

Ghi had no honest opinion. He had other things on his apparently whacked-out mind. "Yeah, good."

"Alright then, you take it easy. You know the drill. Call a nurse if you need anything."

"Okay."

The doctor looked at him once more, in a piercing, uneasy way, and then left the room.

Ghi waited only a few seconds before scrambling out of bed. He put his bare feet to linoleum and staggered into the suite's small bathroom, locking the door behind him.

Inside, there was just enough room to lay flat on his back, to feel the cold of the sterile floor and the goodness of being alone. When the fluorescent lights above interrupted this feeling, he shuddered and averted his eyes, as if reacting to unwanted flirtations. Something like a groan was trying itself in his throat, but he didn't make a sound.

This was bad.

This was so bad.

He decided to let himself think about it, which was about as scary as deciding to open a terrarium full of jumping spiders. He clenched his eyes shut and covered them with his hands.

Ghi had lied to Dr. Avery for the first time. He'd had a dream, alright. He'd had a full-color Discovery Channel documentary fire off in his head.

I know exactly how it went. Jesse Cannon told me all about it.

I spent about fifteen hours in the waiting area, surviving on energy pills, vending machine muffins, and bad cafeteria coffee. I was on and off the phone with Margot and the insurance company the entire time, assuring them over and over again that no, Jesse had *not* overdosed on anything the night before. He hadn't even had three whole drinks yet, and no, he wasn't purging again as far as I knew.

His collapse was all over the news, even though there was little to report. Nothing changed, and there were no conclusions about what had happened, medically speaking. Every couple of hours, someone came in to have me sign something or ask me questions, and all they would tell me was that Jesse was fine, just inexplicably unconscious.

Finally, at about two in the afternoon, right when I was settling down to sleep on one of those short, impossible hospital couches, a nurse came in and told me that Jesse was alert and asking for me.

I was afraid I would have trouble finding his room, but once I found the right corridor, there was no mistaking it. The flowers that had accumulated within the past couple of hours alone now overflowed to a table across the hallway. Cards and well-wishing notes covered the door, sent from every source imaginable, from celebrity acquaintances, from the governor of Tennessee, from obsessed fans. You'd think the Pope himself was in there with a corroded artery. I found the door handle among all the cards and slipped inside.

Jesse was alone, sitting straight up in bed, and he greeted me with a look of pure panic.

"Quick! What's a Cat's Can?" he demanded.

And here we go.

"A what?"

"A Cat's Can."

I sighed wearily and moved farther into the room, maneuvering over baskets of flowers. "A *CAT Scan* is when they take an X-ray of your head, pretty much."

His fearful expression didn't go away. In fact, it grew worse. He gasped audibly. "Are they going to cut my hair?"

I immediately missed the waiting room so very badly. "I really don't think so..."

"You don't *think* so, or don't *know* so!?"

I pulled up a chair, trying to seem as encouraging as possible, but I was exhausted. Unlike him, I hadn't just taken a fifteen-hour nap.

"Jesse. I am *fairly certain* that no one is going to do anything to your hair, but I don't even know what's wrong with you." I looked him over as I sat down. "So what happened? What did they tell you?"

He was calmer, but he didn't look any more relieved. His face, I suddenly noticed, was shockingly pale and unsettled. Something was on his mind, now that he could no longer distract himself with the hair uncertainty. It was easy to see, and it scared me instantly.

I asked again. "Jesse? What did they tell you?"

He shook his head like it was hard for him to pay attention to my question, like he was brushing it off. "They said I'm fine. Said it was exhaustion."

My shoulders sank with instant relief. "Jesus, Jesse...," I immediately started to tear into all the reasons he was exhausted, but something stopped me short a few lines in. He wasn't finished, and he wasn't listening. He was staring off into space, ahead of himself with thoughts, trying to hold them all together. A nervous stillness fell between us, and he broke it quietly.

"It's not exhaustion, Jordan."

A knot formed behind my navel. The person looking at me was not Jesse Cannon, at least not any side of him I'd seen in five years' time. This person was not frivolously frightened about hair alterations. This person was serious and shaken. Scared.

The knot tightened when Jesse leaned closer to me, concentrating on the familiarity of my eyes and face, reminding himself that he could trust me. The door was closed, but he spoke in a low, somber tone, not once taking his eyes off mine.

"Something is about to happen to me."

PART II

ORIGINS

There was a river named Ket.

The Ket used to empty into another river, and that river eventually emptied into the Nile, long before the people along its famous banks had assembled into anything but small tribal nations. Along the Ket, there were only two such nations, vastly isolated yet separated from one another solely by the river running between them. The larger one to the west was called Amphet. The smaller one, settled on the eastern bank of the river, was called Nifushunm.

Amphet was the reason there were no other people around. Prosperous and relatively metropolitan for its time, it had a substantial population, an impressive defense, and territory expanding widely into the feral deserts—things any respectable one-goat town would look for in a neighbor. Amphet's neighbors, however, had this historical way of being driven away, razed to the ground, or enslaved. The valleys on Amphet's side of the river were fertile, and so were the women. Hence, Amphet had no use and no place and no tolerance for another people anywhere near it. The only exception was Nifushunm.

Nifushunm was small and sparse, not much more than a walled cluster of communal tents, and it hadn't produced a soldier for hundreds of years. Instead, it produced great diviners. Necromancers and healers, seers and priests, people with strange but undeniable gifts. It was these diviners who had made the smaller nation so invaluable—and therefore so remarkably invulnerable—to Amphet. The very walls around Nifushunm were built and maintained by Amphet, and Amphetians guarded its perimeter by night. The diviners of Nifushunm were not spiritual zealots or deceptive magicians. They performed no painted dances or petty tricks, and they didn't babble in tongues. Their craft was a science, methodological and measurable, and known only to them. And it was highly profitable to be their friends.

The diviners lived unquestioned. Their method of reading the surrounding world, of interpreting its messages to fit the context of their mortal existence, was seemingly as old as human life itself. They liked to claim that the shapers of the universe—namely the forces governing nature and life—actually breathed these gifts into the first generation of diviners. From then on, the people believed, the diviners could breathe their powers into newer generations of chosen students. Literally. As in through the mouth.

Whether or not their gifts came from the breath of gods, no one could deny the diviners' accuracy. By means of trances and instruments, personal sojourns, coordinated sacrifices, careful mathematics, and risky alchemy, the diviners were able to understand the world around them in layers which others could not see. They read events in the stars and in the patterns of the sand. They could chart the movement of the wind and know when to hunt, when to slaughter, and when to make love. Their advice doubled crops and fattened livestock. They could heal wounds, listen for news in the water, and hear the voices of the past.

And one of them, a man called Dahrkren, would learn how to speak with death itself.

Dahrkren was a revered necromancer in Nifushunm during a period of low spirits and soaring tension. Though the diviners themselves were as potent as ever, fewer and fewer young citizens were showing the inherent abilities necessary to respond to the breath of divinity. The stars and sands had been telling mixed omens of oncoming terror and misfortune, but it was difficult to determine just what these messages applied to. There was a lot of misfortune going around.

The shortage of diviners was not the worst of Nifushunm's problems, not by a long shot. Of greatest concern, actually, was a serious case of neighbor drama. Warring tribes were beginning to swallow one another, competing for land in the river valleys and relishing the growing concept of empire.

Amphet's king in that time, whose name is lost to prehistory, was no exception.

This king was as inclined toward conquest as any other warlord king during his day, only he believed himself to have the most formidable advantage of all: he had the diviners of Nifushunm on his side. Or so he liked to think in the beginning.

The diviners had been offering up their guidance and talents to Amphet for centuries, in exchange for peace and protection, and so the king began dogging them repeatedly for counsel on matters of battle and strategy. And each time, they gave him the same unwelcome answer: that he would lose.

That didn't sit well with the king of Amphet, who was said to be a notoriously determined and mistrustful man. He began to suspect treachery from Nifushunm, and feared that the diviners were conspiring for his defeat. He also feared the diviners' powers, as all misunderstanding minds did, and so he would not dare attack them outright. But he could, he thought, secure them as his own. And he tried. First with open arms, then with clenched fists, then with a sword in hand.

The rift began with the messages, these polite little invitations for Nifushunm to be peacefully annexed, for its own sake and security. The king believed, truly, that by exercising fuller authority over the diviners, he could force them to increase his nation's strength and influence. What the king failed to grasp was that the diviners were not shapers of events; they could only read what was to be and guide others accordingly. And sometimes, as was the case for this stubborn king, their guidance was not pleasant to hear.

When annexation was refused, the messages became more confrontational. Amphetians began blaming battlefield defeats on the diviners themselves, claiming that they were being sabotaged by supernatural craft. The accusations mounted higher and higher, and soon moved beyond the realm of military failures. Suddenly every illness in Amphet, every day of drought, every still-birth, every dead cow and lost bet and hangnail, was marked to be the work of the insidious diviners of Nifushunm.

The people of Nifushunm balked at the accusations. They made no plea of innocence. They had other things to worry about, droughts and dying infants of their own, not to mention the increasing onslaught of bad omens. And worst of all, at the height of all this smack talk, their own aging king died.

Nifushunm was not ruled by a blood heirship, nor were any of the nations around them. That trend wouldn't catch on in the region for a few more centuries. There were other ways to choose a king back then—ordination through mysticism, tests of valor, duels to the death. The kings of Nifushunm, in particular, were traditionally chosen by its eldest diviners, who customarily spent days fasting and hallucinating in the desert before making a decision.

This time around, their divining led them to a young citizen named Ahmul. Ahmul was an upstanding enough young man. He was said to possess a gentle heart and a faithful respect for the divine gifts. He had none of these gifts, however. Not a lick of them.

That fountain had apparently run dry into his five older sisters, who were some of the most gifted individuals Nifushunm had ever seen, despite the recent drought of talent. Ahmul's sisters were unprecedented seers, tried-and-trusted interpreters of the constant natural messages around them. And when they heard of their brother's ordination, the sands issued the five of them a specific and strong warning:

Get the hell out of town, girls, said the sands.

So those sisters did as they were told. They packed up, wished their brother love and luck, and left Nifushunm without knowing if or when they would return. Unaccompanied, they travelled into unclaimed desert, watching for instructions from the stars. The stars told them to stay put. The stars had plans for them. And so they waited.

And while they waited, their only brother was making a desert sojourn of his own. Before Ahmul could fully accept the title of king, he was to spend some customary time in the wild himself, where he was supposed to listen to the desert's voice, seek its counsel during his people's time of distress, and ask for its guidance at his coronation. He was supposed to find answers.

Unfortunately for the rest of us, he found Zabur instead.

He found her on the final evening of his soul-searching trip, while he and his attendants were hunting along a ravine. Alone on the trail of a wild dog, Ahmul found himself running further up the ancient river's path, deeper and deeper into the stretch where it had long dried up. Far from the rest of his party, he came across the ruins of a small, forgotten settlement. Ahmul entered the site carefully and paused, startled by what he found there. The dog was nowhere to be seen, but a solid black horse stood among the ruins, its coat gleaming in the barred sunlight that was flooding down into the cragged earth.

Ahmul's gaze shifted upwards to the light, where a broad, broken pillar of sandstone lay across the ravine's edges overhead. And stretched out upon it, spread out before the great red sun, was a woman—bronze, beautiful, and completely naked.

Ahmul wanted that woman very badly and very suddenly. But a heavy despair entered his heart just as quickly, competing with these overwhelming desires. As king, he knew, he would be denied a great many of life's pleasures. He was not to drink wine or sleep outdoors, and he was not to love a woman.

That last part did him in.

Typical man.

The woman noticed him. And instead of screaming and hiding her body, she stood up straight with the disc of the sun quivering behind her. She placed her hands on her ample, athletic hips, howled like a beast, and jumped to the bottom of the ravine.

This frightened Ahmul immensely. It must have also really turned him on, because he dropped to his knees instead of running away. The woman advanced towards him, demanding that he name himself. Her eyes were wild and round, so round that the whites of them circled their singular black ornaments completely.

Ahmul readily declared the truth, that he was Nifushunm's new king. And to that, the woman smiled a smile of unmatched power and pride, as if she were crushing a planet the size of an insect between her lovely fingers. That smile drenched Ahmul with fever. Was she flesh? Was she a vision? He begged to know her name.

The woman laughed, and the sound multiplied against the walls of the ravine.

I am the mouth of the desert, she said. The witch spirit of this place. I have no name.

As she spoke, the wind moaned through the ruins, and the black horse paced a nervous circle behind her.

You are a king, the witch said, and your people are sick with fear. You come seeking my guidance.

Ahmul, shocked by her accuracy, could only nod his accord.

The witch laughed a soft, drunken laugh. Her lips seemed to drip the words formed by their motions. She asked him to swear obedience to her counsel, to bind himself to her instruction, lest she release a storm of ruin upon his nation.

Ahmul, still on his knees, agreed. He had to wonder if his five sisters saw this sort of thing all the time. If so, then he had really been missing out. As the woman backed away in slow, graceful steps, his eyes drank their fill of her flesh, but his ears were desperately dry. He wanted her, he wanted her words, but why was she backing away? In the distance, he began to hear the calls of his men, searching down the ravine for him.

The witch hastened to give her instructions. She stood rigid, her voice resonating the hollowness of the wind as if speaking on its behalf. When you return to your people, she said, there will be a message waiting for you from Amphet's king. A proposition. You will answer it 'No'.

The calls of Ahmul's party drew closer, but their voices were not enough to pull his eyes away from her.

In a week's time, the witch continued, the king will send another message. Again, your answer will be 'No'.

Ahmul nodded.

In yet another week's time, she said, the king will send a third and final message. Here, the witch paused, contemplating, listening to the wind maybe. Her strange, wild eyes bore deep into Ahmul's.

Answer it 'Yes', she said.

Ahmul tried to catalog all of this in his mind. He was more focused, however, on the feeling that this woman was about to disappear forever. He rose to his feet.

Your people will rage at you, she said in haste, and say you betray them, and betray the order of things, but do not sway. Answer it 'Yes'. For me.

Before Ahmul could speak his pledge, laughter broke over the witch again. She turned away, lunging for the steep ravine walls, and the black horse ran another way, knocking Ahmul to the ground and taking the breath from his lungs. When his attendants came within sight moments later, he was alone, shouting and scrambling to the top of the ruins, frantically seeking the horizon in all directions.

The woman was nowhere. The horse was nowhere. Ahmul was a fool.

It was during these times that Dahrkren had begun speaking with death.

In a way, Dahrkren had always known how this worked. He was a necromancer, after all; death was his bread and butter. Knowing all about death, naming its many forms, understanding how to please it, recognizing what it looked like and how it was going to happen—all of this was his craft. It was his arena to attend to the dying (primarily the more important ailing individuals from both Nifushunm and Amphet) and to ensure that they departed in the proper manner.

Just as importantly, he kept a good correspondence with the deceased.

From their dreamy, other-planed existence, he could glean cryptic messages about the future and reminders about the past. To do this, Dahrkren used all manners of carefully calculated processes and states, tools and trances, some too old to have names. He lived by himself and worked with no one, yet he was rarely alone. The shadows of the dead and their voices filled his thoughts often; they had a near-constant, combined presence. But these were beings who had already lived and walked the earth and died. They were not death itself.

Death, Dahrkren knew, was not a being. It wasn't anything which would've warranted a capital letter in some holy book, had the diviners lived in a late enough century to write one. Like the winds that moved the shape of the earth, or the hand that held the Ket in its cradle, death was simply a force. It did what it did according to the order of things, and at times, in readable and measurable ways, it responded to the actions of the living by behaving differently. But it did not think or speak. It did not change. In doing so, it would disrupt the seamless engine of everything else.

As Dahrkren and other necromancers understood, the force of death lasted only a moment. It was a negative force, a vacuum, and it was permitted only a glimpse of the living plane while it worked. Its only purpose was to detach something living from its earthly shell and then send it along. Along to where, not even the necromancers knew. The dead had to be *somewhere*, of course, because the necromancers could still hear them, but not even Nifushunm's most anointed could determine where exactly they had gone.

Or if they were happy.

And that itself was the big mystery, the reason that necromancers of all people, of all diviners, were the most sober and joyless individuals. They knew everything there was to know about what happened when a person *died*, down to a science, but after that? Nada. Where do you go? How do you feel? Is there suffering? Is there peace? Are you alive again? Do you become part of something else? Something that shapes the universe? Like water or air?

Oh, they asked. For centuries, necromancers asked the dead these questions. But the dead ignored them, always continuing with their unrelated advice. The possibility of a famine. The outcome of a battle. So most necromancers had to settle for their best guess, that the energy of the dead got caught up in the rest of the universe and forever coursed through the earth, in flames and rays of light, in wind and water.

Something like that.

Well, Dahrkren wasn't so sure. And he was immensely troubled by this uncertainty, more so than his predecessors had ever been. The more death he encountered, the more uneasy and terrified he became, the more he became aware of how each day was bringing him closer to his own death, his own variable eternity.

So he started looking straight to the source for certainty, secretly attempting a connection that no other necromancer would have dared to even endorse. Line after sacred line was crossed, and by the time he attended to the passing of his own elderly king, Dahrkren had already begun to question death itself for the truth. And death, that nameless, starving vacuum, seeing an open window, was more than happy to answer him.

It answered him with deceit. He fell for it. And together they threw a big, crooked monkey wrench into that seamless engine I just mentioned.

That desert witch hadn't been kidding around. When Ahmul returned to Nifushunm as its newly appointed leader, a message from Amphet's king was already waiting for him. It was long and recited by heralds, who repeated word for word their king's congratulations and blessings. They also repeated his proposition, which was not unlike the invitations he'd sent before things had soured: a stated need for the diviner's unanimous assistance; a request that Ahmul become part of Amphet's own court, and for Nifushunm to likewise become part of Amphet.

Ahmul already had his answer: No.

Nope. No thanks.

Nifushunm's citizens were pleased by that. They liked this kid. In stark contrast to the battles raging out in the desert on all sides, the tiny state of Nifushunm was in a jubilee, throwing celebration after celebration and thriving on new hope. Maybe now things would turn around for them. Maybe all they'd needed was this young and fearless king.

One week later, more heralds from Amphet came with a second message. In so many parroted words, they claimed foul play on the part of the diviners. In retribution, the king threatened to revoke Amphet's long-standing protection of Nifushunm. He warned of the warring tribes ebbing closer, and reminded Ahmul of how defenseless his small nation would be without the protection of Amphetian armies. He demanded that Ahmul cease the meddling of the diviners, and offered him peace and protection should he join Amphet's court.

"No," was all Ahmul had to say.

And the crowd went wild. Again, the citizens of Nifushunm praised their new king and celebrated his sass. Again, they scoffed at the absurd idea of becoming barbaric Amphetians. Amphet's threats were empty, these people believed, so long as the diviners were feared, and so they gloated without worry.

A week passed, and again a message came. Ahmul's blood bubbled. This was the third message. And this time, it wasn't just the heralds who showed up—there was an envoy at the gates.

The message began with the usual complaints and requests, a list of grievances blamed on the diviners, a plea of logic outlining why Nifushunm should accept Amphetian citizenship. And then it got right to the point:

Marry my daughter, Amphet's king proposed through the talking heads of his heralds. In short, he wanted to include Ahmul as a figure of Amphetian royalty, thus orchestrating a more peaceful, enticing merger. Ahmul could continue ruling Nifushunm as he pleased, and would answer only to Amphet's king.

The people in Nifushunm's court laughed openly at this desperate attempt. A king of Nifushunm, bowing to another king, taking a wife. A barbaric Amphetian wife! What a riot. They turned to their crowd-pleasing leader, ready to hear some cheek.

But Ahmul was silent. His heart was crushed and divided. Was this really what the desert witch had meant? Was this a mistake? It had to be. She had said his people would rage against him, but this? The idea was too cruel. He cursed her face in his mind, which had been so full of the rest of her these past few weeks, and so empty of any original thought.

The laughter gave way to silence as more of the envoy entered. In the middle of it, Ahmul suddenly noticed, was a solid black horse. And sitting on top of it, now fully and finely clothed, was Zabur, the daughter in question, the desert witch herself.

She was controlling herself, doing everything in her power not to laugh. The result was stunning. Her face was like the Datura blossom at sunset, just about to burst open for the night.

Yes, was Ahmul's final answer. Absolutely, yes.

The Luna Latum historians always liked to point out that what happened next was not Ahuml's fault. Yes, they'd say, he was enamored enough by Zabur to go against his people's wishes. But it's been speculated that he made the decision with his head, too, and not just with his hormones. The safety of Nifushunm, however self-assured its people liked to be, had been in real jeopardy for too long. And sooner or later, powerful diviners or not, they were going to have to give in to Amphet or face annihilation from any number of sources. As it happened, Zabur was simply the most attractive solution to this problem.

I personally never gave Ahmul so much credit. But I did agree: What happened next would have happened eventually anyway, maybe not to

Zabur, but to someone else.

There was outrage. Ahmul's people, his biggest fans, turned on him in a matter of seconds, calling him weak and treacherous, accusing him of betrayal and crying of disregard for the diviners. But Ahmul put his decision into immediate practice. He left with the envoy, bringing only a few attendants and high priests with him, reasoning with his people that the merger was a necessary reaction to a dangerous world. An increasingly dangerous and uncertain world, and not even the diviners could deny that.

Ahmul's people didn't know that beneath his facade of rationality, he had nothing, no firm standing on whether or not he was doing the right thing. But he left the devastated mob anyway and boarded a barge bound for the other side of the Ket, because he was certain of *one* thing: his own complete incapacity to deny Zabur.

The merger had been entirely her doing, beginning with her instant and artful portrayal of a witch, and ending with the careful implantation of the marriage idea into her father's brutal mind. Amphet's king surely thought of the proposal as his own scheme, but it had sprung from Zabur's rapid fancy out there in the ruins, born the moment Ahmul had revealed himself to her.

The girl adoringly whispered all of this to Ahmul before the barge even left the eastern bank of the Ket, while the heralds lit colorful fires to show their king what the answer had been. Ahmul was at once impressed, terrified, outraged, and impassioned, but there was no turning back. This clever, royal wild thing beside him, who liked to lounge naked and unattended in the wilderness, who would manipulate centuries-old political structures on a flimsy romantic whim, would be his wife before the sun went down.

The connotations were not good. Clearly he'd made a reckless choice. Yet he could not help feeling that the order of things was guiding him, that this was the most sensible, peaceable conclusion for both nations.

Or maybe he was just telling himself that because he'd gotten a good look at Zabur's bazonkas already. Who knows?

Music and shouting met the envoy on the other side of the glassy waters, and the sand of the Amphetian banks could not be seen beneath all the people waiting to welcome Ahmul. His arrival marked a fantastic victory for Amphet, and all its people had their party sandals on. The envoy was immediately swept away in an impromptu parade through the city's passageways, and Ahmul walked with his attendants and diviners as if in a dream, deafened by the music and cheering, dodging the jewelry, food, and live animals that were being tossed every which way.

Maybe Zabur wasn't that wild after all, at least not by Amphetian standards. Ahmul consoled himself with this thought, watching her as she rode ahead on the black horse, trying and failing to hold onto every flower and bracelet being handed to her. And as quickly as a warm admiration fell over him at the sight, a hard and swift shadow fell over Zabur.

In every direction, people darted and screamed. A column of stone had crumbled, toppled onto a swath of the crowd ahead. And most directly, most significantly, onto Zabur and her horse.

There was a wash of panic followed by a glimmer of relief. Zabur had not been crushed, just dashed against the ground as the animal fell beneath her. In fact, as the dust settled and people regained their bearings, she appeared as lovely and whole as if nothing had happened. Her warm hands still clutched at flowers; her eyes were still liquid with light. The only sight betraying her life was a fast trickle of blood between her lips, dampening the earth beneath her, announcing her death.

Ahmul had no time to react. Hands were suddenly upon him from every angle. Mass confusion and hysteria erupted, and he and his attendants, his priests, were beaten to the ground. The Amphetians were baying like animals, shouting about the diviners, about the murder of their beloved daughter.

Ahmul was going to be ripped apart, he was certain of it. Everywhere, there were feet kicking him, hands pulling at his limbs, blunt objects striking him in the face. In the corner of his battered eye, he saw the skull of one of his diviners split open by a stone, and a group of people stabbing and stoning someone else over and over; he couldn't tell who.

And then he saw Amphet's king, bellowing wretchedly from where his favorite child now lay dead. The volume of his grief and fury was enough to command the attention of the entire gruesome mob, until every last living ear was waiting for him to speak.

The king was quick in his judgement. He surmised that this was base villainy, the work of none other than the diviners themselves. He no longer cared for their help. He no longer feared their power. Whatever the consequences, he would crush Nifushunm before the sun buried itself, and burn to death every man, woman, and child within its walls.

He would start with their young, newly anointed king, who was at that moment too shocked and petrified to do more than chatter his teeth behind bleeding lips. A torch was set in the older king's hand, and he waved it violently with each promise of what would become of Nifushunm, of his Zabur's vengeance, of how Ahmul would burn before their eyes here and now, and the livid Amphetians shouted louder at every promise.

But someone else was shouting. It was not the loudness of his voice, but what he was proclaiming which made the Amphetians—even the king—halt and go silent before Ahmul could be set ablaze.

This man was literally screaming for his life. He was, in those days, an older man, just under 30 years of age, frail but handsome, dressed in the telltale robes of white. The man was Dahrkren, the high priest and gifted necromancer of Nifushunm.

Like all the other priests who had accompanied Ahmul across the Ket, he now lay crushed under the punishing feet of several vengeful Amphetians. But Dahrkren alone knew a truth that could instantly halt the execution of his brethren, himself, and his own king. And so he was shouting it as loudly as he could, again and again, the words ringing out across the baffled square:

"I can make her live! I can make her live!"

Dahrkren had been told where people went after they died.

He had spent hours, days and nights at a time, shut away in his tent, drinking and drugging himself into darkness. At first, he'd stuck with the things that he knew. He had cut his skin and read meaning in the colors of the scratches. He'd huffed snake venom, cracked bones, and examined the innards of chickens and toads.

It wasn't until he strayed into questionably illegal territory that he found results. He began to dig around, somewhat literally, into the dead themselves. He lay with them for hours, matching his pulse to where he had once been able to feel theirs, listening for answers.

What he discovered, or what the voice of death led him to believe, was that the afterlife was more miserable than he could imagine. He was told it was a place of eternal waste, suffering, and powerlessness. Death itself, as Dahrkren had seen so many times, was sweet and gentle. It gave a person power and invincibility. But fleetingly—the actual force of death could never hang onto a person. It could not rescue one from the unending sorrow of the afterlife.

Or could it?

On that day, when Zabur met death, and all of Nifushunm faced it, Dahrkren was already sure of the answer. Death had shown him the way. He need only heed its orders and live forever. And here was his chance.

But convincing the king of Amphet of his sincerity was no cake walk. The man, you'll recall, had just seen his own daughter dashed to death against the ground, and he sincerely believed Dahrkren to be among those responsible. It took a lot of pleading indeed, a lot of powerful descriptions, to stop the king from blazing his hot trail of revenge right there.

Dahrkren had to think quickly. There was no way to convince the delusional king that this was a mistake, so he proposed that an anonymous faction of diviners had committed this atrocity. He apologized shamelessly for their actions and professed a grand hatred for them. But most importantly, he promised that he could restore Zabur to life to make amends. He claimed that within a matter of days, if he could take Zabur's body across the river and into his own necromancer's tent, that she would walk out again, alive.

It's no surprise that this offer was met by more immediate hostility, nor that the king was furious at the very idea. But the air was uneasy, strangely sour as Dahrkren spoke, and the rioting did not immediately continue.

By then, the great necromancer had been thrown into the center of attention, and was free of the crowd. He continued, mostly unharrassed, to where Zabur's black horse lay. Once more, everything quieted, and everyone, including both kings, watched him carefully.

With quaking hands, Dahrkren pulled something from a bag at his side, something small and yellow. Holding it cupped and concealed in both hands, he paced the length of the horse, and then stopped to kneel by its head. Its eyes were wide and rolled back, sunken into its hollow face, empty of all life. He closed the eyes carefully and ran a hand down the bridge of its velvety black nose, over its nostrils and lips. He did not look up to watch for anyone's reactions. As far as he was concerned, he was alone, and the silence of the mob affirmed that feeling.

Dahrkren again took the yellow object in both hands. His whispered, unheard chants stopped abruptly just before he twisted the thing between his fists, snapping it—whatever *it* was—in half. With immediacy, he then stooped to the ground, opened the horse's mouth, and pushed the broken object down its throat.

No one moved. For well over a minute, Dahrkren continued to kneel, staring fixedly for signs of life from the horse, watching with fear—for his life, and for what it would mean if the animal's own life were restored.

His eyes didn't waver even as people started to shout again, calling him a fool, eager to get on with razing Nifushunm. But even these outbursts were half-hearted. The air was still heavy and acrid; to make noise in it felt deadly wrong. A few more moments passed. And then came the sound.

It was a low sound, not a whisper or a groan, but something deeper, an older sound.

It was the sound of the horse exhaling.

It breathed in with a grunt, and Dahrkren, with his trace of a smile weighed down by a heavy terror, stood cautiously to move out of its way. The horse twisted its head off the ground with a miraculously unbroken neck. It squealed and groaned, pulling its back legs away from the slabs of the fallen column. These legs, which had moments ago been crushed and broken, now moved freely, filling out to their normal shape before every eye within view.

As the animal heaved itself to its feet, it hacked something up into the dirt. Dahrkren looked to the earth, seeing what he expected: a small yellow bird, newly dead.

No one else even noticed the bird. Every other eye was surely fixed upon Zabur's horse as it lunged in circles, snorting, breathing, magnificent, acting very much alive.

Less than two days later, Dahrkren was sitting in his tent, in the dark hours beyond midnight. Zabur's body and the wooden bench it lay on were the only other objects of stature in the room. The rest of the place was a disorder of pots, skins and feathers, and the strange and varied instruments of necromancy.

He had been given seven days.

What he needed to do would only take seven *minutes*, and he could do it at any time. But he waited. He spent the first day and night pacing through the tent, debating with himself, never once lifting the linen covering to look at the girl's lifeless form. By dawn he was sitting on the earthen floor. He sat this way all day, motionless, never once rising, until long after the sun had set again.

He didn't have to worry about being bothered by anyone else. Amphet's king had ordered that no one disturb the process, which did little good. Dahrkren was plenty disturbed by himself as it was.

He knew the course of action, and now he knew its result. The black horse, as he'd requested, was tethered behind his tent. All day long it had raged and squealed, running in tireless circles, neither drinking nor eating, attacking anyone who came near it with gnashing teeth. Despite its behavior, it had been examined and said to be in fit condition, probably only stressed by events it couldn't comprehend.

Stressed. Sure.

Dahrkren stared across his dark tent, the little mound of his life, all the things that would remain for someone else's use should he die. *Should he die.* Death's reminders crept through his imagination, all the uncertain, eternal horrors of the afterlife. All that had awaited each spirit he had sent on into death. Everything that awaited him. Everything that now awaited all the people in Nifushunm.

Unless he sided with death.

He had consulted with no one, knowing that the other diviners would have abhorred what he'd done already. They were not ones to meddle with forces meant only to guide them. But they hadn't been guided to *this* truth, to this level of action. They'd never been promised this kind of power. Death had *chosen* him. He would show the rest of them how, if they asked. And if any stood in his way, he would move them. He would not willingly pass up this divine offer, to go on and suffer, only because so many others had done so before him. He had decided.

Just before midnight, he stood and crossed the length of his tent. Without hesitating, he gently pulled the unstained linen away, revealing Zabur's unwounded—and unadorned—anatomy in its entirety.

Her dark, grape-skin eyelids were closed, and her white teeth glowed in the darkness, visible through the gentle snarl of death, the shape of an unfinished breath. She reeked only of the floral oils that had been spread over her icy, blanched skin; decay's stink was not yet detectable. She was perfect.

He did as death had instructed. It was very simple, what he'd been told to do, but he used every extra precaution to ensure success. He put out the fire in his tent, leaving only a few lanterns lit, and tied the tent entrance tightly, just in case of an unauthorized interruption. Once his eyes had adjusted to the new degree of darkness, he walked all around the bench, testing it from all angles for sturdiness. Satisfied, he placed three items on the edge of the bench, just beside Zabur's shoulder: a ball of moist clay, a lump of black resin, and a clean bone dagger.

He then grabbed a handful of glittering white sand. Moving around the bench, he chanted an invocation of protection while leaving a complete circle of sand behind him, a circle he was not to step outside of again, not until he had seen this through.

Dahrkren centered himself, straightened his white robes, and stepped onto the bench. He lowered himself gently, carefully, onto Zabur's body, and seated himself about her waist. His breathing increased, and the blood rushed hot in his ears. He took three deep breaths, faltering, and finally forced himself to utter the first of those ancient words, words that no one else has ever heard or known since.

The wind stopped rattling the tent. The horse ceased its raging and was still. The air grew cold and the lanterns went out, leaving Dahrkren in a temporary darkness, until a sudden and unexplained silver light illuminated his surroundings.

Dahrkren paused, confused by the light, listening, watching. His mind and heart were in tumult, but there was no turning back. He looked at Zabur's face, fear stinging his eyes in the form of hot tears, and stammered on, stuttering the words until something took them from him in a quick, pronounced stream. Upon uttering the final tones, he picked up the lump of palm gum.

With shaky but expedited movements, he rolled the gum into four small balls. He stuffed one in each of his nostrils to seal them off, and tested them for any leaking of air. Finding none, he then issued the same treatment to Zabur's nose.

Next, he pulled out the black resin, kneading it until he found the runny, gluey center. He carefully parted Zabur's lips, and, with his finger, painted them with a layer of the sticky substance.

His chest was heaving uncontrollably as he applied the remaining resin to his own lips, his breathing verging on hyperventilation. Enough of that. He didn't allow himself pause. Holding tightly to either side of the bench, he inhaled deeply and plunged forward, sealing Zabur's lips securely with his own and willing himself to breathe no more.

With resolve, he fumbled for the nearby dagger, his wide eyes now fixed in position, unable to take in anything but those thick purple eyelids below him. His fingers found the handle, and steadily, cautiously, he guided the blade through the empty space between Zabur's throat and his own, where he let it hover in his hand. Only then did he allow himself to hesitate, to tremble and tighten his grip, to choke on the foul air drifting into him, to feel mortally afraid. He squeezed his eyes shut.

With a sure, hard motion, he sliced his own throat open from one side to the other.

@

"Jesse!"

"Just hear me out. I'm almost finished."

"That's sick! What is *wrong* with you?!"

"Oh, honey. Just you wait and see."

For the remainder of that night, Ahmul's sisters stared at the desert sky with solemn grief and awe. They had just witnessed the moon lurching from its position in Earth's shadow. Trembling, they had watched it move from the darkness, become a crescent, wax full, and then accelerate into shadows once more, all within the hour.

It was the first time they had seen the moon.

Before that moment, the moment Dahrkren had spoken the words no one else would ever know, the moon's orbit had always been fixed within the earth's shadow, never showing itself. And at his incantation, it had accelerated senselessly, defying what we call physics, causing oceans and rivers to shift, and the earth to tremble and break in places. The sisters knew this, even though everything was still and quiet where they watched. Though they did not know what the moon was or what role it played, they understood that it would follow another routine from that night forward, the path and pattern it would stay on for thousands and thousands of years to come, the logical orbit we know today.

They listened and waited until morning, learning from the surprised stars, from the astonished wind and sands, what had happened.

They were told what Dahrkren had done and how. They knew that as he had fallen forward in his own tent, the life gushing out of him by his own hand, that his precautions proved effective. The resin had held his lips fast to Zabur's, and his dying breath had passed into her.

And for awhile after that, nothing had happened.

As the moon shifted to its new course, they were told, Zabur's death-closed eyes had opened. Her dead body flooded with panic. Her dead lungs struggled to fill themselves, but were constricted. Flailing, she'd pulled the gum from her nose and pushed Dahrkren's slumped body to the ground.

She sat straight up, staring wildly into the silver darkness, breathing in and out and in and out, a learned motion, a habit.

She didn't need to breathe anymore.

She smeared at the warm blood that had been spilled on her, feeling no horror or surprise, just a quizzical calm. Its strong smell, its bold flavor on the tip of her curious tongue, filled her with sensations of overwhelming lightness and untested strength. She jumped straightaway to her feet and down from the bench, thoughtlessly laying waste to that silly circle of white sand.

The citadel all around the tent was awake with sounds of shock and disbelief, as people fearfully sought an explanation for the moon. Zabur heard this. She could feel the pulsations of a hundred beating hearts prickling against her skin. She could smell sweat and life pressing in all around her, as strongly as she could smell the blood curing on her hands. Peering through a small tear in the tent's folds, however, she saw only the moon and her beloved black horse, which was staring back at her, motionless and expectant, possessed of the same fantastic energy. She smiled knowingly and whirled back around into the tent's darkness.

She knew exactly what to do. A new force was guiding her instincts now, one that would never weaken her body or leave her soul unprotected. It was death, raw and unchecked; it saw through her eyes and touched with her hands. And now, it wanted to taste through her teeth.

She easily found the wet, open massacre of Dahrkren's throat. Although the remainder of his blood wasn't enough to satisfy her instinct, it was enough to placate it, and she drank him dry in minutes. The blood soothed her head, sped up the vibrating, twisting sensations inside her body, and made the instructions of her new conscience ring loud and clear. There was more to do. So much more.

She lifted Dahrkren with tremendous ease and lay him out on the bench, drew open his mouth with reverent gentleness. And then she breathed into him, filling his chest with the same force that had animated her.

Just as she had, he lay still for awhile. And then he opened his eyes and rose up, strong and whole, a waking window for something with no name, a void where a person had previously existed. Zabur stepped back, ravenous but reveling, and bowed at his feet, an action symbolic of the moment that death became an operating force on this plane. The moment the Hollows, as they would one day be called, came to be.

The sisters listened in misery to this, at how these two abominations left the tent and forcibly spread their death disease from one fortress wall of Nifushunm to another, all in the time before dawn. How the morning had passed without any word from Nifushunm's side of the Ket. How anxious the vengeful king had grown, and also their brother Ahmul, who was being held in Amphet until Zabur's return.

And return she did. Just before dusk, Amphet's river sentries began shouting that the gates of Nifushunm had opened, and that Zabur was riding out, alive, returning to them. Citizens rushed the banks to see this for themselves, zealous and amazed. But the joy quickly turned to terror.

Zabur wasn't alone.

No one in Amphet was spared the terror that swept across the river that evening, not the mightiest soldiers or the most guarded courtesans, not even the savage king himself. The historians like to say that Zabur slew her father and devoured him completely, or maybe that is what she did to Ahmul. However she sliced it, every human being within Amphet's walls was dead—or something worse—within three hours of her homecoming.

From their safe vantage point, miles into the wild, the five sisters saw all of this in a shared trance. They understood that this force, this disease, this hunger, would never stop. It would consume life after life, people after people, until there wasn't a beating heart left in the world. And even then it would not be satisfied. It had no conscience or goal, only a bottomless need, and it had learned to speak. Dahrkren, the curious, selfish, gifted, unlucky necromancer, had been chosen as its listener. And he had been deceived in the worst way. He wasn't going to live forever.

He was going to spend forever dying.

And so would all his victims, until there was nothing and no one left, the sisters knew, so they had to act immediately. They begged answers of their usual guides, asking what could stop these creatures and their hunger. What could drive something without life beyond the clinging force of death? The answer came simply and swiftly: other forces. The forces which rightfully outlasted life and death alike and never ended, five essences which any diviner would have known intimately—light, fire, earth, water, and air.

These ever-living forces wouldn't succeed on their own; they would need consciousness in order to act. This consciousness, in turn, would require living hands to guide the forces separately, to physically will them against death. It would take a channel, a medium, a carrier.

A vessel.

The five sisters were shown how to create these vessels, but they would also need witnesses, people to hear their warnings before the act was finished. So they walked until they crossed a warring tribe, armed people fleeing across the desert after seeing the moon. The sisters explained to them what had happened, and all that would come, and these people were frightened enough to listen. The tribe pledged its assistance, and the sisters got to work.

As the sun was sinking into the sand, the five of them began moving in a circle, guarded by their new allies. Long into the night they performed a spell that none of the bewildered onlookers could understand, yet its significance and magnitude held the total attention of all those who watched. Just five lithe bodies winding around a fire, hands linked, whispering fervently. The wind whispered back. The sand shifted. The fire crackled. But that was all.

Still hours before dawn, the sisters abruptly faced out of the circle in unison, with the understanding that they would never again look upon one another. They released their linked hands for the last time and immediately began traveling in opposite directions.

They walked as far as was necessary to carry out the final length of their spell, each accompanied by members of the baffled bedouin tribe. What these escorts saw, they reported, and the story has remained intact for generations, for millennia:

The youngest of the sisters stopped walking when she smelled a thunderstorm, and waited for its coming on a grassy flat, where she remained until struck by lightning.

The eldest of the sisters merely walked to the closest hip of a Nile tributary and refused to stop. She walked until the top of her head disappeared under the current, and did not resurface.

The wisest instructed the bedouins to build a pyre, upon which she allowed herself to burn alive.

The strongest of the five stood in the bottom of a ravine and ordered her escorts to bury her.

And the loveliest sister walked to the rim of the highest canyon she could find and leaped off.

There were no bodies. No burnt embers or crushed bones. Ashes to ashes. Dust to dust. The sisters had successfully *Become*—that is to say, they'd wholly given themselves up to these forces, and in turn, the forces had consumed all of them whole. Their atoms, their essence, their souls—however you want to think of it—had already begun to spread into every grain of sand, drop of water, particle of air, flicker of flame, and ray of light that touched the earth.

They had given these forces a living conscience. And though that was still only *half* the plan, it was enough to win part of the battle. By dawn, the bedouin tribe had regrouped a safe distance from Amphet, on a hilltop where the sisters had told them to meet. And at sunrise, they watched the Ket erupt from her cradle. The structures along the riverbanks tumbled to the ground, and the earth beneath both cities sank away, devouring not only several centuries' worth of divining legacy, but also death's origins: nearly all of the Hollows were buried that morning

By the hundreds, they fell with their cities into the caving earth, where they would wait indefinitely, suffering, starving without nourishment, dying without completion. Only Dahrkren himself managed to escape the flooding of the Ket and flee across the desert for cover. He ran not from the destruction, nor from the bedouins, but from a curse, the most direct result of the sisters' spell.

Thanks to their individual sacrifices, Dahrkren found himself suddenly and considerably crippled, unable to roam and feed unchecked. Every ray of sunshine or raindrop scalded him. To touch the sand with his bare flesh was agony, as was the heat of any flame, and the gentlest of breezes was enough to torture him. What was to be an eternity of power and inhuman strength had suddenly become an everlasting and constant torment.

That's what you get for trusting death, I guess.

The same fate fell upon any Hollow he created from that day forward. Where he began his collection, no one is certain, and so the story ends on that hilltop with forty people. Forty dumbstruck bedouins, who would guard the secret of what they had seen and pass it on to their children like a curse. Children who would centuries later name themselves the Luna Latum, or "the Burial of the Moon". These people alone knew what waited beneath the sand—and what ran loose above it. They also knew what could stop the Hollows, and it was something they sure as hell didn't have.

Amphet and Nifushunm, even the very banks of the Ket, were gone. There was no indication, not so much as a dent in the sand, telling where the cities had once stood, nor to which spot Dahrkren would inevitably return to raise them. The bedouins had no understanding of divinity, so they could not even ask the sands or the dead what to do. They had only the explanations the sisters had given them. Explanations about what that kind of power had felt like, about how Dahrkren had abused it, and how this misused force would continue to spread.

And they had the following words, the last half of the sisters' plan, the part that made Ghiyath Ayman, Su Kim Khan, Whitney Leroy Jackson, Corin Livingston III, and Jesse Cannon shake in their sleep about seven thousand years later:

"Keep all of this known well among yourselves and your children, and keep it secret, as others would invoke more evil out of panic. Have patience, remain vigilant, commune with the divine, and wait.

"We will send others to finish what we ourselves began, in the form of great men, born of woman's flesh but constructed of the divine forces, five beings of terrible power, fierce and indestructible.

"They will move light, water and air, flame and earth, with courage and conscience, and they will seek death's origin together, as it will seek them in turn. It will find no place without suffering until that day, when by the sacrifice of Becoming they will defeat the crueler force, and banish its pale eye from the heavens.

"So preserve yourselves and watch for signs of them; prepare to defend and serve them. Forget our names but heed our forces, for through the coming Vessel, we will again touch the earth with new hands. Until that day, we remain only a part of it."

CHAPTER 5

When Jesse finally seemed to be finished, he watched me. Carefully.

I said nothing. I was too tired, too stupefied, to come up with a response. The mere fact that Jesse had produced something so complex was the only thing that had kept me awake that much longer in the first place. Now that his story was over, I sat back and waited for more, for something else. For him to ask what kind of drugs he'd been given to explain this bizarre dream. Or for him to immediately request more of them.

But he said nothing else. He just stared at me with an impatient and anxious hope in his eyes.

I finally just shrugged. What the hell was I supposed to say?

"Jordan," he started, already pleading.

I shook my head wearily and adjusted myself in the chair for the billionth time. Was he kidding?

"Jesse," I said softly. "You're just tired." *And delusional.*

"Jordan, *please*, I'm serious." He sat forward, trying to look me in the eye while I avoided the invitation. "Do you think I *want* to sound like an idiot?"

I bit my tongue. Why? Why did *this* have to be the first occurrence of him asking me that? I cringed.

"Jesse? Seriously?"

"Seriously."

I froze for a moment, just a moment. No. Nope. No way. I shook my head resolutely and started to stand up, getting defensive when he shot me one of his desperate looks.

"Oh, come on!" I threw my hands up. "It sounds like you just—"

"I know what it fucking sounds like!" Jesse shouted, loud enough for the morgue to hear, and wind rattled fiercely against the picture window. The last time he'd sounded remotely that angry, he was blitzed on vodka and reading a negative red carpet outfit review. This was incomparably worse. I sat back down stiffly.

"I *know* it sounds crazy. It was in *my* head, remember?" he waved his hands about his head while searching for any trace of agreement on my face. "But it wasn't a dream, Jordan. It wasn't, I'm telling you. It was real. It was a signal or a message or something and it was real. It's real and it's going to happen. To me."

His head dropped, and all that hair, still perfect even after a night on hospital linen, fell over his face. He laced his long fingers through it to massage his forehead and moaned. "What am I going to do?"

What was *he* going to do? What the hell was *I* going to do? This was the kind of crap I got paid to prevent. The dream description had been strange and disturbing enough, but now this? Now he's taking it as some kind of divine appointment? Alright. Fine. Okay. I could handle it. I'd gotten him through that month when he was totally convinced that mirrors caused cancer. I could get him over this. And I wouldn't even have to do his eyebrows.

Three more days, I reminded myself. Just three more days, and you're done.

I sucked in a deep breath and stood up.

"You're going to take it easy today, that's what you're going to do," I commanded. "Margot already cancelled tonight's show for you, and the press release went out this morning. You don't have to do a thing. Just one happy photo of you hugging a nurse and we're out of here."

He remained slumped over, shaking his head limply from side to side, hardly listening.

"And then I'll book you a place to get a deep tissue massage, huh? Acupuncture, lemonade, whatever the hell you want."

"No, no, no . . ."

"—and from here on out you're going to start sleeping like a civilized human being, okay? And you'll be fine. We'll stay on the tour bus tonight and we'll still be on schedule for tomorrow."

"No, no, no, no," he flipped the hair out of his face and rubbed his forehead some more, in obvious agony. And then suddenly he straightened up, his almond eyes round as bottle caps, as if he had just realized that he'd overslept on the most important day in history.

"I have to go to New York," he said, quick and matter-of-fact, looking around the room like he was just going to grab his shoes and be off. "I have to. Tomorrow morning. I have to be there."

"What *are* you talking about?" I bent low and snapped my fingers sternly between his eyes. I'd had about enough. "Don't do this, Jesse. Don't crack up on me now, right before I go. That's why you're acting like this, isn't it? You're trying to guilt me into staying . . ."

"What? Jordan, for god's sake! No. This isn't about you at all."

I shook my head and turned away.

"Look! Forget about it then, okay?" he snapped. To my horror, he started throwing the sheets off, his angelic face sullen with anger and disappointment. "Just don't tell anyone about what I said, then. But I'm going."

"Whoa!" I put my foot down. Not on my watch he wasn't. I wasn't going to answer for him, not this time. I backed towards the door. "If you're really serious about that, then I swear to god I'm getting a doctor right now. Because your head is obviously more fucked than they thought."

Of course I said that; of course I was serious. And of course I wasn't giving his whack dream any thought whatsoever. I'd experienced too many of his nervous breakdowns and hair-brained notions for this to really phase me much. Granted none of them had ever been so downright weird or vivid. But I thought I was saying the right thing. And maybe I was. Maybe everything would've been better off had he listened to me and ignored it all.

He couldn't ignore it. I understand that now.

"No, no, don't!" he started to come after me, lunging halfway out of the bed, then squealed. He'd ripped an IV needle out of his arm. "Son of a *bitch*!"

I had little pity. But I didn't leave the room. I crossed my arms and watched him struggle.

"What then? What am I *supposed* to do? Huh?" he hissed, pulling the mess of tape and cotton gauze off his arm. "Yeeegh..."

"Well, for starters, you're *supposed* to be on Oprah tomorrow, remember? So you better drop this Planeteer crap right now."

That got the response I wanted. Jesse paused. You don't flake out on Oprah. It's celebrity suicide, and he knew it. Still, he appeared to be deliberating. I honestly couldn't believe what I was seeing.

"Oprah!" I screamed.

It's a powerful word.

"Alright, alright, Oprah, Oprah!" he lifted his arms in defeat before settling into a scowl, and from there we stared at one another in a silent showdown.

"I'll go," he finally confirmed. "But you have to promise you won't tell *anybody* about what I saw."

"Dreamed."

"Whatever. Nobody. No doctors. No Margot."

"Fine."

He watched me, suspicious. "Double pinky kiss-kiss?"

I rolled my eyes and walked back over to him. "If I have to."

We locked pinkies and kissed our respective thumbs while glaring at one another.

"That's my girl."

Jesse was all smiles after that, which I ignored. I literally could not process another concern or suspicion; I couldn't even begin to analyze his dream of zombie Egyptians. I'd sort out that apparent head trauma when I had more strength. First I needed to factor how few calls I could afford to make before getting some goddamn sleep. There was Margot again, at least twice, the insurance company, Jesse's holistic specialist back in Los Angeles, Toby the driver, the party host . . .

I fell asleep on the chair.

It wasn't even for a whole hour. The pain in my neck woke me up, or else I would've slept for the rest of the day. But I was curled up in that chair like a chicken embryo, and eventually it got to me.

Why are all the freaking hospital chairs like that? Can anyone tell me this? It doesn't matter where you go, all of them, I swear . . .

Jesse was gone.

I jumped up, which of course wasn't the tender thing to do for my neck, or my back, and scurried Quasimodo-style toward the door in a panic. Was it really four-thirty? How far could he have gotten? Why hadn't my phone woken me up?

The door swung open and hit me in the face.

"Ladies, please!" Jesse was trilling theatrically, lingering just outside the door, "I'll be right back to sign those scrubs, I promise. Keep your top on, Linda!"

Raucous feminine laughter followed from the hallway, and Jesse slid in, closing the door behind him and grinning coyly. He was dressed and looking well, an extreme contrast to an hour ago. I staggered out of his way, clutching my nose to stem any possible bleeding.

"Oh good, you're awake," he prattled on and broke into some half-hummed disco song. Grabbing my arm, he dragged me back to the accursed chair, somehow getting me to sit down.

"Jordan, this is very important," he put a sealed envelope in my lap. I left it there, stunned, still rubbing my face. "Everything will be just fine, but I need your help."

I didn't like where this was going.

Jesse sank to his knees, which put us eye-to-eye, and took both of my hands in his.

"I need you to do something for me, not as my assistant, but as my friend."

His honey-browns were pleading. Oh brother, when he does that . . . I forced myself to remain stoic.

"I need you to go to New York," he said. "Like, right now."

@

A horrible screeching woke Su Kim Khan up. His body burned. It was numb with cold, and his ill-fitting, bright orange jumpsuit was wet and freezing.

He was moving.

He was in a boxcar, and it was slowing down.

Khan grimaced at the cold and at his incredible headache, forcing himself to uncurl out of the large shape he was huddled in. The boxcar was empty and black. He had closed the door after jumping in, he remembered that much. In the blind darkness, he peeled the soaked orange prison garb off and dropped it in a heap. He needed to get rid of it. And he needed to get warm.

Kneeling, he steadied himself against the rumbling and halting of the boxcar, staring hard into the blackness. He reached out, feeling the damp clothes with his rough fingers. Khan knew how to do this. Somehow, he knew.

He emptied his mind and thought only of *her*.

There was a spark. The wet clothes made a sizzling sound. And then an orange flame started multiplying over the damp material, drying it, burning it.

Khan warmed himself as the fire grew. Watching it, feeling it, breathing in the smoke, he had never felt healthier in his life. He laughed at himself for a moment, stood up to his full height, and started investigating the box car. It wasn't empty after all, he noted; there were some boxes piled in the other end. Khan dragged one to the fire and opened it, felt around inside. Some kind of heavy, soft material. Fur? He laughed and laughed. This was his lucky day.

He pulled the heavy garment on and warmed himself while there was still time. The fire was starting to die; his prison suit was almost completely reduced to ashes. Khan made his way to the large, rusty door and slid it open a little. He squinted.

Outside, frosted evergreen trees rolled by. The ground was blinding white, and an icy highway wound along the valley below. Khan frowned, wondering what time it was, and how much time had passed. There was no telling whether he was in Arkansas or Alaska.

The boxcar balked and squealed. Any minute now it would stop at its final destination, and Khan was smart enough not to wait for that. He ducked and rolled.

He didn't roll far. He just kind of sank. The snow was well over two feet high. Cursing silently, Khan danced barefoot to the bottom of the hill, towards the highway. He scanned the roadside until he found a sign and squinted hard.

Toronto: 22 km

Oh, lucky day.

Driving in Manhattan really put Stella Rosin on edge. She found it difficult to subdue the urge to run red lights and weave through traffic, but breaking laws would attract too much attention, police attention. And she knew from past experience that police attention often ended with lots of dead police. That was precisely the kind of idiotic mess Stella Rosin liked to avoid.

Besides, it would have been a feat even for Stella to weave through downtown gridlock in a '96 Buick. Luna Latum hunters, for innumerable practical reasons, preferred speed bikes and auction-acquired ambulances, and indeed Stella's favored Honda had been flown out to Long Island at her request. Abe, however, had insisted that they use a car to get around. It would be less conspicuous, he'd said. Stella Rosin suspected that he was just a pussy.

Abe had quite a lot to do with her sour mood.

Dr. Abraham Sharma. The high-ranking specialist she was shadowing for this most unusual (and undesirable) assignment. This was very clearly *his* hunt, not hers, and it was about as exciting as a tax return. The urgent situation addressed at the Consulate meeting—that proverbial shit nearing the proverbial fan—had turned out to be the apparently imminent union of the Vessel.

That had been Stella's first shock. According to everything she'd ever been taught, the Vessel story was complete rubbish, a fairy tale, a parable at best. Most alarmingly, however, it had nothing to do with hunting down and disabling Hollows. Which frankly made her wonder why it had anything to do with her, since that was the one and only thing hunters were good for.

We want you there as a precaution, a consul had said. *For Mr. Sharma's sake, but more significantly, for the protection of the Vessel. That is of utmost importance. Other hunters will be in the area if you need them, but they will not be briefed on the situation to the extent that you have been.*

Protection. As if she were some sort of bodyguard. The thought made her teeth grind.

Stella's second shock had been Abraham Sharma himself—or, more precisely, his title. Abe was the head of an isolated research department which existed solely in anticipation of the Vessel. The fact that Stella had never heard of this department was no great surprise; it was not in a hunter's job description to know the doings of other Luna Latum units. What shocked Stella was the troubling fact that any so-called Vessel "department" existed at all. Mostly because Stella—along with all other hunters before her—had been conditioned to regard the Vessel the way most women her age regarded Santa Claus.

So imagine if you will, that at the tender age of forty-one, someone told you that you'd been lied to, that Santa Claus was indeed real, along with all his impossible abilities. Then imagine being told that he's actually one of the reasons you have a job, and oh, by the way, you're supposed to go find him and deliver him safely to the North Pole.

That's about how Stella Rosin felt.

Now imagine trying to drive in Manhattan weekend traffic with a know-it-all workshop elf chattering incessantly in the passenger seat.

Abe's enthusiasm was unbearable. He carried with him an arsenal of unidentifiable gadgets, and had the most annoying habit of making sudden exclamations while using them, blunt facts that often trailed off unfinished through a thunderstruck smile. The way he bounced in the passenger seat, thumbing the buttons of some hand-held device with unbridled eagerness, he appeared more like an eleven-year-old playing a Game Boy than the fifty-something Nobel-laureate doctor that he was.

"Almost, almost . . ." He squinted his graying eyebrows together with delighted concentration, keeping his eyes glued to what looked like a slightly oversized GPS unit. On its small screen, patches of coded color layered a modular street map of the city. Abe deftly filtered through them until only blue patches highlighted a perfect outline of New York's many islands and peninsulas, then zoomed in closer to the Buick's location.

Too much blue. Way too much. He increased the concentration of the reading and scrolled around until he saw what he was looking for: a tiny but blindingly bright pinpoint of blue on Staten island. "There you are!"

"Which one?" Stella asked flatly.

"Water."

"Which way?" she forced the question, clenching her hands on the wheel. Acting as chauffeur was not within the boundaries of her temperament.

"Left." Abe braced himself while she gunned for the correct lane and sped through the first seconds of a red light. Seething with excitement, he sat up and looked around, then checked the map again, "Yes, keep going and take the bridge. This one's definitely much closer."

Stella glanced subtly at the monitor herself, unable to quell her curiosity. She still had a lot of questions, even after all the briefing, but she knew how to be careful with them. Hearing a little of the wrong thing could severely limit future assignments; knowing too much of the wrong thing meant forced retirement.

"Clarify this for me, Dr. Sharma," she said testily, cutting off a delivery truck in order to pass a cab. "How do they know how to find one another?"

"We don't know exactly," Abe shrugged wistfully. The bouncy, East Indian cadence in his voice made him sound all the more inappropriately cheerful. "We suspect it's similar to the way Hollows hear each other."

Obviously, the five beings in question were figuring *something* out. High concentrations of divine activity—undoubtedly the Vessel themselves—had only started showing up on Luna Latum radar little more than a year ago. In the beginning, when the signals were faint and infrequent, they had appeared on four different continents. As it was now, they were all constant, and all in North America: two were in New York, and the other three appeared to be headed that way.

Stella frowned at his vague answer. "And you don't know what happens when they do find each other?"

"Correct."

"Correct, what?"

"We do not know." Abe smiled in the apparent wonderment of it all.

Stella's razor-colored eyes narrowed. "Don't you think it might cause some kind of natural disaster? Some enormous crisis?"

"Could be," Abe tapped his knee with his free hand, drumming along to his own little song. He hardly took his eyes off the monitor.

"And you still feel that we absolutely should *not* interfere until they come together?"

"Nope."

"What?"

"We should not interfere."

She gripped the wheel and took a hard right, following directions for the Verazzano-Narrows Bridge. "Why is it so important, then? That they find one another before we approach them?"

"We do not know."

Did this insufferable quack and his department know anything at all? Stella cursed herself for ever accepting this assignment. Opting for retirement after all that briefing would've been less tedious.

"At least," Abe said, clicking through the monitor settings with brimming anticipation, "we can identify them first."

Stella Rosin gritted her teeth. There was a forced detour ahead, screaming pink signs and countless police officers. One look at the bridge and she understood why.

"Identify them," she repeated. "And just how do you propose we do that?"

Abe looked at her as if that had been a silly question, and wagged the divinity monitor in reply.

Stella curtly gestured at the windshield.

Thirty thousand or more people were packed together along the full length of the bridge, mulling around with their registration numbers, their water bottles, and their running shorts.

The New York City Marathon was about to start.

Abe looked at his monitor, at that indiscriminate little blue pixel, and then over again at the endless forest of spandex covering the bridge. He frowned. His bottom lip quivered.

"I'll guess." Stella Rosin looked across the seat at him mirthlessly. "You do not know?"

CHAPTER 6

Corin stared at his Rolex in horror for the tenth straight minute, listening to the chortling over the long distance line. He was never going to get to the marathon in time. Never. Making it out of the ER without a passport or any form of ID had taken long enough. Now he was being subjected, for the hundredth time, to his father's story about losing a bet in Morocco and spending the next day wearing a beach towel. The humor was somehow lost on Corin, now shoeless in the November chill, hopping from foot to foot in a Chinatown phone booth.

Twenty minutes later, after hop-stepping speedily for ten blocks (it's impossible to get a cab without shoes and a wallet, no matter how outrageously wealthy you claim to be), Corin returned to his room at the Wellington, activated his backup Sabre phone, cancelled the stolen credit cards, requested a duplicate passport, devoured six packets of oatmeal, properly hydrated himself, threw on his running gear, and successfully hailed a cab. He used the time in traffic for followup emails, explanations and apologies for missed meetings. He had to keep his mind busy.

He had to keep his mind busy or else he wouldn't be able to run. Out of the country, maybe. But not in the marathon.

Corin had seen, in his head, what Jesse and Ghi had seen. You'd think he wouldn't have been able to do much in a coherent, professional manner after that, and you'd be right. There were plenty of errors in those emails, and his running shorts were on backwards. But he made it to the marathon registration somehow, breathless, dizzy, and with fifteen minutes left to stretch before go-time.

The day's air was cold and sharp, with a patchy overcast blanket admitting bold rays of sun. Several news helicopters waltzed around over the island, and sponsors were granting their well-wishes and advertisements over an obnoxiously loud speaker system. Everything was shining and splendid. Corin tried to focus on that and found it impossible. He slapped on his number and took his place in the eager throng of people behind the starting line.

He was terrified.

None of this was logical. It couldn't possibly happen. Over the heads of the ten thousand or so people in front of him, he could see Liberty's torch, and his mind rushed to the morning ahead.

He just wanted to focus on running. That was all.

The pistols flared and cracked the air. The marathon mass lurched forward towards the bridge, and Corin started pacing along just as he had for the past seven years, not expecting to place, just excited to be there.

But this year was doomed to be difficult. No matter how hard he consciously tried, he couldn't appreciate the feeling of striding with all those strangers across the bridge, watching the Manhattan skyline bob in front of him as he ran, or feeling the chilly, stale New York air pushing into his lungs.

He was thinking about what was supposed to happen. He was thinking of what he could do to convince himself that nothing was *going* to happen.

By the time he had reached Times Square, somewhere in the first third of all the runners, he had structured a total solution for himself. He would finish this race and walk back to the Wellington for a relaxing evening. He would put off work until morning, then hunt down and confirm logical, medical excuses for his recent afflictions. He would go down to the hotel's lounge to watch marathon coverage, reward himself with several drinks before calling it a night, and get back down to business the next day.

By the time the marathon route took him past the Wellington itself, he was so pleased with this idea that he was almost enjoying himself.

Then he saw Ghi leaving the hotel through the front doors.

Ghi saw him too.

Ghi ran. Fast. Down the sidewalk. In the opposite direction.

Shouting some unintelligible religious profanity, Corin darted sideways mid-stride. Some *thing*—some roaring, crashing, impulse of a thing—took over, and before he knew what he was doing, he'd cut in front of countless other runners, hurtled over the marker tape and through a glob of spectators, and started sprinting down the sidewalk.

He kept shouting. Ghi kept running. People along the sidewalk showed only mild interest. There was a marathon going on, after all, and this *was* Manhattan.

Ghi fled into a wide alley and pushed himself forward faster, looking back over his shoulder again and again at his pursuant. His veins exploded with adrenaline terror. He had seen that face. He had seen it in the dreams. He should have never come here. *Call Dr. Avery. Call 9-1-1. Run inside somewhere.*

Just keep running. That was really the only feasible option. He ran into every connecting alley he came to, hoping to put some more distance between himself and this berserk runner, maybe lose him at a turn. Eventually, he found himself at one end of a long, greasy stretch between interconnected rows of gigantic buildings. The back streets were gated off. There was no way to run but straight ahead.

Ghi's head buzzed. His vision split erratically and he felt a nose bleed coming on. He'd been told to take it easy, to avoid excitement so as not to wreck the results of any immediate testing. But he didn't think about that, not with a marathon runner chasing him, yelling like a European dictator between sharp puffs of breath.

He could feel himself slowing down despite the effort he was throwing into his strides, but he could hear Corin losing power, too. The pace faded steeply. With the open street still over a hundred yards away, they were all but pathetically loping along. Ghi was moving just fast enough to stay ahead of Corin, and together they looked like a couple of senior citizen Olympians.

Out of breath, Corin decided to quit yelling and start negotiating.

"*Please!*" he gasped, giving it all he had to sound sincere. "Just stop!"

Ghi ignored him.

"Come on!"

Ghi tossed a look over his shoulder, kept going.

"I just!—wanna talk!" Corin slurred between breaths.

"Why!" Ghi squawked back with a short gasp and then galloped on ahead, shouting back one forced word at a time: "—should!—I trust!—you!?"

"Because!—I don't!—want!—to run!—anymore!" came Corin's desperate, fatigued reply. Feeling totally absurd, but seeing no other choice if he was to save them both from cardiac arrest, he simply shouted the word.

"Vessel!"

That tripped a gear in Ghi's pace. It did not make him want to stop. In fact, it had quite the opposite effect. However, Ghi reasoned with himself, he was going to have to stop soon. His legs could not guarantee him that they wouldn't stop before Corin's did.

He looked over his shoulder again, still jogging ahead. "Let's stop! Same time!"

"Agreed!"

"Promise!" Ghi warned.

"Okay!" Corin screamed.

"Now!" Ghi screamed back.

Their footsteps drummed to a stop.

With many yards still between them, they both doubled over and heaved in air for a solid minute. The sounds of the city hummed in and bounced off the buildings, filling their ears between breaths. Ghi maintained a cautious watch out of the corner of his eye, ready to run again, but Corin kept his word. He didn't move an inch closer.

The moment they stood upright to face one another, Ghi's caution barrier began to dissolve.

Corin was exactly as Ghi remembered him from the steps of that star-shaped platform. He was sporty and solid in build, yet his mannerly posture made him seem tall rather than broad, just as it made him seem leaner and less muscular than he really was. His pale, noble face flushed red with pumping blood under a layer of freckles, and his usually rust-colored hair was darkened with sweat.

He was smiling in a friendly way, realizing with a sense of self-defeat that he, too, fully recognized Ghi. Here, without a solitary doubt, was a live fragment of that maddening, recurrent dream.

In contrast to Corin, Ghi had little in the way of shape—from what Corin could glean anyway, given the fact that Ghi was packing at least two sweaters under his outermost Red Socks sweatshirt. If one had to guess, he was a slouching, noodly individual beneath all that, wearing only as much muscle as testosterone naturally alloted him. His skin had a pale quality, yet appeared to have the capacity to be much darker—like coffee overloaded with cream—and his features were implacably Middle-Eastern: intense, golden eyes (one was disproportionately dilated and lazing to the left at the moment), a prominent nose, wildly spiraling black hair, and what appeared to be a permanent five o'clock shadow.

Gusts of wind blew the pickled alley air between them, carrying the distant sounds of traffic and marathon cheering, while they stared at one another in total wonderment. Neither of them spoke for some immeasurable time, until Corin shrugged and stepped forward, diplomatically reaching his hand out.

"Corin," he introduced himself. "Corin Livingston."

"Ghiyath Ayman. Ghi's fine."

They shook hands.

And then they stood in complete silence again. What the hell would you say next?

Hi! I'm made entirely out of light energy and I have dreams about you.

Nope. No good at all.

Ghi gradually resumed his natural position: arms folded, shoulders up as if trying to guard his ears, feet shifting back and forth. And Corin began to put his hands in his pockets, realizing only then that his running shorts were on backwards. He tapped his fingers casually on his sides instead, rocking back on his heels.

"Are we on the same page here?" he asked finally. "Do you understand? What . . . what we *are*?"

Ghi's eyes darkened. The lazy one was beginning to come back into alignment again. He sighed. Definitely should've stayed in Boston.

"Probably not any more than you do," he said.

Corin watched his own breath puff out in front of him, and he nodded. He'd expected as much.

"Yeah, then. Same page."

The way he saw it, Jackson considered it pure lucky timing that he had lost consciousness behind the wheel of a speeding fire truck. That incident had been more than enough, after all, to warrant him a few days off. And he was going to need time off immediately if he wanted to make it from Filbert, Missouri to New York City in little more than one day.

Armed with AC/DC, tire chains, a gallon of Gatorade, and a duffel bag full of lovingly made Wonderbread sandwiches, Jackson was all set to blast his Chevrolet pickup off onto I-70. First, however, there was one small detour he needed to make, and so it was westward that he drove first, not east. About five miles from Filbert city limits. He pulled the Chevy over to the side of the highway, next to a creek. The creek where he had come face to face with Su Kim Khan.

Su Kim Khan, who was wanted in six countries on multiple counts of theft, property damage, border violations, piracy, patronization of prostitutes, illegal firearms smuggling, drug trafficking, first-degree murder, and arson—his apparent favorite.

Su Kim Khan, who was apprehended September 28th outside Kansas City with two Japanese convicts and several American AK47's. Su Kim Khan, who was scheduled to be sent back to South Korea in January for trial.

Su Kim Khan, who'd reportedly killed a man with a . . . a hairbrush? Is that even possible? That couldn't be right.

Jackson squinted hard at the printed text, taking a contemplative chug of Gatorade. With a shudder, he tossed the sheet of paper to the passenger seat, back atop the heap of pages which represented two hours' worth of Google searches. Zipping up his coat, he stepped out of the truck and turned towards the creek.

The authorities hadn't found Khan. Which obviously meant he wasn't anywhere in the area, judging by the tenacity of the search effort. But Jackson couldn't leave without making sure, offering a ride at the very least. They were headed to the same place, after all. Hell, why not let the arsonist-murderer hitchhike along? Not like life could get any weirder at this point.

But of course, Khan was nowhere to be seen. The only things visible through the flurry of snow were a couple of scattered homes and, in the far distance, a train depot. A cluster of black cows dotted the flat white field in between. So much for that ride.

Would've been one darn uncomfortable trip anyway, Jackson thought, climbing back into the warmth of the cab. For a moment, he humored the idea of the colossal, tattooed convict sitting in the passenger seat all the way to New York, sharpening a hairbrush with his switchblade. Then he pushed the Chevy into gear and headed east.

CHAPTER 7

The Crescent's entrance was a few steps below street level, buried under a mammoth cluster of storefronts and apartments on the corner of 62nd and Columbus. The image of a severely arched ballet slipper, bright red and encrusted with shellacked glitter, was painted above the heavy door.

It was the first suitable place they'd come to; not at all busy, with music just loud enough to drown out conversation. Mainly, a place where they wouldn't draw attention to themselves. The dusk-dim dining room had thick wooden floorboards and unsanitary-looking velvet walls, their color that of raw liver. Close to the door sat a man whose styled, highlighted hair stood in clear defiance of middle age. He paused over his sandwich when they entered, and winked as they passed.

"Nice fanny pack."

"Thanks," Corin muttered. *It's a runner's pack,* he reminded himself with some dignity.

He and Ghi headed for a secluded, cramped booth in the far corner, half hidden by a shoddy wooden piano which had quite obviously seen better days. As soon as they scooted into their seats, a tall, reed-thin young woman emerged from a door behind the bar and made her way over.

"Didn't finish, huh?" she smiled and pointed one long, graceful finger at the number pinned to Corin's running shirt.

Corin shook his head. The charm practically tumbled off of him. "No. I'm afraid I just got too thirsty."

"I can help with that." The waitress placed her hands on her hips, which didn't seem to be more than a foot apart. "What'll it be?"

"I don't suppose you have any Glenlivet in the house?" he asked, and the air of hope in his voice was met with a blank stare.

"Any what?"

"Right," Corin sighed. It had been worth a try. "Just a scotch, please, rocks. And my friend here will have—?"

Ghi blinked. "Dr. Pepper?"

"—a Dr. Pepper."

The waitress nodded, turned, circumvented the sorry piano, and was gone.

Which meant that, for the first time since exiting the alley, the two of them were alone. And there still seemed to be nothing sensible to say. This was getting old fast.

"So," Corin shifted, trying to get comfortable in the high-backed, somewhat sticky seating. Clearly, it was up to him to get any kind of conversation rolling, since Ghi was presently drumming his hands on the table's edge, staring intently at his lap. "You're a Red Socks fan, then?"

Ghi stopped drumming and looked back at him in complete puzzlement, until it occurred to him what sweatshirt he was wearing. He shrugged, his shoulders lost somewhere inside it.

"It was a gift," he said. "I live in Boston."

"Oh, Boston," Corin said pleasantly. "Great town. Always wanted to do the Boston Marathon, but something seems to get in the way every year."

Ghi nodded, searching desperately for some kind of normal thing to say. All he could come up with was: "So you came all the way here for the marathon?"

"The marathon, yes, and work," Corin said. "I'm in the philanthropy business. You'd think I was in the bloody mafia, though, the way some people run things."

The arrival of drinks rescued Ghi from having to come up with something to say in reply. The waitress retreated, and he poked idly at the straw in his Dr. Pepper, watching the tiny brown bubbles.

Corin took a test swill of the scotch. Rather bad scotch, it was. "So what do you do then? In Boston."

Ghi sat straight up and drew both hands away from the glass.

"I do dry cleaning," he proclaimed. "I am here legally."

"Whoa, friend." Corin put his palms up in a peaceful gesture. "Never said you weren't. Ghi, is it?"

Ghi nodded and took a fierce, sullen drink through his straw.

What an odd, jumpy person, Corin thought, looking across the table. Understandable. He was a nervous wreck himself. And small talk wasn't going to ease either of their minds. He took a moment to scan the room again: not a soul was close to their table. The waitress sat at the bar, chatting with an equally tall, slender girl who had just walked in. The man with highlighted hair was getting up to pay his check.

Time to get to the point already. Corin refocused his attention on Ghi until they were holding eye contact.

"Well, Ghi. I think we've seen some of the same things, you and I."

Ghi froze. He freed his lips from the straw and then nodded. In the thick, dark air of the Crescent, his eyes looked as yellow as the eyes of an owl.

"The statue," he said softly, making the words a kind of question. "Many times."

"Too many," Corin confirmed. "And that history lesson, my god . . ."

"The desert?"

"The diviners."

"Those women."

"Those *things*."

Ghi leaned forward. "You're—?"

They stopped. The waitress was approaching. Corin slid his glass slowly across the coarse wooden surface of the table, from one hand to the other. He watched the cubes of ice slip against one another, fighting for space.

"You two need anything else? Lunch?"

"Water," Corin replied, meaningfully lifting his sea-gray eyes to Ghi before addressing her. "Just water, please."

Ghi swallowed reflexively. His throat felt dry and tasted of sweet syrup and carbonation. He was not comfortable. He liked Corin, but he suddenly wasn't sure that he wanted to be talking to another Vessel. He had pretty much decided already that he didn't want to *be* a Vessel.

Not that it was going to change anything.

"Light," he said.

They stared at one another in silence for some time, until the girl returned and set two glasses of ice water between them.

"Are we crazy?" Ghi asked, when she was gone again. "Is this real?"

"Oh, I think we both know it's real." Corin released a brief, despairing laugh. "And I think that makes us both crazy. Cheers to that."

"Cheers."

They clinked glasses.

The room became lighter momentarily when the door to the street opened, admitting two women. They joined the waitress and her friend at the bar, each of them as tall as the last. Dancers maybe, thought Corin. The Juilliard School wasn't far from here. He settled further into the booth and lifted his glass to his lips again.

"So I guess this means we're visiting Miss Liberty in the morning, yeah?"

Ghi's eyebrows dropped into a nervous line. He stared resolutely at the table. "I don't know if I'm going . . ."

Corin coughed and thumped the glass down.

"What do you mean you don't know?"

"I'm supposed to be somewhere else."

"Somewhere else?" Corin leaned forward. "Do you know how many people are counting on me to be in a boardroom tomorrow morning? I'm sick just thinking about it. But as far as I'm concerned, there isn't any 'somewhere else'. I won't be able to stop myself from going, I already know it. Don't you feel the same way?"

"I do. And that's what I'm worried about." Ghi continued staring at the table. "If I go, it will cause trouble. They'll look for me."

Clearly, Corin shouldn't have skipped the small talk.

"They?"

Ghi sighed. When he did look up, it was with a guilty, worrisome expression. "I'm here with my doctor. I'm not supposed to go anywhere without telling him. I shouldn't even be here. I'm here—in the States, I mean—because he wanted to treat me."

Yes. Definitely should've covered more small talk.

Corin proceeded with appropriate caution. "Treat you for what, exactly?"

One slightly awful pop song ended, and another one began. Ghi sat back, despondent. He was used to this question, and he was used to people not understanding the answer.

"Protracted fugue state."

Corin stared back blankly, a response which Ghi was very much accustomed to. But then he shook his head in skeptic amazement.

"Wow. *Wow*. And I thought I was having a hard time. No wonder you're such a mess."

Ghi frowned. "What are you saying? You know what I'm talking about?"

"Of course I do. Minored in Psychology before switching to Anthropology. Let's see, fugue state . . ." Corin tapped his fingers on the table, mind wandering its own catalogues of information. "A kind of amnesia, yeah? Lost all sense of self, very sudden, am I right?"

Ghi opened his mouth, shut it. Couldn't have said it better himself. He shrugged, palms up.

"How long ago did it start?"

"Five years."

"Christ, man," Corin shook his head, threw back the last of the scotch. Truly awful, that stuff.

And then he froze. Any further questions he had for Ghi would have to wait. His ears were demanding his full attention for something else. The music. The song was familiar, heavily over-played in Europe. Piano acrobatics over a driving dance beat. And the voice.

Jesse Cannon.

"Christ, not *this* guy," Corin groaned, before the true recognition hit him all over again. He slapped his hands abruptly on the table, coming very close to spilling both ice waters. "Wait! This guy!" He pointed a finger upwards, as if toward some omnipotent being. "He's one of us."

"Oh, I know!" Ghi nodded eagerly. Half of him seemed grateful for the subject change, the other half of him was strangely enthused. He began bobbing with helpless, earnest energy to the music. "I recognized him from the dreams right away. I'm a little nervous about meeting him, aren't you?" He paused to take an especially exuberant gulp of Dr. Pepper. "Have you seen his newest video, the one with all the panthers?"

"Pardon?"

"He used to be a regular here, you know," the waitress startled them both, coming to lean against the piano. "Before he dropped out of Juilliard. One of my ballet directors had him in class."

"No way!" Ghi practically squealed.

Corin, though not as vocally, was equally interested. "Jesse Cannon used to come here?"

"Yes. And he made this old thing sound like a Fazioli. No one else even plays it anymore," she shrugged her narrow shoulders and touched the piano's keys lightly, "but people often pay their respects."

Corin and Ghi immediately stood for a closer look at the decrepit piano, and saw that the yellowed keys were covered in a reverent festoon of lipstick marks.

"Lovely," Corin remarked, recoiling slightly, until he noticed the framed photo propped up on the piano's splintering mantle. It was an enlarged snapshot of the statuesque blonde seated at this very same instrument, mouth photogenically open in mid-song, a suffocating number of people around him. Flashy strokes of permanent ink along the bottom corner proclaimed:

There will never be another Crescent. Jesse Loves You! XOXOXO!!!

"Too bad I didn't work here back then," said the waitress wistfully. "Isn't he amazing?"

Ghi nodded vigorously.

Corin fished out a fifty-dollar bill out of his runner's pack and placed it on the table.

"Thanks, miss," he said, and began to steer Ghi away, for fear that he would linger to touch the piano and thereby acquire some disease. "We'll give Mr. Cannon your regards."

I'll tell you now that I did, in fact, drive from Nashville to Manhattan, and that I did it in thirteen hours flat. That I ate only Pop-Tarts and gas station burritos on the way, that I only dozed off once, on a particularly lulling stretch somewhere in Pennsylvania—and that the resulting panic of being honked awake by a neon pink semi-truck was enough to keep me alert for the next eight hours.

But before you think for one second, *one second,* that I bought Jesse's "do me a favor as a friend" bullshit, think again.

Before I walked out of that hospital room, I had my final paycheck in hand, in advance, and it had been doubled. I also had a signed six-month severance agreement, hammered out on a piece of hospital stationary.

Do I feel ashamed now, for working that money out of Jesse in his hour of need, instead of accepting his mission out of goodwill?

Do I feel guilty that he probably didn't know what the word "severance" meant?

Hell no, I don't.

Didn't I consider myself his friend? Of course I did. But a complete idiot I was not. Or at least I didn't think I was at the time.

I arranged a rental car on his tab, a little purple Honda, and left the hospital within an hour, eager for the solitude and quite pleased with my compensation. Everything was set. Jesse had been released and was safely on his way to Chicago aboard his beloved tour bus. And even though I was technically still doing his bidding, even though he called me at least twice an hour during the long drive, he was nowhere near me. I was free of him, finally free, and once this bizarre detour was over, that freedom would be complete.

I neglected to take an overnight bag, which was pretty stupid. It was also pretty stupid that I'd worn only a sweatshirt, since I was headed to New York in November. All I took along was a wallet full of cash, a cell phone, and the envelope Jesse had given to me, which held the message I was supposed to give to the other "Vessel", as he called them. That was all he'd asked me to do: spot these guys, give them the letter, and split.

Sure, Jesse. Sure.

I hit the early Jersey traffic in darkness and sat in the 24/7 gridlock that surrounds New York City, skipping through the radio and grinding my teeth every time I heard a Jesse Cannon song. Finally, in that bleak part of morning before dawn, after the madness of downtown traffic and the unbelievable quest to simply find the correct parking lot, I boarded the morning's first ferry to Liberty Island.

The New York skyline glittered in the gritty dawn, and I watched it without feeling, having seen it before, countless times. I had seen the Statue of Liberty before, too, but never in this light. Never quite this way, while so much was going through my mind. Everything suddenly seemed so ridiculous, there on that boat with the envelope folded stiffly in my pocket. I honestly couldn't decide whether I'd been paid enough or not, to drive all this way just to stand up on that platform like an idiot all morning. It was hardly the worst thing Jesse had ever asked me to do, but I couldn't get over the reasoning behind it. I wondered if he was going to start wearing a mask in public, or join some cult and start waiting for the mothership and become *that* kind of celebrity. Wouldn't have surprised me, honestly.

I bought a cheap cup of coffee on the island and marched up the entrance steps of the star-shaped platform. Liberty's back was turned to me. More out of necessity than duty (my legs were greatly in need of a good stretch) I did a quick lap around the entire platform, feeling conspicuously silly in front of the twenty or so people milling around. Assured that no one out of the ordinary was there, I took up a post near the entrance steps and stood there, freezing in the bitter breeze, tasting the rank, horrible coffee and wondering how long I should stand there to be fair.

And that was when I saw Jackson.

Jesse had described (in more detail than I'd cared to hear) the people I should be looking for. This guy just so happened to meet one of the descriptions, that was all. I couldn't help but take a good hard look.

He was square. As in the shape. His shoulders, his face, his jawline, even his neatly trimmed sideburns were broad and cornered off at the edges, though he wasn't particularly what I'd call angular. He was definitely more on the beefy side, and he was well-equipped with a thick canvas coat and utility gloves. Casual, worn jeans. Muddy boots.

Jesse had also described him as "delicious."

I stepped closer to the entrance to get a better look, feeling like a moron but unable to tame my curiosity. He definitely fit the bill of fare, for Jesse anyways. I'm not partial to a lot of muscle myself, but this guy was certainly attractive in his own right. His face, I could see from where I stood, was handsome and somehow endearing. It neared the border of rugged even, except for one notable quality: his mouth.

Cute, I guess, is the word. His mouth was too cute to get him onto the rough and rowdy list. Pinioned between dimples, it stretched as wide as the square face it sat on, existing in this perpetual, irresistible smirk. Not like a weaselly smirk. Like the smirk of a kid, an ornery little boy who was hiding something. His eyes, I would see later, added to the effect. They were a dewy green, too big and full of expression to match up with the beefy exterior. Again, just like a little kid's.

I continued watching him for a few minutes, and not just because he matched up with Jesse's description so perfectly. I've seen a few square-shaped people in my lifetime, and believe me: many, *many* are the men whom Jesse Cannon would label delicious.

It was Jackson's actions, or his lack of actions, which made me stay. He stood with his feet apart and his arms crossed, watching the entrance steps like Lady Liberty's big, stocky bouncer, as still as a statue himself.

He wasn't there to sight-see.

He was waiting for someone.

And so I drank the rest of my coffee and watched Jackson watch the steps. He didn't even notice me, he was so interested in those steps. I told myself a number of things. *He works here; works for Homeland Security, I'll bet. No, he's waiting on some girl.*

Eventually, I got mad at myself for even wondering about him at all. My time was up, I decided. I was finished with this final act of employment. Scolding myself, I walked to the top of the steps.

And then I stopped cold.

Jackson saw who he was waiting for. He stood up straight.

There were two. I'd come so close to walking into them that I had to turn on my heel—back towards Jackson—to avoid doing so. They came up the steps together, separating only to walk around me while I stood there in the way, dumb, feet braced, staring at the ground. My face went hot and my ears hummed as they passed, very close. One of them brushed my arm accidentally with his elbow, and I looked up.

"Sorry," he said over his shoulder with a sincere smile, crazy black hair moving in the strong wind like a living thing.

Ghi.

He and Corin didn't look around for anyone else. They walked straight to Jackson and began introducing themselves, all three of them awkward but immediately friendly. I turned away quickly, realizing I was staring, and wavered near the top of the steps.

I couldn't leave.

I couldn't believe this.

This had to be a coincidence. Had to be.

I flicked a few fast glances. They were as described: Corin with his reddish hair, dressed like a *GQ* cover. Ghi's shrugged shoulders and mulatto skin, the disheveled spirals.

I looked away, realizing that I'd stopped breathing and was staring again. There had to be some kind of explanation. I looked all around. Was I being *Punk'd*? Who would prank an assistant, a simple drink mixer? What else could it be? An overreaction on my part?

Or was Jesse absolutely right?

I wasn't about to go down that road. I wanted out of there, plain and simple. The letter was stuck in my front pocket. Hand it over and walk away, hand it over and walk away . . . *Ridiculous!* What kind of *idiot* was I? I pulled it out and flipped it over in my hands, took a deep breath, and turned around.

Jackson was passing around the Google printouts, and all of them seemed to be nodding with recognition at Khan's mug shots. They were talking over one another, debating something, though not loud enough for anyone else to hear them.

I thought fast. There were supposed to be four other Vessel. Did I have to wait until they were all there? Did they know who Jesse was? Would they be upset that I knew about them? Would I have to stick around for a message from them?

Oh, for god's sake.

"Excuse me!" I called over the wind, louder than I'd meant to.

They stopped talking and looked at me, all of them. My mouth stopped working. It gaped open a couple of times and I held the letter up, gripping it tightly. I moved quickly forward by some miracle and stopped in front of them.

"Hi," I said, as normally as I could, and thus sounded like a robot or a very old woman.

They just stared back at me, unmoving. Corin looked overtly cautious. Ghi appeared to be utterly petrified. And Jackson just looked slightly impatient.

"I think I'm supposed to give this to you," I choked, holding the letter out.

And that could have been the end of it.

Jackson and Corin both reached for the envelope, but a strong gale blew it right out of my hand. Swooping, it slapped Ghi between the eyes and then fluttered onwards. Before we could so much as lunge for it, Jesse's letter blew right over the platform's edge and out across the park.

"I got it!" Ghi volunteered abruptly and darted for the steps, hurtling down them in a jumble of far-flung limbs. The three of us who remained moved to the side railing. Unacquainted and awkward, we watched him sprint across the lawn, chasing the envelope halfway around the platform. It cornered itself against the high walls, and Ghi jogged in to snatch it up before it had a chance to blow away again. With a triumphant motion, he stuffed it between his sweaters and started coming back around the jutting corners of the platform walls, back to us.

But then Ghi turned a very significant corner of that wall. He stepped around it and came face to face with Stella Rosin. He saw her face register shock, and then ferocious outrage.

And then he saw the concrete.

CHAPTER 8

Stella Rosin barked two syllables.

With his face scraping the sidewalk, and his arm twisted in the air behind him, pinned in an iron grip, Ghi struggled to assess the situation. A boot was crunched into his spine, that was significant. Most significant, though, was the barrel of what he feared to be a pistol digging into the back of his neck. That fear was confirmed when he heard the unmistakable sound of it being cocked.

Stella repeated herself, then unleashed a string of other demands. The sound of her voice was drilling and forceful, but with a trained volume—no moseying tourists above would hear her. More arm twisted. More spine crunched. But Ghi realized very suddenly that he didn't understand her, not a single word.

"I don't know!" he coughed into the ground, for what it was worth, desperate. "I don't know what you're saying!"

Stella paused momentarily. "English," she murmured.

With a deft, harsh motion, she flipped him onto his back and pressed the pistol to his throat. She hardly needed to. This woman scared the shit out of him. He wasn't about to move. As she examined his face with quick intensity, he got a good look at hers: angular, older, light hair, blue eyes, getting angrier and angrier . . .

"Explain yourself!" she shouted.

"What?!"

"What are you doing here?" she nearly inverted his adam's apple with the gun. "Where are they?"

"Lady, *please!*" he squeaked. "I don't know!"

Corin, Jackson, and myself, meanwhile, were already running down the steps towards the commotion. Well, *they* were running. If given the chance, I would have sprang for the next departing ferry without so much as a good luck sentiment. But Jackson—a hefty guy, I'll remind you—had taken hold of my elbow and was yanking me along. He let me go as we rounded the corner and onto the scene. And then he did the stupidest thing imaginable.

He tackled Stella Rosin.

The pistol went off with a muffled, wet pop. Ghi's limbs spasmed out and then fell limp. I screamed. Jackson jumped back and knocked Corin forward in the process.

Stella Rosin whipped around, now with two pistols outstretched and trained on the closest thing that moved, which was Corin. He ducked his head and threw his arms out as if this would save him.

It did.

There was another pop, but a different kind—a crackling, hardening sort of sound. Stella stopped completely. Her eyes still stared forward, focused on Corin. Her pistols were still trained on him. Her body remained in a poised lunge. But she didn't move. She *couldn't* move. And for a moment, as we grappled to comprehend what had just happened, neither could we. We were petrified.

Stella was covered in ice.

Solid ice.

From the tips of the gun barrels, the ice followed the line of her arms back to the rest of her body, and encased her from the top of her head to her knees, slick and smooth, curved out behind her in the captured shape of a watery blast.

She fell backwards to the ground.

Corin screamed. It was the kind of immasculine scream that friends make fun of you for. We weren't friends yet. And now wasn't the time.

It wasn't the time for anything but running. No time to wonder why

Ghi, instead of lying dead with his throat blasted apart, was suddenly coughing and fumbling to his feet. No time to marvel at this frozen phenomenon, or to stop for the extremely excited Indian guy who had appeared from nowhere to chase after us.

We just ran. Jackson dragged Ghi along, Corin grabbed the nearest pistol off the ground, and we ran as fast as we could for the loading ferry.

❦

There was no way to tell if anyone else had noticed the incident. I'm not even sure how we got aboard that ferry. Jackson was the only person among us who could still form a complete sentence at that point. Corin stowed the gun in his jacket and kept staring at his own hands, and Ghi—well, I'll get to him.

We watched the ramp for an agonizingly long five minutes, but saw no signs of Stella or her apparent accomplice. When the ferry shoved off at last and the other passengers moved into the warmth of the cabin, the four of us slumped down against the railing of the deck, alone, finally able to freak out properly about ambushes and ice explosions.

Keeping a nervous eye on the island behind us, we moved to the first concern: Ghi, who was clutching his throat with both hands and staring ahead without blinking, generally shell-shocked. He sincerely believed, in the horror of the moment, that he was holding his neck together.

"Let's just see here," Jackson pried Ghi's hands away, not at all gently, and moved in closer. After a quick inspection, he smirked shrewdly and pushed Ghi's shoulder. "Quit your panicking, Sally. There's nothing wrong with you."

Ghi raised his hands back to the spot in disbelief, finding that his throat was cold and clammy, but whole. The collar of his sweaters and the hood of his sweatshirt, however, were soaked. Jackson pinched the material and then smelled his own fingers.

"Jesus!" he grimaced and wrung his hand. "Kinda smells like my aunt's house . . ."

Ghi didn't respond. He was just thrilled that it wasn't blood.

"What?" Corin moved in and performed a similar examination. After considering the substance carefully, he sat back against the railing again, totally dumbfounded. "It's just water."

"Water?" Ghi and I said at the same time.

"Smells like . . . fish and cat piss." Jackson was still sniffing at his own hand.

Corin discreetly pulled the gun out of his coat and looked it over, shaking the thawed ice from its surface. It was made of a tough, heavy plastic, not metal, and though it otherwise resembled a normal pistol, its chamber was designed to hold and propel liquid with great force and precision, using a small cartridge of nitrogen. That explained the smell.

It does *not* explain why Jackson's aunt's house smells like nitrogen, and I never thought to ask him.

Corin shrugged, incredulous and almost amused. "A water gun."

"Water gun?" Jackson grabbed it and looked it over. "Now I know New York is full of lunatics and all, but a water gun?"

Corin plucked the gun back and tucked it into his coat again. "I have the feeling she wasn't just any lunatic."

"No," Ghi agreed softly, unsettled. "It's like she knew exactly who I was."

Things got very quiet. We watched the island recede behind us.

"You don't suppose . . . ," Corin began.

No one wanted to finish.

I huddled against the railing, trying to connect everything, using Jesse's rambling story as a reference and wishing I'd listened better. I spit out the word as soon as I remembered it:

"Hollows."

Three pairs of eyes looked at me like I'd dropped the f-bomb at the Vatican.

I frowned. "Well, that's what she was, right?"

"Wait *just* a minute," Jackson pointed at me before anyone could consider that thought. "Just who the hell are you, anyway?"

I was immediately defensive, outraged by his accusational tone. Ghi and Corin seemed equally interested in my reply, and I practically bared my teeth at them.

"I'm somebody who has nothing to do with this," I answered bitterly, ignoring their continued, combined stare. I crossed my arms to the freezing wind and retreated into my sweatshirt. From there, I glared at Corin. He was going to ruin reality for me, depending on how he answered my question.

"How did you do that?" I asked suddenly, sharply. "The ice?"

He looked at me carefully, then at the others. In one sense, he didn't know the answer himself. He certainly hadn't expected that to happen, much less intended it. But in another sense, he knew exactly how it had happened. He'd panicked. He'd needed protection. And it, *she*, the water, whatever, had protected him.

"You already know, don't you?" he asked, patient but direct.

So this was real.

I bit my tongue stubbornly. I didn't want to answer, to condemn my own half-sane little world to the impossible, and they couldn't make me.

"My boss was supposed to meet you here," I snapped. "But he couldn't, so he sent me."

They all spoke at the same time.

"Who is he?" Ghi asked.

"*You* work for Su Kim Khan?" Jackson's square jaw dropped.

"For Jesse Cannon?" Corin butted in.

"Hey! Whoa! Nope, no way!" I tossed my hands up and backed away a few steps. It was time to draw the line. "This is where I get off. When this boat lands, I'm gone. That letter should tell you all you need to know, who he is, where to find him, everything. I am *so* done here."

Something clicked in Ghi's head while he was looking at me, and his face blanched. He reached into his sweatshirt.

"Oh no."

"Oh no what?" I demanded.

"The letter. I lost it."

"Well," I snapped, "That's too bad. Like I—"

Care?

A possible crisis slowly seeped in. My eye twitched. Whether I liked it or not, I was starting to care.

"Did *she* take it?" I asked, glaring down at Ghi.

My expression must have looked particularly murderous, because Ghi immediately put his hands over his mouth in a way that would've been comical had I not wanted to strangle him.

"I don't know," he said quickly, eyes looking from left to right. "Maybe. Yes. I think."

Shit.

The letter. That woman. Jesse.

"What is it?" Corin watched the changing degrees of panic on my face. "What's the problem?"

I could hardly hear him, I was thinking so far ahead. To the instructions in that letter. To a massacre on the set of Oprah. To Jesse, struck dead by an artillery of water guns . . .

The jarring of the ferry surprised us all. It was beginning to dock. Corin shifted his attention from me to look back across the water, watching as another boat prepared to leave Liberty Island, worrying about who might be on board—if she'd thawed out already.

"Alright everyone," he prompted. "Where to now?"

❦

Su Kim Khan didn't like how the people in this little Toronto truck stop were looking at him.

The moment usually passed so much faster. You just don't stare at Su Kim Khan for very long before getting back to whatever you were previously doing. Because once you got a good look at him, you definitely didn't want him looking back at you.

Today was different, though. It's not easy to look away from a tattooed, six-foot-ten Asian man wearing a full-length ladies' ermine coat and no pants.

With impressive indifference, Khan took a seat at the counter and picked up a menu. Some older men in a corner booth, all of them bearded, stopped talking and proceeded to stare. Khan stared back. The men hadn't been paying attention to the countertop TV before, but they quickly turned to it in unison. Khan turned to it as well, and it was a good thing he did.

A commercial was on. A preview for a live talk show, something about the anticipated second appearance of Jesse Cannon. Khan squinted at the screen, taking in the clips of Jesse's previous appearance, hearing his voice through the dusty speakers. Before the commercial even ended, he stood up and lay the menu down. Not a soul looked his way.

He walked immediately out of the truck stop diner and over to the first running car he spotted, a little tan sedan with foggy exhaust humming out the back of it. A big-haired woman was behind the wheel. Whether she was just parking or just about to leave didn't make any difference. Her day was about to change dramatically.

Khan coolly opened the passenger side door and climbed in. He reached across the woman and grabbed her door handle with one hand, and with the other, held his switchblade up where she could see it.

"Take me to Oprah," he said.

CHAPTER 9

"What were you thinking?" Abe questioned in hoarse disbelief. He pried another curved chunk of shattered ice off the back of Stella's hand. She snarled when a microscopic layer of skin went with it.

"I *th-thought*," she began, managing to sound commanding despite the stutter, "he was was w-working for *them*."

Violently, she beat some stubborn ice from the front of her coat. Most of it had shattered when she'd fallen, and Abe had gotten through to her face before she'd suffocated. The remaining ice clung to her in bitter pieces, clumps of it hanging onto her hair and clothes. Her skin was red, raw, and freezing, and her furious breathing came out in trembling gusts, but she was already moving again. Moving and mad.

"Working for the Hollows?" Abe scurried to follow, grabbing the instruments he'd dropped along the way. He was mystified. "Why would you think *that*?"

"Instinct," she said, walking fast around the base of the platform, leaving a trail of ice chunks behind her.

"I beg your pardon?"

Stella Rosin ignored him. She stopped without warning when the dock came into view, thrusting a hand into the lining of her coat and frowning. Abe sailed into her, dropping nearly everything he had gathered in his arms. Stella did not seem to notice; she was too preoccupied with the revelation that she'd left her binoculars in the Buick. Cursing, she turned abruptly and started back up the platform steps.

"Where are you going?" Abe scooped everything into his arms again, following her. On his way up the steps, he bumped into at least three people, totally oblivious to the dirty looks he earned. "We've lost them already! What about the other two? This is a disaster!"

"We haven't lost them," Stella Rosin said firmly, calmly. She stepped to the edge of the platform, looked down the length of the stone bannister, and moved down a few paces to where an apparently unattended child was peering through a tourist viewer.

Stella promptly hoisted the speechless boy out of the way, stuck her eyes to the viewer, and swung it towards the parking lot on the Ellis Island shore, where the first ferry was releasing its passengers.

"Get a pen," she snapped.

Abe grumbled and set everything down so he could fish a pen from his pocket, wincing uncomfortably when the displaced child started whining and pulling at his coat. He hastened to unwrinkle a grocery receipt to write on. Stella was already dictating her observations.

"Alright," she said, "They're in the parking lot. The big one is getting in a blue and gray Chevrolet pickup, not sure about the model, can't see the plates—are you getting all of this?"

"Yes!" Abe scribbled furiously, mildly aware of the staring tourists as the child hugged his knees and wailed. He tried to both ignore the kid and gently shake him off at the same time, while also attempting to write coherently.

"No, wait," Stella corrected. "He only got a few things out of the truck. Now they're all getting into another car. Honda, compact, dark purple, Tennessee plates AFJ-662." She stopped again to process what she was seeing before speaking up again. "Any idea who the young lady might be? She's driving."

"Ow!" Abe squawked when the child kicked him in the shin. "No, no idea who she is," he groaned, rubbing the spot gingerly and watching the little shit run back to his parents.

"Thought so," Stella muttered. Before Abe could ask exactly what she was implying, she backed away from the viewer. "They exited south-bound. Let's get going."

Abe scrambled to see the car she was talking about, but couldn't. When he turned around again, Stella was of course gone, already hurrying down the steps. And from that direction, a small group of angry adults were headed his way, sobbing child in tow.

Frantic, Abe pocketed the notes, gathered everything up again, and chased after Stella, down the steps and in the direction of the ferry landing. "So now what?" he panted.

Stella Rosin answered without interrupting her step. "Now, I order a scan on those plates, you track where they're headed on your little gadget, I call in backup, and we head over to Long Island."

Abe looked confused, but impressed.

"How do you know they're going to Long Island?"

"I don't," she said, "But wherever they're going, we're following on my bike."

I went a little over the top, I think, when I called Jesse. I shouted. I threatened to do some pretty terrible things when I saw him again. Genital mutilation of some form or another was certainly mentioned. But I was sincerely worried, too, so I calmed down soon enough and got to the crucial point:

"You can't go on Oprah."

"Oh? So now I can't?"

Judging by the way Jesse was talking—in frustrated, whispered squeaks—he was in a room with other people. Or other people were in *his* room, more likely, raining powder and hair products down on him. "Isn't it a little late for that now?"

"Jesse—"

"Someone was pretty damn determined that I not cancel, I remember. Do you remember?"

"Shut up and listen to me!" I yelled. "Where are you right now?"

"In pre-*pre*-show brunch."

"Well get out," I commanded, switching phone ears. I was driving, and fast. "Be creative. Make yourself throw up or something. You're excellent at that."

"Jordan, what the hell? Just tell me what happened." I heard excited voices emerging in the background.

"A lot happened. You were right."

"Really? So they were there?"

"Yes, and now they're *here* and we're on our way *there*."

"Well that's the plan, isn't it?"

"Jesse," I said sternly, "There was someone else and they're not very friendly."

"What?" Jesse's voice was hard to hear. There seemed to be a lot of cheering going on around him. He gasped. "I can't hear you! She's here, I have to go!"

"Jesse! Someone is coming after you!"

"Great! Oh, darling, hello!" The phone was obviously nowhere near his face. For a split second, he came back to me. "Just call me when you get to Chicago."

And then he hung up.

I shook the phone, shoved it into my pocket, and swerved into another lane to go faster.

Jackson, Corin, and Ghi sat in nervous silence, looking like scolded giants in the tiny car. I seethed air between my teeth, focusing on the road.

"So," Corin spoke up congenially from the passenger's seat. "You know Jesse Cannon."

"Yes." I glowered. No one had said anything about directions yet, but I was taking streets that would lead out of the city. I knew where *I* was going. If they didn't like it, they could get a goddamn cab.

"So are you his girlfriend or something?" Jackson popped his head between the seats.

"I'm his *handler*," I corrected, disgusted. "Put your seat belt on."

"So why didn't he come here himself?" Corin pressed. "Was he afraid of drawing too much attention?"

Had I been in a better mood, the question would've made me laugh. To Jesse, there wasn't such a thing as too much attention.

"No," I said. "He couldn't come because he's on Oprah today."

I allowed some time for that to sink in.

"I see. So we're chasing after him now? Because of his schedule?" Jackson seemed annoyed. Understandably annoyed. Like me, he'd been more or less awake for over 36 hours now.

"Not at all," I said curtly. I looked over my shoulder to check the next lane before passing over. "You three can do whatever the hell you want. But I'm going to get to him before *they* do."

That made Ghi pop in between the seats with renewed alarm, his memories of the icy femme fatale still very fresh. "Can't you try to call him again?"

"Seat belt." I waited for him to disappear before continuing. "And no. There's no reaching him now. The show taping isn't until after four, but he won't have a moment to himself for hours. I'll just have to *go*."

And every bit of me hated saying this. I was tired, so extremely tired, of rescuing Jesse Cannon. Whether it was from a critic's remarks, or a deranged groupie, or whatever *this* was. The horror of the morning, the sheer freakish nature of it all, stood second—if only for a few minutes—to how angry I was.

"She's absolutely right," said Corin. I liked him immediately. "I say we all go," he added, and I liked him less.

"Yeah, but what about Khan? What if he shows up?" Jackson started to lean forward between the front seats again, but he caught my glare in the rear mirror and decided to stay put. "How are we gonna find him?"

I was guessing that this 'Khan' person was number five, and I didn't particularly care. I would've happily pulled over and let Jackson or any of them out right there. Chicago was a long ways away, and I wasn't looking to waste any time.

Corin frowned. He shook his head. "There's no telling where he is, none at all. At least we know exactly where to find Jesse at the moment. Khan will turn up somewhere eventually. I mean, given his circumstances, he won't make it to Liberty without getting arrested anyway."

Ghi muttered something indecisively. He was looking rather sick.

The Washington Bridge lanes were coming up fast. I gripped the wheel, and my voice was sharp, impatient. "So? Where are you boys headed?"

"I guess Chicago," Jackson scratched a sideburn and shrugged. "That'd be what—twelve, fourteen hours?"

"Ten," I said convincingly, mostly in order to believe it myself, but also to keep from thinking about the more obvious problems at hand. My idiot employer's life was in danger, and despite what I wanted to believe, I possibly had a rental car full of gods on my hands. That's not something anyone should ponder in Manhattan morning traffic.

CHAPTER 10

In case you were wondering, Hollows are exactly what they sound like: empty voids, heedless vacuums. It would be a mistake, however, to think of them as stupid. Nor should they be thought of as the Vessel's darker opposites. They are earthly manifestations of some higher force, yes, and their ticket to existence involved a sort of sacrifice, but their similarities to the Vessel end there. The differences are too numerous to list, but it should be noted that the Hollows' most dangerous distinction concerns not what they are made of, nor what they can do, but what they lack: conscience. They have none of the stuff, not a drop.

Whereas the Vessel are free-thinking individuals, the Hollows are all parts of a primal but calculating whole, coexisting with the singular goal of consuming life. They can see and hear for one another, and share information seamlessly within one combined, violent mind. If they are the eyes of death, then they are all separate eyes on the same gigantic head, connected by an invisible but vividly real network. A network too hideous, thank your lucky stars, to take shape in a discreet enough manner for our plane of existence.

As an individual, a Hollow is merely the lasting imprint of a dying person. Not a dead person. Not a zombie. When a Hollow breathes into you, extracts the life from your body and takes you over, you don't *die*. You never really make it all the way there, because the actual force of death itself constantly has you in its grasp. You're always on the brink—you're always just dying, and death lives *in* you, and *as* you, and you become just a home, a shell, a window.

And no, you don't start shuffling around moaning with your arms straight out, voicing a desire for brains. While the Hollows do demonstrate a strong palate for human tissue and blood, they are smart about their hunger, smart enough to blend in. That which drives the Hollows is organized, intelligent, and able to mimic intact human beings in every way. So the Hollows speak to one another, though they don't need to. They drive, though they could walk for centuries without rest. They can read and pay rent and laugh, if necessary. But it's all a learned ruse; a kind of careful mirror trick, one that is less of a chameleon scheme and more of a defense mechanism within the beholder's own mind. Because there's nothing there that you want to see. When you look at a Hollow, you're looking at yesterday's meal.

It can take a day, it can take a century, for a Hollow to completely consume the body of a human being. When a Hollow's breath is passed successfully into someone who is dying, the victim's body immediately begins to preserve. It literally embalms itself, so as to remain as it appeared when overtaken. Hence, there are Hollows of all sizes and all ages. There are elderly Hollows, and handsome Hollows, and obese Hollows, and even little kiddy Hollows (and trust me, those are the scariest).

This preservation takes place on a level of appearance only. It's skin-deep. Everything that lies beneath, everything inside, has been consumed, eaten alive, swallowed out of existence. Even the skin itself, at some point or another, is no longer there. But you see it, regardless. You see it because you don't know *how* to see it any other way. In order to view a Hollow as it truly is (and don't try this at home), you have to hold your breath and face it with your eyes closed.

If for some idiotic reason you *do* try that at home—if you take a deep breath right now, close your eyes, and turn to your bedroom door—and you actually do *see* something, then you should run. Immediately. And very fast. That's pretty much your only option, because on top of being amorphous masters of disguise, the Hollows are physical marvels. Their abilities don't quite breach comic book proportions, but they are much stronger and faster than the average living Joe thanks to the almighty emptiness which animates them. The Hollows are divine, so to speak, as divine as dying can make someone. And beyond the limitations they've learned to deal with, the torments and inconveniences of being exposed to the hateful elements, they are untouchable. Sure, they'll shriek when on fire, or slow down in the sunlight, but they'll be up and biting again in no time. Point is, *you can't kill a Hollow*. Period.

There are ways to repel them, even subdue them, but running is always the best policy. Shoot one, blow one up, push one off a building—just don't expect any spectacular results. Assaults like those actually make things worse, in ways I'm not eager to describe just yet. The important thing to know is this: Only five other forces are able to *completely* destroy a Hollow, to shake death off it and let it die. And those applied forces have to be divine. Cue the Vessel.

Considering all of that, you can imagine why the Hollows and the Luna Latum had both been seeking the Vessel so obsessively since day one. And, given the advanced methods acquired by the Luna Latum in the meantime —divine energy monitors and high speed motorcycles and all—you'd be surprised if the Hollows found the Vessel first, wouldn't you?

Well, put on your surprised face, because that's what happened.

Jesse's letter may have had nothing to do with it. For all we know, it could have disintegrated in the Upper Bay. I've looked back countless times to that day, trying to recall the other people visiting the Statue of Liberty, and I don't remember anyone unusual, excluding the obvious exceptions. Just typical visitors, parents and kids, a school group, tourists. I don't trust my memory, though, not in this case. I know I was too busy watching Jackson or running from Stella to have noticed much else.

So maybe there were Hollows sniffing around Liberty Island that day, who chose not to act in front of an audience. Maybe they found the letter. Maybe they could sense the Vessel as distinctly as they could sense one another. Maybe they heard the songs, or saw the movies, or the commercial that tipped Khan off. Maybe Dahrkren is an Oprah fan.

We don't know.

But we do know that the Hollow world was buzzing that day with a name. It was repeated in their connected minds and their phone networks alike, raising up like speed bumps in their slick trails of ancient speech: Jesse Cannon, Jesse Cannon, Jesse Cannon.

It didn't take long for the subject of Jesse Cannon to reach the rented Honda either. We were somewhere in Eastern Pennsylvania when the questions started, which is like saying we were somewhere on a plate of plain yogurt. Driving across that particular part of the country is unforgivably boring, even when the horizon is full of demons and gods and who-knows-what else. And Jesse Cannon was like the only tabloid in an emergency room lobby with no television: he was simply the closest sane distraction.

I can't say I didn't see it coming. Still, I was wholly unprepared for the ferocity of the onslaught. Seriously—these three were more relentless than a pack of twelve-year-old girls.

"What is he like in real life?"

"Where is he from?"

"Is he really that tall?"

"Did he actually get an Olsen twin pregnant?"

"Can he really do that thing with his hips or is that digitally animated?"

(You'll see. St. Petersburg. Yes. Definitely not. And yes, yes he can.)

"How did you end up working for him?" Jackson inevitably asked, and I told him the same thing I tell everyone else:

"I made him a drink he couldn't refuse."

❡

Need-to-know basis. That was my policy for the first hundred miles or so. I didn't ask a question unless it was absolutely vital that I knew the answer. Most of my inquiries involved the gas gauge. And more than once I consulted Corin's phone for traffic alerts and route decisions. That was it. The rest I tried my absolute hardest to tune out.

So when Ghi squinted at the dash clock, fished two separate orange pharmacy bottles out of his pocket, and swallowed a handful of pills in the back seat, I very actively paid no attention.

Corin was driving at the time. I use the term "driving" loosely here, mostly because I have yet to decide on a word that accurately describes what it is that Corin does behind the wheel of a car. It hardly resembles driving, I know that much. Corin could not operate a motor vehicle to save his damn life. He was the worst driver I'd ever seen, worse even than Jesse, who once—I kid you not—confidently drove a limousine full of male dancers *into the lobby* of a Vegas hotel because he believed the valet sign indicated a parking garage.

It's not my job to make this stuff up.

Anyway. Back to the Honda.

I vividly remember watching the guardrail sail by, precious inches away, and looking over my shoulder occasionally to see if anyone in the back seat understood that certain death was near. Ghi would smile politely back each time, oblivious to our peril. And Jackson would do nothing. Jackson slept. He slept in a way that was more like a special ability, a super power, than a simple biological activity, and I envied him for it.

As soon as Ghi started popping his noon-time pills, Corin turned in his seat, dragging his arm—and the steering wheel—a little to the side as he did. The right tires and the rumble strip began a lengthy duet.

"Ghi," he said over the grating sound, retrieving his Sabre phone from a nearby cup-holder. "Don't you need to make a call or two?"

Ghi froze up, forgetting for a moment how to swallow. Call? He hadn't even left Dr. Avery a note. What would it have said? *Off to battle Death Incarnate. Real important. Be back later.* He honestly hoped the doctor would assume that he'd gotten lost, wandered off into a second fugue, drowned, been hit by a subway train, anything. But he also doubted that life would be so forgiving.

He coughed hoarsely, dislodging the pill from his throat and willing it to go down quietly.

"Um, no, "he said. "No, it should be fine."

We arched boldly into a ramp lane, and I locked eyes with a merging driver, sharing with her a moment of primal fear. Then I squeezed my eyes shut and curled into my seat.

I will live. I will live. I will live . . .

"You sure?" Corin asked.

Ghi cleared his throat again. "Yeah. I don't know what I'd even tell him."

Didn't need to know what they were talking about. Didn't care. But I clearly heard Jackson sit up a little straighter at that point. His superhuman sleep was apparently triggered to shut down whenever there was potential for interesting conversation.

"Tell who what?" he asked through a yawn.

Corin opened his mouth to politely fend him off, but it was Ghi who answered. He shrugged naively. "My doctor."

Jackson stretched in the compact confines of the seat, yawned again. "What would you have to call your *doctor* for?" he cocked a perfectly rectangular eyebrow, looking over at the pill bottles. "You some kind of junkie?"

"Honestly!" Corin snapped. I opened my eyes and immediately shut them again—we were now taking up most of two lanes.

"Bugger off and drive, Tea Time," Jackson smirked dismissively. He turned back to Ghi and shoved him on the shoulder to show that he meant no harm, which of course had the opposite effect. Ghi shrank away, disappearing just a little more into his sweatshirt.

"Doesn't bother me what you do for fun, man," Jackson said. "But we have to stick together here, play for the same team. All I'm saying is that if something's up with you, we got a right to know about it—"

Corin's jaw tightened. Mostly because Jackson had a point.

"—and I got a feeling something is definitely up with you."

"I am here legally!" Ghi insisted reflexively.

"Good to know," Jackson said. "And this doctor guy?"

"He's going to wonder where I am, that's all."

"Why?"

"For Christ's sake, he has a condition," Corin exclaimed.

"So?" Jackson sat back expectantly, hands behind his head, getting comfortable. "Then let him tell us about it. Unless of course it's something really gross or embarrassing . . ."

Corin looked over at me. As if there was something I could do.

Ghi sighed. He looked across the seat at Jackson, who smiled back at him. "Same team," he pledged.

"Same team," Ghi repeated. He paused for a long moment, organizing his thoughts, how to word them all, how to explain them in a way that would cause the least amount of alarm.

"My standing in this country depends on my doctor," he started. "I could be deported if I don't follow his treatments."

"Deported to where?" Jackson cut in.

"Jordan."

"Hngh?" I grunted without opening my eyes.

Ghi's confusion lasted only a moment, and then he laughed. "No, no. Jordan the country. I'm *from* Jordan."

"Oh. Right. Awesome." I settled farther into my seat, doubling my efforts to ignore the conversation.

"About six years ago," Ghi continued, "I survived a hotel bombing in Amman. The medical short story is that I had severe burns and a bullet injury to the head, and I spent more than a year in a pretty deep coma. They'd just about written me off as a lost cause when this fluke power outage at the hospital knocked me out of it, and that's it. Waking up in the dark is the earliest memory I have. Of anything. I was already in the fugue state."

The car was silent for a moment. Except for the rumble strip.

"Bombing?" Corin asked.

"Bullet in your *head*?" I blurted, abandoning my policy. Too interesting.

"*What* state?" Jackson made a face.

Ghi took a moment to describe what a fugue state was, for the benefit of those in the car who had *not* studied psychology. He explained that, upon surfacing from his coma, he'd had no recollection whatsoever of his life before—and, despite a range of treatments, still didn't. He had awoken able to speak, to read, to do almost everything normally, but without any sense of self or identity. Where he had lived, who he had known, nothing. He hadn't even remembered his own name.

Dr. Avery, he said, worked specifically with survivors of head trauma, and had offered to help him after three years of unsatisfactory progress. Ghi's memory continued to be the main point of concern. The physical recovery was mostly behind him, though the medication he took now was for migraines and muscle tension, side effects of a somewhat delayed sensory motor cortex.

"Sometimes," he said factually, "when I'm not paying attention, I still drift slightly to the left."

Jackson listened, wide-eyed. His jaws had been hanging open on their square hinges, but he finally got them working again.

"So, you're like one of those people on the The Learning Channel or some crap?" he prodded. "You had to come over here and see, like, the *one* doctor in the world who'd know what was wrong with you? And even he's totally stumped about you? Something like that?"

Corin rolled his eyes. But Ghi started laughing. An honest, relieved laugh. "Yes, actually. Story of my life." He shrugged, adding, "What I can remember of it, anyway."

"Well, I'll be damned." Jackson's perpetual smile shifted to maximum mode. He slapped Ghi on the shoulder again. "See? Telling us all that wasn't so bad, was it?"

Ghi's smile froze, then converted into an ashen grimace.

"Well, no," he said. "But that's not the part I'm worried about."

Oh boy.

We waited, and after a moment's weary hesitation, Ghi carried on. "No one could confirm my actual identity, not officially. I had no records. And nobody ever recognized me or came forward to claim me," he explained. "So, well, since that's the case, and because of the bombing and everything, I was accused of faking my condition."

Just wait. It gets better.

Ghi cringed, then blurted rapidly: "They suspect I was a terrorist."

"Awesome!" Jackson, naturally.

I turned completely around in my seat, swinging from piqued apathy to total outrage in an instant. Really. A loose terrorist was all I needed.

"Well are you!?"

Ghi cringed. "I don't *know*! If I was, then I'm not anymore. Really!"

"Dude." Jackson scooted to the middle seat, eyes wild and serious. "Are you, really?" He winked, punting an elbow into Ghi's arm. "You *are* just faking it, aren't you? You can tell us. Come on, you probably haven't killed more people than Khan—"

"*No!*" Ghi threw his hands up in surrender, panicked and pleading. "I swear! But don't you see? That's what they'll think, now that I've disappeared!" He sank into the seat with a miserable expression. "What if they're already looking? The police, the FBI, the CIA, the National Guard . . ."

Clearly, deportation was the least of his worries.

I looked at Corin. Corin looked at me.

Correction: least of *our* worries, as of this morning. That woman he'd frozen, maybe she hadn't been a Hollow after all. Maybe that was why she'd gone straight for Ghi. Still didn't explain why she had a water gun. Unless Jordanian terrorists had a collective aquaphobia I wasn't aware of.

"Relax," Jackson drawled loudly, waving a casual hand through all the tension. "The man ain't going to catch up to you, not today." He started rummaging through his duffel bag on the floor, and pulled out, of all possible things, a sandwich.

He tossed it onto Ghi's lap.

"Just calm down and have a sandwich."

I was still too stunned to react with anything less than hostility when he pulled out three more and tossed two of them at me. I held one up, appalled.

"What is this?"

"Baloney," Jackson rolled his eyes as he sat back, his mouth already full. "You want a different kind? My mom probably packed more'n twenty."

"Your *mom*?"

"Yep," he shrugged his imposingly square shoulders. "I told her it would be a long trip."

I spun back into my seat and stared out the windshield, at the open highway ahead. I held the slices of bread in my lap and very carefully, very thoroughly, picked the situation apart piece by piece, to make sure I had it right.

I, Jordan Murphy, a perfectly innocent individual, a twenty-four year old woman of sound mind, was trapped in a rented Honda with a driver who may as well have been geriatric, a wanted terrorist with amnesia, and a grown man whose one solution to it all was a bag full of sandwiches *that his mother had made.*

Also, it was a likely possibility that the CIA would gun us down at any second.

And, my boss was probably already dead.

"Jackson's right, actually." Corin interrupted my list, looking in the rear mirror at Ghi. He took a bite of his turkey and swiss and then rested it against the wheel. "There's nothing we can do about it just this second, is there? I mean, even if they are looking for you, it's sort of irrelevant now, isn't it? We really do have bigger problems."

Oh yes, that too.

The whole Vessel thing. The Hollows. Undead soul-suckers and all of that.

I twisted around again and grabbed the strap of the duffel bag. I never have cared for baloney. "What else did your mom put in there? I'm starving."

The earliness of the still day felt unreal. When my eyelids were telling me it had to be at least two in the afternoon, it was still only eleven in the morning. When my restless legs suspected a sunset, it was hardly three o'clock—and still over 250 miles to Chicago.

The tiny car seemed to grow smaller and more cramped by the hour, a speeding purple time capsule with no means of communication to its only destination. I called Jesse frequently to leave messages, knowing he wouldn't answer, and grew more and more anxious with every mile. Jackson dozed, off and on. Corin theorized out loud. I worried. Ghi fidgeted. And all of us talked.

Corin talked about traveling, overseeing the projects his father had financed, detailed long stays in places like Papua New Guinea, Laos, Tibet, Johannesburg, and Bengal—just one marvelous feat after another. Listening to him was like listening to a James Bond audio book (complete with the accent). He'd gone to the same prep school as Prince William, claimed two masters degrees, dated a duchess-to-be, swam the English Channel, and surfed five continents. He'd been treed by an Alaskan grizzly, broken a femur halfway up Mt. Everest, and had assisted the successful emergency landing of the rescue helicopter. With a fractured femur.

Which stumped me even more as to why he drove like a one-eyed centurion, but I digress.

When Jackson took the wheel somewhere in Ohio, Corin spent about an hour answering all the emails that had accumulated on his Sabre, canceling appointments and penning apologies. When he was done, he was done. I guess if you own just about everything, you can disappear anytime you like.

As for Ghi, no one could think of a disaster-proof way to account for his sudden disappearance, and so it was decided that he should contact no one at all. That was a debate I stayed out of. I didn't know how long they all planned to be absent from their normal lives, and I didn't ask. I just knew that Ghi likely represented a national threat by that time, and that he was traveling in a car that was rented under my name. Which meant I was potentially harboring a terrorist—not something I wanted on my résumé.

Jackson didn't make any calls, either. He told us about the incident with Khan, and about wrecking the fire truck. He'd told everyone back home that he was visiting a friend in Maine, just taking a little vacation to clear his head after both ordeals, and no one had questioned him. Which was good, since he didn't actually know anyone in Maine.

"They don't worry about me none. We're not the worrying kind, not where I'm from. And by the way, I haven't *always* lived at home, you know," he said, jabbing a mustard-flecked finger over at me. "I went to college for engineering, actually. Football scholarship. But I didn't finish. Tore a knee ligament my sophomore year and lost it all.

"I wound up volunteering at the fire hall the next year and just stuck with it. And then I moved back in with the family," he shrugged. "We have a beef range down in the Ozarks, and I just thought, what the heck, you know? They always need extra help anyway. There's twelve of us kids, but we didn't all stick around so close."

"Wait," I stopped him. "Twelve? As in twelve brothers and sisters?"

Jackson proudly confirmed this with a nod, then slapped his forehead correctively. "No, no. Thirteen. Bill. Goddamn, I always forget Bill . . ."

Thirteen kids? I bit into a sandwich—my third—with renewed respect for its maker. Popped out *thirteen kids*. "Is your family Catholic? Mormon?"

"Nope. Just big," he winked. "Kids are cheap labor."

"I'm guessing you don't all go by Jackson," Corin mused. His phone beeped and he involuntarily plucked it up to check the screen.

Jackson smirked. "Yeah, Whitney was Mom's idea of a handsome name. Some soap opera star or something."

Ghi nodded mystically. "Whitney Garret. *Passion Seasons.*"

A mildly uncomfortable silence followed, of which Ghi was wholly unaware. Jackson shook his head and continued, deciding not to comment.

"Eh, I forgive her. I'm her favorite, after all," he thumbed his shirt collar. "She always teases me about being the only one who came out looking like her. Everyone else looks more like my dad."

Corin didn't look up from prodding his phone as he spoke. "Well, that makes sense. He's not technically your father."

I blinked at that presumption, especially since it came from Corin, who was in all ways the opposite of presumptuous. Or so I had thought. But there was not a trace of outrage on Jackson's face. If anything, he looked vaguely thrilled. His jaw dropped with a kind of gratified awe.

"Oh, that's *right*," he gasped, tapping the wheel. "I'd sorta forgot *that* part. Wow. It's weird to think about . . ."

"What part? What's weird?" I demanded, sitting forward. Before either of them answered, my memory answered for me. In the voice of Jesse Cannon, relating his ancient dream: *Men, born of woman's flesh but constructed of the divine forces . . .*

My spine prickled. I felt like a stranger to myself even saying the words. "Immaculate conception?"

"More or less," Jackson grinned, then spoke over his shoulder. "Mind handing another Gatorade up here?"

"It sure makes a lot of sense in my case," Corin pulled a bottle of fluorescent orange liquid out of the duffel bag. He thoughtfully unscrewed the top before handing it to Jackson. "My parents tried for years to have kids, never could, and then I came along. My mother was fifty-four."

I tried to wrap my head around the physics of that statement, and then realized that there were no physics. No sane biology either. There was only magic, for lack of a better word. I looked over at Jackson, who had declared himself the Vessel of all things earthen earlier that morning, and forced myself to recognize that I was sitting next to a guy who had been sired by dirt. *Dirt.*

How in the hell were they coping with all of this? How could they be sitting here talking about their mothers and drinking *Gatorade*?

Corin turned to Ghi, and, realizing just in time that Ghi would have nothing to contribute on the subject of parentage, spared him the question and addressed me instead within the same breath: "What about Jesse?"

"Jesse?"

"Yes, his parents. What do you know about them?"

I shrugged. Jesse was forever interested in the first-person present tense. He didn't expound upon much else. I had learned more about his past from Wikipedia and tabloids than I had from him personally. But I offered what I could recall.

"Well, I know his mother was some famous Russian opera socialite. She was in a handful of movies, too, I think, and she died when he was in high school. Car wreck. National news. She had a lot of affairs, from what I've read. And if she ever told Jesse who his father was, then he's never mentioned it, not to me. But, if what you guys are saying is true, then I guess it was never *any* of them . . ."

Corin nodded, adequately sated. Jackson took a pensive swill of Gatorade. Ghi sneezed abruptly, and I offered a blessing.

That evening developed slowly in Illinois, painfully slowly. The sun, which had chased us out of New York so many hours ago, did its ancient disappearing act somewhere near Springfield. Flat farmlands gradually relented to small townships, then into a sprawl of suburbs, where the straight highway left the ground to become a long series of tunnels and bridges, mergers and overpasses. We were getting so close, less than an hour to go, but the remaining miles seemed to stretch out ahead of us like a chain of cheap rubber bands, tense and uncertain.

The night itself was a clear one, but an orange haze blotted out the stars —the lights of Chicago, still too far ahead to see. I took over the driving again, and Jackson almost immediately began to snore in the passenger seat. Behind me, Ghi and Corin spoke in lowered voices, their quiet tones probably more for my benefit than Jackson's. Ghi was trying to explain how the light now appeared to him, how each one made a different sound, like separate streams of sonar. How street lamps, fluorescent bulbs and stars, the wiring through walls and the headlights of passing cars all buzzed and clamored for his attention constantly. And yet he didn't have a clue what to say back to a single one of them, how to command them, to *move* them.

Corin nodded knowingly, listening. I thought immediately about the frozen blast of water, how it had hardened, moved as if with its own life, behaved in such an impossible way—all to defend him.

And then I thought about what Ghi had said earlier, wondering what it would be like to wake up one day without a reference point, without an ounce of self inside. How could anyone be prepared for that? And where do you go from there? You arrange your life into this sturdy composition, but all it takes is a bullet to the head or a divine vision or one courier mission to Manhattan to demolish it all. You get handed another blueprint and told to build elsewhere.

"This is our exit," Corin spoke up, startling me.

I opened my mouth to argue otherwise, but realized just as quickly that he was correct. There it was, in big white letters: Exit 51D, Madison Street. Frowning at my own negligence, I hastened to get into the correct lane.

"Thank you," I said, glancing up at the rear-view mirror. Corin was smiling at me.

"You're taking all of this in remarkable stride, you know," he said, leaning up against the side of the passenger seat. "If I were you, I'd have written us off as complete lunatics from the start."

I shrugged modestly, not quite knowing what to say to that. Mostly because

I *did* think they were complete lunatics. And also because he didn't know jack about my threshold for dealing with lunacy. He still hadn't met Jesse Cannon.

CHAPTER 11

We arrived at Harpo Studios just after 7:00 p.m., with the time zone change acting in our favor. A set of studio passes and a dressing room key were waiting with the gate attendant. That was evidence of more foresight than I'd ever deemed Jesse capable of, a shock I was too nervous and exhausted to fully appreciate. We all held our breath as the attendant wrote down Ghi's name, expecting a SWAT team to fall from the sky at any moment, but he was added to the list without so much as a second glance.

With relief, I relinquished the Honda to a valet. I wonder if it's still in rental circulation, and if anyone who has driven it since could feel the magnitude of what it once carried. I wonder if it still smells like baloney.

I handed out the passes at the rear of the studio, pausing with my shoulder against the door.

"Just keep your heads down and stick with me."

Chaos. No matter how many potted plants and lint-free surfaces there are on set, the behind-the-scenes habitat holds nothing but chaos, and that goes for any production. Cameras and furniture rolled by, hustled between groups of backstage tourists. Everywhere, there were crew members, set managers, guest wranglers, and my own brethren, the assistants, recognizable by their darting pace, cups of coffee, and suicidal expressions. But nowhere on that vast linoleum battlefield did I see the tall physique, golden hair, or oversized sunglasses I was looking for.

I pulled aside the closest manager I could spot, showed him my pass, and asked him where Jesse Cannon would be.

"All his autographs and after-show stuff wrapped up about an hour ago," the guy said, eyeing my three companions with curiosity as they shuffled anxiously behind me. I knew he wouldn't question me about them, not in this environment. Escorting fans is part of being an assistant. As is delivering dessert, if you catch my drift. These three didn't look like Jesse's typical fare.

Shaking his head, the manager checked a clipboard and found our man. "He's in 11B. Down that hall and to the right."

"Has anyone been back to see him yet?"

He thought for a minute, then nodded, "Yes, actually. A bunch of girls with a group pass, I think. They might still be back there if you—"

"Thanks!"

We left him standing there, watching us panic off into the direction of the dressing rooms.

"How come that guy looked at us like that?" Jackson asked, close behind me.

I flashed my pass at the attendants guarding the hallway, never breaking stride. "Probably because you're not wearing assless chaps," I panted. There was no time to explain what that implied. We hustled to the next corridor, which was quiet and empty, and then broke into a full sprint down to 11B.

I smacked the heel of my palm against the heavy door. "Jesse!"

No answer.

"Jesse, it's me!" I knocked several more times and waited. I pressed my ear to the door. Nothing. With a sinking, hollow feeling in my stomach, I found the key the gate attendant had given me, unlocked the door, and swung it open.

"Oh my god."

My breathing halted. The sinking feeling turned into free fall.

The room was a wreck. Everything, every chair, every lamp, every item on the vanity, was overturned or thrown to the floor. The wardrobe was gutted. The television was smashed and the mirror was broken. Shards of glass and promotional photos littered the floor.

No one moved. For a moment, in my mind, this was the end of the trail.

Jesse was gone. All possible conclusions were the same: these things had broken in, and they had killed him or taken him or *something*, and he was gone.

I couldn't breathe. I couldn't see. The room phased into one blur of color, and then it was eclipsed, with a face, with arms. Corin had placed himself in front of me and grabbed my shoulders.

"Think. Is there *anywhere* else he could be? Or anyone else who would've been with him?"

My mind raced. It was perfectly reasonable to assume that whatever had happened, Jesse had been here for it. But that wasn't *totally* certain. Not yet, I told myself. I scrambled to hold on to that, to process any other sequence, and then—a sudden ray of hope with ten wheels.

"The bus," I gasped. "The tour bus."

"The what?"

I turned and fled the room with stupid hope, and the three of them followed in unquestioning silence. Instead of going back toward the stage area, I sought out an exit to the back lot and made a dash for it, chanting in my head a single *'please'* with every sprinting footstep down the long corridor. An eternity of seconds later, we burst into the freezing Chicago night air to find ourselves on a vast and gated lot where—glory of glories—Jesse Cannon's tour bus was still parked.

The bus was a big, sex-red behemoth of a thing, with iridescent trim and black-tinted windows. The tint didn't really keep the general public from guessing who might be onboard, since both sides of the bus featured a rather provocative image of Jesse himself, naked and stretched out on top of a piano.

Despite the circumstances, Jackson burst out laughing the second he saw it. I can't say I blame him.

I ran, yanking my extensive set of keys from my pocket, finding the right one just as I made it to the bus. My hands were shaking so uncontrollably they could hardly get it into the keyhole.

"Just a minute, we don't know what's in there," Corin warned behind me, and Ghi wheezed in agreement, out of breath. I ignored them. The bolt slid, the door unlocked. I didn't knock, didn't call out first, just yanked the handle and stepped up into the bus with the three of them following close. It was dark. The heater was humming. Something moving to the left almost gave me a heart attack.

"Jesus, girl, I've been trying to call you for an hour."

Jesse peered out from the back room, pulling a T-shirt on. His hair was wet. I could smell the leftover eucalyptus-flavored steam of a shower. He emerged, looking first at me, then tilting his head at the three individuals behind me. Before he could acknowledge them, though, I moved. Correction: I propelled myself forward and threw my arms around him.

"You idiot!" I screamed, squeezing him violently, smashing my face so hard into his chest that I am not sure how my words came out clearly. "Someone tore your room apart! What happened?!"

He stared distractedly over my head at the others, as transfixed as they were, then looked back down at me.

"I don't know," he said, gently prying me off. "I didn't go back to the room at all. I've been in here, listening to your messages."

"Oh, thank god. *Thank god*," I gasped for air.

And then I pulled away and slugged him. Hard. It was a beautiful shot, truly beautiful—square in the eye. The thick, resonating sound of it was followed immediately by my roared declaration:

"I quit!"

And I did. Employment terminated. I was done. Out. Finished.

Jesse reeled away, entirely stunned, and I whipped around to face the others. They stared back, speechless. Ghi cringed as if I might hit him, too.

"I'm sorry, really sorry," I said, with Jesse still gaping and grasping his face behind me. The rest of my words rushed out in a nerve-racked stream. "I won't say a word about any of this. Consider it forgotten. Good luck with the entire thing. Goodbye."

None of them made a move or said a word as I stepped around them. And before another second could pass, I tossed my keys down on the bar, stomped out the door, slammed it securely behind me, and started walking.

There.

One foot in front of the other. Away, away, away. My throat felt hoarse with a forming lump of emotion. My eyes burned with salt and my face flushed red. I was furious, positively furious. Because of everything that had happened to me in the past day. Because Jesse had knowingly involved me in something beyond any reasonable person's control.

Because I now had an inkling of what could've happened to him. To any of them. And some dim understanding that this was only the beginning of it.

I didn't even know where to go first. A hotel room for starters, then maybe a plane ticket or another rental car. I was quite aware that almost everything I owned was either on that bus or in Jesse's L.A. beach house. It didn't matter. I didn't get far. I took maybe twenty steps before I saw them.

There were four. All women, standing together about fifty yards away, close to the studio door we'd run out of only moments ago. They stood in perfect stillness, watching me.

I stopped cold. Something about these women, other than the fact that they were collectively staring at me, made my blood turn to slush. Two things, actually. The first thing is hard to describe, but I could see it. Even at that distance, and under the harsh street-lamp lighting, I could tell something about them was off, weird, *wrong*.

You know that house in your neighborhood that no one has lived in for awhile? It looks just like all the other houses. There's nothing specific about it to indicate that no one lives there. Maybe a neighbor is still mowing the lawn to be nice. The shingles and gutters are still clean. It might even have curtains.

But somehow you can just *tell*.

That, my friends, is kind of what Hollows are like.

CHAPTER 12

My feet would not lift from the pavement, my mind would draw nothing but blank after blank. The Hollows did nothing immediately. They stared. And I stared back, mesmerized by how positively motionless they were.

And while I stared, I tried to make sense of the second thing about them that frightened me so much. This one's fairly easy to explain:

They were all wearing Jesse Cannon T-shirts.

That's right. Un-dead groupies.

Who knows how much longer our staring contest would have lasted. Maybe all night. Or maybe they were about to spring, to tear me into pieces on their way to the tour bus. Before that or anything else could happen, though, a scalding roar and a wave of distant screams erupted close by. The Hollows were just as surprised as I was, and our startled focus converged at a corner of the building, where bursts of orange were blooming upward against the night sky.

The back of Oprah's studio was on fire.

I didn't pause to consider why or how. Neither did the Hollows. Without a single word between them, they bounded into immediate action. Two of them darted around a corner, moving like beads of sweat around the perimeter of the building, running towards the flames.

The other two ran towards me.

I motored backwards frantically and smacked into the tour bus door. Had I locked it? Had they? I started banging on the it with everything I had, gawking over my shoulder at the two Hollow fangirls moving closer with fluid, steady speed.

Corin opened the door. I shamelessly toppled him to the floor on my way back into the bus, then spun to shut the door immediately, scrambling with the locks.

"Back so soon?" Jesse said loftily, holding a cold can of orange Fanta to his eye.

"Drive," I gasped to no one in particular. The word was an empty wheeze.

Corin picked himself up off the floor. "What?"

"Drive."

Something thudded against the door. The handle shook. I heard the sound of what I correctly believed to be a metal stair-step being broken off. And then a dent the size of a perfect karate chop busted into the door.

"Hey!" Jesse frowned against his Fanta.

Jackson peered out a tinted window, seeing exactly what I expected he would see: women in Jesse Cannon shirts going absolutely crazy. He let out a low whistle, then looked at Jesse. "You deal with this all the time?"

"Drive!" I repeated myself to the top of my lungs.

The window above the bar shattered.

Jesse dropped to the floor. Ghi ran in an ambiguous circle, falling all over himself and knocking Corin down again. Another dent appeared along the door frame, and the door itself was starting to buckle in like a piece of scrap metal. I braced my back against the bar and looked to the driver's station.

Jackson was already climbing into the seat.

"I got this!" he shouted. "Keys!"

Without pausing to consider the similarities between fire trucks and tour buses, I grabbed my set of keys from the glass-sprinkled counter and tossed them into his waiting hand. "The black and gold one!"

"Got it."

He fired the bus up, just as the window above the door was smashed through. And then he floored it.

Ten wheels left rubber all over that parking lot. Jackson steered in a huge circle to get us going, and I dropped to the floor. Loose objects—magazines, shoes, sunglasses, martini glasses, CD's— went flying. The bus bounced as we ran over something (or someone), and then bounced again as Jackson plowed right through the flimsy, unmanned gate and onto the access road. He picked up some speed, but not much—the street was short, ending at a busy intersection.

"Where to?" he shouted over his shoulder.

Ghi and I answered at the same time. "Anywhere!"

I pulled myself to my feet with caution, one inhalation away from a sigh of relief, when something thudded loudly on the roof. I snapped my head upwards. Whatever was up there, it didn't hold my attention for long.

"Oh, god! Oh god!" Jesse was bouncing up and down, pointing at the bar.

A bloodied woman was climbing through the broken window.

We screamed in perfect four point harmony.

My mind reeled. This girl couldn't have been more than twenty, younger than all of us, her face pretty except for its starved sneer, her tour shirt tidy except for fresh bloodstains. In my short life, I had fought off my share of groupies. I had been trampled by stiletto heels. I had tackled nearly naked men, men much larger than myself. But I had never been up against anything quite like this bitch.

She poised in the jagged frame, stretching a hand down to the bar to steady herself, eyes darting between us. Her arm streamed with ribbons of blood, but she took no notice, showed no pain—nor did she seem to care that the blood itself was turning darker and darker and darker . . .

Ancient words slid out of her mouth, words with lots of menace and very few vowels, and with them the dark, almost syrupy substance trickled from the corner of her chattering lips, oozing down her chin, down to the glittered marble countertop. She ducked further inside with one fluid motion, suddenly way too close to all of us, her wide eyes clouding over with that same inky material.

Corin was closest to her, his back pressed to the connecting counter, his arm reaching around wildly for something, anything at all. The Hollow's attention snapped to him. She calculated. She got some traction.

She lunged.

Corin met her with the first available blunt object, which happened to be my weathered George Foreman grill. Wielding it like a shield, he drove her back towards the window, and she grappled and hissed and squealed, spewing black matter all across the countertop. After several clumsy seconds, during which no one could decide exactly how to offer any assistance whatsoever, Corin reared the grill back in both hands. He swung out, cracking it against the Hollow's head with such force that I fully expected excess grease to spew from her ears.

No grease. She took the blow without insult or injury, wiped a tar-like liquid from her nose, and in one inhumanly fast motion, grabbed Corin's wrist and bit down. His hand disappeared between her gnashing, sawing teeth. Then his wrist. By the time his forearm disappeared, physics and logic were out of the question. She had swallowed him up to his elbow—and she was still going.

The George Foreman grill fell out the window and to the roadside.

"*Christ Sakes Mary Mother!*" Corin bid it a blood-curdling farewell. And with the better part of his arm still down her gullet, the Hollow lurched through the shattered window, yanking most of him out with her.

By some miracle of unprecedented valor, Ghi and I both acted to grab his flailing legs. We braced and heaved, attempting to haul him back in, but it was a useless of tug of war. The Hollow kept ripping away at his arm, he kept yelling religious obscenities and kicking us into one another, and we kept losing hold on him, inch by inch.

"How's it going back there?!" Jackson hollered.

Our very loud reply did not come in the form of actual words, but he got the idea. He sped up.

Dents were starting to dot the ceiling, as if the tour bus were driving through a triple-gravity hail storm. Something banged heavily on the emergency escape hatch, which just so happened to be positioned above the very spot Jesse had chosen to hop around and do nothing in. A frustrated shrill sounded from the roof, and I glanced up to see the hatch get pummeled a second time.

"Jesse, what are you doing?!" I shouted, fighting to maintain my grip on Corin's bucking leg.

Just dancing around, that's what he was doing. Just staring at the damn hatch and waiting for it to open.

"Lock it!" I roared.

Jesse reached up to turn the little red knob, and then withdrew his hand the instant another dent appeared. He cringed at me. The hatch flapped open for a fraction of a second, before the jet stream of air against the bus slammed it shut again.

"LOCK IT NOW, JESSE!"

He grimaced, stood up resolutely on his toes, and turned the handle. The lock clicked.

With an entirely disproportionate amount of relief on his face, Jesse turned to me, expecting I don't know what. A high-five? A medal? I glared at him with as much resentment as possible before Corin kneed me sharply in the nose. And then the hatch door burst off of its hinges.

It dropped onto Jesse's head, and he threw his arms out, falling flat on his million-dollar ass as Jackson cut the bus sharply onto Randolph Street. We swerved widely into a second lane as our newest threat slipped her head and shoulders through the small opening above, emerging upside down into our current chaos and absolutely exceeding even the most horrifying of expectations.

There was no comprehending what we were seeing. There was only confusion, confusion which momentarily paused all horror. Though she was much the same as the first Hollow, there was one largely important difference about this one:

Her head was on fire.

Her body dropped through the hatch and landed on top of Jesse, her limbs ablaze and flapping. She twisted, she shouted. Jesse wailed. Ghi and I screamed, side by side. Corin was all out of breath by then. Jackson, because he felt left out I guess, just kept sounding the air horns.

In all this hellish noise, the competing tension on Corin's upper half suddenly went slack. He tumbled back through the window and Ghi and I dropped his legs, abandoning him on the black-splattered countertop. I didn't pause to see whether or not he still had two arms. I had more immediate concerns. The hems of my jeans were on fire. There was a demonic being writhing on the floor, much too close to me. She flung herself to her feet, shrieking, roaring with what sounded like several different voices at once, and the rest of us scattered.

I dove for the couch. I don't know why. The immediate threat was a five-and-a-half foot flaming woman, not a rodent. The bus tilted dangerously as it curved around the loop of the interstate ramp, and we merged onto 1-90, westbound, doing eighty, smoke pouring from the broken vent. The smoke detector inside the bus was screeching, and above its noise and the Hollow's howls, I heard sirens.

Ghi rushed for the main door and fought it open. Through the smoke I could see the guardrail flying by at nauseating speed, and orange sparks arching out from where the broken steps were scraping pavement. I looked to him in horror. "What are you thinking!?" And then—

"OUT OF MY WAY!"

The snarl made me spin around, not the Hollow's snarl. A familiar snarl. A platinum record, pitch-perfect snarl. I could believe my ears alright, but my eyes had to be kidding.

Jesse Cannon was driving the Hollow—wrestling her, flames and all—toward the open door with his own bare hands.

The sight was both worrisome and strangely inspiring, and it was brief. One exaggerated stage kick, and the Hollow's journey with us was over. She hit the guard rail with an unforgettable snapping sound and rolled out of sight, still burning and bawling.

"*Bitch!*" Jesse screamed lividly after her, planted by the door. He dusted his blackened hands against the front of his designer jeans, muttering rapidly about custom carpeting and smoke stench. Jesse really loved that tour bus.

The howling faded, and as the interstate took us on a wide turn, we caught a surreal glimpse of our wake. The Hollow was rolling to a stop in the wet grass beyond the highway. Already far behind us, a second twisting ball of flame lay in the road—the other Hollow, the one that had tried to shred Corin's arm off. And beyond her, fat plumes of smoke were rising against the lamp-lit sky, hovering over the studio. The flashing lights of several ambulances and other emergency vehicles were converging at the scene.

My knees spasmed together. I sank into a sitting position on the couch, heaving, quaking, checking my extremities for damage, finding none. The smell of burnt flesh was thick, filling my head and gut with unpleasant sensations.

No one spoke. The door slammed shut against the rushing night air, though I did not see Jesse close it. He turned and, with the prim composure of someone who'd just administered the ass-kicking of a lifetime, walked over and sat down stiffly beside me. Ghi stood by the refrigerator, wobbling. The smoke detector continued to screech until Corin, who had been sitting on the counter gripping his own mangled arm, punched it off the wall without looking up.

Jackson gradually eased to a less illegal speed. He turned to look over his shoulder.

"Everyone okay?"

Something huge pounded on the roof of the bus.

This time, I was the only one who screamed. Hysterically. I dove behind Jesse, buried my face between his shoulder blades, and inhaled in order to scream again.

Jesse sighed and snaked an arm around to touch me.

"It's fine," he said wearily. "He's with us."

What?

"Has he been up there this whole time?" Corin wondered aloud.

I forced myself to look up. Jesse and the others were watching the ceiling, exchanging knowing, tense glances. There was another thump. A set of large feet dipped through the open hatch, followed swiftly by legs, then not so swiftly by a jammed tangle of torso and ... and *fur?* And—*!!*

Jesse gasped and clamped a hand over my eyes.

Ghi winced. "Is he stuck?"

"Unbelievable," Corin remarked, monotone. "A little push, Jackson, if you please."

Jackson whooped and happily slammed the brakes, providing the abrupt force necessary to separate twisted fabric from broad shoulders, and broad shoulders from the narrow opening of the emergency hatch.

Somewhere near mile fifty-four, one very expensive ermine coat landed on the wet highway.

And, smack in the center of the bus's plush interior, landed one very dangerous, very pissed-off, very naked escaped convict.

And so let it be known to history that the Vessel, the long-awaited divine punishers of death, united at last on that fifth night of November with the addition of one Su Kim Khan, on a customized tour bus merging onto Westbound US Interstate 90, after leaving a few Hollows and the set of Oprah in flames.

No one spoke or did anything because no one knew where to start.

Not that there was any confusion as to what needed to be said or done. A great deal needed to be said and done. Broken glass and black Hollow juice needed to be cleaned up. Corin's arm needed attention. Jesse, whether he liked it or not, needed to make some phone calls pretty damn soon. Khan needed pants.

And polite introductions. We still hadn't gotten around to those.

Jackson accelerated, settling the battered bus as best he could into the evening traffic while we waded out the stunned silence. Someone (I don't know who—Jesse hadn't removed his hand from my eyes) offered Khan a towel, and he wrapped it around his waist, having not yet uttered a syllable to any of us. Sufficiently decent, he stalked to the table booth and sat down, assuming a kind of waiting posture, staring blankly ahead as if expecting to be left alone and ignored.

Leave him alone, we did.

Ignore him, we did *not*.

We couldn't ignore Khan any more than one could ignore a Great White Shark in a kiddy pool. At that innocent point in our lives, he was right on par with the Hollows as the most frightening thing we'd ever seen. Imagine, if you will, the scariest escaped convict that you can, the baddest guy you can come up with. Someone you don't ever want busting out of jail in your neighborhood. Someone you don't ever want at large anywhere in your *country*. Big, mean, bad-ass, probably hairy, missing teeth, bulging muscles, am I right?

Okay, that guy? That guy would've been Khan's bitch.

He was tall—just shy of seven feet, enough to dwarf even Jesse, too tall to stand upright in the bus. His arms and legs were solid and lanky, chiseled of hard, sinewy muscle and elevated veins. And all of this was wrapped in a rough casing of tawny, calloused skin, stubble, scar tissue, and colorful ink. Flames, waves, dice, busty women, tigers, koi fish, lotus petals, kanji, and ornate cloud patterns—tattoos of every kind wound up his arms, covered his chest and back, circled the base of his neck, and streamed down to his calves, all of them interlocking into a permanent, seamless body suit.

His hair was almost as colorful. A stringy mess of it fell over his face and neck, in natural black, peroxide yellow, and dyed lilac. He'd obviously not had the opportunity to fix his roots in awhile. The face beneath all this was long, stout, and solemn, if not positively emotionless, and it was decorated with an array of scars from previous piercings and who knows what else. Probably knife fights. And I'm guessing a good head-slamming or two, judging by the nose, which looked to have been broken more than once.

What made Khan truly chilling, though, the icing on the cake if you will, were his eyes. They were handsomely tapered and steady—quite placid, actually. Their color, however, was indeterminable. In fact, nothing about his eyes were determinable, not even the direction in which they were looking. Both of them were coated with a dingy film, murky translucent clouds which covered both his corneas. You could just make out the shape of the iris in each eye, and nothing more.

Khan was as blind as your Dear Aunt Sally.

Right.

So there we all were, the whole damn circus. We needed a facilitator. We needed Jerry Springer. We had Jesse Cannon instead.

Jesse had almost no threshold for silence. When confronted with silence, his immediate reaction was simply to make sound of any kind. By singing. By doing unimaginably wonderful things to the closest piano. By turning up some Aretha Franklin. Or of course, by enacting the most unfavorable alternative—he'd talk.

Jesse stood up. My insides sank immediately.

"Well!" he clapped his hands together once. His smile and stance would have been just as suitable for attempting party tricks at a funeral. "Welcome, everyone, to the Jesse Cannon Tour."

He placed a hand eloquently over his heart. "I'm Jesse Cannon, of course. And most of you have already met Jordan, my darling assistant, yes?"

He gestured at me as if presenting a game show prize. I bared my teeth.

Without pause, Jesse moved on, leaning languidly against the passenger seat, inclining his head toward Jackson. "And our handsome driver this evening is—?"

"Whitney Leroy Jackson," Jackson shot out a fearless hand. "But you can call me Jackson."

"*Ooob*." Jesse shook his hand, almost civilly. He winked at me and I quickly looked away, rolling my eyes.

"It's actually you. I can't believe this, I really can't," Jackson rambled, really hanging on to that handshake. "Jesse *Cannon*. My sisters love you . . ."

"Do they?" Jesse purred. I am certain that the rest of the bus dissolved from his mind at that point. So much for the remaining introductions.

Oblivious to this attention trap, Jackson continued. "Are you kidding me? They play that one song of yours over and over. The one with the . . . ," he trailed off, attempting a vigorous weaving motion of the shoulders. The bus did not deter from its course.

"*Sexodus*," I supplied flatly.

"Yes!" Jackson punched the wheel. "Yes, that's the one. Man, I thought I had you figured out until I saw that video. All that latex and lipstick—damn. Seriously, what *are* you?"

Silence.

A vengeful laugh barked out of me before I could stop it. Ghi and Corin looked away from anyone and anything as fast as they could. I guess they had their own confused feelings about the video in question.

The smile on Jesse's face stagnated on the spot. Normally, he reveled in the worship and controversies surrounding his gender-juggling image. He thrived on it, really. Under these delicate and trying circumstances, however, he took Jackson's statement as a direct insult.

The results were spectacular. You could almost reach out and touch the wall of contention that rose up between them. Jesse countered carefully, joining in with my laughter, waving a hand in showy indifference.

"Oh, I'm all man, honey," he teased, leering closer to the driver's seat for good measure. "What? Liked what you saw, did you?"

Jackson slapped himself across the thigh. "God yes, I did!" he said. "I *love* women with thick, bony necks."

Jesse's jaw dropped indignantly. He looked to me. I laughed again. And it felt very, *very* good.

"Just kidding, man," Jackson winked, shoving Jesse on the shoulder just a little too enthusiastically. "And thanks for clearing that up for me."

Game over.

"Anytime," Jesse seethed, snapping his teeth back together. He set his face straight, flipping the switch that restored his fabulous facade, and then turned his attention quickly to Ghi. A murderous flash was still left in his eyes.

"How about you?" he demanded. "What's your name?"

Ghi appeared too frightened to speak.

"His name's Ghi, " I rescued him. Ghi waved cautiously with one hand. Jesse then whirled to face Corin, who was preoccupied with coaxing bits of glass from the mauled parts of his forearm.

"Corin," he offered off-handedly, and yet remarkably polite, considering that he was prodding through his own broken skin. He paused to look up then, but not at Jesse. It was Khan who held his attention. Khan, who was biting serenely at a hangnail, ignoring all these niceties. It seemed unwise to ask his name, to attract his attention in any way. But that is exactly what Corin did.

"How did you do it?" he asked, frowning in a dreadfully serious way. "You set those things on fire. You set a prison on fire. How?"

Khan did not look up, but the corners of his mouth lifted slightly in response. He made a soft, single-syllabled laughing sound, but he didn't say a word.

This made everyone slightly more uncomfortable.

Corin slid down off the bar and took a step—one step only—toward Khan.

"How?" he asked again, brow creasing, then looked to Ghi and myself. "When I did that, er, *thing*, with the ice, back in New York, the water acted on its own. Sort of. Look, my point is, the water was already *there*.

"But that fire . . ." He turned to Khan again. "I don't get it. Where did it *come* from?"

Khan stared ahead, unheeding. He slid one hand into a multi-colored snarl of hair at the side of his head.

"Who cares about that right now?" Jackson spoke up. "Did you toast them all or what? If they're still following us, I need to know right now."

"Yes," Ghi prompted nervously, already shying away from the nearest broken window, just in case. "Are there any Hollers left back there?"

Khan laughed subtly again, and shook his head, fingers still digging through his hair.

"No," he said, very softly, in a tone suggesting that the very question amused him. It was the first thing he'd said at all. His voice was deep and reedy, like an oboe.

Jesse turned to me and dramatically mouthed the word '*creepy*'.

But I didn't see. I was still looking past him, at Khan, who had pulled a cigarette from the tangle of hair behind his ear, placed it between his lips, and was proceeding to light it.

With his finger.

A droplet of flame balanced upon his flexed fingertip, igniting the slightly rumpled cigarette within a nanosecond of contact. Khan tilted back leisurely, taking the initial puff, and the flame itself dissipated, leaving no trace whatsoever on the surface of his skin.

Corin considered this small miracle for a moment, incredulous. "So, that's how," he stammered. "You—you *make* it?"

Ghi shook his head. His golden eyes were wide with amazement and admiration, and they never left Khan.

"He *is* it."

"Mr. Su Kim Khan!" Jesse pushed between them both and placed himself in front of the alleged murderer with pleasant authority. "I'm afraid I'm going to have to ask you not to smoke in here."

Oh dear.

The round shapes floating in Khan's eyes shifted beneath their swampy surfaces. He took a drag of the cigarette and stared at Jesse like he was about to eat him. I must point out that, much like your Dear Aunt Sally, Khan is only legally blind. Which means that in good lighting, he can see well enough to get around. Or to pummel someone into a bloody heap.

We all watched in helpless terror, waiting for Jesse to burst into flames. But Khan simply butted the cigarette out against the upholstered seat and let it drop to the floor.

Remarkably, Jesse seemed just as eager to verbally disapprove of that as well. He opened his mouth to do so. I lunged. I realized that, formally, I was no longer his employee. But when you've been paid for five years to protect someone from his own stupidity, it just becomes second nature. I power-pinched the back of Jesse's arm as hard as I could and knocked him sideways.

"God, I'm not even thinking!" I declared madly, gesturing at Corin's bloodied arm, at my own scratched up hands, at the cut on Ghi's forehead, which he evidently hadn't noticed yet. He crossed his eyes and poked at it with alarm.

I tightened my talon grip on Jesse's arm, speaking loudly so as to cover up the sound he made. "There's a first aid kit in here somewhere," I said, marching him towards the rear of the bus. "Just give us a second to find it."

@

Stella Rosin knew the Hollows. And, regardless of the Vessels' significance, she was sure the Hollows would not try to harm them in the middle of New York City, or anywhere else. Not in broad daylight. Not when there was much easier blood to find.

The Hollows were not interested in trophies. Their objectives were and always had been simple and straightforward: feed, grow, multiply. So Stella had doubted very seriously that they were interested in the Vessel enough to be a threat. She doubted that they even knew about the Vessel.

She had been wrong.

The backup unit had reached the Chicago fiasco long before she and Abe had, a circumstance which only added to her ire. The entire group was now gathered on the sixth level of a parking garage about two miles away, a vantage point far removed from the fading smoke trails and flashing lights still visible below. There looked to be ten or fifteen hunters in all, waiting around a row of parked ambulances, the only vehicles on the entire level.

Stella cut the bike's ignition and removed her helmet. Her face was hardly a happy one, but it was as composed as ever. Behind her, she felt Abe slide awkwardly off the seat, mumbling something about ergonomics. He then staggered off, rather bowlegged, towards the ambulances and the other hunters.

A solitary hunter approached Stella, his paramedic jumpsuit half unzipped to reveal the telltale black under-armor. The second in command—or "beta", as he was to be called according to protocol—for the length of this assignment. Stella watched him, setting the kickstand and releasing the bike, waiting for whatever it was that he had to say. This beta did not offer his name, and it was unlikely that she would ever know it. But she quickly noted that the irises of his eyes were the same as hers—a snowy gray, a borderline silver—and among hunters that counted for something. He may have looked younger than her, but he'd been around long enough.

"Thank you for coming here first," he said. "There have been some important developments."

Stella barely acknowledged either statement. She got straight to business. "How many were there?"

"Just four. Very young. But they definitely knew what they were after."

Her eyes flicked to the ambulances. "I take it you've subdued them all?"

Here he paused decisively.

"Yes and no," he said finally. "Not much was necessary on our part. Not this time."

Stella did not need to verbally ask for elaboration. She let her glare do the talking.

The hunter paused again, gravely serious. He moved closer in order to speak in lower tones. Not for fear of being overheard, but because this was almost painful for him to admit.

"Look, it's true. The Vessel—whoever they are—they live up to the hype. Fire does, at least. Those Hollows were dead. All four of them, burned to death."

It took a great degree of muscular control for Stella not to flinch.

"Dead," she said.

"Dead."

Stella tapped a foot. Dead Hollows. As incredible as the idea sounded, it just didn't seem right. Didn't seem . . . *natural*. However intrigued she was, she decided to save any additional reaction for actual proof. There were other concerns at hand.

"And the Vessel? You didn't stop them?"

The hunter shook his head. "We were under instruction not to approach them without you or Dr. Sharma. But we're tailing them. And we've got word back already that they're all together. All five."

Stella nodded. "Any idea yet where they're headed?"

"Too soon to say," the hunter shrugged. "Headed south so far. They're not aware that our people are following, and there's no threat on board with them. Just fleeing blind, if you ask me."

Stella paused to align the facts for herself. The Vessel were all in one place now. They had seen the Hollows first hand. They had evidently *killed* said Hollows. And now they were bolting.

Three other things seemed very obvious. One, judging by the ice mishap and the recent fire, there seemed to be no doubt that the Vessel were aware of their own abilities. Two, they did *not* seem to be aware of the Luna Latum's existence, or its purpose to assist them.

Three. Considering the aforementioned facts, any direct attempt to surprise or corner the Vessel seemed extremely and unnecessarily stupid, in her opinion.

"There's no way we'll let them out of our sight," the other hunter assured her. "The next move is up to you."

Stella adjusted a pin in her helmet-flattened hair and stared at the rows of lights weaving along the highway system. She stepped around the bike, removing her gloves. Break over.

"Alright," she said flatly. "Find out what you can about this arsonist. The singer, too, whatever you can dig up. Let's keep back for now, see if they're heading somewhere specific, and try to contact them in the meantime. Dr. Sharma would be the best person to . . ."

She trailed off and turned slowly on her heel to look around the garage. And just where was Abe? She could not see him, but she could hear his voice among the cluster of vehicles, commonly excited, mingled with the lower, tamer tones of other hunters.

"He's examining the four I was telling you about," her colleague explained, walking hurriedly behind her toward the furthest ambulance. Its back doors were wide open, casting a garish yellow light into the murk of the garage. "We got lucky. Picked them up before a single police car even showed up. No mess. Listen, they're not properly put away, but I assure you—"

It didn't matter what he was trying to assure her of. Because the instant she stepped into the ugly yellow light behind the ambulance and saw what was inside, she had a gun drawn and aimed before the next instant ever knew it was due. A flame-thrower this time. No chances. No time.

"Stella, you *must* see this!" Abe gushed above the cross-hairs.

Stella did not even notice that he'd spoken her name out loud in front of twelve other hunters. Had she noticed, she would likely have kicked on the flame thrower and toasted him then and there. But Abe's fatal faux pas was overlooked utterly, because he was kneeling, pulling aside the flimsy sheets that covered two unrestrained Hollows.

Charred Hollows.

Motionless Hollows.

But Hollows all the same.

"Dr. Sharma, *move!*" she roared, barrel still trained on the twisted remains. Her composed expression fleetingly awoke with shock and aggression. He was *touching* one. He knew better. They all knew better. "Move. Now."

Abe didn't move. No one moved.

"I told you," said the silver-eyed beta, very calmly. "They really did it. Just look."

Stella did not lower the gun. She did not take her fingers from the trigger. She looked from one of her fellows to another with stern misgiving, and then she looked back at the two Hollows.

She closed her eyes. She halted her breath. And in the darkness behind her eyelids she saw—

Nothing?

"Come and see for yourself," said Abe.

Stella opened her eyes. Without further hesitation, she holstered the gun and stepped forward to examine the first Hollows ever to die.

CHAPTER 13

I knew precisely where the first aid kit was. I had used it many times. Gravity didn't treat Jesse kindly when he was drunk, which was often. And life in general hadn't treated me kindly ever since I'd started working for him.

I bypassed the sleeping berth where the kit was known to be buried beneath a mound of promotional materials, however, and pushed Jesse into the rear room of the bus. His room, with its heaps of new clothes, flat screen TV, karaoke machine, and of course, the custom circular bed, installed at his request.

I backed him into its cushy, curved edge.

"Jesse, what are we doing here?" I demanded in hissed tones. My instinct to take control of a situation wasn't going to go quietly. "We can't do this. This can't continue, it can't. Those things, those guys—"

"Oh, I know," Jesse grabbed my shoulders, his eyes wide and affirming. "That tall one is *too* weird." He shuddered dramatically to emphasize his point. "And can you believe that Jackson guy? Huh? Who does he think he is? Did you hear what he said about my neck?"

There. Right there. Something inside me screamed, popped, shriveled up, and died.

"Jesse!" I backed away and threw my arms in a downward motion, the universal sign of grief and despair, for my patience had just breathed its last. "We almost get eaten alive by teenage girls, a known murderer is out there breathing fire, and you're upset upset because some jerk said you had a fat neck?"

Jesse cringed. "Do I?"

This time, I went for the throat.

"And *you*!" he gasped, palming my forehead and holding me at arm's length as I swung and clawed uselessly. With his free hand, he prodded the bruise beneath his eye, which was beginning to darken to a greenish purple. "You hit me! What's gotten into you?"

"What's gotten into me? *What's gotten into me!?* You dragged me into this, you prick, that's what." I wriggled away and poked him in the chest. "I can't believe you *paid* me to get involved in this. Didn't you care? If you would've told me all that stuff was really going to happen—"

"Uh . . . hello? I did so tell you."

I stomped my foot. "Yeah, but you didn't tell me it was *real.* Like, *for real*-for real."

His eyebrows arched cattily and he looked from side to side, jutting his chin out. "Uh . . . *yeah.* I did. Maybe you should take me seriously once in awhile."

He had me there. I was still trying to think of a counter statement when Jesse's phone began to proudly sing the chorus of "It's Raining Men". Together, we looked down as he slipped it from his pocket, and stared at the caller ID with identical horror.

Our eyes met.

"Margot."

Margot. Jesse's agent.

The phone turned into a singing hot potato. He dropped it. I saved it and flung it back to him. He tried to push it on me, but I threw my hands up, glowering vehemently and backing away.

"No. N-O. I'm not here anymore. Ever."

"Fine," Jesse spat, lifting the phone to his face, his voice melting to sugar at once. "Go-Go, hello!"

An angry string of sounds jumped from the phone to his ear immediately, and he winced away from it. I didn't have to hear a word to know how this would go. After releasing any initial wrath, Margot would get straight to business as usual, first by assessing any possible damage incurred to her six-foot-six flaxen-haired money machine.

"No, no. I'm fine," Jesse said brightly, at the same time shrugging hopelessly at me. "Why wouldn't I be?"

More garbled yelling. I caught myself straining to hear, then moved correctively back out to the sleeping berths. Margot had undoubtedly heard about the fire by now, and there were a million ways Jesse could screw this up for everyone, but none of it was my problem anymore. As soon as we got far enough from Chicago, I'd decided, I was getting on another bus. One that would get me as far away as possible from Jesse Cannon, from convicted arsonists and amnesiac terrorists and burning buildings and baloney sandwiches and flesh-eating demons.

I pulled aside the curtain. Tour shirts. Giveaway "Confession" cologne samples. No first aid kit. I started digging.

"You're *kidding*," Jesse gasped into the phone, feigning shock. "A fire? It started where? From *my* room?" He put a hand to his mouth for good measure, and I actually wondered for a moment if this were a real reaction, if his attention span was truly so remarkably small.

"My god. We must've left right before it happened. Is everyone okay?"

He paused, listened, sank down to sit on the bed, adding a "Seriously?" or an "Omigod," wherever necessary. My search for the kit was not an adequate enough distraction; I simply could not drown out all of his fumbling explanations.

"Oh, the driver?" he looked to me with a pleading stare of sheer panic, to which I shook my head callously.

"Jordan fired him and called in someone else," he said flatly. His eyes flicked to me and narrowed to malicious slits. "No, she's not here. She's slutting around somewhere with a bodyguard from Dave Matthews Band."

I shot him an open-mouthed look of pure poison, then turned away. My fingers finally closed around the handle of the first aid kit. I yanked it viciously from beneath the heap of shirts, jerking it open.

"Well good," Jesse was prattling on. "As long as no one was hurt. Hey,

I've got another call coming in. Right, yes, okay ..."

I flipped furiously through the kit, making sure there was plenty of antiseptic and ace wrap and—

My fingers froze on a tube of burn ointment.

As long as no one was hurt ...

I slammed the kit shut and whirled around at Jesse.

"No one was hurt?"

Jesse arched his eyebrows at me, still babbling through whatever closing words Margot was trying to get out. I made a move to grab the phone, but he held it out of reach as he hung up.

"Jesse!"

"What?"

"No one was hurt!" I wailed. "No one was hurt?"

"That's what Margot said," he affirmed, giving me a cautious look, confused by my outbursts. "The fire did some damage to the studio, that's all, and they already suspect Khan. Did you know he hijacked some poor lady's car? And—oh, get this, Jordan—they think he's obsessed with—"

"Jesse!"

"What!?"

I rushed over and sat down beside him, closing the kit on my lap, my mind playing a horrifying game of leapfrog with itself. I didn't know the Luna Latum had cleaned up after us. I just knew that Margot should have had more news, more than the fire and Khan, more than the confusion over drivers and the deathblow possibility of being sued by Oprah.

There should've been some mention of the four female fans burning to death.

Suddenly the prospect of staying on the tour bus forever didn't seem so bad. Both a nauseating dread and a resigned sense of calm fell over me. And also a sort of giddiness, to know that I would never again have to talk to

Margot, since I was pretty certain at that point that something would kill me by morning.

"Think about it, Jesse." I pieced it together for him. "She said nobody was hurt. Don't you think she should have mentioned some severely burnt groupies?"

Jesse paused to consider this, and I got to witness his face blanching as the image sank in, maybe the same one I was envisioning: the charred Hollows rising from the highway and slithering off into the night, to regroup, to put themselves back together. To finish what they'd started.

His eyes met mine. "Oh."

I pushed the first aid kit into his hands and nodded towards the front of the bus. "Let's go tell them."

We moved dazedly out of his room. I paused again by the sleeping berths as an afterthought, pilfering there until I found an extra-large tour shirt, and Jesse passed behind me. He was about to slide open the privacy door, to saunter into the front end of the bus and give the bad news, but I stood up straight and turned around.

"Wait."

I had to make sure. If I was going to be on this bus another minute, I had to get a few things straight, for my own sake. Everything I'd seen so far had confirmed it, but I hadn't given myself a moment to decide what I believed. Or where I stood.

I took a step back so that I didn't have to crane my neck to see his face: the black eye, the supermodel lips, all of it. And suddenly it was difficult to speak. I found that I could hardly do more than grimace.

"You know I can't help you, Jesse." The words just fell out, and they were strangely terrifying words to hear myself say. "I can't. Not with . . . whatever this is."

Jesse listened with rare patience, not smiling, not frowning.

"But I'm trying," I blurted, bracing myself as the bus accelerated. "I'm trying to at least understand it all. I really am. So are you really . . . ? Some kind of . . . ?" I shook my head and smiled helplessly, stealing Jackson's words: "What *are* you?"

To that, Jesse's mouth stretched into a sly, camera-ready grin.

"Oh, the rest of the world has known that all along, honey," he said, tapping a finger under my chin as he turned again toward the door.

"I'm a god, that's what."

The Jesse Cannon tour bus, much like Jesse Cannon himself, rarely went anywhere without receiving loads of attention. The waving and honking and winking, the occasional carload of girls baring their jugs as they passed. Men's bikini briefs flung at the windshield. Things I'd stopped noticing long ago, plus things I had learned to notice right away, such as crazed stalkers in station wagons, or the occasional paintball-happy death metal fan out seeking musical justice.

The fact that it was close to 11 p.m. on a rural Indiana highway did not change matters much.

"I could really get used to this," Jackson said, admiring the suggestive salutations of yet another female driver in the next lane. Having appointed himself the only person onboard qualified to drive the bus, he had been at it for over three solid hours now, minus one stop for gas and cigarettes. "You need a new driver anytime soon?" he said, without taking his eyes off the side window.

"Darling, you can drive my bus anytime," Jesse yawned boredly from the couch.

Considering all this highway attention, and considering the apparent fact that the Hollows were aware of Jesse's identity (we could not otherwise explain their tour shirts, nor their presence at the Oprah show), it seemed rather unwise for all the Vessel to be riding around in a thirty-two foot diesel tour bus with Jesse's picture all over it. The issue was certainly debated more than once, but there was truly no alternative. No place to get a rental car this late, no way we were going to face the exposure of public transportation, and no sane reason to sit still. Not in a hotel. Not in an RV park. Not anywhere.

More immediate problems had already been seen to. The broken windows were patched over with flattened designer label shoeboxes and duct tape. Corin's right hand and most of his arm was wrapped in a thick mass of ace bandage, held firmly in place by additional duct tape. And Khan was dressed. Sort of. The seams of the extra-large shirt I had given him were in a strained state, to say the least. No duct tape had been necessary, but it was on hand just in case.

This shirt, by the way, was hot pink, the kind of hot pink that should be unlawful in amounts exceeding one square inch. And across its front it read in bold, white, glittering letters:

JESSE CANNON SEXODUS TOUR
I went. I saw. I came.

In addition, Khan had somehow zipped himself into a pair of *my* cut-off denim shorts, provided to him after a second private argument between Jesse and myself, this one over whose waistline was smaller. I will admit that Jesse won that one, but not before getting slapped a few more times.

The woman in the next lane took her exit, and Jackson returned to the ongoing conversation, which, for the second time, had found its way to the bedouins. The ones who'd watched Amphet sink into the earth. The ones whose ancestors were supposed to be waiting to assist the Vessel.

In short, the ones who weren't around.

"I bet they don't even exist anymore," said Jackson. "Probably all got picked off a long time ago."

"That's certainly possible," Corin forced himself to agree. He was staring his Sabre phone down for information, prodding it crossly with his bandaged fingers. "Do you think the Statue of Liberty has anything to do with them? Symbolically, I mean?"

Jackson snorted. "Like what?"

"I don't know," Corin was starting to sound slightly defensive. "Why else would the dreams have told us to meet there?"

"Maybe because it's a place we'd all recognize," Ghi offered peacefully. "Even me."

I was hunting around under the table as they talked, searching for the coffee pot, which had tumbled through the bus back when we'd been doing doughnuts in Oprah's parking lot.

"Look, we wouldn't have to reveal anything about ourselves initially," Corin was saying, cautiously, "but I would like to again point out that perhaps the FBI—"

Oh, this again.

I spotted the coffee pot, which was close to one of Khan's enormous feet, snatched it up, and then got out of the way.

The idea of contacting the FBI met the same fate it had the last time it was mentioned. Jackson and Ghi were strongly opposed. Jesse put his hands over his ears in a tired way, and Khan, before anyone could reassure him, caught the carpet on fire.

"Would you just relax!" Jesse stamped at the short flames, exasperated. "No one's going to arrest you!"

Corin threw his head back. "I'm just saying—"

"Are you out of your mind?" Jackson barked. "They'd haul Ghi and Khan off in a heartbeat, and put the rest of us under a scalpel—"

"—they're *bound* to have some record of—"

"—and if anyone else wants to drive this bus to DC, then go right ahead. Cause I won't, and I ain't ending up in no goddamn petri dish!"

"—and if we just demonstrated to them that—"

"What's a petri dish?" Ghi frowned.

"It's French," Jesse replied sagely.

"—then they would have no choice but to listen—"

"—neighbor called the Feds about that mutilated cow, and we didn't see him again for weeks! Sold everything. Started growing onions."

"—Bloody never mind."

"—Onions!"

I stepped around the last dying flicker of Khan's outrage, placed the pot in its proper place on the coffee machine, and flipped the brew switch.

"What if you just went to sleep?" I said. "Maybe another dream would tell you all what to do."

There was sweet silence for a moment.

I turned around and leaned against the counter. All of them were staring at me. Even Khan. It's hard to tell with him.

"That's brilliant, actually," said Corin.

I shrugged.

"I volunteer!" Jesse jumped to his feet, stretching grandly and making way for his bedroom. "I'll let you all know the moment I know anything."

The door shut behind him. We looked at it for a moment, as if fearful that he might come back out. He did not.

"No need to thank me," I sighed and took his place on the couch.

A restored calm fell over the bus. The words *"Ohio Welcomes You!"* blurred by on a sign by the highway, and Jackson took the speed up a notch. Corin sank further into the armchair, giving his eyes a moment's rest from his phone, and Ghi eyed him from the far end of the couch.

"How's your arm now?" he asked.

Corin had been growing sweatier and generally more uncomfortable-looking by the hour. He'd assured us already that the bandages were tight enough to stem the bleeding. But we all remembered how things had looked underneath.

Dry. The bites, the scattered craters of missing flesh, had looked unnaturally dry. And dark—greenish black around the edges, to be exact.

The broken skin had darkened before our eyes before he'd covered it up.

"It's fine," Corin said.

Dry and dark. Flaky. Sick. Waxy. Unhealthy. Corin's arm was many things, but it was definitely not fine.

"You're not going to turn into one of those *things*, are you?" I asked bluntly. I didn't need anymore surprises. Or anyone else trying to gut me.

Ghi shook his head. "It doesn't work that way."

"And if it does, you're fully authorized to set me on fire." Corin nodded at Khan, who offered the minutest affirmative gesture with his thumbs in response.

Reassuring.

Shrill squeals and cheering interrupted the moment, leaking in with the night air as a carload of girls sped by. High school cheerleaders, fresh from the game, still in their uniforms and glitter hair spray, were hanging out of the windows and waving.

"God bless America," Jackson uttered feverishly under his breath.

I fought the urge to roll my eyes. "Look," I said, "I'm glad you're having fun here, but seriously, where exactly are we going now?"

Jackson's shoulders, stout enough to be visible on either side of the seat, bobbed up and down. "Just moving for now," he said. "I guess we can rent something else in the morning, wherever we end up. We can probably make it to Charlotte by sunrise."

"I am not abandoning this bus in some honky town!" said an indignant voice from the back room.

"Then we'll leave you on it!" Jackson shouted back. "Go to sleep!"

"Yeah, and then what?" I pressed. "Then where do you guys go? Are you just going to run from these things forever?"

Ghi blinked "Well, no—"

"Or defend yourselves? How the hell are you going to do that?" I demanded. "Ice tricks? That's not going to cut it. Setting them on fire didn't even do the job, apparently."

Khan blew air out of his nose, clearly offended.

"I bet I could float like David Copperfield if I tried!" Jesse shouted through the closed door.

"Go to sleep!" we screamed back.

"See?" I snorted, sinking back into the couch, folding my arms. "Floating. That'll be real helpful, too, I'm sure."

I looked around the bus. There was a general contest between Corin and Ghi over who could stare at his own feet the longest. Jackson's focus hardened on the road, which was empty and practically straight.

"None of you have a clue, do you?"

Corin sat forward. He looked at me, very closely, and his eyes drew up into shrewd, slightly worried lines.

"How much did Jesse tell you?" he asked. "About where the Vessel came from?"

"Everything."

"And what did he say about how this would all end?"

I had to think about that for a moment. Certain things stuck out more than others. I felt that there was a particular word or name which should fit here, but all I could think of were the more vivid details. Zabur. The throat-cutting. The sisters. The last divination.

"Those cities are going to rise out of the sand," I said, remembering that much. "The moon's going to roll backwards, all of that."

"Christ, Jesse." Corin rolled his eyes toward the ceiling, looking very disappointed.

"It all depends on Dahrkren," Ghi explained. "When he's gone, they're all gone. All we have to do is last long enough to find him."

That made sense. And the fact that it made sense should have been a clear warning that I had invested way too much thought into these things—things I was planning to forget as soon as possible. I did not pause long enough to consider this, however.

"Yeah? Well, where?" I asked. "And when?"

Ghi shrugged. "That's what we don't know."

"What we *do* know," Corin cut me off before I could further expound upon their complete unpreparedness, "is how to kill him."

"Hold it right there!" Jackson called from the front. "I do *not* want to be here for this."

"For what?" I snapped.

"Becoming," Corin sighed.

"What?"

"Jesse didn't say anything to you about Becoming?"

"Not in here, man!" Jackson warned, shaking his head. "I can't abide a crying woman."

I ignored him, thinking back to the hospital room, wading through all the crazed hours since. And once again, the final divination replayed in my mind, each word direct and meaningful, until I recalled the right part.

. . . and by the sacrifice of Becoming they will defeat the crueler force, and banish death's pale eye from the heavens . . .

"Becoming," I thought out loud. I had not given the phrase a speck of consideration earlier, and so I worked for a moment to decipher its meaning. And then I smiled.

I did more than smile. I sat forward and hugged my knees, holding back a good minute's worth of baffled giggling. "Wait a minute," I said, emitting the tiniest snortle. This was too good. "Becoming? Does that mean you're all going to physically turn into women? Into those sisters?"

Corin looked at Ghi. Ghi looked at Corin. Jackson looked at the road. Khan looked at nothing.

"No, Jordan," Corin said. And then he knocked the smile right off my face. "It means that we all die."

CHAPTER 14

There's only one easy way to say this, and it's not actually all that easy.

The Vessel were never supposed to exist. Just by asking the divine forces to create them, the sisters had essentially broken the same rules Dahrkren had. They had been aware of that. They had also been aware that their future creations would be permitted to exist solely because they had a purpose to serve. And once they served that purpose, all bets were off. They'd go back to where they came from. The end.

The coffee machine filled the toxic, tense air with rich aroma and ghastly gurgling sounds, but no one had moved to fill a cup. No one had answered my confounded, grasping questions, either. *Can't you just refuse? You could just ignore that part, right?* and all of that desperate nonsense.

No one had humored me with alternatives. There were no alternatives, and they knew it.

I looked to the microwave. Its primary purpose, other than storing bagels, was to tell me the time. It was fifteen after eleven. Without seeking consensus, I picked up the remote, turned on the TV, and didn't stop flipping channels until I found the evening news.

Ghi was relieved—we were all relieved—not to see his face on the screen anywhere. If he had indeed been labeled a terrorist who'd entered the country under the guise of a rare and tempting psychological disorder, at least it hadn't been leaked to the public yet. One worry checked off the list.

But the breaking story of the evening was, of course, a fire on the set of Oprah. That much was unavoidable. Coverage on all networks were flooded with comments by the studio's press people, interviews with the sobbing woman who'd driven to Chicago at knife-point, and warnings to the public about escaped convict Su Kim Khan, who, among other things, was now suspected of attempting to murder Jesse Cannon in a crime of apparent fan passion.

Honestly. The things these people come up with on their own.

Khan coughed, an action that seemed to have less to do with the allegations and more to do with something actually irritating his lungs. I wearily shoved the remote under Ghi's nose. He took it, and readily surfed through channels until finding something that was neither a commercial nor news-related. A cooking show. Mushroom quiche.

Then the dividing door swung open.

"I had a dream!" Jesse proclaimed, throwing himself into the room. Instantly, every ear on the bus was trained on him, and we all waited with the unreasonable hope that he might actually have useful, applicable information to tell us. Such was the level of our desperation.

"There was a huge tornado," Jesse said, stalking closer, eyes wide. "And you were there," he continued in his best Judy Garland, gliding past Khan. "And *you* were there, and you ..."

"Don't you take anything seriously?" Corin asked severely.

Jesse shrugged, unrepentant. "Couldn't sleep," he said, taking stock of his surroundings. The panting coffee machine, the mushroom quiche, the general acrid silence. He seemed to gather that something was amiss.

"And," he punctured the air carefully, "I could really go for a drink. Anyone else? Vodka? Jordan, be a dear and—"

"Go to hell," I said darkly.

"Coffee, Jesse," Jackson interceded. "I'll take coffee."

Jesse blinked. He gave me a cautious look before pressing the button on the coffee machine, at last putting it out of its misery. Somehow, he must have guessed the meaning of my sour glare and all the tense stillness. Maybe he'd heard the entire conversation about Becoming. Or maybe he was just distracted because Jackson (whom he still undoubtedly considered delicious, despite their differences) had addressed him.

He filled a cup and, without spilling a drop, settled smoothly into the plush passenger seat, handing the boiling drink over to our tireless driver. They began a pleasant conversation. And, much to my indignance, everything settled again. Corin reclined the armchair and stared thoughtfully at the ceiling. Khan and Ghi both appeared to be very interested in how the quiche was turning out.

Without a word, I stood up and withdrew to the back of the bus. I closed and locked the dividing door behind me, passed the bathroom and the sleeping berths, and went directly to Jesse's room, where I flopped face down into the bed.

The coverlet was still faintly warm from Jesse's attempt at dreaming, and the memory foam mattress sank under my shape, luring me into that wonderful limbo between heaviness and weightlessness. *I'll leave as soon as possible, in the morning*, I thought with firm resolve. I wouldn't stick around a minute longer than I had to. I'd say goodbye, and I'd go home.

I was asleep before I could decide where home was.

When a person goes without sleep for days (and how many had it been now? Two? Three?), the sleep that eventually comes is of a certain breed. Heavy, dreamless, yet miraculously restless. And inexplicably short-lived.

I snapped awake in the dark, in a puddle of drool, for absolutely no apparent reason.

The bus hummed and swayed. Highway speed. Still moving. Still dark out. Many thoughts occurred at once. Recent events organized themselves in my memory, simultaneous with the stunning realization that they had not been a dream. And one thought rose above all of this, more urgent and more powerful than all the others: I really, *really* needed to brush my teeth.

I rolled forward and blinked through a murky haze until the digital clock came into focus, which took several seconds. Priority number two: clean the contact lenses.

It was 5:55 a.m.

The dividing door was still closed, and I hovered close to it, listening carefully. Everything sounded quiet up front. I could just make out Jesse's voice, and Jackson's, though what they were saying was unclear. Keeping one another awake, presumably.

I didn't want to go back out there, not yet. Teeth first. Contacts. Maybe more sleep. I crept backwards and opened a narrower door, entering the closet-sized lavatory and flipping on the lights at the same time.

My face hit something very big and very fluorescent pink.

I leaped backwards into the doorway and gazed upward at Khan, who was crouching over the sink so as to position his face, one hand, and a lit cigarette close to an open window. He turned around to face me, which required a surprising amount of maneuvering from him, considering the small space.

It occurred to me that he had, in some criminal way, unlocked the dividing door to get back here. I was offended. Outraged. I wanted to tell him to get out, in the most ferocious voice possible.

"Sorry," I stammered instead, as the blood drained from my face.

I retreated to close the bathroom door, but Khan shook his head and shot out a hand, firmly holding it open. He flicked the last of the cigarette out the window and advanced toward me—or toward the door, I realized with knee-shaking relief. I moved aside.

Khan contorted himself through the slim passage one shoulder at a time, shuffled past me, and turned around again, gesturing into the bathroom. "Go ahead," he said, in a mechanical, blood-chilling, do-as-you're-told, polite sort of way. I readily complied. Had the shower been full of venomous snakes, he could have probably convinced me to dive right in.

I immediately noticed that there was no sky outside the open window—just steep walls of stone racing by without end, cut away from mountains to form the highway. One leftward glance to the mirror showed Khan's shoulder disappearing beyond the door, on his way back to the front of the bus.

"Hey!" I said, and the shoulder froze. "Where are we?"

Khan did not answer, at least not with the name of a place. He laughed, opened the dividing door, and disappeared.

Jerk.

I glared into the mirror, flattened my bangs, coerced my hair into a ponytail, and snatched up my toothbrush. I had been brushing for about five seconds when I realized that the closest bottle of contact solution was somewhere in my overnight bag. Still brushing furiously, I ventured out of the bathroom and over to the sleeping berths, where I plunged a hand into my overnight bag.

I was still digging through its contents when a bright light over my right shoulder caught my attention. A pair of headlights, muted by the thick shades in the back of Jesse's room—the very rear of the bus—grew in size, driving closer at what seemed to be excessive speed. The bus's wheels clacked sharply beneath me as we drove over something metallic, and the sound of the road itself changed, as if we had entered a tunnel.

The headlights swung out into the passing lane and became four. There were two cars, one in front of the other, moving like one unit.

They accelerated.

I accelerated, too. I dove into the bathroom to spit.

Wiping frantically at the corners of my mouth, I looked up to the small window and froze, unable to make sense of what I saw out there. Gone were the carved mountainsides by the road. There was only blackness, endless space. And the two vehicles—two rather battered-looking U-Hauls, to be exact—sped past, interrupting the nothingness.

I bolted out of the bathroom and tumbled through the dividing door.

"Guys!" I barked in one harsh, minty breath, racing to the front of the bus, startling both Ghi and Corin awake as I passed. "What just happened?"

"Relax," Jackson smirked, nodding at the road ahead, which stretched forward into darkness. "We're just crossing a bridge. A really big bridge."

"The New River Gorge Bridge," Jesse corrected, reciting from one of the many *Wild and Wonderful West Virginia* brochures he'd evidently picked up at the last truck stop—along with what appeared to be a gallon of apple butter and a coonskin hat, which was perched at an angle on his head. "The longest and highest vehicular bridge in the nation at nearly nine hundred feet above—"

"Well what are *they* doing?" I pointed at the U-Hauls speeding past.

Corin and Ghi blinked groggily out the windows to see what all the commotion was about. Jackson shook his head as the first truck made headway past the bus.

"Probably just some assholes in a big hurry," he said.

The assholes cut sharply out in front of us and hit the brakes hard.

Jackson cursed and braked, stiffening his arms to steady the wheel. I grabbed the back of his seat as the bus shimmied, seeing that the rear truck had sidled up to our driver's side door to keep pace, blocking entry into the passing lane.

These weren't just any assholes. They were assholes with a premeditated formation.

I looked ahead. There was still plenty of bridge to go.

"Shit," Jackson growled. He ground the clutch and switched gears.

"What are you doing?" Corin rushed forward.

"Reminding them that we're bigger," Jackson replied, then floored the gas. Before we could so much as decide what to hold onto, the nose of the bus rammed into the rear of the front-running truck.

"The paint job!" Jesse cried, raccoon tail bouncing.

The truck popped forward but then accelerated, nearly matching our pace, nullifying the impact. With the front of the bus pressed persistently to its rear bumper, it began to brake again. Jackson cursed and pushed the gas harder, but the bus only groaned, strained, and shook, unable to muster the leverage for momentum.

Less than two feet from the glass of our windshield, the back hatch of the truck rolled up.

And poised in the close wash of our high beams was a whole line of people. Men and women. All with guns.

Large guns.

Pointed at us.

"Back back back back!" Jesse screamed, bailing between the seats and knocking me to the floor with him. Jackson slammed the brakes and struggled to downshift. Khan lunged forward, to do god knows what, but Corin and Ghi grabbed him from either side and wrestled him down, just before the first deafening shots fired.

The windshield shattered. Jackson threw an arm over his face and battled to steady the steering wheel with one hand. He looked sideways, shouted, and ducked. More people were hanging out of the truck in the passing lane, armed, aiming. The driver's side window burst and fell over Jackson in one sparkling sheet.

Shots took out a front tire. The bus lurched and swung wide, hit the concrete railing and scraped along it for a good forty yards before it was steady again. We rolled along the floor, shouting, tangled in one another.

And then there was a roar from Jackson, as bullets tore into the meat of his shoulder, and everything that came next seemed to occur simultaneously: another shot punching into his chest, the rupture of two back wheels, the sideways leap of the bus, the sudden ramming from the truck beside us, and the firing of a bazooka—yes, a bazooka—into the side of the road directly ahead of us.

The boom filled our ears and left a shocking silence in its wake. Jackson dropped, cutting the wheel wide as he went. The concrete guardrail crumbled and gave way. The bus fishtailed, leaned dangerously, and then pitched headlong off the bridge, out into world famous heights.

In an agonizing, slow, screeching way, it came to a stop with its rear third still gripping road. The back-most tires hooked over what was left of the railing, and, while we held ourselves in rigid stillness, feeling that so much as a drop of sweat would end us, the bus halted, moaned, then swung downwards, jerking to a vertical stop.

We rolled like a burst sack of potatoes. Brochures, glass, and cups of coffee all rushed down into the blackness. I grabbed and gripped and clawed blindly until I found myself clinging to the front of the passenger seat, legs sprawled and kicking in the air where the windshield used to be, kicking above 870 feet of nothing. From there, even in the dizzying darkness, I could look down and see just what that height looked like.

It was a fucking long way down.

I looked over. Jackson was dangling in his seatbelt, staring straight down at the river, limp and undistressed. Someone else was hunkered over the back of the passenger seat, clamping down on my slipping forearm without even realizing it. The dual textures of ace bandage and expensive wool told me that it was Corin. Khan was bracing inside the couch alcove. I could not see Ghi or Jesse, but I could hear them, shouting in frantic medlies of their native tongues, shouting until another sonic boom from a bazooka drowned them out.

And then everything and everyone dropped.

CHAPTER 15

There are rules to falling.

We learn the rules in junior high physics. We learn that all things, a mouse and an elephant both, will fall at the same acceleration—9.8 meters per second squared—until reaching their separate terminal velocities.

So you might be falling hundreds of feet, maybe down into one of the deepest gorges in the United States for instance, and even though the wind chill of the air skinning by you feels like fire, even if your gut is doing double axels around your heart, all the things you start out with—a cushion, a friend, a coonskin hat—they're all right there with you the whole way down, right where they started. Relatively speaking.

The pre-dawn blackness made spatial sense impossible. The little white ripples on the water below provided no clue of distance, of when impact would come. There were just the G-force spasms in my stomach and the shrill sound of my own long scream, replaced by the howl of air in my ears once I'd run out of breath.

The other screaming trailed off too, but I could see no one. Suffocating, I plummeted, frozen in total free-fall somewhere between the front seats, limbs sprawled and reaching. This was it. This was it. This was really, really it. I braced for impact. Waited, waited.

Waited.

Terminal velocity, we're told, is achieved when the downward force of gravity acting on a falling object meets the upward force of drag, or air resistance, at which point the object begins to fall at a steady speed.

What we never stop to think about, though, is all the air creating that drag. We spend our whole lives walking right through air like it's nothing, sucking it in, belching it out, lancing through it with our cars. Air takes a beating, but it's there. It's made up of solid little particles just like everything else, just like you and me.

And when it wants to—when it's willed to, more correctly—air can and will push you back.

Impact came. And it was painful, a sudden smack upon every limb. An awful upward pressure, like the sting of a belly flop at the pool, but all over. It increased steadily and quickly, pushing, scooping under me, until I was no longer falling. Until the dizzying motions in my stomach and the drunken spin of the watery shimmer below were only in my head.

There was a stillness. For the first time in my life, my mind was completely, utterly empty. I was grappling again at the upholstery, curling around it with my entire body, sucking in breath after breath before any sense returned to me. A set of arms—one of them half encased in duct tape—hauled me onto the ledge formed by the now horizontal seat. It provided only a few square feet of refuge, upon which Corin and I were both shaking so violently that we could hardly keep from pushing one another off.

I didn't understand. I looked all around, seeing in clear pictures again, not blurred motion. We were not falling. The water still ran beneath us, the bus was still nose-diving, but we were not falling. I looked up, saw what Corin was looking at. Saw what we were all looking at.

"Oh my God! Jesse!"

But what I saw was impossible. I couldn't make sense of it, of this sudden pause, of anything at all, because here was the most bizarre scene yet. Yards above us, centered perfectly in the open space between the table and the bar area, arms at his sides, feet dangling, perfect hair rising in every direction, was Jesse Cannon. He was holding onto nothing, he was standing on nothing. He had all the appearance of a person underwater, and for a mind-squeezing second I thought we were all underwater, that we were sinking into the river. Then the incredible truth registered, sudden and hard:

Jesse wasn't floating in the water.

Jesse was floating in the air.

And if you happened to be down on the New River that dark and early November morning, just under the famed bridge, you would have seen that the Jesse Cannon tour bus was floating in the air, too. Nose down, fifteen feet above the rolling river, as sedentary as a part of the landscape, its bulk supported by the trillions of rebellious air particles under the command of their astonished, air-headed leader.

I wobbled at the edge of the seat, straining to look up without falling. "Jesse?!"

"Don't talk to me right now," he snapped, as if I'd interrupted an important phone call or a delicate self-waxing procedure—not the levitation of a five ton bus using only hitherto untested supernatural abilities.

I repositioned my grip on Corin and counted heads. Jackson was still fastened to the driver's seat. Behind it, Ghi and Khan were propped awkwardly in the small space afforded by the couch alcove, clinging to one another rather immasculinly in order to avoid falling out, both of them carefully watching Jesse. Below us, the black water ran fast but shallow. We were hovering very close to the bank.

Without warning, the bus shifted slightly, just enough to draw a rainbow of exclamations—in Arabic, Korean, and the King's English.

"Please remain calm," Jesse said loudly, about as calm as a stewardess with a burst aneurism. The look of concentration on his face was pricelessly unattractive. "I'm going to put us down."

We braced as the bus swayed and halted, rocking back a few degrees toward its normal orientation. Whatever Jesse was doing, it was working. At his directing, the bus lowered a foot or so more towards the river, tilting until it was nearly right-side-up again. Not bad at all. A thrilled expression crossed Jesse's face, an overjoyed, cocky look.

"Yes! Look at this! Can you believe this!?" he shouted triumphantly. "David Copperfield can suck my—"

WHAM!!

All the invisible arms of air at our defense were not prepared for a second poorly-aimed bazooka shot. Nor was Jesse's frail concentration, which snapped like a thread when the water beneath us exploded into a column of white spray. Everything slammed sideways with jarring, breakneck suddenness as the bus dropped the remaining few feet into the riverbed.

The emergency lights kicked on. Gravity had us all scrambling to stand on the walls instead of the floors as water began rushing in through broken windows. It took only a moment to assess that the bus had landed on its side, in the rocky shallows of the bank, and that there was no danger of sinking. Not quite solid ground, but at least the normal rules of physics seemed to have reinstated themselves.

Except for one rule, that is. Most of the incoming water, instead of taking the course gravity naturally suggested, rushed to Corin instead. It surged upwards toward his knees like an eager pack of dogs, and he shrugged at us helplessly. Either I had seen enough at this point, or I was in actual shock, but this was the first of the Vessel phenomena which failed to amaze me.

Corin quelled the geyser with a glance, to his own brief amazement, and then moved past me, along with most everyone else. I turned to follow and understood the urgency immediately. It wasn't the notion that another blast might strike us at any moment. It was Jackson.

He was still alive. He made that clear with a groan as he undid his seatbelt—an ill-planned action, considering he was still dangling several feet off the ground, and no one was close enough to stop him. He dropped through the length of the cab, landing beyond the dashboard with an ominous, pitiful thud.

Then he popped up onto his feet.

"Is everyone okay?" he bounded over the passenger seat, looking to each of us. "Everyone? Any compound fractures? Does anyone need CPR?"

"Jackson," Corin attempted to halt him, loud but calm.

"Seriously? No one?" Jackson paused, frowning, apparently disappointed that part of his emergency training was going unused. He quickly moved on to other protocol, instructing us to exit the bus in an orderly manner, which we did not.

We did nothing but stare, because Jackson was covered in blood.

His own blood. It streamed down from gashes in his square forehead, criss-crossed down his bare arms. It darkened his cotton shirt, drenching it in outward circles from the holes gouged by bullets. Lots of bullets.

"Alright, let's all stay calm and exit through the windshield."

"Jackson," Corin reached an unsteady, beseeching hand. "Sit down."

"No time, England!" Jackson dismissed him crossly and continued to make sweeping, shepherding motions towards the front of the bus. "Get going, people. Stay low. Move it."

Ghi stepped forward carefully. "Jackson, please," he said, as diplomatically as possible. "You've been shot. Multiple times. And cut up with glass. Look at yourself."

"What, you think I'm blind?" Jackson hardly glanced down. He jerked a thumb towards Khan. "And this guy stabbed me in the face last week. I'm fine. Trust me."

Unremarkably, no one did. As he gestured once more towards what he had deemed the safest exit, we continued to stare at him in horror.

"Okay, look," Jackson dropped the fireman routine for a second and crossed his thick arms impatiently, rubbing a finger across a streak of drying blood as an afterthought. "Knife? Steel. Bullets? Metal. Glass? Sand."

Where he'd smudged the blood away, only a fading streak remained, barely a scratch. "And what am I?"

Earth.

All of those things. Technically speaking.

Jackson lifted his T-shirt.

"Oh . . . ," Corin and I both said, as comprehension sank in. Jesse made a similar noise, but for entirely different reasons.

Jackson's body had absorbed it all, closing itself back up where the bullets or glass had pierced him. No wounds or deep gashes remained. Just a lot of drying blood and some distinct reddened areas, the beginnings of bruises. It looked as if he'd just finished a round of paintball.

"Jackson, that's incredible," Ghi blurted. "If bullets can't hurt you, or knives or—"

"Can't *hurt* me?" Jackson frowned his wide frown. "Son, that hurt like hell. You've been shot before, you ought to know."

Ghi let every last wrong thing about that statement go with a benevolent sigh.

"Now," Jackson pulled his shirt back down and straightened up with authority. "I am the safety expert here, and I want everyone off this thing."

We filed through the warped windshield frame and continued around the overturned bus, staying as close to the roof as possible. Slabs of rock afforded everyone a semi-dry foothold, except for Corin, who was experiencing another watery revival at his feet. I sidled away from him to avoid any splashing, and turned to Ghi, who was leaning around the bus's far end, watching the mountainside where it connected to the bridge.

"Are they gone?" I asked, picturing what would come next. A chase through the pitch-black woods, jarring camera angles and guttural screams. A scene from every B horror movie, and then cut to black.

Ghi shook his head. "They're driving down."

Everyone's guts sank collectively. I testify that it made a sound.

"How long before they're here?" Corin asked.

"Another minute, maybe." Ghi swung back around and leaned against the roof. Not an inch of him fidgeted. He looked over my head at Corin. "How deep is this river?"

Corin seemed to understand where this was going. The water at his feet settled and he paused for a few seconds, his face reaching the kind of focus one assumes for reading very precise instruments, even though he wasn't looking at anything in particular. He was reading something beyond himself.

"Little over a meter," he reported. "Crossing's a bad idea, though. Too rough, and too cold. I could try freezing it? Or moving it out of our way, maybe..."

"I could just fly us across," Jesse offered, having appointed himself an expert levitator already.

"Why are we talking about running?" Jackson demanded. "We're supposed to fight, aren't we? Come on. We can handle them."

"Easy for you to say," Corin balked. "We're not all bullet-proof, you know."

"Fine. Part the water, Moses. We're all waiting."

Ghi ignored them, leaning around the rear of the bus again. There wasn't time for arguments, for decisions, for over-thinking, for much of anything but direct action. Three more sets of headlights were coming down the mountain, not far behind the initial two.

He turned back to us, significantly more fidgety.

"Khan."

Like a statue brought to life, Khan swiveled in the direction his name had been spoken. Ghi scrambled over to him, ideas running mad behind his eyes. He slapped the roof of the bus.

"How fast can you burn this thing to the ground?"

Khan positively beamed.

"Excuse me?!" Jesse cut between them. "My alligator Berlutis are in there!"

Ghi did not have the fashion caliber to know what Berlutis were. He looked around imploringly, overwhelmingly conscious of the fact that all eyes were on him, but not wavering. "We're not going to get far if we run. But if we torch the bus and hide, they might think we're dead, and they'll leave."

"And if they don't?" I asked.

"*Then* we run."

"Or fight," Jackson added.

No more time. Everyone moved.

Jesse's lip quivered. I grabbed his hand and started stepping over stones behind Ghi and Corin, staying low, coaxing him along. Jackson followed. Khan stayed behind, slinking around the underbelly of the bus to start the fireworks.

"I never even got to *wear* them...," Jesse whispered.

Not far up the bank, a cluster of steep rock formations jutted out of the shallows, forming what looked like the closest and most sensible place to hide. We were almost halfway there, maybe thirty yards from the bus, when we began to feel the rising heat at our backs. Khan was already outdoing himself. Jesse stiffened, and I gripped his hand a little tighter.

"Just don't look back," I suggested.

That was when Corin stopped suddenly and looked to Jackson, wide-eyed.

"You did cut the engine off?" he asked. His face was so white it somehow rejected the orange glow from behind us.

"Of course I did." Jackson smirked. "Like it matters anyway. Buses only explode in movies."

And he may have been right. But do you know what else explodes in movies?

Bazookas.

The next instant was nothing but movement. And that sound. We were running before we'd consciously processed it—that whistling whine the air made, like the scream before fireworks, the kind of noise that is always followed by something much louder. We darted over slippery stones and smashed into one another in the knee-deep currents of frigid water, racing to be as far away as possible when the fuel tank of the Jesse Cannon tour bus exploded. Which it did, about two seconds later.

Just before the thunderous sound of it filled the gorge, a sonic wave of heat lifted us upwards and outwards, and this time it was not Jesse's doing. I remember the next couple of seconds as clearly as if they'd happened this morning. I remember the incredible sound and the hot force hitting me like a wall. I remember being launched forward by the blast as if I were no more than a wet leaf, and then slamming into Ghi midair.

And I remember that it was simply a natural reflex, what he did then—he was just trying to brace us both before we hit the ground. I know that now, and I knew it then, but this is what happened anyway:

Ghi swung out with both hands and clamped them around my upper left arm. There was a pop, a brief sizzle, and an ugly scream. I didn't realize, not until after my body struck a rock and stopped rolling, that the last sound had been me.

The first two sounds had been a couple hundred volts of electricity going through one side of my arm and out the other.

I was face-down in water. Ice water. I sat up, coughed up a burning lungful of river, and rolled to a crouch behind a large shelter of rock. A strange pressure was mounting around the biceps of my left arm, an oncoming something that I wasn't truly feeling yet. I dared a look down, and saw the two blackened holes in the sleeve of my sweater.

A fine veil of smoke snaked from them both.

The pressure began to grow, becoming heat or something like it, dull but angry and picking up momentum with every rapid heartbeat. I swallowed hard and plunged my arm into the river. Big mistake.

The cold water burned like bleach on my naked nerves, gouging into the void that had been blasted out by the electric current. Chunks, I realized. Chunks were missing. Missing from the meat of my arm. Dribbling around loose somewhere inside my sleeve.

Any of the noises I should've made at the moment were held in by the tide of vomit that jumped up my throat. I fought it down, yanked my arm out of the water, and pressed myself against the boulder, biting my lips together until I tasted blood.

Something moved out of the corner of my eye. Ghi. He was standing yards away, half golden in the glow of the flaming wreckage, staring with dumb astonishment. At me, at himself, at everything. It was hard to tell, because his eyes were completely white.

"What did I do . . . ?" He staggered toward me, and I ducked, motioning fearfully at him to back off, as if he were some kind of monster. And he was. Crackling fingers of white light were darting across the water at his feet, raking over his shoulders and through his hair. He froze, groaning when he noticed the light sizzling over his own hands.

But even that horrific moment—stark as it was with the explosion, my arm blown all to hell, and Ghi lighting up like something straight out of *Poltergeist*—it provided no pause at all. Headlights washed over the trees. I heard gravel crunching under tires, rolling to a halt. Somewhere, Corin hissed at Ghi to get down, and he did. He also stopped glowing, for what it was worth.

Car doors slamming. The back hatches of the U-Hauls rolling up. But no voices. No other noises. Just the sounds of rushing water, and of fire. The ragged roar of the bus and all the fuel burning away, filling the base of the gorge with a throat-stinging haze of thick black smoke and brightly lit ash.

Our ears strained; our feet and tendons were at the ready. I didn't dare move, didn't dare look. And the only thing I could see without moving, the only thing that wasn't part of the landscape, was Ghi, his back pressed to a rock about fifteen yards to my left. He watched me with round, vocal eyes, begging me not to cough, or gasp, or scream.

More tires. Thumps. Raking, metallic sounds. The blast of gunfire and the ricochet of bullets. And then Jackson, shouting a wordless, cowboy battle cry.

Ghi closed his eyes and breathed deeply.

"Fuck," he said. He tilted sideways to take a look, and I did, too.

Somewhere between the bus's descent from the bridge and its explosive death, the sky had tinted lighter in one small but perceptible increment. Dawn was on its way. And out there in the first charcoal hints of daylight, visible only between swirling blankets of smoke, at least thirty Hollows were swarming out of the two parked U-Hauls.

They were frightening to see in their number, in their overall silence, in their swift movements and slightly disheveled but normal clothes. But they weren't the strangest thing I saw out there. No, that title goes to the fleet of ambulances that had followed them down the mountainside.

It took me a moment to physically acknowledge the things. Five run-of-the-mill ambulances, driving along the riverbank as if they were just out testing the terrain. Bullets and Hollows bounced ineffectively off of them as they plowed along, and it dawned on me that I was about to see a bunch of innocent, terrorized paramedics get ripped apart. It never occurred to me that these ambulances had arrived far earlier than any emergency responders should have been able to. However, it *did* occur to me that gravel wasn't the only thing I heard crunching. The ambulances were running over the Hollows at any given opportunity. And as far as I knew, running over people—even murderous, death-infested people—was not something ambulances normally did.

I remembered Jackson's war cry and spotted him in less than a second. He was charging toward the bank—much to my extreme horror—with Jesse, who was trying to position all of his height behind Jackson's bulk in case of gunfire. Whatever heroic deed they intended to do, they didn't do it. They both stopped in their tracks when the ambulance doors started springing open. You would have, too, believe me.

What I saw then, what I *thought* I saw, were identical people wearing identical black body armor. And identical black masks. It was immediately evident that these folks were not your friendly neighborhood paramedics. There were perhaps eight of them to each ambulance. And each and every one of them was armed with one of the following:

A flame-thrower.

Or a pair of machetes.

Things got very ugly, very fast. Violent, surreal, and impossible to recount in any sensible order. The Hollows descended upon the armed newcomers with savage disorder. Gunshots and lightning-fast metallic flashes followed, along with the whir of blades and blasts of flame. But there were no words, no shouts. Only inhuman squeals, sharp gasps, and the incessant spray of something dark and thick, something like silty mud.

They were getting closer. I panicked, fought with myself about which way to run. Downriver, I spotted Khan's unmistakably huge silhouette, standing upright amidst molten bus parts, in the center of a massive column of flames. He staggered sideways, paused to spit something out—a tooth, I believe—then lurched for the bank. The pair of Hollows who rushed to confront him simultaneously ignited. They screamed madly but did not veer off-target.

Ghi was no longer anywhere to be seen. I moved just in time to see a blur of Corin, sprinting onto the bank and bringing a great deal of river along with him—in the form of a great, cresting wave.

Okay. More of a smallish cresting wave. Had the Hollows constructed a sand castle by the river, he may have knocked it down. It did make them back up for a second. I'll give him that.

Jackson paused to stare at him.

"You do something then!" Corin screamed, voice cracking.

Jackson opened his mouth, almost certainly to say something cocky, at about the exact moment Jesse was swinging him into immediate gunfire. Point-blank range. Judging by what Jackson then shouted about Jesse's mother, I'd guess a bullet or two got him near the groin.

Part of the hillside was on fire by then. Nearby rock faces began to split and topple to the ground—Jackson's contribution, no doubt—uprooting burning trees. Stars and fuzzy darkness bloomed at the perimeter of my vision while I watched and listened, getting good and high on blood loss, shock, and smoke inhalation, fully expecting another explosion at any moment. The bridge maybe. With any luck, I thought, the biggest part of it would fall directly on me. But I could no longer see it. I couldn't see what was happening on the bank. I couldn't stand. I sure as hell tried. But my best effort was more diagonal than vertical.

Shots sang and spat into the water at either side. Something—part of an arm or a leg—bounced off my rock and then disappeared into the rapid currents. A masked figure went sprinting by, never breaking stride when a tree came down at his heels.

Someone lifted me.

The thick smoke was suddenly backlit in irregular white flashes, revealing everything within it. The vehicles, the baffled Vessel, the eerily silent war raging on the bank—all lit up as if under a powerful but offbeat strobe light. And somewhere, someone was screaming in broken English for people to get out of the way.

Someone was half-dragging, half-carrying me to the bank.

"It'll be fine," I said serenely, clutching my arm to my chest. "There's Neosporin on the bus."

I saw Ghi knee-deep in the water, his whole body tremoring, his eyes nothing but discs of light. Blinding ropes of lightning arched wildly away from him like the arms of an octopus, lancing out across the bank and through the water, turning the smoke as white as steam.

I saw Hollows blacken and fry and fizz before my eyes, all around him. Wherever the scorching light grazed them, they dropped into twitching, howling heaps.

I saw Corin drive a second, more impressive wall of water forward. It crashed over the nearest grouping of Hollows, forcing them into Ghi's path of involuntary destruction. The result was a fantastic barbeque.

I saw the smug look Corin gave Jackson.

I saw the Hollows begin to back away or turn and run. I saw Jackson's sly, knowing grin as another ledge high above gave way under burning trees, creating an avalanche of fire and stone and smoke and ash. I saw all those cables of light whip back into Ghi's own body, saw him drop out of sight in the streaked darkness that followed.

And I heard all about what happened next, but I didn't see it. I was suddenly somewhere flat and dry, a place that reeked of blood and gas exhaust. A door rolled shut, and, lucky for me, it was too dark to see anything after that.

CHAPTER 16

Jesse paused on the rocky bank and stood very still. He wiggled his fingers and toes, read himself for any damage, and was relieved to find that everything of importance was as it should be—heart: beating, hair: still there, member: intact. He was fine.

But something was sensationally wrong.

He watched the tail lights of the retreating U-Haul fade into the deepest smoke at the base of the mountain and disappear. A light rain had started, but it was no match for the forest fire which hotly lit up this small corner of dawn. The occasional burning tree caved, sending up spectacular whirlwinds of gray and orange ash. It was only a matter of time before emergency crews showed up.

Or so Jackson was saying. He was marveling out loud at the county's slow reaction time as he meandered towards Jesse. Khan was close behind, sucking a busted lip. His last cigarettes were soaked and he was most unhappy.

Jesse frowned. He could not quite put his finger on what was so horribly wrong. There were the obvious things. These very odd strangers in black, for instance. But it was so hard to think. Because everywhere, *everywhere*, there was the smell. The humming. This crawling, gnawing sense of *enemy*.

Hollows.

Hollows who were burned beyond recognition. Hollows who'd lost limbs, who'd been twisted and mangled beneath tires. Jesse and Jackson watched with a quiet, numb curiosity as a woman writhed indignantly in shallow water, several yards from her own head.

I'll explain.

This woman was moving so frantically because decapitation doesn't feel all that great, especially when you don't die immediately as a result. There was also the water, the breeze, the stony shore—things that are bound to feel unpleasant against your skin. If you're a Hollow.

But pain and inconvenience aside, she was fundamentally fine. Fine because the water and the sun and all those pebbles she was rolling in hadn't been commanded to destroy her. And fine because her blood vessels and her spinal cord and all the things which normally hold a human together have nothing to do with what holds a Hollow together.

What holds a Hollow together, actually, was at that moment pouring out of the woman's neck and clouding through the water like dirty oil, swirling towards her wayward head, drawing it back to her. More of the stuff stained the riverbank around other Hollows, hundreds of splatters which had begun to wiggle with life, smears that physically slithered over the ground. It dripped from torn shreds of burnt flesh, evaporated into muddy steam. It was everywhere.

To you or me, that would all just be really gross.

But to the Vessel, it was maddening.

The Vessel could smell it. They could hear the silent crawling, hissing of it, the way dogs hear training whistles. The stench of it clouded their thoughts, filled them with a nagging hostility, and made their names disappear in brief, barbaric flashes. Flickers of identity vertigo. The stuff, whatever it was, pleaded to them for violence.

Their only distraction was the hunters, faceless under their carved blinders, down to their stoically unparted lips. Besides the occasional pronounced gasp for breath, they were weirdly silent. They spoke to one another only in the briefest, most direct commands. And with the exception of the occasional confirming glance, they took little notice of the Vessel. There was still work to be done.

Work to be done with very big knives.

A common saying among the hunters, a fun little motto of theirs, starts with the question: *How do you outrun death?*

Jesse watched a solitary hunter pause in the path of the last Hollow still intact. I say 'intact', but the thing's features were burnt beyond crispy, melted and warped like an action figure left on the dashboard, its burns covered in masses of what resembled black worms. Evidently, it had gotten too close to one of the flame throwers. Or Khan. Either way, it was still standing, still running, and fast. The hunter faced it, unmoving, a soiled machete in either hand.

How do you outrun death?

Any hunter will answer that question the exact same way:

You cut off its fucking legs.

The Hollow zeroed its eyes—or rather, the molten caverns where its eyes had been—in on the hunter, sprinting close enough to lunge. And with a patient, unflinching movement, the hunter pitched one machete into a low, powerful spin. The blade became a whistling, silver blur before clattering into a spray of pebbles, and in that instant, the Hollow's stride broke. It toppled forward to the ground, still yards from reaching the hunter, its left leg slanting off separately like a felled tree.

And here was what Jesse saw, what Corin and Jackson saw, what we've all seen since. This was what distinguished a Hollow as a vehicle of death, and not just some human being that refused to die. This was what animated them, thought for them, saw for them, spoke for them. It connected them, linked them to their source. It held their bodies intact, and even put them back together if, for instance, a Luna Latum hunter hacked off a leg.

It was the decided form of something never meant to be seen, and it had decided to look insurmountably, incomprehensibly revolting.

In the void left behind by the cleanly severed leg, more dark, wormy organisms amassed, swarming rapidly, thicker and thicker. The sight made good old-fashioned gushing blood seem desirable, yet it was merely a prelude. With sickening quickness, whole tendrils burst from the wound without explanation, improbable and much longer than any human leg should ever be. They twisted and flopped along the ground, undecided between being solid, gas, or liquid with each new angle, but always opaque and putrid-looking, coiling out of the wound like some nightmarish, alien limb while the attached Hollow thrashed furiously.

And what was it? Was it death? Decay? Hell? The Vessel marveled at this sprawling thing, and at the many identical scenes around them, cooling their divine vehemence with human shock. It didn't have a name to them, whatever it was. But it was why the five of them existed. That much they understood.

The hunter stepped deliberately around the writhing mutations, lifting the remaining machete over his shoulder, swinging it downward.

Jesse flinched away. And he noticed immediately that he was standing by himself again. The others were walking over to two hunters who, instead of dicing up Hollows, were standing around having some kind of debate. Ghi was on the ground between them, flat on his back, hands over his eyes, groaning.

The problem seemed to be that they were afraid to touch him.

Jackson stepped in, and Ghi wheezed his disoriented gratitude as he was hoisted to his feet, blinking with wildly unfocused eyes. The hunters assumed immediate silence, and Corin, with all appropriate caution, turned to acknowledge them.

He was close enough now to notice that their blinders appeared to cover their eyes completely—no holes. And yet the hunters still seemed to be looking right back at him. He cocked his head, took a sideways step to get a different angle, and got the eerie result he anticipated. They followed his movements in silence.

"Who are you?" he demanded, doing his best to sound bold instead of thoroughly creeped out.

No response. Jesse, who had wandered over to regroup, paused to watch this exchange. He waved a hand in front of the unblinking blinders, and the hunters did not flinch. They merely frowned. More sourly than they had been frowning before, if it were possible.

Jesse turned to Corin and shrugged.

A shorter, presumably female hunter joined them, flicking black matter off her blade before sheathing it over her shoulder. She dismissed the stoic pair with a few foreign words, and then her full attention landed heavily upon the Vessel. With a gloved hand, she lifted the face of her blinder, and looked at them. All of them.

"Well," said Stella Rosin, with frank disappointment. "You're certainly not what they're expecting."

Ghi, having wrangled both his eyes back into proper alignment, focused them immediately on her face. He jumped and backed into Jackson, who responded quite like a solid wall. Jackson remembered Stella, too—her compact stature, her mercury eyes, her small nose, as petite and pointed as the rest of her.

Corin hadn't forgotten either. The three of them were suddenly shoulder to shoulder, waiting for Stella to act, anticipating the worst. Khan towered menacingly behind them. He had no idea what all the sudden tension was about, but he sensed that something might need to be set on fire.

Other hunters emerged from the thick smoke then, abandoning their grisly duties as if answering some call to contention. But they froze just as suddenly, limbs taut with caution. The water closest to the bank was beginning to swell and circle. The pebbles underfoot vibrated ever so slightly. Khan bristled, the air above him wavy with heat.

"Who are you?" Corin asked again, this time with a deliberately threatening tone.

All of the hunters stood very, *very* still. All of them except for one.

"Oh, enough," Stella snapped. "We're on your side. Isn't that obvious?"

No, it wasn't. The earth didn't settle. The heat didn't extinguish.

"We got off on the wrong foot, I know," Stella proceeded, her tone bold and informative, not at all apologetic. "My mistake."

"Why did you try to kill me?" Ghi croaked. "Back in New York. That was you."

"Didn't you hear me?" Stella stared him down. Her steely eyes ran over his face, closer and more thorough than a new razor, before she repeated herself. "My mistake."

"How do you know about us?" Corin demanded. He nodded at the nearest Hollow carcass, one that had been utterly fried by Ghi. "And them?"

Stella's shoulders sank. So these punk excuses for gods didn't know anything. Except maybe how to start landslides and forest fires. Great.

At her gesture, the other hunters returned to their grim work, leaving her alone with the five of them, and with no sure idea where to begin. Explanations, by conditioning, were not something she was comfortable giving.

"We're the Luna Latum," she offered sullenly. "Ring any bells?"

Not a jingle.

"The good guys," Stella summarized. "We've been around for awhile."

There was a collective, enlightened "Oh" from the Vessel. Slightly reassuring.

"Well that's *great* news," Corin said, sounding genuinely relieved and relaxing his stance. "We've been wondering how to find you this entire time."

Stella nodded. "And *we've* been following you since New York," she said, flicking an errant black glob off her forearm before adding: "Sorry about the bridge mishap. Their trucks slipped past us somehow." This was said without inflection, as if she were apologizing for coughing in the library. Not for the flaming bus wreckage lighting up the morning behind her.

"What exactly are they doing?" Ghi asked, staring past her. He appeared no less nervous than before. Hunters were hauling coffin-sized steel boxes in and out of the ambulances, collecting the Hollows—the ones which were still moving, anyway—into them separately.

"Putting those things where they can't hurt anyone," Stella said, with a subtle sting in her voice. "That's our job. And we've been doing it just fine for a very long time."

"But what's with the masks?" Jackson indicated his own eyes. "How do you see?"

Stella shrugged. "Hollows are deceptive to the naked eye. It takes practice, but it's easier to look at them with other, more refined senses. Same goes with you five, we've discovered. Which reminds me..."

She flipped her blinder down over her eyes again and smiled.

"Yes. You all look much better this way."

"Hey!" Jackson objected, taking a rather self-conscious stance.

"Interesting," Stella noted. "I don't have to hold my breath to see you." Her smug smile then retreated into a familiar, strict line. This Q&A could go on for hours, judging by how little the Vessel seemed to know. And she couldn't afford much more time humoring them.

"Look, boys," she said. "I have a friend up on that bridge who is dying to answer every single one of your questions. But right now, I need some information from *you*. Starting with whatever you can tell me about the young lady you've been traveling with."

It only took half a second. And then the daze of shock dropped off Jesse faster than a pair of generic-brand pants.

So *that* was what felt so very wrong. My absence. He turned around. They all turned around, around and around, to see that I was nowhere in sight. After all the chaos and panic, they had only just noticed.

Thanks, guys.

Jesse raised his hands to his mouth and gasped. "Jordan."

"Yes, let's start with her name," Stella said patiently.

Ghi scanned the river frantically, turning on his heel and tripping. Corin wheeled on him. "I thought she was with you!"

"Does it *look* like she's with me?!"

Jesse pushed past them to go searching in the shallow water, and they fumbled to follow. None of them made it far. Stella raised her voice to them, although its tone remained maddeningly calm.

"She isn't out there."

That stopped all of them. Jesse's jaw dropped. Horrible things dawned on him. He swung around.

"Where is she?"

Stella ignored his question. "I need to know who she is. Why she was with you, and what she knows."

"Jordan Murphy. She's just my assistant," Jesse sputtered, marching over to place himself in front of Stella. "She's not part of this."

Stella shook her head. "I'm afraid she is now."

"No, really. She won't tell anyone about this. Never. She's very dependable. Just let me talk to her. Where is she?" he pleaded, glancing to the ambulances farther up the bank, and pausing when Stella showed no immediate reaction. "You're not going to hurt her, are you?"

"Hurt her?" Stella said, sounding slightly disgusted at the presumption. "Of course we wouldn't hurt her. But they might."

She turned and pointed to the mountainside, at the dawn-faded brake lights of a U-Haul. It was all the way up the access road and about ten seconds from reaching the highway, and there wasn't a thing anyone could do to stop it. A single ambulance was tailing it, but it was far behind.

You can imagine the hysterics which followed. Primarily from Jesse. "Oh my god," he repeated rapidly, over and over again. "Oh my god."

God my ass.

@

Everything was moving too slowly. More rain picked up, and less fire spread. The sun was all the way up now, low enough to shine beneath the clouds, lighting the dissolving smoke up like morning mist.

The hunters were dragging expired Hollows into a heap, marveling quietly at them, and packing the live ones away in those ominous cases. They scoured the bank and shallows for overlooked body parts, many of which were scooting around on their own, trying to reassemble themselves. A hunter passed close by, carrying a severed head at a careful arm's length. It was gurgling and spitting obscenely, sprouting drippy black noodles from its open throat.

Corin turned away from the sight abruptly, his jaw slack with spasms.

"I need to sit down," he said.

He sat. Jesse was already flopped on the damp earth beside him, wordless, miserable, face in his hands. They had been asked to wait while Stella "saw to the issue." And so wait is what they all did. Mostly because there was nothing else they *could* do.

After spending what looked like ten very heated minutes on a satellite phone, frustratingly just out of earshot, Stella returned to them. She looked just as collected, just as unfriendly, as before. No more, no less.

"Very capable people are in pursuit of your friend," she said, and then added, in order to block the inevitable questions: "As soon as something happens, I'll let you know about it."

The Vessel more or less accepted this passively, with the exception of Jackson, who did quite a bit of contentious huffing and head-shaking.

"We'll do everything we can, as fast as we can. You have my word," she continued, sounding callous as ever, despite her best effort at a reassuring tone. Also, her blinder was raised again. She had read in a magazine once that access to eye contact made people feel more at ease.

"What's most important is getting you five where you're supposed to be, before we have any more surprises. I don't trust the roads anymore. I've arranged for a helicopter to meet us at the closest suitable landing—"

"Now hold on just a minute, lady." Jackson could no longer contain his flaring ego. "You people seem to know a whole lot about what's going on, which is great and all, but we're perfectly capable of—"

"Of what?" Stella switched from serene to severe in an instant, an effect which cut him off completely. "Driving off a bridge? Catching everything on fire? Almost getting my people killed, after we've chased you all over the country, trying to help you? And I'm assuming you told Ms. Murphy all kinds of valuable details while you were at it."

Jesse winced guiltily, an expression not missed by Stella. Not for a second.

"Exactly," she drilled on. "Do you have any idea what Hollows do when they want inside someone's head? Any guesses?"

Stella looked from face to face, and in the increasing light of dawn, the Vessel could see that her eyes were the color of aluminum foil, or a mirror. Just reflections of everything else, not really a color of their own.

No guesses.

"That's what I thought," she said, backing away. "So I suggest you let us do our job. And right now, my job is getting you to the Elysium without any further incident. Come with me."

She turned and stomped toward the closest ambulance without checking to see that they'd followed. She knew that they would, and they did. Stella Rosin wasn't a high-ranking hunter for nothing.

"What's this Elysium?" Jackson asked, more as a form of protest than out of actual curiosity. But Stella showed no signs of having even heard the question. She was finished with questions. It was Corin who replied.

"The Elysium of Greek mythology," he recited blankly, "is the resting place of gods and heroes."

They stopped at the rear of the closest ambulance. Stella opened the hatch doors before stalking off to make another call.

"Get comfortable," she advised. "I'll only be a minute."

The Vessel peered inside before complying. If the thing had ever been an actual ambulance, then it had been thoroughly gutted of all equipment as far as they could tell. There was nothing inside, nothing except one of those steel boxes, the ones meant for containing Hollows. Up close, they could see that it had a handle on one end—and a slot for an identification tag.

It was a giant drawer. A person-sized drawer.

"That one's empty," said a passing hunter, noting their hesitation.

Ghi stood in a patient daze as the others climbed in, feeling a peculiar prickling on top of so many other unpleasant sensations. Pain, fatigue, apprehension, fear—all skirting the edges of this sudden and heightened paranoia. He hesitated before stepping into the ambulance, planting both feet on the ground. He wasn't sure what he was waiting for, looking for, but his eyes landed on Stella.

She was not on the phone. She was standing among some of the last wisps of smoke, her blinder still lifted up from her solemn mask of a face. She pulled the thing down immediately and turned away then, but not before Ghi had caught her staring at him again.

CHAPTER 17

I'll go ahead and say for the record that the ride was the hardest. Worse things had happened, yes, and worse things were yet to come. Things that will bend your mind and twist your stomach, I'm sure. But all of that other business—the falling off the bridge, the shock to the arm, the horrors that were headed my way—they all came with a generous supply of adrenaline and some feeling of finality. When you're dropping hundreds of feet or hearing bullets whistle by, you tend to think, *Oh, okay, this will be over soon.* There's just the moment and and no assumptions that the next moment will come. And that's manageable.

Sitting in absolute darkness, feeling dead hands and shoulders and knees brushing past, listening to the sounds of decaying bodies putting themselves back together (it sounds a lot like juicy chow mien getting twirled around a fork, to give you some idea), and not knowing when the ride will end—that isn't manageable. I don't care who you are.

The Hollows, for the most part, left me alone, which was fine and dandy by me. The only thing they seemed the least bit interested in was my arm, something I was paying an awful lot of attention to myself. I couldn't see a thing, but in the bumpy darkness I imagined that everything between my shoulder and my elbow must have swelled to the size of my head and beyond. Every nerve in the area of the shock throbbed and hummed with a raw sting. I wanted to squeeze the living daylights out of it. I wanted to rip my arm off. But I could not bring myself to touch it, so I did a lot of ghastly clenching and puffy breathing instead, while bubbles of heat fizzed up in my brain and made my eyes water. I was grateful for the dark. I probably looked pretty stupid.

Cold hands pinned me down near the beginning of the ride. Someone prodded at the burn, smelled it, and dragged a dry finger (or maybe a tongue?) across the hole in my sleeve. Fully expecting the thing to start chewing, I stayed rigidly still and did my best not to piss him off or seem too delicious. When he began rolling up my sleeve, however, and I felt my own loosened flesh moving with it, I lost my damn mind. I shredded his soap-like skin with my nails. I screamed until I forgot how to breathe.

The next thing I knew, I was sitting upright, wiping snot off my face. A strip of cloth was wound around the uppermost part of my left arm, pulled tight and knotted of—a tourniquet. My pulse throbbed against the pressure, but the swelling was dissolving, along with the dizziness. I wasn't in great shape by any means, but I was no longer bleeding to death. And for the hundred-billionth time that day, my life continued when it should not have.

Joy.

I didn't understand such treatment at the moment, but I was being preserved. These Hollows didn't want me to die on their watch. They didn't want to kill me, and they didn't want to breathe into me or eat my guts. Those kinds of pleasures had already been reserved for someone else. Someone they knew better than to disappoint.

And so I was mercifully ignored for the rest of the trip's duration, which was maybe an hour or more. During that time, I did all the things any Bruce Willis movie had ever told me to do: I counted stops the U-Haul made, and attempted (with pitiful success) to memorize the direction and order of the turns. I had no way of marking the time or determining how fast we were going, but I definitely noticed when we hit a gravel road near the last leg of the journey. A series of rolling hills followed, up and down, up and down, punctuated by sharp hairpin turns and staggering potholes.

I was pulled to my feet before we rolled to a soft stop. The door rolled open with an ugly screech, and I blinked my dark-stunted eyes, confused because there was no light outside. It felt like I had been in that thing for a day, sure, but my body knew better. My body still expected morning.

Only after I was dragged out of the truck did I understand. Twigs of distant daylight were coming through the wiggly edges between panels of corrugated steel. We were indoors, in some enormous, old, industrial space, like a factory or an aircraft hanger. Just one big open floor, soft with dust, and not a light on in sight.

Once its hold was empty, the U-Haul sped away across that vast space. A door, small and impossibly far away, opened for it, and in the faint light that rushed inside I could see more doors along the closest wall. The Hollows hustled me towards one of them—a flimsy metal door, rusty and banged up, chained shut. A key hung in plain sight and the Hollow to my right grabbed it, fumbling a little to fit it into the lock. Most of his left hand, and part of the left side of his face, I noticed, was covered in limp little strings of pink flesh, as thin and dangly as jellyfish legs.

Hollows don't always heal in perfect ways.

I was totally mesmerized by those little strings. They seemed to be the most hideous thing I'd seen so far, and the thought of what they would feel like made me queasy. I became terrified by the idea of being touched by them, so when the door was pushed open, I moved through it without any encouragement.

Nothing touched me. Nothing at all. I turned around and saw that all the Hollows were still outside the door. And then it closed with a painfully loud creak of rust. The chain clinked while Spaghetti Hands fiddled with the lock, the key pinged against the wall, the footsteps shuffled off, and I was alone.

I stared at that door for what felt like a very long time, simply because it was the only thing in the room I'd seen so far, and I was afraid to see just what else might be around me. When I could no longer bear to stand still, though, I took a solid look around.

This room wasn't as dark as the factory floor had been. It was large but not immense, about the size of a two-car garage. The floor was concrete and covered in grime, and from what I could tell, the walls were made mostly of cinderblock and sheet metal. The halogen lamps above were off, but they were so thick with gray dust that I doubted any light could escape from them at all. The only light I saw was muted daylight, filtering through teal green panels of rigid plastic, the kind you see patching up the tops of greenhouses.

Large shop tables were parked directly in the center of the room, heaped with dirty tarps and cardboard boxes. Along three walls, metal shelves were put up in disarray, holding more boxes, bulging trash bags, piles of clothing, toolboxes. Looked like your average suburban basement. The fourth wall stretched halfway across the room and then it recessed to form a large, shadowy nook in the far corner.

I stood there awhile, watching the breath condense in front of my face, clenching my fingers to keep the feeling in them. The fingers of my left hand were becoming slow and stubborn. Gradually, I worked up the will to get my feet going, and suddenly I was rushing to find a light switch, childishly, as if light would make the situation better.

Whatever this place was, the Hollows were evidently still paying their bills. I did find the switch, and, despite the dusty bulbs, the lights did come on.

They did *not* make the situation better.

One step at a time, I moved toward the center of the room, lightly touching one of the heavy tables as I came to it. I pushed a corner of stained canvas aside to uncover a cluster of disassociated items. Dingy glass jars full of clear liquid. Tools, sharp and caked with a dried ruddy brown. A pair of reading glasses. A human tooth. Things that made me swallow and shudder.

I pulled my hand back to myself, and my elbow bumped a box. A huge box, probably big enough to ship a mini-fridge in. Its contents were heavy. Tentatively, I took a step closer to the table and leaned forward, holding back one of the cardboard flaps to peer down inside.

Shoes. Just totally full of shoes.

Something behind me made a sound.

Something behind me was moving. Groaning.

I wasn't alone.

I stared straight ahead, right over that big box of shoes. My nostrils flared and the rest of me tightened and turned to stone.

It moved again. It moaned, thrashed, made a rustling sound. I turned my head first, taking days to swivel it in the right direction, not daring to breathe, my eyes straining so far to look left that they ached. From the edge of my vision, I caught up with the sound.

That shadowy nook in the corner had more light cast into it now, and I could see the network of pipes running across the back wall. Hanging from these pipes were four large bags of rubberized canvas. The kind of thing you'd see in a garden store. Or a morgue. Zippers ran down the front of them, and plastic funnels had been stitched along their bases. From these funnels, a coiling maze of rubber tubes tumbled down to the ground, all of them winding to one place: to a flat, plastic tank.

The tank was filled halfway with something scarlet and opaque.

Blood.

Hollow Cocktail.

I was already upset. Very upset. And this development, understandably, upset me more. But what took my upset-ness to an unthinkable level, what really did it, was the bag all the way to the right. The one farthest into the corner. It moaned again. It shifted and twitched.

I took a step toward it, which sounds like the last thing anyone would want to do, but remember: I still didn't have all the pieces of what had transpired on the river. Not the foggiest. So in my mind, it could have been Jesse. It could have been any of them.

I tried to say "Hello." Hi. Hey there. You know, just a reassuring greeting. What anyone hanging inside a bag, letting blood, would like to hear. No sound made it past my frozen trachea, though, so I crept over silently, forcing each and every step. With some serious self-prompting, I managed to reach up and grab the top of the zipper, flinching and jumping every time the bag moved. My breath moved in and out in dry gulps, like empty sobs.

I pulled the zipper down a few inches. I saw bare feet. Farther down, the bunched hems of denim jeans. As I continued, unzipping a little more quickly, waves of conflicting emotions slammed into me.

I was horrified. This was a person.

I was elated. This was a person.

I was not alone. That's what mattered most.

I uncovered knees, a waist, a navel. Arms lashed to sides with nylon cords. Open wounds, flaking and bled dry. I had to stop for a second there. But this person was still moving, still breathing. And so I had to keep going, keep pulling the zipper down. A bare chest, a panther tattoo, a stubbly neck. A face. A man's face, an older face.

I pulled away and smashed my palm against my mouth.

The man's eyes were black, as if oil had spilled through him after he'd been left upside down. His mouth was wide open, croaking, dribbling more oil. And lolling out of that mouth was something my mind couldn't begin to comprehend. Not a tongue, but a ghastly black tendril, waving and unravelling like a time lapse film of a growing plant.

That's what you look like after they breathe into you, for awhile. Until that's all that you are.

With one flailing, flapping move, I managed to zip the bag back up halfway before I lost control and fled, tripping over the tubes, throwing myself through the room. My body quaked, my knees knocked together, my breathing was that of a Lamaze instructor.

I didn't bother with the door. It would make too much noise, and it would never open, and even if it did I would only see more things outside that I never wanted to see. I didn't bother with anything, just hurtled to the other side of the room, crashed into some shelves, puked until I couldn't puke anymore, while the guy in that bag just moaned and moaned and moaned. And then I slid down to the floor and had myself the most hard-earned cry of my career.

While I sobbed nauseously and awaited death, the boys were feasting on breakfast burritos in the fresh morning air.

They were just sitting there on a dry patch of asphalt, passing around packets of hot sauce in the most inconspicuous place imaginable: the far end of a Wal-Mart parking lot, waiting for the helicopter Stella had arranged. In addition to the quick zip through one auspiciously placed Mexican drive-thru, the ambulance had made another stop along the way—it had paused at the top of the bridge to pick up one last passenger.

Abraham Sharma had been in absolute heaven ever since.

The Vessel, in the flesh. Walking, talking, chewing chorizo. It was a Luna Latum bio-chemist's wet dream, and you couldn't have pinched him awake with a pair of pliers.

The feeling was overwhelmingly mutual. To the Vessel—who had spent the last thirty-six hours just trying to figure out what continent they should be on—Abe was like some kind of Book of Answers on tape, read by an informed man with a pleasant, East Indian accent. To them, he knew *everything*.

"The Elysium is actually a small island."

"At some point during the Black Plague, the Luna Latum were down to twelve members."

"Hollows prefer polyester."

"Agent Rosin is Swedish."

They listened as if he were the Messiah.

"You're lucky," Abe interrupted one of his own tangents, an explanation of the modified antibiotics he was currently swabbing Corin's massacred arm with. "I examined these Hollows myself. They were very young, not even finished with the change, or else your arm would've fallen off by now."

Corin watched thoughtfully, stoic as a medical intern, as if he didn't feel the solution being swiped through the troughs of torn skin. The others listened intently, but were doing their best *not* to look. They were still eating, after all.

"Of course," Abe continued, "I can't be totally sure. I haven't had a chance to study whether the five of you react to a Hollow's touch differently than average people. But I'd still wager that if they'd been older, or more potent, then you wouldn't have lasted an hour without this stuff."

By *potent*, as they understood it, he was referring to the degree of separation from death's wellspring. How many breaths down the family tree an individual Hollow was from Dahrkren or Zabur. As far as Hollows go, that's the difference between making someone's arm rot off slowly just by biting it—or being able to rip an entire crowd of people limb-from-limb in seconds without lifting a finger.

"So it's an antibiotic, then?" Corin navigated back to the previous train of thought, and Abe nodded.

"An antibiotic, yes, with a divine kick. Chemically, it's almost identical to the type used to treat recluse spider bites. Same principal." He cracked open another tube of the stuff and continued working with steady, accomplished hands as he explained.

"That black matter you saw, that's the real trouble. Think of it physically, like an acid, or a topical poison. It'll start killing tissue wherever it touches you—skin, fat, muscle, whatever it can get to. Technically speaking, all that damage will cause your blood to clot up, which eventually leads to renal failure and ultimately, to death. And the older the Hollow is, the faster it feeds, the less time you have.

"Now if a Hollow *breathes* into you, as opposed to merely touching you, it technically does quite the same thing. The only difference is that the death simultaneously regenerates you as it's destroying you. And so instead of dying, your body becomes another Hollow, just another vessel of death—if you'll pardon the association. The complete process can take a very long time, long after you're one of them. It slowly breaks down everything organic and recreates the victim in its own image—or recreates itself in the image of the victim, to be more precise.

"So a Hollow may look human, because that's just the easiest and most discreet form to assume, but some of the older ones don't have a drop of blood or an ounce of bone left in them. That's why they drink blood so often, or eat living tissue, because that's what *it* exists to do—consume anything living. Once it's done with a whole body it'll still want more."

"But what *is* it? That black stuff?" Ghi wiggled his fingers like tentacles. There was a fleck of hot sauce on his chin. Mild.

Abe's brow lifted; his surprise at the very question was enough to move the spectacles down his nose a full inch. He adjusted them before producing a roll of standard first-aid bandages.

"The very thing you are here to confront," he shrugged, winding the dressings firmly around Corin's arm. "It's death. Just death. In whatever language—too tight?"

"No."

"Right. Well, on its own plane of existence, we don't know what form it takes. But in ours, it tries to appear. It manifests itself beyond its host. And the laws of our physics simply don't apply to it. That's why it can change and move so illogically. Same goes for the breathing. There is nothing chemically altering about the breath of a Hollow, nothing that *should* change a human body, scientifically speaking. The act is merely a symbol, but because it's being played out on death's terms, it elicits an equally symbolic and uncontainable response. That's why some of our best practices don't always work against it, why the best we can do is simply contain Hollows to keep them from multiplying. Which is why we need you all. You five are foolproof."

At that moment, a pair of police cruisers tore loudly by on the distant highway, on their way, no doubt, to the the bridge and the empty wreckage below. It would have been an opportune time to further discuss the false report being planned for the authorities, had Khan not bolted to his feet at the first recognition of sirens. The others froze collectively, watching him sprint to the edge of the lot, cringing as he neared a moat-like drainage ditch, which he promptly fell into.

"Foolproof," Corin reiterated.

"I'll get him," Jackson sighed. He hastily wrapped what was left of his fifth burrito before trotting off.

The driver's side door of the ambulance swung open, and Stella emerged, satellite phone held firmly to one ear. "What's going on out here?" she demanded crossly.

Corin waved his neatly bandaged arm in an assuring gesture. "It's all under control," he said, at about the time Jackson geronimoed into the ditch and disappeared.

Stella stepped down to the asphalt to make a better assessment, at which point Jesse paused the preening of his cuticles to look at her, his eyes glossed attractively with cartoon puppy hope.

"Any news? Did they find her?"

She ignored him. Her eyes stayed on the drainage ditch and her ear stayed against the phone.

Jesse scoffed. He leaned back on his elbows, coming as close as he could to lying down without allowing hair to touch asphalt, and looked sideways at Abe.

"Does *everyone* at the Luna Latum have such a stick up their ass?"

Abe cleared his throat loudly enough to drown that out.

"Hunters are not quite the ... eh ... the norm within the Luna Latum," he answered with polite caution. "Subduing Hollows—well, you can imagine it's a very unpredictable, dangerous job. Quite stressful, really. So hunters can sometimes come off as a little ..."

He paused when Stella sliced a glance in his direction.

"Assy?" Jesse supplemented.

Ghi rescued them both with another question. He was carefully picking the cheese out of his third taco. "What happens to the Hollows? Once the hunters have ... um ... *dealt* with them?"

"Well," Abe said, rubbing smudges off his bifocals, "most of them are simply put away, since we've had no way to eliminate them. And some are studied for practical purposes—to create that antibiotic, for example, or to devise ways to prevent their communication.

"That sort of work is originally what the Luna Latum had in mind for me, but it just wasn't my style" he shrugged, the cadence of his voice resolutely cheerful. "I requested a change of departments, and eventually wound up developing ways to find you five."

Corin furrowed his eyebrows. This, I have long come to recognize, meant that a very sensible and appropriate question was about to be asked.

"How did you find the Luna Latum in the first place?" he asked, sensibly and appropriately. "How did you even know they existed?"

They all paused when a wave of intense heat brushed by, immediately followed by Jackson shouting choice words, unseen in the smoke and dust whirling up from the drainage ditch. Abe was so mesmerized by this that when he turned back to Corin, he had completely forgotten the question.

"The Luna Latum," Corin repeated himself patiently. "How did you find them?"

"Oh," Abe laughed abruptly. "Oh, that's a good one. The Luna Latum found *me*. They always find the people they want."

Corin did not find this nearly as funny as Abe did. He and Ghi exchanged looks of nearly equal unease, clearly reaching the same conclusion. Jesse's attention span had timed out minutes ago. He was back to the cuticles again.

"They're really very good with all the arrangements," Abe continued. "Everyone thinks I left the Human Genome Project to work on my own influenza vaccine. It's never been an issue. Mother still hears from me on holidays."

Ghi's nerves failed him. He applied too much sudden force to a packet of hot sauce, and some of it came fatally close to hitting Jesse's shoes. Armani.

"You mean they *abducted* you?"

Abe shrugged.

"You might say the Luna Latum found my expertise crucial to their cause," he said, in a careful but giddy attempt at modesty. His expression was coy, bashful at best. Apparently, getting kidnapped and forced to do paranormal experiments for a clandestine organization was considered a high honor among men of science. Or at least men like Abe.

"I mean," he blathered on humbly, "Dr. Ivor would have probably been a better fit, but he had all those children. And Mechtild was a total alcoholic. Not that you heard it from me—"

Corin stared at him, wide-eyed. "You've never tried to escape?"

Abe blinked at him as if waiting for a punch line, and then laughed despite the absence of one. "Are you *kidding*?"

Heavy coughing interrupted them. Jackson had emerged from the ditch—sooty, but otherwise unmaimed—with Khan just behind him, smoldering. Visibly. Literally. As in a small fire had broken out across his shoulders.

"You have to learn to calm down, man," Jackson coached as they walked back together. "Take it easy. Imagine yourself in a meadow or some shit. Lord."

As he said this, Abe was already rushing over to examine this divine fire himself, eager to see it up close. Khan, perturbed by this sudden invasion of space, faked at Abe with Rottweiler malice, baring his teeth. An arch of flame lashed out, and Abe's sleeve ignited.

The doctor laughed an awestruck, thrilled laugh and slapped at the spreading flames with his own hand, looking back to Corin and Ghi with resolute delight.

"Why would I want to be doing anything else?"

CHAPTER 18

There is positively no doubt that he came to me from another direction. The loose motorcade of unmatching vehicles, unimpressive and inconspicuous except for their darkly tinted windows, simply could not have come within five miles of that lonesome parking lot without incident. Serious incident. That Wal-Mart doesn't know how lucky it is to still be standing.

He wasn't in the area by chance, though; this was no mere coincidence. He had been following—far behind the tour bus, far behind the U-Haul brigade and the hunters' many ambulances. Way behind.

He stayed behind because he wanted to know more. He wanted to wait awhile, to draw his answers from a number of sources and senses: from the unconsumed blood spilled by those Hollow groupies, from the shock of their unprecedented deaths, from the collective thoughts of his U-Haul posse. And with these gleaned references, he patiently pieced together small fractions of the Vessel—what they were capable of, what might hurt them, what defenses they had, and who they knew.

He still wanted to know more. So the motorcade steered clear.

They will seek death's origin together.

He wanted to know more in order to make it count; in order to make it hurt. He wanted to swallow any fact he could sink his teeth into. The rest of it could wait. He had forever, after all.

As it will in turn seek them.

The nature of the divine is strange. To the divine, the action is nothing, and the meaning is everything. The action is merely a symbol, something palpable to make sense of the meaning behind it. This explains how Khan himself can ignite without the clothes burning off his back, or how water rushes uphill to exalt at Corin's feet. How that 13-ton tour bus floated like a feather on frozen air.

It also explains why Dahrkren decided to carve out my heart and eat it.

He almost didn't get the chance. It was James Brown who almost killed me.

An hour had passed. The guy in the corner had eventually settled down again, had gone back to dying or mutating or whatever he was doing before I'd so rudely disturbed him. He was quiet, and so I pretended he was not there. I pretended *I* was not there.

Rain drummed against the steel edges of the building, some of it leaking through the middle of the room in heavy streams, creating a uniform din of sound, a loud and steady silence. I hadn't moved, and I was afraid to try. The cold had already transitioned to numbness, then to burning, then to throbbing, and now it was just a strange heaviness on my limbs and in my chest.

I sat against one of the shelves, going over each bleak outcome in my head just to stay awake. Freeze to death. Bleed to death. Or wind up like one of those things in the corner. I was wondering which of the first two would be faster when a box on the shelf, the one I happened to have my head propped up against, screamed directly into my ear.

Or, more specifically, the voice of James Brown screamed directly into my ear.

I saw stars. My entire body defied gravity. My shriek bounced off the shabby walls. My heart did something new, something that hurt.

The box stopped screaming and started playing "Get Up Offa That Thing".

I recovered. I ripped the box off the shelf, opened it.

Pagers, iPods, cell phones.

Cell phones, cell phones, cell phones.

I followed Mr. Brown's advice. I got up off of my thing. I grabbed the singing phone—the most beautiful object I'd seen in my entire life—and silenced it with quaking, fumbling, stupidly joyful hands.

A quick dig through the box told me that this was the only phone with any charge left. Two bars of service, low battery—not much, but still all that I could ask for. I steadied my fingers and dialed the only number I knew by heart.

Stella Rosin liked certainty. You'd think that would make her fairly ill-suited as a hunter, but you'd be wrong. If you're face-to-face with a Hollow, you better be very certain you can take it down before it gets to you.

Doesn't guarantee that you can, of course, but it sure helps.

Stella was certain of a few things at the moment. For the first time in several days, things were going her way. Her payload—all five obnoxious units—was accounted for, and according to her calculations, the helicopter would be arriving in about fifteen minutes. She was also certain that those fifteen minutes could not pass quickly enough.

Stella glanced sourly to her right, where all of Khan's presence was crammed into the passenger seat. The rain had picked up again, forcing the Vessel to pile back into the formerly sane haven of the ambulance, bringing with them the faint smell of hot sauce and something like wet dog. One of them was currently snoring like a jackhammer, and Abe was spouting off classified Luna Latum information—much to the Vessels' welcome distraction, and much to Stella's overworked chagrin. It was not in the best interest of her career to overhear such things. She found herself staring at the sky through the windshield with manic hope, willing the absent helicopter into sight.

Fifteen more minutes, she reminded herself, and she would have peace. No more Abe. No more of this insulting babysitting nonsense. No more wild chases or uncontained explosions. No more uncertainty.

And no more singing.

I could have told Stella that he was just nervous. When dogs are nervous, they run in circles. When hamsters are nervous, they eat their young. When Jesse Cannon is nervous, he sings.

Or when he's bored. Or excited. Or drunk or horny or sad.

Jesse was nervous because the runaway U-Haul had been surrounded and disabled. Stella's colleagues had informed her of this development well over twenty minutes ago, and so far there had been no report of "collateral damage" (a fancy term for dead celebrity assistants). In fact, there had been no report at all. Which meant that Jesse had been passionately humming "Stormy Weather" for an intolerable length of time, despite Stella's reminders that the hunters were busy assuring my safety, and that they would be in touch again when the incident was over.

In the meantime, Abe had steered his lectures toward the Elysium, a subject of immediate interest to the Vessel, since a helicopter was evidently coming to take them there. According to Abe, the Elysium was precisely what Corin had defined it as: the resting place of gods and their mortal heroes. Apparently, it was also prime real estate. And the place where Abe just so happened to work.

"Does it have a pool?" Jesse stopped singing long enough to ask.

The Elysium was, in fact, an island. A lush dot on the map which had remained in Luna Latum possession ever since they claimed it at the onset of the thirteenth century. The idea, even back then, was to shape it into a glorious haven for the Vessel. A sort of luxurious, pre-destiny waiting room for their mighty gods. Something really classy.

Except the Luna Latum had jumped the gun a little on the planning and implementation bit. Construction on the main complex was officially complete in 1562, if I have my history right. The four centuries of stewardship that followed meant that something had to be done to pass the time, leading to an unrecordable number of renovations and additions. Updated facades. Complimenting structures. Laboratories and training facilities built and rebuilt with evolving technology. Breathtakingly beautiful gardens. Intricate murals. Water slides.

"It has twelve pools, not counting the ones in the study facilities," Abe replied from memory. He nodded in Corin's direction. "Three of them are in your room."

Corin's eyebrows disappeared into his hairline. He was undeniably pleased by this.

"A bar?" Jesse ventured.

"A few of them."

"A disco floor?"

"A proper disco floor could be arranged, I'm sure."

When Jesse opened his mouth to ask what would have certainly been another frivolous question, he was sharply interrupted by the chorus of "It's Raining Men" coming from his own pocket, an event which surprised absolutely no one at all.

Panic pulled his eyes wide open. Margot had no doubt heard about the bus by now, and must be out of her mind with worry, fury, and financial rage. He struggled to remember what he had been directed to tell her as he wrestled the phone from its tight denim prison. But one look at the slender screen cancelled his worry. He breathed a short sigh of relief.

"Unknown caller," he announced.

"Don't answer that," Corin and Stella commanded sternly at the exact same time.

Jesse nodded obediently while contradictorily lifting the ringing phone to his ear, two things he was hardwired to do. Corin, Ghi, and Abe stared at him without breathing. Stella's eyes bore into him from the rear mirror. Martha Wash wailed and wailed.

The pressure was just too much. Jesse caved. He accepted the call and opened his mouth.

"Hel—"

"Jesse! Jesse?!" I blurted, doing my best not to scream with maddened relief at the sound of his voice—of any voice—on the other end of the line. "It's Jordan."

"It's Jordan," he echoed blankly.

Other voices erupted around him at once.

"Where is she?"

"Who is she with?"

"Is she a Hollow now?"

"What? Give me that phone. Don't tell her anything."

There were definite hushing, swatting sounds from Jesse.

"Jordan, honey, are you okay?" he asked, coveting the phone close. His voice was crystal clear. "Where are you?"

"I'm not okay!" I answered, surprising myself with my own level of hysteria. "I don't know where I am!"

"Slow down. What's happening?"

"They're going to eat me," I sobbed shamelessly, unintelligibly. "They're going to hang me upside down and throw my shoes in a box with everybody else's!"

"But where *are* you?" he pleaded. "How are you calling me? Are you still in that truck? Are you with the Luna Latum?"

"The what? Maybe?" I heaved, trying to maintain a sense of calm and finding it impossible. I could fit only a limited number of syllables into one breath. "Not the truck. I'm inside. Some huge building. Really old."

"But whose phone are you on?"

"Guy in the corner. His."

"What?!"

There was massive confusion in the background. Stella was trying to dictate the things Jesse should ask me, while at the same time attempting to communicate with the other hunters. Corin was demanding that everyone be quiet, and creating more background noise in the process. And yet somehow one of Jackson's loud, drawn-out snores made it through to me.

I closed my eyes while they argued, concentrating. I tried to think of what would be the most important details to give. It also occurred to me to list off some final wishes while I still had someone on the line. *All my savings go to Mom and Dad. The memoir manuscript is in the L.A. beach house, in the upstairs linen closet. And please: dispose of my* Gilmore Girls *complete series deluxe box set, before anyone ever knows—*

"Jordan? Are you still there?"

My eyes snapped open, zeroing in on the dust-encrusted hard hats that had been lying in a pile by my feet. Each one had a dull metal tag on the back, too filthy to read. Of course! I snatched one onto my lap and scratched away at the brittle gray dirt until I could make out the words engraved underneath:

PROPERTY OF THE WHALEN QUARRY
BEARD'S FORK, WV

"Jordan?"

"Whalen Quarry," I said.

"Wailing what?"

"That's where I am," I spouted hastily. "I'm at the *Whalen Quarry*. In some town called Beard's Fork."

I listened impatiently while Jesse relayed this information, and frantically corrected his many botched pronunciations. I gave him all the details I could about the building, what I'd seen of it from the inside, and warned him that the Hollows were likely still around.

It was at this point that Stella made a very uncharacteristic mistake. It had of course dawned on her that I was not in the U-Haul. Which meant that the other hunters were nowhere near me. Her mistake was getting out of the ambulance to call them.

What followed was another explosion of voices and sounds. Corin, ranting about rural areas and the "bloody slow" internet service. Abe, asking whether I had been bitten, breathed into, or otherwise mouthed by any Hollows. Jesse, very sweetly asking Khan to lock the ambulance's front doors.

The phone beeped into my ear, and my stomach plunged. Low battery.

"Jesse!" I warned, trying to pull him back from the garble of voices.

A scuffling sound answered me.

"Hello," said a polite voice—not Jesse's. I had been handed over.

"Ghi?"

"Yes?"

"Listen! My batteries are dying!"

"Oh," he said. "Um."

"Got it!" Corin practically screamed, no doubt waving around his beloved Sabre phone. "Whalen Quarry. End of Beard's Fork Road—"

"How far is that?" Jesse asked, just before slapping Jackson's cheeks. The ones on his face, I feel the need to clarify. "Look alive, soldier!"

"The hell?!" Jackson barked.

"—less than thirty minutes," Corin was saying. "It's on this side of the bridge. Middle of nowhere."

Beep. Battery. Fuck.

"Hello?" I begged.

"Yes?" Still Ghi.

"Will you please tell me what's happening?"

"Um. I guess we're coming to get you."

Jesse's prattling in the background immediately confirmed that guess.

"—we just need you to drive again, darling."

"Yeah, what else is new?" Jackson asked groggily. "Where's that blonde broad? Won't she be mad?"

"Oh, yes," answered Abe's unfamiliar but merry voice. "Very."

Loud banging noises followed, and yelling. Although no words could be made out over the sudden revving of the engine, the general outrage conveyed in the yelling itself was loud and clear, even to me.

"She'll get over it!" Jesse called brightly. There was another ominous beep as he took the phone from Ghi.

"Save your batteries, girlfriend," he said to me. "See you in thirty!"

He ended the call.

And I was alone again.

Alone. Freezing. Bleeding. Doomed to die. *See you in thirty!* Thirty minutes. The room's general gloom closed in around me at once. Cold rain continued to scour over the plastic roof, dripping down the concrete walls in dirty brown rivulets, pooling around the hard hats at my feet. In the corner, a second suspended body bag started thrashing, screaming.

I hugged my knees and hoped to god no one ever found that *Gilmore Girls* box set.

About fifteen miles north of the New River, down a one lane road off Route 60, a motionless U-Haul straddled the gravel curb, tilted sideways into a grassy drainage ditch. Three ambulances and a total of five speed bikes were converged around it, parked and unmanned. A quarter mile in either direction, someone stood in the road to turn away traffic. So far, there hadn't been any. It was still very early in this particular corner of nowhere.

Both the U-Haul's back tires had been blown out, and the driver's side window had been smashed in with a crowbar. Most of the cab's interior was now incinerated. The latch of the back door had been dealt with similarly to the aforementioned window, and the door itself was rolled completely up, revealing the truck's hideous contents to the light of day and to the thin spatter of rain.

Among these contents was a floral patterned love seat, which had been pulled out into the grass. Part of the love seat was on fire, and a hunter was busily dousing it with an extinguisher.

The love seat belonged to Charlotte Pickens, soon to be Charlotte McCormick.

Charlotte soon-to-be-McCormick Pickens was standing at a removed distance from the U-Haul, holding a pack of ice to the side of her head from where she'd banged it into the windshield. Her hair was blackened and singed in places, but she had not otherwise been burned. Charlotte wore an awful lot of hairspray. It had to do with her upbringing.

Beside her stood Jeff McCormick, dutifully holding Jelly, their miniature Pomeranian. Jelly had absolutely peed all over him, or so Jeff contended. As for Biscuit, well, there wasn't much of Biscuit left to mention.

The hunters hadn't said very much. They'd put out the fires from their own flame-throwers, and they'd given Charlotte an ice pack, and that's about it. Everyone seemed terribly embarrassed.

These sort of mistakes are bound to happen, the beta hunter reminded himself, breathing in the smell of charred upholstery—with a hint of dog. *Everyone drives these damn things now.*

Another hunter approached him, carrying a satellite phone and a rather strained demeanor. It was possible that she had news about other U-Hauls spotted in the area, but that hope shrank significantly when she held up the phone, extending it as if to hand it over.

"It's our alpha," she said. "She's pissed. Been trying to get us for over twenty minutes."

"Well of course she has," said the senior hunter. "But before we give her any details, we need to redirect—"

"The hostage is no longer an issue," she interrupted. "We've got a bigger problem."

"Oh?"

"Yes. The Vessel have ditched. Alpha believes they've gone after Hollows."

"Oh."

"Ran over her foot apparently."

"Ah."

"Indeed." The junior hunter pushed the phone at him persistently, expressionless. He took it and watched her stalk away for several seconds before lifting it to his ear. Grimacing, he pressed down the button.

"Beta speaking," he said, scarcely getting a syllable out.

"How quickly can you track down the ambulance I was driving?" Stella Rosin demanded from the other end of the connection. The sharp calm of her voice thinly veiled the hottest wrath of multiple hells.

The hunter surveyed the small mess around him. His colleagues were already gathering around their vehicles, quite aware that it was time to move on. A cluster of them, including the woman who'd handed over the phone, were gathering around a GPS server mounted on one of the bikes, no doubt locking down the location of the ambulance in question.

"Already on it," he confirmed.

"Good. Send a bike to pick me up, just one. I want the rest of you after the Vessel immediately. Your little mishap is not of consequence at the moment. Just leave it."

"Will do."

"I expect Sharma will be in touch with us shortly, if our divine idiots haven't gotten him killed already. He's quite aware that they're not capable of . . ." There was a screech on the line, an extended interruption. " . . . god knows how many . . . unless we catch up to them."

"Sorry, bad connection," the hunter cut in. "Can you repeat that?"

He could hear Stella responding, but her words sounded as if they were coming through a sponge. More static followed, and then a voice that was not Stella's. This voice could have belonged to a moldy, rattling shower drain.

"They will seek him," it said, rusty and metallic and wet.

Color drained from the hunter's face. It was the oldest voice he'd ever heard—and he'd heard some pretty old ones. Several yards away, Charlotte was rubbing her forehead, hoping her eyebrows would grow back in time for the wedding. Jeff was thinking about fire and machetes and his dad's Vietnam flashbacks. Jelly was pissing on a speed bike. He was the only one who comprehended how very small his problems were.

"Alpha?" the hunter said. There was silence on the other end, a pop, and then Stella, cursing. "Alpha? Did you hear that, too?"

"Of course I did," she snapped. "God. I *hate* it when they do that."

There was another screech, a piercing one, but the hunter could not take his ear away from the receiver.

"They will seek him," the voice said again. "And he will seek them."

CHAPTER 19

Beard's Fork Road is a featureless, one lane road off Route 61, just a trail following one of the area's countless mountain trenches. On this road, you won't see much—a small cluster of 30s-era bungalow houses, an overgrown field, a tangle of rusting cars, a nervous gathering of deer, and—if you look hard enough—the shrubbery-coated mouth of an ancient gravel road, marked by a barely legible sign which reads "Whalen Quarry Road: No Trespassing".

If you take your chances and trespass, and follow Whalen Quarry Road for a few slow, descending, nauseating miles, you'll find Whalen Quarry itself. And if you stop right there and turn around, you might just live.

The road itself ends abruptly on the mountainside, sloping off into an unorganized pathway of worn tire ruts leading straight down to the filled-in valley that had once been the gravel quarry. The valley is nothing now but eroding piles of pebbles and deep, stagnant pools of gray water. Its far side is bordered not by another mountain, but by a humungous, rectangular monster of rust and chipped paint, over a half a mile in length. An old gravel processing plant, a place no one wanted or needed anymore, a place that would have been torn down long ago if it hadn't been purchased.

Purchased, of course, by the Hollows. They positively love places like this, mostly because no one ever stops by. And also because the people who occasionally *do* stop by are usually criminals or drug addicts or wayward teenagers—people who are expected to turn up missing anyways.

Easy pickings, Abe had explained.

The ambulance sat parked where the gravel ended, because there was no sensible place to hide it, nor any sane reason to risk getting it stuck in the mud below. The Vessel stood alongside it, squinting into the heavy rain, surveying the valley below and feeling mutually—yet silently—stupid about coming here.

Corin squashed the toe of his shoe into the sloppy tire tracks. He turned to the others, contemplative, unblinking. Instead of collecting in droplets on his face and arms, the falling rain spread evenly over his skin before disappearing, fast and clean as rubbing alcohol. "Well?"

Everyone else was already soaked to the bone.

"We could try calling her again," Jesse suggested from the shelter of the ambulance's rear door.

Ghi shook his head, which was harder than it looked. Wet, his hair appeared to have shrank two sizes and gained twenty pounds. "That might be a bad idea. What if she's not alone now?"

The driver's side door opened, and Abe slid back out into the weather, protecting his eyeglasses by making a visor with his hand. Everyone looked his way.

"I've sent out a general distress signal," he announced. "No one's answering. Even if they're already on their way, it'll still take the hunters just as long to get here as we did."

The mood dropped a few more degrees at that point, as did my chances for survival. Nothing was moving near the enormous building below. No cars, no Hollows. For all they knew, I wasn't even there anymore. There was no way to tell. Maybe the place was empty, or maybe it was teeming with waiting Hollows, wall to wall. Maybe I had never been there. Maybe I'd been forced to deceive them on the phone, and this was all some lethal set-up, a trap. Maybe I was already dead. Or worse. These were the things running through their minds as they watched the rain move in heavy sheets across the valley.

Jackson cleared his throat.

"Look, we kicked their asses back at the bridge. We can do it again," he insisted, weary of the suspense. "I say we just go for it."

"Oh? And what would your contribution be?" Jesse snorted behind him. "Caving the building in on us?"

He had a reasonable point there—that none of them were even close to using their forces in any precise manner, with the exception of Khan. Which wasn't all that reassuring.

"Actually, Dorothy," Jackson shot him a warning look, "I was thinking I'd just step out of the way and let you flutter all around. They won't know what hit them."

Jesse kicked a fleck of mud in his direction. Jackson responded by sending an entire sheet of vengeful mud right back. Jesse, outraged and suddenly brown from the neck down, lunged. No one did a thing about the violent smacking match that ensued. It was only making the obvious fact even more painful not to say:

Coming here had been a terrible idea.

Khan stood with his weathered pink shirt pulled up over his head to ward off the rain, absently running his tongue through the newest gap in his teeth. Abe looked at his watch. Corin paced, stopping every few seconds as if about to suggest something, then saying nothing. His expression was defeated, self-admittedly blank. There was nothing he could draw from his Sabre phone—nor from his extensive experience with conflict resolution, mountain climbing, or the many dialects of the Indonesian language—which seemed helpful.

Ghi turned suddenly from staring at the building, a flash in his golden eyes.

"Jackson's right," he declared.

"I am?" Jackson glanced up from where he was holding Jesse in a bent arm lock, pressing his furious face into the mud. "About what?"

Ghi moved back towards the center of the scattered group, his back to the valley. Every second that passed was another second they weren't using, another second during which something preventable could be happening. At the very least, after leaving Stella in a parking lot and driving here, it seemed totally irrational to spend anymore time standing there on the side of the mountain, waiting and wondering. No matter how bad of an idea the next step was.

"About the bridge, you know?" he said. "We might not know what we're doing, but the Hollows were still afraid of us. And that's enough."

Corin shook his sorry, lost head. "Enough for what?"

"Enough to make it out in one piece," Ghi said. And somehow, even though the knob in his throat bobbed to an incredible height when he said it, he sounded unshakable. Convincing, even.

"Why do I end up with Goliath and Peter Pan, that's what I'd like to know," Jackson grumbled to everyone within hearing range—Khan and Jesse, respectively.

Jesse rolled his eyes, trudging along behind him, the thick mud sucking loudly around his sinking feet with every step. He resentfully noted that Jackson's feet weren't even leaving boot prints. Jesse wasn't exactly thrilled about this arrangement either, but when all the decisions had been made twenty minutes earlier, he'd been busy de-twigging his socks.

"Are you seriously still bitching?" he asked. "Shouldn't you be paying more attention to what we're doing here?"

The three of them were moving up a slope alongside the perimeter of the building, which seemed even more mind-bogglingly huge now that they were right up against it. At this juncture, Jackson stopped abruptly so that Jesse would walk right into him, then whipped around. He cocked his head to the side and drew his eyebrows together in a most authoritative manner. "How many fire exits are on the top level of this side of the building?"

Jesse's lips went slack. In lieu of an answer, he flicked his mud-soaked hair behind his ear and stuck his nose in the air.

"Seven. You're welcome. So I'll bitch if I want," Jackson mandated before turning and marching off again. "I'm not responsible for your asses, just because I know what I'm doing, that's all I'm saying."

"Oh yes, a firefighter, I forgot," Jesse directed a sigh back to Khan, who was keeping a silent pace behind them. "Thank heavens."

Khan, of course, didn't respond. Jackson waved his hand urgently and made a shushing sound as they neared the corner of the building. He highlighted the importance of stealth by pressing his back to the wall and hesitating to peer around its edge.

Jesse skipped past him without pause and hopped beyond the corner.

Jackson's eyes popped. A wave of heat pulsed away from Khan, sizzling and popping in the rain. But Jesse smirked and turned around, clearly amused by both of them. "*Puh*-lease. There's nothing here."

He was entirely right. Around the corner, there was nothing whatsoever. Just the shorter side of the building, about a hundred yards wide, and several large doors, each one big enough for a tractor-trailer to pass through. The door closest to them stood wide open. Nothing moved beyond it, and nothing made a sound over the falling rain.

They approached the door with quiet caution. Even Jesse was silent when they paused there together, at the place where shadow cast a hard line in the mud. The three hesitated on that line as if for the last breath before a dive, and then they walked inside.

For the next several seconds, Jackson and Jesse's eyes strained to adjust, to comprehend what they saw—or didn't see, rather (for Khan, this wasn't really an issue). Though barely classifiable as daylight, the dreary glow behind them *should* have been enough to define a few shapes inside the building. Yet for some reason, the light wasn't doing its job.

After quite a bit of blinking, they understood: there was nothing for the light to fall on.

Decades ago, the gravel had been ground up and cleaned here, then funneled through to the lower level to be shipped away. Now the place was gutted of all machinery, leaving only a vast, open floor which stretched the entire length of the building, a featureless plain of wooden beams and dust as far as the eye could see—which wasn't very far at all. The drenched daylight from the open door succumbed to absolute darkness about forty yards ahead of where they stood. The rest of the level's interior, the full half-mile of it, was utterly untouched by any light source. It looked like the perfect place for a rave. Or like a portal to hell, with no light at the end.

"This is fine," Jackson said, psyching himself up, sounding uncharacteristically nervous. "It'll be like spelunking. Without lamps."

Jesse sneered under his breath. He didn't know what spelunking was, but evidently he thought it sounded icky. "Would be nice if Ghi were here."

They both jumped when a glowing gush of heat materialized beside them. Khan, naturally. His right arm was suddenly alight with a rippling sleeve of fire, and he held it up like a torch, looking bored but wearily patient.

"That works, too," Jesse forced a smile.

They started forward.

The fire created only a small dome of light around them in the enormous space, not nearly enough to reach the other end of the building. They could, however, make out the distant side walls, and knew that they were moving through a single chamber—not some sort of hallway. They passed the occasional fire exit, but no other doors or rooms. No Hollows. And no Jordan.

A minute or two passed without interruption or incident. Just more and more empty, featureless space ahead. Behind them, the open door floated like a perfect gray rectangle in the distance, and all else was blackness beyond their little orange orb of space.

"She can't be up here," said Jackson. His lowered voice went forth into dust and darkness, never returning as an echo. "Any word from them yet?"

"No." Jesse was quick to answer. He'd been checking his phone constantly.

"Must be a lot more to look through downstairs," Jackson squinted at the side walls. "There's gotta be stairs or something at the far end of this. We could—"

And just like that, with an abrupt catch in his voice, Jackson dropped from sight.

In the very same instant, Jesse stopped, flung a halting hand in front of Khan, and swept his other hand in a rising motion.

Calling all air particles. Someone's fallen down the well.

Jackson tumbled silently upward out of a gigantic hole in the floor, still too surprised to yell. With a withheld sigh of relief, Jesse dropped his hand, and the air obediently dumped Jackson onto solid ground. The entire ordeal, from fall to finish, hadn't lasted two whole seconds.

"Shit," Jackson grimaced and sucked in a breath, physically feeling his mortality. He rolled to his feet and stood beside Jesse, staring down into the depths of the rectangular chute. It had once been used to funnel gravel into trucks on the lower level, some forty feet below. Now it was just an opening to an even deeper darkness than what already surrounded them.

"Thanks," he said graciously.

Jesse's mouth was a hard, nervous line. "Still going to call me Peter Pan?"

Jackson thought about that for a second, and then sighed.

"Yep," he said. He was nothing if not honest.

They continued on for more than twenty minutes, finding nothing noteworthy or hopeful. The same pattern persisted for the entire top level of the building—fire escape doors every fifty yards, two more chutes through the floor. Until all at once, something began to come at them from the darkness, taking shape ahead in the faintest outer glow of the flame. A flat, vertical plane. A wall. The end of the line.

The three paused. Without being asked, Khan lifted his flaming arm so as to better illuminate the wall from one end to the other, grumbling tiredly. At one corner, the wall recessed into a short alcove, leading to the wide, trap-like door of a freight elevator. The only other feature was a single door directly in front of them, one metal door with a narrow, thick-paned window, its glass obscured by the dingy film of time.

The stairs.

Jesse rested his hands on his hips. He checked his phone, shook his head. Nothing yet.

"Can't just turn around," Jackson said, scratching his ear. "I reckon we should go on down and meet them in the middle."

Khan exhaled smugly.

Jackson glared up at him, craning his thick neck. "If you got a better idea, Sideshow, then you best say it now."

Whether he had one or not, Khan said nothing. He rolled his eyes. Maybe. It was hard to tell in the firelight.

The rain was so heavy on the rigid plastic siding that I didn't hear them moving outside or whispering. But I did hear the chain clanking against the door, and that was enough to get me moving again.

I rolled dizzily from my position against the wall and scrambled to get beneath a large, moldy heap of canvas under one of the shop tables. Pulling it down around me, I squeezed my eyes shut, trying not to think about what kinds of things I might be huddling up against. The door creaked on its hinges. Always with this creaking. Don't the Hollows know about DW-40? God.

I stayed very still and held my breath. As if it would help. As if those things wouldn't feel the vibrations of my heartbeat.

There was the treading of feet. Murmuring, questioning, careful voices. One of them in particular stood out to me. It was soft and sensible and very, very British.

"Jordan?" it said, in a hesitant, amplified kind of whisper.

I burst out from under the table and bolted to my feet, causing an avalanche of boxes and jars. It's a miracle that lightning didn't strike me dead that very second, because Ghi was standing right there, practically on top of me. The startled look on his face clearly indicated that he was rushing to tell every photon in the room not to fry me on the spot.

Corin stared from behind him, along with Abe, who I of course did not recognize. I didn't care who he was. He wasn't a Hollow, and I wasn't alone anymore. I wasn't going to die by myself in this cozy horror shack, and that was all that mattered. The unprecedented joy from all this was causing my sluggish circulation to speed up, which made my face hurt. It made everything hurt so much I could barely see. I was unable to utter a syllable before the questions started.

"Are you okay?"

"How long have the Hollows been gone?"

"What about your arm?"

"Are they still in this building?"

"Jesus, your lips are blue."

"Can you feel your fingers?"

I threw my hands up and clasped the sides of my spinning head. "I don't know," I finally gasped, so baffled and deliriously happy. Until I counted the three of them. A red flag went up in my fizzling mind, flooding it with a sudden, gut-eating worry.

"Where's everyone else? Where's Jesse?"

"He's with Jackson and Khan. We split up to find you," Corin explained calmly, instantly dissolving that particular concern. At the same time, he shrugged off his coat and threw it over my shoulders, pulling it around me securely. Ghi seemed to have had the same idea, but he'd gotten his head stuck in all his layers of sweaters. Abe hummed and began waving some pronged instrument over my head. It beeped at intervals, and he seemed happy with whatever it was telling him.

"We'll meet them outside," Corin continued, pulling the Sabre phone, that Excalibur of his, from the coat pocket now at my hip. We waited while he texted nimbly, gathering ourselves for an exodus of questionable risk. I took one look at Ghi, who now had both his head and one arm completely trapped inside his own clothes, and reminded myself that, somehow, these people had made it this far without getting killed. Chances were we could still make it out here.

"What's that?" Ghi asked, peering over the collar of his outermost sweatshirt as he pulled himself free.

Oh no.

He was staring into the place I had done my best not to notice for the past hour. The dark corner of the room where the four occupied body bags hung in a row. The one on the end was swinging again, wheezing forcefully, awakened by all our racket.

I grabbed Ghi's arm with gusto, dragging him to the door. He continued to stare at the corner, transfixed. "It's nothing," I pleaded. "Please, let's just go."

"Someone's in there?" he started to step away, all curious and helpful. I almost screamed at him to get my point across, but remembered in time that making loud noises here would be a very bad idea.

Abe swiveled to see what the stir was about. His eyebrows soared the moment he saw those bags, and he quickly stepped into Ghi's path, rerouting him back toward the door.

"Yes, yes. She's right. Let's just leave that alone."

"But—"

Abe shook his head firmly. "Nothing can be done, Ghi."

Text message sent. Corin was now staring at the same corner with grave concern. "Done about what? What are they?" He took one investigative step—

—and I stomped down on his foot, looking sharply at Abe. "Who are you again?"

"Oh, do forgive me," he said, and held out a hand. "I'm Abe. Dr. Abraham Sharma."

"Jordan," I said, and I shook his hand for a nanosecond before turning on Corin and Ghi. "You two shut the hell up and listen to Abe."

The stairwell was lit. Dimly, but lit. Fluorescent lamps shuddered weakly on the cinderblock walls, strobing throughout the tall, square chamber of concrete steps and steel handrails. The smell of rot and mildew churned up from beneath, rushing for the open door as if the air had been trapped in this place for a very long time.

Jackson paused just inside the threshold, waiting for some reaction to the startlingly loud moan the door had made upon being opened, but there was none. The only sounds that answered were the hums and taps made by the feeble lights. Looking down, they could see that the building had an unexpected depth: it appeared to have a basement, something they hadn't noticed from outside. Four flights of steps above the basement entrance was the ground floor landing; and four above that, the upper level, where they now hesitated. Not a thing moved beneath, and they felt sure that the stairwell was empty.

Jackson and Jesse did, anyway. Khan, apparently quite sure of something else, lurched past them and began hurtling down the steps in threes and fours. He moved as if a pistol had gone off for a race only he was aware of, his feet slapping violently on the concrete, somehow never failing him.

Something had his attention.

"What the hell, man?" Jackson leaned over the railing, surprised by the volumous echoes of his own voice. Below, the steps formed a deep square spiral of gray shapes, hard shadows, and rigid angles. Khan was already halfway down to the unexpected basement.

Jackson growled and started stomping down the steps at a normal pace. "Seriously. What is his *deal*?"

"Oh, who knows," Jesse sighed, moving lithely down the steps to catch up. He swayed in close, intentionally allowing his shoulder to bump Jackson's. "Maybe he knew how badly we wanted to be alone . . ."

Jackson pushed him away with enough force to flip him over the railing, and as he expected, Jesse righted himself effortlessly in the air. He wafted down to the next landing, where he paused to wait with a devious, triumphant grin. A grin that disappeared when his back pocket began to buzz. His phone. The message. He reached to pull it out—

And froze. Jackson did, too. With one foot still hovering above a step, he locked eyes with Jesse. Together, they looked over the railing, down towards the new sound.

It was Khan, racing back up the steps, kicking distance between himself and the basement. When he reached the landing just below Jesse, he flung around and stopped.

And then the basement door flew open with a startling noise, steel slapping into cinderblock. The stairwell exploded with footsteps, so rapid and dense they sounded like pouring water against the concrete floor.

Way too many feet to just be me, Corin, Ghi, and Abe.

Jackson and Jesse stepped away from the railing and started backtracking upwards quickly, exchanging glances of horror. Jesse lent a sliver of attention to the phone, then put it away.

"They found her," he confirmed hastily, but there was no space for relief in his voice.

When they were nearly out of stairs to climb, Jackson chanced a look down through the vertigo spiral of steps and rails. His eyes snapped against their tendons. The basement level of the stairwell was crawling with bodies, all rushing upwards. More of them flowed from the basement door with every second.

"How many?" Jesse whispered over the incredible sound.

Jackson wordlessly pushed him towards the top of the stairs.

Too many.

Of course the upper level door made the same ungodly moan when opened again, and the footsteps of the Hollows quickened pace in response. Jackson looked down again, searching for Khan and spotting him at the ground floor landing, where he was sticking close to the wall like a tattooed shadow, poised and unmoving. There was no mistaking Khan's intent: he was a land mine lying in wait.

Jackson's brow set itself into a horizontal line, parallel with his mouth, which even then was upturned in the faintest hint of a smirk. Those Hollows didn't look so tough.

"Is he coming or what?" Jesse hissed impatiently, waiting by the door. Behind him was the pitch-black, hellish sanctuary of the upper level, empty and safe.

Jackson shoved him through the door and slammed it shut.

He gripped the knob firmly and waited, not allowing it to twist so far as a millimeter as Jesse fought to turn it. Jackson forced himself to focus, to let the vibrations of the cool metal drown out all the other sounds, just for a second.

"Hey!" Jesse shouted, drumming on the other side of the door. "Hey! Are you crazy? Come on!"

Jackson tuned him out. His senses invaded the steel, all its separate pieces, solid and resilient, malleable only to him. He flashed his teeth with satisfaction when the bolt locked, expanded, bonded to the doorframe itself and became part of it. He dropped his hand.

Jesse wasn't at all impressed by this neat trick. He gave up on the doorknob and began banging frantically on the door itself. "What the hell are you *doing?!* Get out here!"

The dust on the door's narrow window fell away in grimy clumps as Jackson smeared it with his hand, casting quick glances over his shoulder toward the growing noises of the Hollows. There was instant gratification in seeing Jesse's face, outlined in darkness, panicked of course, but above all utterly outraged.

"You got five minutes to get out of this building," Jackson shouted calmly through the thick glass. "Send a message to the others, tell them the same thing. Tell them Khan and I will be a little while."

Judging by the berserk way Jesse began throwing himself at the door, he did not agree with this plan.

"Stop wasting time, idiot!" Jackson slapped the glass. "Five minutes! Go!"

He turned away from the continuing protests and didn't look back. Jesse would eventually muster the common sense to do what he'd been told—Jackson hoped he would, anyway. There wasn't time to negotiate. There was only noise, and the violent scent of death, rising through the stairwell, buzzing up and down his spine, both invigorating and revolting. These things weren't going to get out of the stairwell, not if he could help it. They weren't going to get out of the building. By the time he was through, there wouldn't even be a building left.

He reached the ground floor landing and halted for a second, steeling himself at the sight. Khan had not moved; he stood facing down the rest of the stairs, shoulders squared, his sightless eyes unblinking and unflinching. And below him, a grotesque spectacle. Tens upon dozens of Hollows were packed rail to wall, all the way down to the basement door, writhing and grinding against each other. The ones closest to the top were blocking the way for all the others, paused just steps beyond Khan. They snarled and gaped up at him, unnerved and unsure, their bodies swaying eagerly from side to side, unable to hold still, yet not willing to leap.

Jackson had never seen anything less human in his life.

Shaking off the revulsion, he slapped Khan's shoulder and bounded over to the door.

"You want out?" he offered.

Khan's murky eyes never left the Hollows. His answer was a snort, an amused sound. *Are you kidding?* The shadows swarming across the cinderblock walls began to surge upwards. The dying could no longer hold themselves back.

Jackson grinned. "Well, don't bottle it up on account of me," he said, locking his hand around the door handle, nodding over his shoulder. "Roast 'em."

He heard Khan's soft laughter. And as he welded the door shut, just as he had welded the one above, he saw its metal surface reflect the sudden splash of orange, felt the bold wave of heat on his back.

Turning, Jackson saw what he expected. Pandemonium. The first wave of Hollows swathed in rolling flames, sweeping upward towards Khan, who was now standing within a pillar of white-hot fire. They stormed the landing even as they were falling over one another and over the rails, screaming and cursing in ancient tongues. Beneath them squirmed countless more, unsinged, clawing their way through their burning brethren.

Jackson pressed his back to the door, surprised by the suffocating heat. He wasn't going to collapse the entire stairwell just yet, not with Khan still in there. But maybe he could cleave a section of the stairs away and trap the Hollows below, in a kind of giant concrete barbeque pit. He leaned out over the railing, chewing on the idea. The basement door was still wide open, and for a second, he thought he heard something—a voice or a warning—coming from it. Which was stupid. Nothing, not even a Tyrannosaurus in heat, could have been heard over all the noise around him—the fire, the Hollows, the awakening hiss of the long-dormant sprinklers.

They will seek him.

The landing was filling up fast, and the Hollows diverted their eager attention toward Jackson, who was easily the more attractive target (being that he wasn't on fire). The first one to reach him was shoved over the railing immediately, and then another. A third Hollow dug jagged fingernails into Jackson's face before going down, and another wound its shifting black octopus of a hand around his arm. Jackson wrenched free and dove for the stairs, ducking under smoke, under burning, scrambling feet. A few bodies fell heavily around his waist and legs, trying to bring him down, but they didn't know he'd once been star receiver for the Filbert High Falcons. No sir. He drove through, flung himself to the edge of the landing, threw his hands down on the first step, and told the solid construction of stone what he wanted.

With massive and very satisfying snapping sounds, the entire length of steps fell away, along with all the Hollows who were fighting to get to the top of it—and also about half of the main landing.

"*Gae saeki!*" Khan screamed wrathfully behind his veil of fire, leaping back from the crumbling edge just in time. Far below, the falling section of steps flattened at least a dozen Hollows.

"Sorry!" Jackson cringed and jumped to his feet, dodging the remaining Hollows. Though aggravated, Khan got the general idea right away. At his prompting, the basement level quickly filled with fire, transforming into a sort of hell that the Hollows could no longer climb out of. Nor could they exit any other way, Jackson noticed, stealing a fast downward glance. The doomed were throwing themselves against the locked basement door, a sight which made Jackson do a double-take. Had that door not been open just a moment ago? Was all the heat and stench messing with his head?

There wasn't time to wonder about it. Jackson still needed to give Jesse and the others—Khan, too—plenty of time to get out of the building before he brought it down. And there were *still* more Hollows on the landing. More open, screaming mouths, more black coils, lashing and snapping towards him, circling around Khan. Jackson got back to work trying to force them off the broken ledge of the landing, with little success. There were just too many. Dozens. And they weren't waiting in line to tear him apart. They were at him like a pack of dogs.

Were they climbing out? He could no longer tell. The stairwell was tar black with smoke, putrid with the scent of scorched death. And there was something else in the air, too, something that twisted like the shadow of a flame, striking at the fire surrounding Khan, shrinking and diffusing it, forcing him into a corner. Something was wrong.

And something *hurt*.

Jackson grabbed a handful of tangled hair and yanked at the Hollow who had her teeth buried in the tendon behind his knee, hurling her into the basement.

Reeling, he backed away from the countless fingers and teeth, and slacked against the scalding metal door, forsaking all his firefighter's training for the emptiness in his lungs. He panted for air, pulling in only smoke and something else, something that felt like thorns against his windpipe. The same feeling coursed through his arms and legs; it circled his throat and filled his chest.

He stared through the black haze at his own forearm, and saw the long gash there, spilling over with blood and thick, gray fluid. Just a laceration, a cut. Nothing. No big deal.

Before his eyes, the gash split another four inches, tore itself wider and deeper.

And behind his knee. Around his neck. Both his hands. It was all over him, spreading and tearing, everywhere they had touched him.

"Jackson!"

The door behind him thumped. "Jackson! Let me in!"

Jesse, you fucking idiot. Jackson slumped around to face the door, cupping his hands against the dirty glass of the tiny window, unable to see out. *Must've jumped through one of those chutes.*

He opened his mouth to shout, to say whatever it would take to make Jesse go away, but the pleas outside suddenly reached a fierce level of hysterics. And then they just became screaming. Awful, wordless screaming. The door banged and shook against Jackson's butchered hands.

Jesse wasn't beating on the door, he realized. He was being beaten *into* the door.

They were everywhere. Not just the stairwell.

Jackson grappled at the doorknob. "Jesse! Hang on!"

The door didn't budge. Shit. Of course. He'd welded the bolt himself. He could un-weld it—

He never got the chance. Bodies slammed into him from behind, pressing him into the door, ripping him sideways. The door spun away from him, along with the floor and the broken railing. He flailed, flipped, twisted in the air, watched the edge of the landing above slip out of reach.

Jesse wasn't going to catch him this time. He fell.

He fell to the bottom of the stairwell. Into Hell, a fiery mosh pit of bodies, still jumping and moving and moaning, spouting gobs of black plasma for heads and arms, sticking and melting into one another amid the flames. Jackson never felt the hard concrete floor, only the hot, squirming forms that crumpled beneath him. Without pause, more of them toppled over him like displaced water, one solid wave of disconnected hands and gasping mouths, pulling and tearing and burning.

He could bring the entire stairwell down and flatten every single one of them. He could do more than that. He could drive all the broken fragments into the earth and compress them until the whole place and the Hollows themselves were nothing but dust—

His reaching, grasping fingers touched the basement door, and he heard *it* again. He heard it somehow without actually *hearing* it, the same way Khan had heard it before charging down the stairs. There was laughter on the other side of that door. Death's laughter.

They will seek him.

And he will seek them.

Jackson roared and banged his fist against the door once, furiously. The side of his mangled hand split open like a rotten peach, and then burning limbs dragged him under.

CHAPTER 20

Everyone stopped walking.

"Thunder, maybe," said Corin. He looked to Ghi. "Would you be able to tell?"

The thought had clearly never occurred to Ghi. He let his mouth hang open for a few seconds before giving an answer. "I—I'm pretty sure I would. And I'm pretty sure it wasn't."

Hell, I could have told them it wasn't thunder. Thunder doesn't shake the ground so hard that you almost fall over.

"And the screaming?" I demanded. I couldn't have been the only person who'd heard it.

"That was just the wind," said Abe, with not quite believable assurance. His explanation did have some credit; no one could deny the cold gusts of air blowing through the old building, kicking up dust and swinging stray doors on their decaying hinges.

We started walking again, much faster than before.

The ground level was way bigger than I'd imagined on the way in. The gray daylight had slightly diluted the solid darkness since then, so much that we could see all the way to the far corners of the factory floor. My empty insides churned and sank when I saw a line of mismatched sedans, caked with drying mud, on the far end. I pointed at them with the hand I could still feel.

Ghi and Corin looked at me.

"I don't think those were here before," I said.

Ghi and Corin looked at Abe.

"Luna Latum?' Corin asked.

Abe shook his head. "Doubtful."

"Luna Latum?" I frowned.

"Friends," said Ghi.

More walking. More quickly.

The quarry's administrative offices were walled off at the nearest end of the building, and beyond them was the fire exit through which my companions had entered. That would be the safest and fastest way out, they told me, less conspicuous than trying to break through the huge loading dock doors, which were locked. They needn't have wasted the breath. *Rip open the biggest, loudest door you can find, boys,* I thought, *and see if I care, so long as it leads out of this place.*

We reached the promised corridors after five more minutes of stop-start motion, pausing at every small sound. A set of flimsy steel doors stood open before us, frozen in mid-swing by rust, and beyond them glowed the dirty yellow beacon of fluorescent lighting. One by one, we stepped sideways through the half-open portal, breathing just a little easier. That much closer to getting out of there.

This relatively small section of the building was nothing more than a few looping hallways—connecting offices, supply closets, bathrooms, all the smaller spaces that required walls. Most of the bulbs along the ceiling were burnt out or busted, and what little light the rest gave off was absorbed by the smudged, drab walls and dull metal doors. We started down the dingy linoleum path to freedom, and I just had to assume that the guys remembered which way the exit was.

Corin compulsively checked his Sabre phone, even though it had done nothing to attract his attention. No buzzing. No messages. His lips were pressed into a hard line. "I don't like this."

No one liked this, but no one said a word. We wouldn't know if the others had made it out until we got outside ourselves.

Turning the first corner, I picked up on a subtle, gradual change of pace, and my anxiety skyrocketed. Corin and Ghi were looking at one another uneasily. They slowed down, breathing deeply through their noses, before stopping altogether.

"That's new," Corin whispered. "That wasn't here on the way in."

Ghi shook his head.

I didn't get what the problem was. I just saw a hallway that split off into two directions at the end. Closed doors. Greasy walls. More old, humming lights. The smell, though, couldn't be missed. I pulled the collar of Corin's coat up around my nose.

"You mean the stench?" I mumbled.

It was beyond rancid. It was rained-on roadkill bad. It was "the fridge broke while we were on vacation" bad. It was was the smell of death.

Dead death.

"I know that smell," Abe said.

He tapped his fingers for a long moment while we stared at him, not wanting to alarm us with his words. When he finally embellished, it was with a very careful tone.

"I *think* there's been a fight."

Corin and I paused to deliberate exactly what he had meant by that. Ghi, on the other hand, started walking again, walking toward the smell. Ignoring the warning curses Corin hissed after him, he stopped at the hallway's end, put his hands to the wall, and leaned around cautiously—so *unbearably* slowly—to look around the corner.

I was standing behind Corin at that point, peering around him, holding my breath. We both jumped when Ghi threw a hand to his face and pressed his back to the wall. Whatever he'd seen, it was astonishing, and apparently disgusting—but not dangerous. He gave us one startled look before stepping entirely beyond the corner, a hand still mashed to his face in clear disgust.

With his other hand, he beckoned us all, and only after turning the corner did it hit us like a wall, too, both the smell and the sight.

"Jesus," Corin breathed.

"What *happened* to them?" Ghi hadn't taken his eyes off the scene.

I gagged down the urge to dry heave and dove into my sweatshirt. Would this never end? Had I not seen the worst already?

No, I hadn't. Because this was hell. I know a thing or two about hell now. And in hell, there is no *worst*. Hell is knowing that there is always the potential for things to be worse, increasingly, over and over and over again without limit.

And in hell, 'worse' is always just around the corner.

I was aware, even without being told, that they couldn't hurt us. None of them were moving. They were mere carcasses, finished shells, no longer Hollows. That part of them was gone, done away with somehow. There was nothing left to them, no black matter to animate the bodies.

Or the pieces.

If I had to guess, I'd say about fifteen. Some of them were easy enough to count, clearly identifiable as individuals. Skeletons with skin, and not in a starved sense, but a literal sense. All their flesh was compressed tightly to the bone, like cling-wrap. Not a molecule of air remained in any part of them, as if it had all been drawn out by some violent and instant vacuum.

The rest were impossible to count. Blobs of skin lay ballooned beyond recognition, stretched to translucence, popped, scattered. A bloated stomach here, a ruptured face over there, littering the floor. The memory of the guy in the body bag seemed appealing in comparison, fond even. There was nothing in my imagination capable of doing this. And yet the proof was lying in bits and shreds at my feet.

Too close to my feet.

I backed a few paces, still holding my breath. Abe brushed past, went straightaway to the closest carcass, and knelt down to examine it. Ghi followed, and Corin passed them both, picking his way to the corner of the L-shaped hallway, where most of the carnage seemed to converge. I stayed exactly where I was.

"These were old, very old," Abe muttered, prodding a ribcage wrapped in greasy brown flesh. "No blood whatsoever. And the smell. The smell can sometimes tell you. Fascinating."

Ghi hunched over behind him, staring at the corpse's blind, cavernous eye sockets, the mess of inverted cartilage that had somehow been a nose before. He fought hard to swallow before he could say what he was thinking with appropriate firmness.

"I think Jesse did this."

Jesse? I panicked at the thought of him anywhere near this place or these things. The image would not register.

But Abe nodded. "I agree. Sucked the air right out of them. Or expanded it. If I had to guess, I'd say he had a tangle with them, alright."

"And I'd say he won," Ghi stood up and immediately almost tripped over a set of imploded remains.

"I hope you're right," said Corin. He was standing at the end of the hall, staring down a shorter, dead end hallway with a blank and sternly composed expression. "Abe?"

"Yes."

"You said there was no blood?"

"That's right."

"Come here, please."

All three of us approached him, not just Abe, and that didn't seem to please Corin. He said nothing, though, and as we drew closer, one of my feet slipped out from under me. I managed to latch onto Ghi's elbow before falling onto anything disgusting, and glanced down. My foot had slid over a splatter of blood, a sticky pool of scarlet shining under the harsh lights.

I steadied myself and looked down the shorter hallway. Blood cut a trail along the floor and painted a broken smear along the wall, making a ruddy chain all the way to the solitary door at the end.

The next few seconds were a race to that door, all four of us fighting to be the first to reach what we each dreaded seeing. I knew what would be on the other side, and I knew that it would cost me the most. I think that's how

I got there first.

I flung the door open, hitting something that was on the floor as I did. A blast of air instantly whipped the hair out of my face, and for one confused instant I thought I had stepped outside. I saw movement and nearly screamed before realizing that it was my own backlit reflection in a mirror. Water was running, and there was a strange, rhythmic rumble against my ear drums. While clambering for the light switch I nearly tripped over him.

The lights hummed on and I saw a small bathroom. He'd left the sink on, and murky, clay-colored water was brimming over its edges and streaming to the greasy tile floor, close to his head. There wasn't a strand of blonde left unstained. All of it was either clay brown, blood red, or black. The blackest black.

Imagine tar. Nicotine tar, the kind you see swallowing the set of lungs in that disgusting poster you were forced to sit next to in Health class. Imagine that festering out of Freddy Kruger's skin. And blood. And shredded, blackened tissue.

Now imagine that it's not Freddy Kruger.

It's your boss.

Okay, sure. Your friend.

Fine. I'll admit it.

Your *best* friend.

My best friend is lying belly-up on a filthy bathroom floor, hardly recognizable under a layer of open, weeping sores—a layer of *decay*. For one awful, eternal moment, I am positive that he is dead. But the breezy rumble in my ears coincides with the jarring rise and fall of his chest, a movement which proves he is not dead. Each time he draws a breath, the air in the room changes. It changes even within my own chest, avoiding the pull of my lungs.

His eyes lock onto me with definite recognition, but he doesn't speak and his face doesn't change. It is distorted, twisted into a picture of fury. He sucks the air between his teeth, which are bloody and grated forcefully together. The spidery wounds covering his skin have soaked his clothes through. His wrists are stripped and mangled, and an indiscernible mire circles his neck, like he's been throttled with barbed wire. A similar mess spreads from the corner of his mouth to his ear, leaking thick black ink. It is incomprehensible, nauseating—but I can't *not* look, because it's Jesse.

This is not the worst thing I have seen. But it is an image which comes to mind more often than I would like: after a nightmare, before opening a door, or whenever I need a reminder of what the Hollows were capable of.

I hadn't moved a muscle. Someone had to nudge me sideways to get through the door. I was vaguely aware of other people sliding into the room behind me. Ghi closed the door and locked it. Corin leaped to shut the sink off, and Abe got straight to business.

He crouched to the floor beside Jesse, one arm already buried in his shoulder bag, digging, producing an arsenal of hypodermic syringes, bottles, thread. Jesse kept looking at me, and I kept doing nothing. Ghi and Corin remained silent. Abe was doing the talking, fast and serious.

"Did they breath into you?" he asked. It was the most important question in the world.

Jesse's eyes swiveled away. He jerked his chin from side to side.

No. They hadn't.

Abe nodded. "Excellent. That's very good."

I had been acquainted with Abe for maybe fifteen minutes, so I didn't pick up on the lack of enthusiasm in his voice, the absence of his aloof, jovial nature. But I did notice the nervous way Corin and Ghi looked at each other then.

A repetitive sound invaded my attention. *Zipp! Ripp!*—a sound like a zip-lock bag being slowly opened. My throat closed around the sting of bile. Jesse's skin was making that sound.

The wounds were *moving*.

They expanded—sometimes slowly, sometimes in surges—as if unseen hands were still pulling apart the edges. More of the dark fluid came spilling out with every additional torn inch, mingling with the blood and the stagnant water which covered the floor.

"You have a lot of control over how well this goes, Jesse. It's very important that you understand that," Abe was saying, positioning himself in Jesse's line of vision. He sounded less like a doctor, and more like someone about to diffuse a nuclear bomb.

"It spreads deeper and more quickly when you move, when your heart rate goes up, when you panic, understand? Help is coming, but you have to be still and focus. Keep it together. Calm. Got it?"

Jesse nodded once but he looked no more calm than before. That was Abe's cue. He didn't count or declare a warning, just swiftly plunged the first needle down.

I turned and faced the wall, and I shook. From cold, nausea, terror, but above all, anger. How was this real, and how was it allowed to happen? To Jesse? To any of them? I wanted to know just who exactly had decided that Jesse Cannon was a god. He so clearly wasn't. And now he was going to die here, very soon, in this ugly place, because someone had made a mistake. I could have told that someone—that diviner, that ghost, whoever it was—that Jesse doesn't think ahead. That he can't focus for more than ten seconds on anything other than a sheet of music or a nice ass. That he's allergic to mildew and most fabric softeners. That his left ankle needs daily attention, whether he wants it or not, or it will get stiff. I could have told them what a mistake they were making, and to leave him alone, to pick someone else.

When I turned back around again, Abe was on his third or fourth syringe. Jesse's eyes were shut tightly. The air had stopped moving because he was holding his breath. I noticed Corin looking on, smoothing the bandages around his own wrist, anxious cynicism carving extra lines on his face. How many needles and little bottles had it taken to stop the death from eating away at just his arm alone?

Abe wouldn't be able to do enough. What was a finite number of little vials, compared to all that damage? It was like tossing two Tylenols down the neck of a beheaded man.

"Jesse," Ghi spoke up tentatively. He had to ask. "Can you tell us what happened to Jackson and Khan?"

Jesse opened his eyes.

"I don't know," he said, spitting the words through his teeth. His voice was raw and cracked. "There were more. In the stairs."

Everyone grew quiet while that sank in.

"More?" Ghi repeated. "How many more?"

The air pressure in the room was starting to change dramatically again. I could feel it with my skin, and with the walls of my lungs. Jesse was losing it. I moved away from the wall, pushing past Ghi.

"Would you back off?" I snapped at him, getting down to my knees beside Jesse and pressing my palms onto the slimy floor. "You're just making him panic."

Ghi closed his mouth mid-breath because I was absolutely right. Beside me, Abe discarded an empty vial and stood up, stepping over to Corin and motioning Ghi along with him. The three started speaking amongst themselves, running over one another with their words.

"What's taking the hunters so long?" Corin asked heatedly.

"I really don't know." Abe's voice. "They should have been here by now."

"Will they even be able to do anything—?"

I blocked them out and watched Jesse's mauled face, trying stupidly to think of something encouraging to say and coming up with nothing. I wanted so badly to apologize for doubting him, to tell him that I wished I'd never found that phone. More than anything, I wanted to say that I would withdraw my two weeks' notice and work for him through retirement, would never complain again about a single demand, would even get that stupid haircut he'd been begging me to try, anything at all, if he would just keep breathing long enough for help to come. I couldn't force a single word out, though, which is just as well. Jesse beat me to it.

"Oh, honey," he said. "You look *awful*."

I blinked.

Jesse, I reminded myself. Still Jesse.

"You've looked better yourself," I said.

The slightest smile caused the side of his face to split open further, and he clenched his jaw ruefully.

"—we'll just have to move him," Ghi was saying.

"Only if it's necessary."

"I'd say it's necessary," Corin balked. "We can't just wait in here for them to tear us all to pieces."

"I should go check the stairs, before we do anything." Ghi again. If anything was said after that, I didn't catch it. Jesse found one of my hands and gripped it tightly, his fingers digging into my palm.

"Go," he ordered.

"What?" I stared cluelessly as terror began to swirl behind his eyes. "Where? With Ghi?"

"Anywhere," he heaved. "Everybody. Out."

The pressure in the room plummeted. I felt something like a pulse rippling against my skin, and an impossible wind began to pick up, circling in an ominous, quickening pattern.

Like a predator.

"Go," said Jesse.

"Okay, okay. Wait." I started to pull away, but Jesse's grip suddenly tightened down like a bear trap around my fingers. He inhaled sharply, ceaselessly, and the air circling the room became a violent gale. Jesse's skin began turning gray all over, and the hem of his shirt was turning a darker and darker shade of red, blooming with blood. The others pushed in around me, looming above us.

"You're not focusing," Abe warned over the moaning airstreams. "You're panicking."

Of course he's panicking, I wanted to scream. He's rotting alive.

And dying. And taking us all with him.

I looked down again and felt my face go hot with horror. Jesse hadn't left the floor, but he wasn't exactly touching it either. The tiles beneath him were all visible in murky, ghost-like detail, and I realized, with shock as powerful as a physical slap, that I could see *through* him.

Jesse's eyes flashed wide at the ceiling, his mouth gaping open in frantic astonishment. The wind was blasting down with almost enough strength to topple me over.

"What's happening to him?" I pleaded for anyone to explain. His hand. I could no longer feel it, even though one look convinced me that I was still holding it with my own. Reflexively, I pulled away from the non-existent grasp, shuddering when Jesse's fingers evaporated into a trail of suntanned smoke.

No, no, no, no.

"How do we stop *that*?" Corin was livid, too loud. "Is this how it happens? Is he—?"

"Becoming?" Ghi finished the question.

I watched that dreamy wisp of color, a fragment of my honest-to-god best friend, vanish into a swift stream of air. My jaw locked in an open position, my only breath was trapped somewhere in the top of my throat.

This is not happening.

Abe began backing slowly, very carefully, towards the door. "It's best for now that we exit..."

Like hell.

"No one's leaving! No one! How could you leave!? I'm not leaving!" I screamed hysterically, filling the hallways with shrill echoes. To my credit, I was suffering from gangrene by that point, had an estimated fever of 103 degrees, and had just watched someone's hand vaporize. My capacity for good sense does have its limits.

"Jordan—" Corin gripped my shoulder as if to pull me off the floor. I flung his hand away and bellowed the basest of four-letter words at him before crouching closer to Jesse.

"Goddamnit! Stop this right now, Jesse!" I shouted, grappling at his phantom arm. His elbow billowed and swirled out of my grasp, dissipating. "STOP IT!"

Ghi clamped his arms around me and snatched me off the floor, smothering me completely with the inside of his elbow and pinning me against his own body. And suddenly it was Jesse screaming and not me. The air in the room burst outward as if from a bomb, coiling and rolling like a wild animal, crushing us against the walls and shaking the locked metal door in its frame. It pounded across our eardrums, howling in a frightening harmony with Jesse's wailing, which never paused for an inhale. If we stuck around much longer, we were going to wind up looking like those Hollows out in the hallway.

"Hurry it up!" Ghi shouted over the top of my head at Abe, who was fumbling to unlock the door. I twisted and kicked unsuccessfully, trying to get back down to the floor, and Ghi locked his arms around me so tightly in response that I could feel his rapid heartbeat through all his sweaters. "Can you lift him?" he shouted at Corin over the crying wind.

Corin glared up from the floor, where he was pinning Jesse's shoulders down, trying to ground him in any way possible. Jesse himself—what was left of him—was alternating between dissolving transparency and opaque rage. How do you lift *air*? Especially when it's mad as hell and about to die?

"I don't think that would be a good idea right now!" Corin shouted back.

There was a loud, resounding crack as the unlocked door blew open and strained against its hinges. Abe tumbled out into the hallway like a man lost in a storm, and Ghi paused with me against the wall, stalled by the obvious conflict. He wanted all of us away from Jesse and out of the building. But simply abandoning Jesse was unthinkable.

He looked to Corin, who was still on his knees, doing all he could to pin Jesse to the floor and to reality. His intention to stay was clear; he made no move to follow us.

"I'll come back," Ghi said. Corin looked up, and the two of them may as well have been in that Manhattan alley again, reading one another, boiling every uncertainty down to trust. Then he nodded, and we left without him.

The same powerful gale that had blown the door open buffered us out into the hallway, slapping the wet clothes against our bodies with punctuated whipping sounds. Ghi threw his weight into the door, struggling to shut it against the wind, releasing one of his arms from me in the effort. He made no progress until the vicious air turned on itself, changing directions and sucking the door shut with such hurricane fierceness that, had Ghi not let go, it would have taken his hand off.

We were cut off from Corin and Jesse instantly, from everything in that bathroom except the sounds of raging wind and seamless wailing from inside. The door itself did nothing to block that, and we didn't stick around to listen, not for a second. With a firm grip on my hand, Ghi charged down the hallway and around the first corner, Abe fast at our heels. I started to speak up several times, to beg or to argue. I didn't want to leave Jesse, and I was afraid to be out here, where *they* were.

There were more, he'd said.

I didn't want to die either way, but I definitely preferred an instantaneous death-by-vacuum to an end spent feeling myself decompose.

There wasn't going to be any bargaining with Ghi, though, and so I said nothing. His feet moved us ahead, unfaltering, while mine tripped along beside him. He looked terrified, just as terrified as I felt, but his terror seemed to fuel him forward rather than petrify him. Without hesitation, he led us down the hall, past the carnival of shrunken and bloated bodies, continuing swiftly around another corner.

"Do be a bit more cautious," Abe panted, hustling to keep up. "Hollows could be anywhere."

I stumbled, and all the lines on Ghi's face hardened. "Then I'll give them something to wait for." He tightened his already painful grip on my hand and kept walking, rightly sensing that if we stopped for one second, then some of us wouldn't be easily persuaded to move again.

The walls of the long corridor rang with our footsteps and the fading, horrible sounds we'd left behind. A sustained rumble from elsewhere was beginning to take our attention, growing gradually louder the farther we went. I wondered fleetingly whether it was storming outside, if we were getting close to an actual exit, when the steady element of Abe's footsteps dropped out of our cadence. He'd paused at a thick steel door with a tiny, sooty window.

"Just a minute," he spoke up, and Ghi halted, pivoting both of us around.

"Stairwell," said Abe. He pressed his hand against the door to push it open, then immediately pulled away, drawing in a sharp breath.

"What is it?" Ghi let go of me and stepped toward him.

Abe wrung his hand, grimacing. "Door's hot," he croaked.

After a second's contemplation, Ghi spun to the door and pushed it with the sole of his shoe. No dice. He added weight to the foot, and still nothing. So he backed away and kicked the door—a fast, downward kick, the kind of kick police use on TV —which resulted only in him shouting, "Beans!" and hopping around on his other foot for a moment. At least I think it was "beans". Maybe it was some Arabic curse word that just sounded a whole lot like "beans". I keep forgetting to look into it.

Abe hadn't been exaggerating. The door was *hot*. The surface itself rippled with heat, enough to be felt from a foot away. Without a doubt, there was one serious fire going on inside that stairwell. And that fact seemed to completely captivate Ghi. Khan could very well be in there, he realized, possibly in a state similar to Jesse's.

Which was a great reason to get the hell away, in my opinion.

Withdrawing his hand into the sleeve of his sweatshirt—and into the two or three sweaters underneath—Ghi gripped the doorknob, turned it, and pushed. The door didn't budge, didn't even a wiggle. *Like it's welded shut*, he thought, not realizing how close to the truth he was. He tried a few more times, kicked the door once more, and banged at it lividly with both forearms before realizing he was wasting time. His hands slid into his hair and he leaned back against the wall, avoiding our eyes.

I've seen this face on Ghi, many times. It's stronger than an expression of despair, stronger than raw guilt. It's the expression that says what he's too stubborn to say out loud: *I can't do anything.*

As someone who'd needed two years of physical therapy in order to function outside a hospital, Ghi was well acquainted with the feeling of not being able to do anything. As a ward of whatever doctor and subsequent nation he'd since been handed over to, he'd pretty much become a pro at it. But now, even with these untold abilities—including the ability to launch fucking *lightning from his hands*—not much had changed. People around him were dropping dead, and he couldn't do anything about it.

"I'm sorry," I said. It was a dumb, meaningless thing to say. It wasn't my fault I'd wound up in that place. It wasn't my fault they'd been reckless enough to come after me. But they had, and so I had to say something.

Ghi looked at me. *I can't do anything.* But he could. He dropped his hands and stepped past me.

"Let's hurry," he said.

He didn't grab my hand and he didn't have to. When he started walking, Abe and I were right behind him. We left behind the burning stairwell and whatever—whoever—was trapped inside it.

A distant, escalating howl rang out. Jesse, without a doubt. I pushed myself to walk faster, choking back a rush of anguished shame. *Just keep walking,* was my disgusted, numbed mantra. *Just keep walking.* A wide set of elevator doors loomed ahead at the corridor's end, where another main hallway started. I don't know if taking that elevator became Abe's idea the moment he saw it, or if he was still trusting Ghi with the original exit plan.

It was about to be the only option we had, regardless.

The sound was incredible. I thought it was an explosion of some kind. A deep, powerful booming, without prelude, and without end. The sound of it drowned out the roar of the fire. It was louder than the distant howling wind, louder than Jesse, and growing louder. I couldn't have been more wrong. It was not an explosion.

Ghi stopped and spun around, and we all froze there, straining to comprehend the tremoring white noise and the crashing, breaking chorus that accompanied it. The linoleum trembled beneath our feet as the booming sound got closer and closer, the vibrations bigger and bigger.

Whatever it was, it was coming.

Abe scrambled to the elevator and gave the "UP" button a good slap, half sure that nothing would happen. To our complete and grateful astonishment, however, the doors slid shakily open. I dove into the rickety elevator without a second thought. Without a first thought, for that matter.

"Ghi . . . ," Abe said, for once using a senior tone. He crossed the threshold after me and held the door open.

Ghi hadn't moved. Still halfway down the hallway, he was a heartbeat away from running back to that bathroom, however useless it would have been. I know he was. But Ghi understood what had happened back there. He understood what was coming, *who* was coming, a split second before he saw it.

He turned and ran to us, to the elevator, as fast as he could.

Behind him, all the way down the other end of the corridor, a tidal wave crashed into the wall.

Floor to ceiling, the massive swell of water rolled back into itself, gathering strength, and then plunged forward down the hall, driven by the inexhaustible torrent behind it. Corin had not survived Jesse's death. And, like

Jesse, his body now had no end—only places to flow, things to smash.

Things like us.

Ghi smacked into the back of the elevator, bounced, turned, searching frantically. He lunged for the control panel and pushed the "close door" button as we watched the thousands of tons of water building, racing toward us. "Come on! *Come on!*" he screamed, pushing repeatedly, his finger tapping so fast it blurred.

The wave undulated upwards, slapped against the ceiling lights, which burst in pops and fizzes as more water rolled forward underneath. Forty yards. Twenty yards.

Ten yards. The elevator doors slid to a close with a tired sound, shutting out the sight, the monstrous fluid wall. There was a hum, a tug. There was upward movement for a fraction of a second. We looked at one another, hopeful that we had made it, knowing that we had not.

Then the elevator quaked and plummeted under the impact.

CHAPTER 21

Fleeting images and feelings. No order, no definitive beginning or end. Something like a meadow. Something like riding a horse, a rushing feeling. A singing falsetto. A hot, tingly, smothering feeling.

It was the blood rushing to my face.

My eyes opened to blindness. My windpipe met a roadblock. I was crushed under a dead weight. Thousands of tons of water? The panels of a crumpled elevator? No. Arms, legs. Warm, heavy. Ghi, Abe.

Something buzzed. My sight returned because there was light. Ghi, flat on his back. Panting, arm stretched toward the top of the elevator, where the dead light flickered feebly at his command and became steady. He let his arm drop, rolled his legs off of us. His face was inches from mine.

"You okay?"

I made a noise that sounded affirmative.

The world bobbed back and forth. I heard the water rushing, slipping by all around the elevator's exterior and down the shaft. Ghi began to roll up to his feet, but grimaced and paused. He rolled to his stomach instead and tried again, ambling up one leg at a time. Using only his left arm, he tugged Abe off of me as gently as possible, while his right arm hung down at a strange angle. Dislocated shoulder.

I looked down at myself carefully, noting with distant relief that all of my bones were right where they belonged—where I couldn't see or feel them. No longer crushed beneath Abe, I took a full breath, and the oxygen made stars dance in front of my eyes. I began to roll forward.

"Hey, don't move yet," Ghi ordered in my direction. He was hunched over Abe. I ignored him and stood up. I was fine. My shoulder blades felt like one gigantic bruise waiting to happen, my head weighed two-hundred pounds, and my ears rang, but I was fine.

Then my vision blacked. It returned seconds later, with a blue tint. I felt very silly, then screamingly fearful, then silly again, all in less than a second.

"He's breathing. I think he's okay," someone said. It took me a moment to remember that it was only Ghi. I rubbed my eyes and ordered myself to pay attention.

"I'm going to need your help here," he wheezed, working his good arm under one side of Abe, trying to haul him off the ground. The doctor's body was limp but whole, and he was vaguely conscious enough to groan when lifted. I nodded and staggered over, and we managed to hoist him between us in a suitable enough position. Ghi and I, just two good arms between us. How hilarious. I giggled and it did not feel at all inappropriate.

Ghi stared at me fearfully and pushed a button.

Somehow, the elevator doors were still in working order. They staggered halfway open on their own, and, with a bit of pushing from Ghi's foot, managed to open wide enough for our passage. A coursing sheet of water fell beyond them, forming a solid curtain that flooded into the base of the elevator shaft. We stared at it for a moment, assessing whether or not it held any threat, but at the moment it seemed only harmless and beautiful, like a normal waterfall. Not like the disembodied spirit of someone we knew, blind and bent on destruction.

No time to think about it. Ghi wordlessly tugged Abe forward, and I had no choice but to follow. We squeezed through the door, passed under the pouring water—which was disturbingly warm—and took one steep step out of the disarranged elevator, soaked and shuddering. First the river, and now this. I wondered if I'd ever be completely dry again.

I blinked. The corridor was gone. Behind my starry red vision, my mind warped. There was a delay, and then I understood. We weren't in the corridor. And we hadn't made it to the top level. The elevator had plummeted down a level, all the way down to the bottom of the shaft.

We were standing in the basement.

I had to guess that anyways, because I could see nothing beyond the glow of the elevator lights, shining faintly through the streaming water. Its splashing echoed out far and wide, and a disorienting nausea twisted in my stomach, the opposite of claustrophobia. This place, whatever it was, was massive in terms of open space. Massive and dark.

I turned my head to locate Ghi and almost gasped. My voice multiplied into sightless space, echoing a hundred times over.

"Ghi, your eyes!"

In the closer blackness, I could make out two mirrory, round planes of light, like cat's eyes. Only these eyes weren't reflecting any light. They were making light of their own. I could just make out the planes of Ghi's face, moving when he spoke back, sounding alarmed. "What?"

"Your eyes. They're ... shining."

"Oh," he started forward again, keeping the pace slow for me. "Neat."

I shifted Abe's weight in my good arm, maintaining focus. "What can you see?"

"Not much," he said. "The foundation. Open space. Machines. Big ones, bigger than the elevator. And they got down here somehow, right? So there has to be a very big exit somewhere."

Exactly where that exit was, that was the million dollar question. We dragged Abe along haltingly, staying close to the wall in hopes of discovering an exterior door. Time kept lapsing in confusing bursts. Deep breaths. Twinkly green spots in my eyes, coating the darkness. A thrilling ache split my head in two and a giddy lightness took my limbs. Had I been talking? Had someone else? What had I even been thinking about? I was walking. I couldn't see. Why?

"Jordan?" A voice. Concerned.

Ghi, I reminded myself.

"Just keep talking to me," I said.

"About?"

"Anything." I remembered the weight in my arm, and that it was a person. "Abe. These Luna Latum people. Tell me more about them."

"Okay, but I don't really know much..."

"Whatever, just—just make something up. Talk to me."

"Right, okay," Ghi cleared his throat, creating harsh echoes. "Well, they're on our side, they know all about us, and even more about the Hollows. That woman who tackled me back in New York? She's one of them. Her name is Stella. She was sent to find us and take us home."

"Home."

"To the Elysium. Some island paradise they built for us."

Hunters. Stella. Elysium. It was enough to keep my mind awake and chewing.

"Do you trust them?" I asked.

"I don't know. I might, if they ever get here."

It was getting harder and harder to breathe in the stifling darkness, and Abe just got heavier and heavier. I kept stopping without realizing it, moving again only after we'd nearly pulled him apart by the arms.

"Ghi?"

"Yeah?"

"Do you really not remember?" I puffed. It was becoming difficult to talk, to push the air out. "Who you are?"

I still have no idea why I was asking this. I guess when you sense that you're about to die anyway, you feel like you have a right to know everything. You feel like it's alright to pry into other people's deepest secrets.

"I won't tell, I promise," I said. "Double pinky kiss-kiss."

Ghi paused for a moment, undoubtedly perplexed by my question, much less by my proposed oath. But his answer was solid and truthful. And frankly, disappointing.

"I really don't remember."

Another pause. I struggled to think of another question, but Ghi spoke again before I could come up with one.

"But I really want to. I'd give anything to be able to remember. Even if all I had was my real name, that alone would be enough for me."

That came as a shock to me, which is kind of funny, considering everything else that was going on. "But why?" I blurted. "What if you were really a bad person, a terrorist, like they think? Or what if you weren't, and you find out who your family is, only now you can't go back to them, and—"

"I still want to know," Ghi said firmly, cutting off my rambling assumptions. His eyes flashed a little brighter. "I've thought about those things, I've thought of worse, but I still want to know. More than anything."

I couldn't think of another question after that, and Ghi stopped talking. Or maybe he said more, I don't know. Time again lapsed without my awareness, because the next thing I remember was wobbling on my feet, abruptly free of my one-armed burden. Ghi was laying Abe out on the ground.

"Here, right here." He grabbed me before I could fall over, and guided me down to a sitting position on the stable, frigid floor. In the sharp glow provided by his eyes, I could distinguish something directly overhead, something rectangular and metallic, a platform maybe.

"I'm not going far," Ghi assured me. "I'm just going to make absolutely sure we're going the right way, before I make you go any further, okay? You just sit here with Abe."

I felt myself nodding.

"Don't. Go. Anywhere," he said, giving my shoulder a squeeze with each separate word. And then he walked away, taking the only light with him.

A few seconds or minutes were lost. When I came back to myself, I couldn't see or hear Ghi anywhere. I realized how quickly I was breathing, how dizzy it made me feel, and so that became my focus. After a moment's blind reaching, I found Abe still sprawled out beside me, and I placed a hand on his chest. Rising and falling, rising and falling, steady and slow. It was all I could do to match the pace with my lungs.

It was so cold down there, and I was still soaked to the bone. I let go of

Abe and pulled Corin's coat tightly around me. Corin, who was dead, I remembered. His endless ghost flooding and rampaging down from the floor above. Thrashed to death by a contained hurricane, by Jesse. And Jesse, also dead. My throat and face began to ache, but I composed myself because it was already hard enough to breathe. Sobbing would not have helped matters.

A grating, metallic creak pierced the gigantic chamber's silence. This did not startle or worry me. Every damn thing in this place creaked. I looked up, and feverish relief broke out over every inch of me. Even from a hundred yards away, I could recognize the miraculous crack of daylight, that wonderful slit in the darkness.

Ghi had found a door.

We weren't trapped down here. We were going to make it out. That thought alone undoubtedly added minutes to my life. My vision started adjusting to that wonderful, faint light. I could just make out my own hand in front of my face, the dull shapes of the distant boilers, the form of Ghi, sprinting back to us.

And then my eyes zeroed in on something else, something that made my heart come to a complete stop with a sharp pang, as if it understood that someone was listening to it. I held in the scream that built up in my chest and felt the terror turn me into an instant statue.

Near the center of the colossal basement, unmoving against the flat darkness beyond him, stood a man. Just one man, so far away and small, so solitary, so totally still.

The body always recognizes it first, I've learned. My heart started ramming in my chest in spite of itself, and a million names and instincts and words exploded through my veins. Scream. Flee. Hell. Dangerous. Pray. Run. God. Fear. Pain. Murder. End. Over. Death.

Death. Death. Death. Death. Death.

"They spoke truth," it said.

You've probably never heard the sound of literal death speaking, so let me tell you what it's like:

It is a unified medley, actually, a few different sounds thrown into one. There's a high shrill to it, like a baby crying. Not the crying of a baby who's hungry at night, but the unrelenting, colicky, piercing shriek of a baby that's just been thrown out of a car and abandoned on an icy road.

There's also this whispery undertone to it, a scraping, rattling, airy noise that's almost like a whisper, but far too loud to be classified as one.

And then there's the booming bass, the element that holds it all together and makes it speech. It's solid and sustained, an ongoing and very loud blast of what might be like a planet belching. And it's deep, incredibly deep. It makes James Earl Jones sound like a little school girl.

The result, I can humbly guarantee you, will make you piss yourself.

My vision wheeled until I found Ghi, and I watched him turn to face that voice in one instantaneous, instinctual motion, a motion that was equally as chilling to me as the nearness of death, of Dahrkren himself.

Ghi moved like a mechanism, and that is the only way to describe it. It is a strangely powerful and upsetting thing to see—somebody you know, moving like that. His body snapped upward fluidly, as if programmed to do so, and he stood attentive while every ounce of his being attuned itself to this sudden, singular threat. It was as though each nerve and muscle and bone in his body had only ever existed in this moment. This moment, and no other.

They spoke truth.

Ghi had never heard this voice with his own ears, or seen this figure through his own eyes. But he had heard and seen it just the same, because the light had heard and seen it. He understood fully what was standing there, speaking to him, and in reaction his body and mind flooded with a powerful and white-hot hate, a bristling intolerance, and a desire unlike anything he had ever experienced in either of his lives, both the one he could remember and the one he could not: the irrefutable desire to destroy.

The hate and the desire overwhelmed all fear, erased any trace of it in his gleaming, golden eyes. This moment was all that mattered, the only thing there ever was. This moment was what he had been made for. And it had come too soon.

CHAPTER 22

"They spoke truth," the brain-burning voice repeated itself, though its source had yet to move in any perceptible way. "We come together. We orbit one another without our own awareness, and seek a collision."

Ghi didn't look like he was seeking a collision. Like the speaker, he was standing completely still. His eyes never wavered from Dahrkren's distant figure—not to me, not to the exit; they stayed as focused and unblinking as painted, glowing marbles.

"Though I dislike the idea of being moved by fate, and not of my own volition," Dahrkren continued. Despite the horrifying quality of his voice, his tone was shockingly conversational. "Don't you?"

Ghi didn't respond; he made no sign whatsoever of even hearing the words. Which seemed, of all things, to *disappoint* Dahrkren. Seriously. The first move I ever saw him make was a shrug. A *shrug*. No sweeping, grand gestures. No shaking with villainous laughter, even. This guy, this incarnation of death, lifts his robed shoulders, drops his gaunt face, lets out this sort of exasperated, hell-rattling sigh, and shrugs.

I guess he'd imagined the Vessel would be a little more engaging.

"You are aware, yes, that your brothers have all perished?" he asked with disdain. "Did you feel it?"

Still no answers from Ghi.

"Please. I am only curious," coaxed Dahrkren. The many pitches of his speech were surreally stoic, strangely gentle. "When you killed my own, I felt it. After all this time, finally, I felt it. They were a part of me, you know. And to me, their passing was like feeling my own fingers being broken."

I heard a startling crack very close to me, instantaneous with a numb spasm in the long-stifled nerve endings of my left hand. I looked down.

The guy had range. My pinky finger was sticking out, broken at the knuckle, perfectly perpendicular to my palm. On the bright side, at least he'd picked the hand I could barely feel.

I must not have elicited the desired reaction, because the adjacent ring finger then did the very same thing, right in front of my eyes. Just snapped at the knuckle and bent backwards. I shrieked out loud, out of sheer surprise and disbelief. Ghi's head jerked sideways, not even a whole inch, before he caught himself. He would not take his eyes off the threat, not for anything.

There was a smile in Dahrkren's voice now. "And when my eldest were destroyed, here in this place, I felt it as if my legs had been crushed."

A fast series of gristling, snapping sounds followed his words. I braced, but there was no additional pain. It was Abe's leg that had been smashed; pulverized at the kneecap by sick thought alone. Being unconscious, Abe merely made a soft sighing sound, almost pleasant. I bit my lips together. No screaming, no screaming, no screaming.

"Did you feel likewise when your brothers died?"

Ghi's skin was beginning to change color. His hands tremored at his sides.

"Then you must understand why I wanted only the witness, to suck the marrow from her bones, to swallow her heart and her memories whole. I simply wanted to see what she had seen, to better understand how you had done these things to me.

"And yet our very natures have brought us together, effortlessly. So very interesting." The voice picked up momentum, a ravenous, scathing edge. "And now it seems that I know all that I require about the Vessel. That you are nothing, that you are not a concern. Do I need her heart now? I think not. I think I will silence it."

I was still putting it all together: the killer groupies, the U-Haul full of Hollows, all sent to gauge the Vessel's mortality. Some of the oldest Hollows in existence—Dahrkren's own road posse—all fried or imploded to smithereens here in this building.

It was as if Dahrkren had wanted to see how *little* it would take to do the Vessel in, to somehow quantify their weakness, while still ensuring that they wouldn't survive long enough to become a problem. And here before him was the last one, singled out, ready for the taking.

So why was he wasting all this time breaking fingers and talking about sucking on marrow memories or whatever? Was he just enjoying himself? Getting his kicks from all the taunting and torment? Maybe. I guess if you've spent millennia in dark, unpleasant places, waiting for your enemy to show up, you'd kind of want to drag things out a little bit.

Or maybe . . . was he afraid of Ghi? Now that he had seen what the Vessel were capable of? Was he looking for a weakness, trying to create a distraction?

And what had he said about silencing what? Whose heart?

Ghi still hadn't moved or spoken in all this time, but I saw the tension in his limbs increase as a pulse shot through the room, dragging the temperature down to an impossibly bitter degree in just one instant. The parts of my body that were not already numbed by cold and trauma seemed to lose all feeling. Beneath my hand, Abe's chest shuddered. The proximity of death was palpable in so many ways; the air was suddenly musky and reeking, nearly too thin to breathe, and it was filled with an awful sound, a booming, gloating, sound, worn out brakes with a touch of giddiness.

Death was laughing again.

"Unnecessary!" Ghi broke, calling out over the sound. "You've saved this for me. I'm here now, aren't I?"

"So you are." The hideous laughter melted into speech. "Now show me. Show me how you will take me from this world," the voice said, and Dahrkren moved forward. I could make out the long pale robe he wore, opened in the front to reveal a bare and shockingly white chest. The garment hardly moved with him as he took that single step forward, and no more.

He knew he didn't need to move any more than that. He knew that Ghi was bound, blind, buried under thousands of years of instincts, all directing him at the speed of light. Sooner or later, Ghi would move, whether he wanted to or not.

"Show me," the voice broke like a wave.

And it started. Ghi stalked forward, fluid and robotic at the same time, as powerless as a moth confronted by a lighthouse. Not a single tendon hesitated, not a moment of his focus shifted. He *wanted* this. His skin lit up like a paper lantern as he advanced, and Dahrkren's hideous peal of laughter raked outwards again in response.

"Yes!" the awful voice said, tenacious, eager, and so much louder than before. Ghi's steps quickened, his arms quivered visibly. Sizzling veins of purple-white light danced on his luminous skin; his eyes were blank porcelain, wide and brightly shining. The air sapped thinner and colder, and the voice ever louder, both deep and shrill, unspeakably loud.

"Yes, show me. When do I shrink?" it squealed and wailed as Ghi drew closer. "When am I overcome? Where is this fury I am supposed to fear?" A million nails against a chalk board. Pure bleach pouring into my ears, into my brain.

Then the loudest sound yet. Ghi's arm swung outward like a boxer's, though yards remained between himself and Dahrkren. A blinding white lance of lightning erupted from his thrown hand and sang out into the open space with a single, ear-splitting crack. I heard a chorus of shattering glass, followed by sharp and overlapping echoes. And above all this, the most unholy scream, a sound that would make you beg to be deaf.

The light was there and gone so quickly, leaving a solid white bar across my vision. I could not tell whether it had hit Dahrkren or whether he had deflected it somehow, whether his bellowing noises meant pain, anger, amusement, or all three. Before I could observe anything else, I saw the snow white skin of his chest burst open.

He split apart from clavicle to navel and released a monstrous cloud of streaming black ink, which—illogically and instantly—became two, three, five, ten, fifteen times the size of his body. This all crashed into Ghi with the solid force of a speeding car.

No defense seemed possible. Ghi's only reaction was a delayed yell of astonishment as the black wave surged outward, bearing him away from its motionless source, solidifying and soaring until it collided with the concrete wall some thirty yards away. The yell ended with a conclusive yelp and the hollow, wet sound of bones breaking.

I didn't have time to turn away or cover my eyes. Irreverent to velocity, the phantom limb retracted from the wall, its many fingers twisting around Ghi and dragging him across the floor at terrific speed. Wild sparks and gnarled claws of light crackled over and around him, sizzling the blackness it touched but never getting rid of enough of it. He was overwhelmed and outmatched. Heinously.

Dahrkren was watching all of this serenely, motionless despite the frenzied tentacles of night writhing out of him. I feared that he intended to swallow Ghi whole, right into his open chest, but the snaking anomaly did not fully rewind. Instead, it arched upwards, jerking Ghi fifteen feet off the floor and slamming him down again.

And again. And again.

I lost count. The violence of it was indigestible, hardly believable at this scale and closeness, something only possible in a cat-and-mouse cartoon. All the slamming, the twisting from side to side so brutally fast, like a dog shaking the life out of something already dead.

I hoped Ghi was already dead. I really, truly hoped he was.

It stopped. Not twenty seconds after it had burst into existence, the blackness melted to the ground and wound itself back into Dahrkren. His skin closed together seamlessly with a sound like fresh paper sifting past fingers.

He strolled, in such a chillingly human way, to where Ghi lay on the ground in one twitching, twisted piece. I understood then what had happened to Jesse, why he'd looked the way he did after facing all those Hollows alone. Only Ghi looked worse, much worse.

My insides sank. He was still alive.

The black wounds were dense and fast, chewing him up at an alarming rate, marring most of him beyond any recognition. His bent arms pushed against the floor but got him nowhere; his legs did nothing. They were dead weight. Broken spine.

The light from his eyes waned; they were wide and rolling, grappling with the comprehension of what had just happened. His chest bowed upward and he gaped his mouth open with shocked effort, marveling that he could not bring air in, nor push any out. Blood erupted in a fountain from his throat instead, spilling with an audible splash out across the floor.

Dahrkren stepped into the ruby puddle and paused there.

Dazzling light crackled and hummed responsively out of Ghi, snapping occasionally into one concentrated blast, like the shock from a downed power line, blind and aimless. Dahrkren ignored this. He pulled one foot back and speared it into Ghi's shattered ribs. Ghi's fingers flexed against the floor. His mouth roared open, but nothing came out but more blood. The rabid, many-toned laughter rang out again, softer than before. It quickly turned into a growl, then a snarling, then a cry of fury.

"Eight! Thousand! Years!" Dahrkren raged, driving each word in with another savage kick. "I suffer beneath you for eight thousand years, and this is your final blow? You can't even survive my outrage? What about my agony? My hunger? My wrath? Who is left to survive that?"

I knew the answer to that one.

All of us.

You and me, folks.

The floor beneath me trembled slightly, coinciding with the fierce rumble of nearby thunder. I watched, dead in so many ways already, just waiting my turn. I watched Ghi's fingers, his eyes, praying that he would just stop, just die already, god or not. The rest of humanity was barred from my mind. I wanted this to be over with. For him, for me.

Dahrkren planted a white, bare foot heavily on Ghi's chest and leaned down low to answer his own question.

"*No one* will be left. *Nothing* will be left."

Ghi's eyes were still on the liquid side of glassy, possibly not seeing a thing, but still alert. It's a comfort now to know that he couldn't give a damn about what Dahrkren was saying, not a word of it. He was not thinking about how the curse had been lifted from Dahrkren, from all the Hollows. He was not lamenting that all the Vessel had failed before they had even begun. Or that death was now free, after thousands of years of cowering, to consume and destroy and spread, wherever and whenever it pleased, to stifle every beating heart until life of any kind became ancient history.

No, Ghi wasn't thinking about any of that. He was only thinking: *Why the hell am I here? Why us?*

The floor shook again, and this time it didn't stop. Another crack of thunder sounded overhead. I heard an explosion, a banging of metal—the door to the stairs being blown right off its hinges.

I heard Dahrkren's surprised gasp, a layered hissing like the brakes of a subway, but I didn't see the look on his face. There was suddenly too much light in that direction, in all directions.

Again, my body reacted before I understood. I shielded my face, buried it into Abe's side. Without thinking, I reached up and clamped my hand down over his eyes, pressed my elbow into his shoulder, trying to anchor us, because my mind was commanding one primal thing:

Hold on.

Just hold on, and don't look.

The wind screamed, thunder cymbaled and snarled without end. I felt the intense, unbearable heat of nearby fire, and heard the crash and spray of water. The ground shook, harder and harder, until it was bucking violently, bringing everything down around us, rattling the platform overhead, our shield. Dahrkren's shrieking, the hideous sound of his pain and shock, was nothing. It all but drowned in the howling and roaring, the thundering and churning, the tremors. The fury he had been begging to witness only minutes ago. The advent of terrible power, fierce, divine, rising.

PART III

ALL THE DIFFERENCE

Every evening during the summer, for a brief period of only about five minutes, the last streams of sunlight coming into the apartment would become unbearably bright. The light bounced between buildings and through the windows in such a direct way, and at just such an angle, that it would blind anyone in the room.

I was protected. I was sleeping on a mattress, in my designated corner, out of the dying sun's aim. So it was Jesse Cannon's voice that woke me up, and not the light.

"All The Difference". That was the name of the song that came out of my CD alarm clock, plugged into the wall next to my head. The same song that had awakened me, always two hours before my night shift, nearly every evening for the past three months.

This was not a coincidence.

I had set the alarm to play that song. It made my roommates homicidal, that particular track, but I wasn't the only person on earth overplaying it. You couldn't go out for lunch without hearing that song at least once, not since it had been featured in some romantic comedy the winter before. And though it thrilled me to see that finally, *finally*, the rest of the world was starting to catch on—the world outside New York, beyond Broadway—it also made me feel sort of . . . *possessive*. I didn't mind sharing him with a city, with opera connoisseurs and lusting fanboys. But I wasn't quite ready to let the rest of the world have him.

Let's get one thing straight: Jesse Cannon was *not* the reason I decided to move to New York. That had been the decision of someone young, bored, and in possession of a useless business administration degree. I moved to

New York because I had this idea in my head that I wanted to be a bartender, and I had friends who'd moved to Queens for grad school. Friends with an extra couple of square feet on the floor of their crumbling, roasting little hot-box apartment. So that's exactly where I wound up, for a little more than a year: on the floor.

New York was incompassionate and tiresome, but it had its saving points. It had cheap thrills and endless opportunities to practice the craft of bartending. It had amusing people and picturesque winters and good pizza. And, for another week at least, it had Jesse Cannon.

Jesse Cannon, born Yeshiv Corsakov.

Jesse Cannon, who'd had to drop out of Juilliard in order to handle all the Broadway acts competing for him.

Jesse Cannon, already huge in Japan.

I had never been a fan before, of anyone or anything. Sure, I had always been fond of the Cardigans and CCR, and I preferred certain brands of macaroni-and-cheese over others, but I'd never been a *fan*. I'd never understood what compelled people to shell out hundreds of hard-earned dollars for tickets, to camp out before shows, to squabble and battle for sweat-soaked T-shirts.

Until Jesse Cannon.

Until I heard one of his songs in a crowded grocery on Boylston, and went, out of inexplicable curiosity, to that first concert. I'll never forget that first performance. I went alone. Seat 32-J. I wept. I clapped until my hands were red and stinging.

Before my first year in the city had passed, I'd sat through maybe fifteen more performances, whatever I could save up for, any chance I could get to see him. He was just so impressive, so original and bizarre and beautiful. The way he played piano, the way he moved, his nightlife reputation in the tabloids. And his voice. Oh, that voice. It was the most perfect thing on earth then, I mean it. It was so clear and full it could just break your heart, without a single catch in it, like a cloudless blue sky. There's no way I can describe how haunting it was, or the way it made people feel. It almost *hurt* to hear it. Can you understand what I mean?

At any rate, it was a good voice to wake up to. It hit me around the first chorus that I didn't really have to be up, that it was my night off, but I rolled off my mattress anyway and cranked up the volume, made the song loud enough to hear in the shower. No one was around to mind. The other two people currently squatting in this one-bedroom unit were still at work—I knew this because we all worked at the same dive bar, a little place frequented by Juilliard kids because of its location, and because it served watercress sandwiches (the ballerinas love those).

Shower. Teeth. Vitamins. All while singing along, as loud and off-key as I pleased. I jumped into a stiff pair of jeans, the ones that made my ass look square, and the "Pink Ivory" T-shirt, the one from Jesse's second solo show. I pulled my hair back, slapped myself awake, and did a quick evaluation in the mirror.

Meh.

My skin always looked peaked then, pale but not in a pretty, luminous way. Puffy blue eyes, hidden artfully behind perfectly normal, wire-rim glasses, a pimple or two, not so bad. Straight, light brown hair, no bangs, not then. No one had shown me yet what choppy bangs could do for my particular face-shape. No one had booted my cigarette habit or whipped my skin into shape, or paid for my Lasik surgery.

My cell phone went off—Jesse Cannon ringtone, of course—interrupting my self-assessment.

Work.

And that was it, right there: answering that goddamn call from work. I cannot tell you the hours I've spent wondering what my life would be like today if I had just ignored that call. I still cannot tell you what possessed me to answer it.

It was Steve, my manager. Long story short, the place was crazy and he wanted me to come in on my only night off.

"No way," I balked. "I have plans."

"Bullshit, Jordan. You have a tube of cookie dough and stolen cable."

I should mention here that Steve was also my roommate.

"What I do with my night off is none of your business!"

"It is when you screw up my Tivo," he countered. "Whatever. Look, you have to come in tonight. *Please.*"

He pleaded, I refused, and this went on for almost a full minute, which, in crowded bar minutes, is a significant amount of time. He was that desperate, the place was that packed.

"Trust me, you *want* to be here for this," he added, with a hint of amusement. "You'll hate yourself if you don't get here quick."

I wasn't falling for it. "For what? Fat tips?"

"Just trust me!" he blurted, hanging up.

I snapped my phone shut, appalled. Just who did he think he was? I'd been holding up my end of the rent. I replaced the milk carton, every time. Did he really think I needed the money that bad?

Prick. I *did* need it that bad.

I was lacing up my slip resistant shoes before the sun was completely down, grudgingly gathering pocket change for the bus, going over the math in my head. Busy night. Empty pockets. And Jesse Cannon's final shows coming up this weekend, the last performances before his impending move to L.A. I could make enough on a busy night to swing a scalped ticket, easy. And now I could negotiate a night off to see the show.

Thirty minutes later I was in downtown Manhattan, trudging toward The Crescent's blinking lights. Steve sure hadn't been lying. People were packing themselves through the front door, forming a jumbled line against the wall. The bouncer looked hopelessly out of his element, funneling in not just the usual types, but an overwhelming mix of clubbers, leather guys, fierce nine-to-five skirts, drag queens, hipsters, scene snobs, and the musical elite.

I ducked around to the service alley and through the kitchen door, stunned to find no chaos in the back of the house. Quite the opposite, actually. The entire staff was crowded by the swinging doors, and none of them even noticed me entering.

What the hell was going on? I strung on an apron, immediately noting with delight that a Jesse Cannon song was playing in the dining room, a welcome but weird omen. "All The Difference", the very same song I used for my alarm. Only it was a version I'd never heard before, a beautiful, more playful take. The original? A live track maybe? Too many voices were singing along to tell.

This is why I don't work karaoke night, I reminded myself. *Too out of control.*

Steve burst through a cluster of cooks while I was washing my hands. He grabbed both my soapy wrists and shook me, shrilly panicked.

"He's here!" he squealed, hopping in place.

"Who? The health department guy?" I asked, more irritated than alarmed.

Before I knew what was happening, Steve had dragged me to the front of the house, stopped me abruptly behind the bar, grabbed the sides of my head, and twisted it around so that I was facing the far corner of the place.

"*He's* here."

My heart bungee-jumped to my feet and my jaw went slack. He *was* there. Way in the back, seated at our dilapidated piano (which had never been tuned, to my knowledge), barely more visible than a mirage between the people who were packing the dining room to see him.

Jesse Cannon.

No one heard me scream. Too many people were singing.

"He's been here a whole hour and I don't know what the hell he wants!" Steve started pulling me back to the other end of the bar, rambling about drinks. "Some sweet thing with strawberry liqueur but not pink? Is that even possible? Something about a sparkling *boy*? Used to get it here all the time, my ass. That was three years ago. I don't even know who worked here three years ago!"

"Boye Sparkle," I said, automatically.

Steve threw his arms forward and hugged me. A little too hard. "I *knew* you'd know what he was talking about!"

"Yeah, it's champagne with—"

"I don't care what it is, just make it happen!" He giddily pushed me to the mini fridge and started hopping again.

"But we don't have the stuff!"

"Make it happen!"

My head was spinning across the shelves, glancing over labels. Jesse Cannon. No mango purée. Jesse Cannon. No champagne in the house. Jesse Cannon, I'm sorry. I cannot make you a Boye Sparkle.

But I can make you something better.

A kind of emergency mode came over me, and Steve gave me a wide berth. I remember it like an out-of-body experience, like I was standing there watching myself turn bottles and pour liquor. Otherwise I wouldn't have been able to do it at all. I would have broken something with my trembling hands or puked into the blender. My nerves were the only hurdle. The drink was the easy part, always had been for me. If it had to get you drunk and it had to taste positively exquisite, then I was your girl.

Steve hadn't hired me just because I was his friend.

I still remember every ingredient, every measurement, every ounce of that drink. Toss four ounces of orange juice and a shot of vodka in the blender with a few strawberries, puree setting. Infuse with soda water in a tall glass, drop in two ounces of strawberry liqueur, peach schnapps, a touch of scotch. Coat a fat strawberry in coarse cane sugar and set it oh-so-carefully on top.

We stared at it in wonder, as if the concoction had been poured into the Holy Grail.

And then the drink was whisked out from under me. I watched, holding my breath, as Steve weaved through the pandemonium, all the way to the piano. I wanted to look away, should have looked away, but I just couldn't take my eyes off *him*, not while he was *right there*.

Jesse Cannon took the drink into his right hand without so much as a sideways glance, his other hand still rolling carelessly across the keys. A break came in the chorus and, still playing, he put his outrageously symmetrical, silken lips to the edge of the glass, tilted it back...

I saw him make a face like something had hit him between the eyes.

He immediately sat the glass down on the piano's lid and went right back to singing, playing with both hands, never missing a single beat.

The bridge came, then the ending chorus. Jesse belted out the last of the song, oblivious to the fact that he had just crushed a young woman irreparably. As all those people continued piling in, lining up around the building, each of them vying to get closer to the decade's most beloved up-and-coming celebrity—*my* celebrity—I just stood there behind the bar, trying to think of a place big enough to curl up and die in.

What had I done wrong? Was it the sugar? No, scotch and vodka don't normally complement, but when paired with just the right—

"Excuse me!"

I looked up and made probably the most embarrassing sound ever produced in the human throat in the history of forever, something between a goose honk and a whimper.

Jesse Cannon was directly across the bar from me.

I had seen him in person many times, it's true, but never this close, never like this. It was quite obvious that he'd been drinking *long* before I'd shown up, yet the effect only enhanced his perfection. Every misplaced hair was spun gold; every bead of sweat was a drop of ambrosia. Those unbelievable lips of his were smoothed into a wicked smile, while his amber eyes were strangely severe, the eyes of a god about to pass judgement. I half expected lasers to shoot out of them.

"I need to know who made this," his demand soared over all the clamor behind him. He nudged the empty glass forward.

Steve sacrificed me, pointed at me without pause or mercy. I was frozen instantly. Helpless to defend myself, I cowered in my own hideous mortality.

"Is there something wrong?" Steve started. "I could offer—"

"You can offer me anything later, honey," Jesse took a moment to wink suggestively at him before shifting his attention to me. "But this, *this*," he purred, tapping the glass, then just moaned, as if there weren't words, closing his eyes rapturously.

I felt my knees liquefy. My eyes stung because I had stopped blinking entirely. I couldn't move, much less respond.

The throng of people behind Jesse were whooping, pressing close. Someone slapped his famous rear, and he swiftly returned the favor before pivoting back to me. He leaned down from his lofty height to put his elbows on the bar, as if to invite continued assaults from behind while he tormented me.

"Oh, you liked that show, huh?" he jerked his chiseled chin at me, and I remembered what I was wearing. *My stupid shirt,* I groaned inwardly. *My stupid fucking Jesse Cannon shirt. Stupid stupid stupid . . .*

I backed up, reaching behind me for the glassware shelf. I must have looked like a girl reaching for something to bludgeon a snake or mouse with. I had never been so terrified in my life.

"D-Do you want another one?" I warbled, getting my hand around a clean flute glass—

"Oh, no, darling. I want *you*."

—and dropped it promptly to the floor, where it shattered into a thousand tiny pieces.

Some guy sidled up, and without even looking to see who it was, Jesse slinked an arm around his waist. He lifted his free hand and rolled his fingers at me hypnotically. "Come, come, come . . ."

Steve pushed me forward and smacked me against the bar.

"Everybody!" Jesse spun away suddenly and shouted in a startlingly loud tenor. The room roared in response, and Jesse leaned back against the bar, so close I could smell the new denim. "Where will I be next week?"

Woeful booing broke out. "Los Angeles!" people shouted. "Leaving us!" they cried. "In my pants!" yelled one of the leather guys.

Jesse laughed, then jumped up straight. "But where am I tonight?"

"New York!"

"New York!"

"My pants!"

"New York," Jesse confirmed. Like clockwork, someone thrust a shot into his hand, and he lifted it into the air. "*Na zdarov'ye*!"

Whatever *that* meant. The resounding cheer was unintelligible and endless. Jesse drained the shot and wheeled back around, beaming, hunting down my eyes again. His face was startling this close up, its glow fueled by all the cheering. And the additional alcohol, no doubt.

"Come with me," he commanded, concealing a slur. "Come to L.A. with me, and drive my car and mix my drinks. Make all of them as good as that one, girlfriend, and I'll never leave home without you. "

Oh God. Jesus. Bloody Mary. Jim Beam. I had no legs at that point. They seemed to have become completely useless. I gripped the bar for support.

"I've been out there!" Jesse was raving. "And those people in L.A. can't pour their way out of a wet paper cat."

Agreeable cheering all around. He didn't have to make sense to work up a crowd.

Jesse outstretched a hand to me. A beautiful, elegant, piano-loving hand.

"Come on," he grinned coyly. "You can't possibly have a reason to say no."

Something in me unfastened and flew away as I stared at that hand, like I'd just gulped down a tank of helium. The feeling terrified me, because I didn't know what it was. There were so many things I didn't know, that I couldn't have known.

I didn't know that one week later, I would be carrying twice my weight in Louis Vitton luggage through the JFK International Airport, or that everything I enjoyed about life at the moment, every friend or aspiration I had, would soon vanish into the vacuum of one person's demands.

I didn't know that at that same moment, it was still late evening in Filbert, Missouri, where Jackson was shaking the fire-marshal's hand at his own induction ceremony. Or that, at 3:00 a.m. London time, Corin was squeezing his elderly mother's hand as she passed away. That in the late and lazy Seoul morning, Su Kim Khan was being dumped on the curb outside his employer's residence, hours after having alkaline poured into his eyes. That a storm had kicked on the generators at the Emirates International Hospital just before dawn, and that Ghiyath Ayman was waking up in the dark after a year of endless sleep, confused, terrified, and without a name.

There were a million reasons to say no. I just didn't know any of them yet.

"Okay," I heard myself say, and I took Jesse's hand.

He was already holding another drink, some electric blue thing. Without spilling a drop of it and without releasing my hand, he leaped onto the bar and hoisted me up beside him. A tall drag queen in neon yellow thrust a shot glass into my hand, and Jesse wrapped an arm around me, pulling me close. I went numb. I couldn't see. I smelled strawberries and vodka and music and sex and magic. He howled and the room howled back.

"What's your name?" he asked into my ear, under all the cheering.

"Jordan."

"To Jordan!" he sang, and punched his glass toward the ceiling. More screams. And then Jesse Cannon, *Jesse Fucking Cannon*, pulled me right off my feet and kissed me fully and fleetingly on the mouth. My toes touched down again. I threw the shot down my throat and never felt the burn, because that was when I passed out and fell off the bar.

Guess who paid for the visit to the emergency room? And guess who had a new job and a minor concussion in the morning?

CHAPTER 23

I wasn't afraid at the beginning. I couldn't remember anything worth being afraid of. I just knew that I was warm. God that felt nice. I could bottle that feeling and become a billionaire.

I tested my eyes and saw that I was in heaven.

I saw an angel.

A radiant angel, with a tranquil smile on her smooth, perfect face. Her fair hair fell forward as she looked down into my eyes, ready to take my hand and walk me to paradise.

"Wake up, girlfriend," the angel sang.

Wrong. I was in hell. My own personal hell simply wouldn't be complete without Jesse Cannon.

"Jesse?"

He was leaning over me, seated beside me on whatever I was lying on. And he was still smiling. Something was wrong about that. I tried to remember why.

"What's your name?" he asked with a bored sigh, flipping the tumble of hair out of his face when he sat up straight. "I'm supposed to ask you that."

I froze for a moment, stunned that I didn't quite know the answer. So I said the first thing I could think of:

"Whitney Leroy Jackson," I slurred. "But you can call me Jackson."

Jesse's face lit up and he stifled a laugh. "Oh, honey," he said. "That one's new."

Why, *why*, did he have to be here? I groaned and scrunched my eyes against a headache, blinking them open again. My surroundings blurred into focus: white walls, a television, my feet, a heavy oak door. I was lying on a bed with railing and buttons and lights. Hospital room. Not the bar. Not Steve's apartment. Not the L.A. beach house or the bus. My heartbeat picked up, faster and faster, and very suddenly I felt the overwhelming urge to hide.

"Where are we?" I could hear the terror in my own voice, but I didn't understand why it was there.

Jesse's bemused smile quickly faded, and his brows creased with an almost maternal sympathy. "Someplace completely safe," he said patiently, pushing a tangle of hair off my forehead. "I promise."

I made the decision to believe him. My eyes roamed for a long time, looking at the same things over and over again, searching for something that would pull everything together in my mind and make sense. It wasn't working.

"You're fine," Jesse assured me, his hand still meandering idly through my hair. "You just have a *percussion*."

I frowned and surveyed myself, realizing that I was wearing one of those stupid, papery hospital gowns. Sleeveless. My left shoulder, from what I could tell, was a mess of tubes and gauze and tape. I didn't dare pull up the blanket to investigate further. The electrical burn was a numb, dull thud and nothing more. Bless you, Madam Morphine.

"A *concussion*," I corrected him in a surly tone.

Jesse yawned and patted my shoulder. "There's my Jordan. Still the smartest girl I know."

Something was still bothering me about him being there. It wasn't that I was necessarily irritated with him, not anymore than usual. I just felt for some reason like he *shouldn't* be there.

I focused on him, then back to the burn bandages, and then I started to remember. It all began to crash back, out of order, the memories dizzying and horrific and indistinct: Rushing water. Ghi, the blood. The elevator. Jesse, writhing and wailing on a tiled floor, his hands evaporating into thin air.

"Jesse!" I shouted, wanting to spring upwards, but I had no leverage. The hand he had been petting my shoulder with was suddenly pressing me down.

"You died!"

"I know," he said calmly.

I became borderline hysterical. "And you and Ghi and Corin and everybody. Everybody died. All of you and ... what? How?"

"Jordan, I know," he said, stern and composed, but also tired. So wretchedly tired. "I *know* what you saw. But you have to calm down. We're okay. All of us are fine, I promise."

The scalding stairwell door. The ghastly white skin, bursting apart, and Dahrkren's mind-numbing scream. Where had it all gone, if this place was safe? How were they alive, if I had seen what I did?

"How?"

"Just relax, *please*."

Relaxing wasn't an option. He looked so perfect, whole. It made no sense at all.

"But ... is it over?" My mind scrambled to filter the images, to put them in order. "That guy, that *thing*, is it dead?"

Jesse's lips stiffened and he shook his head.

"No. It's not over. Dahrkren bailed before we could—" He had to interrupt himself, such was the sudden increase in my panic. "Listen, he can't come here. No Hollow can, I promise. Okay?"

Not okay. I needed details.

"Where's here?" I demanded. "Tell me what happened."

He *owed* me. He owed me whatever I wanted.

I held him in a stern glare, making my case perfectly clear without ever saying a word. And while glaring, it dawned on me how he looked. There was no evidence of his disfiguring wounds, not a single scar, not even the shiner I'd given him myself. Stranger still, he appeared lighter somehow, buoyant, ethereal. His hair a little more weightless, limbs leaner, eyes slightly more slanted. Hell, if I was seeing correctly, then Jesse Cannon looked more physically immaculate than ever before, and that was something I wouldn't have thought humanly possible.

Yet he also looked so profoundly, awesomely tired. Outright worn out and crestfallen. Things were not as alright, as safe, as he was trying to convince me. I was sure.

"Jesse. Tell me . . ."

He sighed, insolent and exasperated. Still the same Jesse.

"It's just hard to explain," he complained, then paused to study me with a smirk. "Not to mention I've sort of told you about it like, *seven* times already . . ."

Right. The concussion.

Like I cared. "Go on, " I coaxed. "What happened after you died?"

"We didn't *die*, Jordan," he insisted. "We were all just . . . something else for a little while."

I thought about his body trailing off into nothingness. The monstrous tidal wave, and the blinding light. I remembered the kicking of the earth beneath me and the crackle of thunder, the heat, the water, and the ripping wind.

"Something else," I repeated.

Jesse nodded.

"Our true forms, let's just put it that way," he said. "We just became our true forms for a little while, out of necessity. That's all. And then, back to this." He gestured at his not-so-true form, which he was obviously still very pleased with. Some things never change.

But I still didn't understand. My mind tried to wrap itself around that concept, grasping to distinguish between relief and horror and morphine. If he was talking about what I *thought* he was talking about, then we should both be dead.

"Jesse? You *Became*? Isn't that supposed to kill you—"

"Oh, no, no, no," Jesse frowned and stopped me, surprised that I'd come to that conclusion. Evidently, we hadn't gotten this far during my previous bouts of consciousness.

"You didn't witness anyone Becoming, Jordan," he said, crossing his arms somewhat haughtily. "We can only do that under certain, *pacific* conditions, you know."

"Specific. Fine. What the hell was it then?"

Jesse uncrossed his arms, opting to place his hands on his hips for more effect.

"Well. I don't know. But it wasn't *that*," he declared, agitated. "It just . . . happened. We all changed, yes, but it was too soon. That's what they were telling us the whole time. Not out loud, but in our heads. Except we didn't have heads, so—"

Okay.

So maybe Jesse Cannon was not the best person to get me all caught up on the Vessel's alleged out-of-body experiences. I squinted my eyes closed, waiting for a brief surge of headache to pass, and then held up a hand to curb his incoherent speech.

"Come here," I said.

It could wait. What mattered was clear: I was breathing, and Jesse was—well, he wasn't dead. He bent toward me, and I reached up with my right hand to touch the surface of his face, the side that had been more or less gone before, just to be sure. He held still and watched me expectantly, unoffended by my soft gasp of surprise.

Jesse wasn't human.

Whether or not he had been before, he definitely wasn't now.

There is no way to describe what he felt like, not a single analogy in existence which really nails it. Sticking an open hand out the window on the highway at 80mph comes to mind, and yet it was nothing like that at all, because nothing was moving and there was more tangibility to him, more substance. He felt how the smoke from a dry ice machine would feel if it were something firm, something solid that you could actually touch.

What had happened, how it had happened, and the impossible physics against my fingers—it didn't have to make sense anymore. Jesse was undamaged, warm, and in one piece. I wanted to keep my hand where it was, afraid he would start evaporating if I moved it.

"So you're really okay?" I asked. "I'm really okay?"

"We're really okay." Jesse smiled. The slight shift of muscle felt almost like a breeze against my palm.

And then his expression changed again. It plummeted to an illustration of serious and resigned melancholy, a very un-Jesse-like expression. He lowered his head down, pressed his forehead into my good shoulder. "I'm so sorry," he murmured.

"Save it," I said. The apologies could wait. I'd never forgive him, of course. But at the moment, I was content to let the morphine keep dripping and to have my closest friend sitting with me. Letting all nightmares melt away into drug-induced oblivion, I closed my eyes, breathed in Jesse's smell—which hadn't changed, I noticed—and put my arms around him.

I put my arms around him . . .

I put my arms around him . . .

Let's try this again:

I put.

My arms.

Around him.

Well, one of my arms was going around him. The left one was—why wasn't it moving? It was under the blanket. All the damn tubes and bandages. It had been numbed. Yes. Yes, that was it.

Jesse tensed, like he wasn't ever going to move again so long as he could help it, like he wanted me to stay just as I was, sleepy and assuaged. I pulled my right arm back around him and reached to touch the other, to feel the bandages, see how much it hurt, assess the damage.

I remember reaching, feeling, for much longer than I needed to.

Like it would just be there if I checked more thoroughly.

"Jesse," my voice croaked, and then it grew a dangerous edge. "Jesse . . ."

He was sitting up, looking at my face. So tired, so tired.

I choked. Heat rushed to my face. I was talking but the words had no sound behind them.

"Jesse! What is this? *What the fuck is this?!*"

That last part came out just fine. I screamed. I threw the sheets and blankets to the foot of the bed, looking at myself in frantic disbelief. I pushed Jesse away, took a frantic swing at him, and he just sat there, saying nothing, doing nothing, looking so completely exhausted and despondent.

Of course he did. I woke up more than once that day, into a fog of total confusion, a murky blank slate. I only remember losing my arm one time.

Jesse remembers all eight times, and it serves him right.

CHAPTER 24

"The blinder is completely unnecessary at this point, you know."

"As you've told me," Stella noted flatly.

The blinder stayed on.

Stella was sitting in a private parlor, her small frame tucked into the end of an impressive antique love seat. Impressive from what she could determine, anyway, given the feel of the silky, pinstriped fabric against her fingertips, and the smell of the lemony polish on the ornate wood.

"Suit yourself."

She heard the speaker ease into a facing chair, maybe ten, twelve feet away. He was a senior consul, one she had spoken to once before, during the initial meeting regarding the Vessel assignment. She had never lain eyes on him, and did not plan to lay eyes on him now.

Stella had seen enough in the past week, she realized, to kill any hopes of further hunting assignments. This reality did not make her happy, but she wasn't about to damn herself with even more information, and so she had stubbornly kept herself blind during most of this week-long limbo. The consul's request to meet with her was no cause for alarm; it was to be expected, and besides, there were a few select things Stella *did* want to know, despite her aversions. She was hoping these same things would be the consul's mind as well.

Unfortunately, his mind—whatever was on it—seemed to be resigned to a leisurely and excruciatingly slow pace.

"Scotch?"

The bass of his voice told her that he was a tall man, and its amber cadence told her that he was black, older, in his mid-sixties maybe.

"No thank you." *Get to the point, geezer.*

There was the pouring of liquid against expensive glass, the rifling of papers, and the creak of the chair as he settled back.

"I had a very long chat with the rest of the Consulate before making my way here," he began. "I think you'll be very pleased with what was discussed."

"Oh?" *Spit it out, then.*

"Yes, yes, but first," he interrupted himself with a sip of scotch, "they did want your opinion on another matter or two."

Stella stroked a finger over the carved edge of the armrest. "Alright."

The consul sighed, took another sip of scotch, "Well, the young lady, for starters . . ."

"A liability." Stella snapped immediately. Was the man joking? "When we arrived at the scene, my order was to let nature take its course, in her case."

The consul didn't pause for long, but his manner of speaking was unbearably slow. "And yet it's my understanding that you are the one who . . . *relieved* her of the afflicted limb, in order to save her life. That's true, yes?"

Push me, grandpa. Just push me. "There was no way of telling if she'd been changed. She would have been an even greater liability as a Hollow."

The consul sighed patiently and assumed a more comfortable position. "Yes, well, the issue still remains."

Stella inhaled sharply through her nose. This dancing around bit was wearing thin on her already. There was no point to this. The correct and sane answer was already obvious.

"I may have been behind this blinder for five days, sir, but I am aware of the situation. Bringing her here was a terrible idea. What you are proposing is worse. Unnecessary, harmful, and dangerous."

The glass of scotch chimed with ice, shaking slightly with the consul's short laugh. "Since when do our hunters care anything about danger?"

Petulant, ignorant . . . I'll show you danger.

"There are other options, other locations. More sensible arrangements."

"Yes. But the other consuls agree, as does your friend, Mr. Sharma," he contended, and Stella bristled at the baseless association to Abe. "We feel that it is wiser at this time to placate the Vessel, to make some concessions at least. And at this point, in her case, what difference does the location make?"

"Probably about as much difference as my opinion makes, from the sound of things," Stella replied coolly.

The consul cleared his throat, and that was that. The shuffling of paper filled the tense pause, and Stella waited with concealed smugness for the next topic.

"Well then, I suppose you're interested in how we'll be covering your tracks this time around?"

Stella said nothing. She was, in fact, not at all interested.

"The bridge fiasco was not that difficult," the consul began explaining, regardless. "We have framed matters to the public so that Su Kim hi-jacked Mr. Cannon's bus in Chicago and then died in the crash. He had no issues complying to that story. I imagine, since he owes money and prison time in several nations, that he is better off dead.

"The others, however, wish to maintain contact with friends and family, so—"

Stella was suddenly interested. She was almost interested enough to stand up.

"You can't be serious," she said abruptly. "Surely. They should all be written off as dead, without exception. There isn't any other reasonable way to extract them from society. Sir, imagine the risks. To our intelligence, to the people they contact."

"We are certainly aware of the risks, Rosin," the consul said, with infuriating serenity. "Any contact they make will surely be limited and very secure. And we are coming up with appropriate alibis for all of them.

"Mr. Cannon, for instance. He escaped with his life before the crash and is currently recovering in Philadelphia. He released a public announcement this morning stating that he is canceling his tour and going on an indefinite private sabbatical due to the psychological trauma sustained during the ordeal.

"Which is really such a shame," sighed the consul. "I do so love his music, don't you? My granddaughter got me hooked on that one song, the one with the . . ."

For a brief and horrible interlude, Stella heard only humming and rhythmic creaking motions coming from the consul's' chair.

And then laughter, another sip of the increasingly watered-down scotch. "Now, as for you, Rosin. We at the Consulate are very pleased with how you conducted the assignment. So much in fact, that we've come up with quite an offer for you."

This honestly surprised Stella. A bridge and a factory destroyed, lost limbs, the Vessel encountering Dahrkren himself. She'd assumed that the Consulate would be mad as hell.

"Oh?" was all she felt the need to say.

Here it comes, she thought. *Just go ahead. Tell me where I'm confined to so I can take this thing off already, so I can go sit around and get old like you.*

"Rosin, the Elysium is, I dare say, our most secure property. There's no chance the Vessel will be under any threat so long as they remain on its premises."

Stella's lukewarm, fuzzy thoughts of retirement suddenly hit a brick wall. Why was he talking about the Vessel, the Elysium? What about the Consulate's offer? Was he jumping subjects? Was he senile?

"But that says nothing," he continued, "as to how secure they will be the day we expect them to face threats. Against the Hollows, even the younger examples, well, you saw for yourself what happened."

Oh shit.

"It won't matter how powerful they become, how easily they can succeed against Dahrkren, if they can't make it to him first. It is absolutely vital that they are shown how to defend themselves against *any* Hollows."

No, no no no no no . . .

"What we've discussed, actually, is retiring you to the Elysium to educate them on that front, so to speak."

Another sip of scotch. It suddenly sounded delicious.

"You're joking," Stella said sullenly.

"Not in the least."

"Someone else," she faltered for words, gripping the armrest. "Anyone else could teach them—"

"We can't spare anyone else right now," the consul said plainly, his charming nature suddenly dissolving. "And even if you weren't perfect for the job, you must realize that your options would still be quite limited at this point."

"For Christ's sake," Stella growled, raising her voice one iota. "Because I've *seen* them?"

"That has little to do with it." The consul paced his words carefully. "I believe you know what I am talking about."

Stella dragged a hard fingernail against the armrest, hoping to leave a scratch.

So that was it, then. Six years. Six years, they let an issue rest, and *now* they decide to address it.

"Is that why I was given this assignment in the first place?" Stella demanded. "To get me out of the way? Because of *that* incident?"

"You were given the assignment because we had faith in your talents," the consul parried, "and you certainly reinforced that faith. None of us could have foreseen the Hollow's level of readiness regarding the Vessel before we could even *find* them. Without your actions, we would have lost them.

"But the incident I suspect you are referring to . . . well, I won't say that hasn't been a factor in this proposed arrangement. I daresay we took risks by keeping you out hunting for as long as we did after that. It's simply best for everyone involved if you lay low from now on, you understand. We are aware of your familial situation, and we are more than willing to accommodate. You'll still have your monthly leave. Twice monthly, if you wish."

Stella allowed her nostrils to flare under the blinder, though her lips remained as stoic and smooth as carved marble.

"Think of it as an active retirement, Stella," he continued consolingly. "Would you honestly rather be set aside so early, with nothing to do?"

You have no idea.

The sound of the door opening did not startle her, since she'd been acutely aware of the approaching footfall out in the hallway. She was irritated immensely, however, when she heard who was entering.

"Hey, sorry! Didn't mean to interrupt anything."

"Knock, you cretin."

The voices spoke over one another but were easily distinguishable. The first being Jackson's loud drawl; the second, Corin's indignant, eloquent half-whisper.

"Oh, Stella. There you are."

And the third being Abe.

"No interruption at all. Do come in," the consul greeted them, his decorum-laced cheer returning instantly. "Rosin and I were just doing some catching up."

The door opened wider. Two pairs of footsteps were entering, followed by the thumping and creaking of crutches. Abe's knee had been shattered, Stella was aware, and he had sustained a minor concussion. What really caused him agony, however, was the fact that he'd been out cold for what he now kept referring to as "the best part".

"Oh good," he was saying, ambling across the room. "So we'll be working together again soon, Stella, am I right?"

"The consul and I will be discussing the matter further," she answered robotically, without a hint of the malice begging to be released.

"What's with the mask now?" Jackson asked with a grin in his voice.

Stella was aware of his large hand waving in front of her blinder. She drew on her innermost store of self-discipline not to reach out and break his thumb. "You said there were no Hollers around this place."

"Just an act of protocol," came the consul's reply. "One which Rosin will soon be putting behind her. Now, would anyone care for some scotch?"

Stella Rosin was the first to raise her hand.

CHAPTER 25

Pill bottles are not made for one-handed people.

Here's where I skip over the whole "trauma of losing a limb" bit. Granted, I don't want it to appear as if I was just the picture of acceptance after the initial shock. I wasn't. I could write volumes on the feeling—any amputee can. It's devastating, maddeningly frustrating, and it's something you never truly get used to. It's a total shit sandwich. It really is.

So yes, I was still furious, and yes, I was sick to death about the whole thing. But there was a lot of other traumatic debris taking up space in my head. Knowing someone who'd turned into a tidal wave and then back into a person again, for instance. The nameless, mindless force that was still bent on slaughtering all of humanity. The voice of death incarnate. Unanswered phone messages from my mother.

So many obstacles, starting with the orange pill bottle I was squeezing between my knees and clawing at.

"Oh, I can't watch any more of this. I'm going to be sick."

Jesse wasn't watching me. His glassy, pining eyes had been glued to the TV for hours and hours, taking in every possible moment of every possible news station. Occasionally, the discovery of an unsanctioned nuclear facility shared second place with the set of conjoined twins born in Germany.

And first place on every network, as you may have guessed, was Jesse Cannon's withdrawal from the public sphere, a story now tied inseparably with the death of escaped felon and crazed fan, Su Kim Khan.

Apparently, you really *can* make this shit up. If you work for the Luna Latum.

Almost as if he believed the fabrication itself, Jesse had been planted in front of the screen for five days, agonizing over the footage of the bus wreckage, of angry fans, supportive fans, hysterical fans. Girls weeping, and sound clips from baffled and empathetic celebrities. The tearful announcement by Jesse himself, filmed in the corner of this very room the night before. Candle-light vigils. Mobs outside of concert halls. Karaoke tributes. Oprah.

"I just can't believe this," he groaned. "Do you think I did the right thing?"

"It's a pretty dumb story, since you're asking," I said, pausing to curse under my breath when I tore a hangnail on the stupid bottle cap, which still refused to budge. "Seriously, Jesse. Who goes on a spiritual sabbatical to Canada?"

"I do."

"Can-a-da." I reiterated. "Why not Tibet?"

"*Puh*-lease," Jesse snorted. "Everyone goes to Tibet. Richard Gere goes to Tibet. Canada is original. *I'm* original."

"Don't have to remind me."

He looked away from the Kleenex carnage on the screen, tipping his head over the back of the couch that he had practically been living on, noticing my ongoing battle with the pill bottle. The brooding ceased and he was in front of me immediately, snatching at it.

"Let me get that."

I rolled my eyes, coveting the pills against my stomach. "I can handle it."

Five whole days in this windowless room, and Jesse's guilt tirade—when he wasn't watching his career fall apart on the evening news, that is—had been nonstop. I'd begun to curse the many times I'd fantasized about *him* waiting on *me* hand and foot, because the real thing was an absolute nightmare. I honestly wished the concussion would've lasted longer.

"Don't be stubborn. Here, hand it over," he urged, reaching out to pry it away.

"Jesse, enough already," I snapped and put on my best exasperated face.

After five years, I had crafted it to perfection. Better than a force field, that face. Jesse backed off and frowned at me, lower lip puffed out.

I sighed. "Why don't you just give me a little time to myself, okay?"

"But—"

"Jesse," I said, as gently, as sincerely, as possible. "I know you just want to help. But if you really, *really* want to make me feel better, you'd go make me a gigantic pot of coffee. Right now."

More frown. More lip.

"And you'd take, like, an hour to do it."

Jesse huffed air from his nose. He tapped his foot.

"Okay," he finally said. He leaned in and covered at least sixty percent of my face with kisses. "I love you."

"I know you do," I said, pushing him away. "*Go.*"

He backed towards the door. "Make sure you keep your temperature elevated. And hold your shoulder down."

Five days of that. Seriously. It really is a miracle that I'm alive.

"Black. No cream, no sugar!" I shouted at the closing door.

And then I was alone, gloriously alone. I would be for awhile, I knew, because short of pouring a drink from the blender or licking batter off the electric beater, Jesse had never touched a kitchen appliance in his life. I slid out of bed and immediately flopped onto the couch, plucking up the remote to turn the TV off. No more news, and no more charred tour bus. For a long, gratifying moment, I drank in the sweet linoleum silence. Then I took up the pill bottle again. It was almost two o'clock, and if I didn't swallow a few of these babies soon, I'd be hurting by two-thirty.

Goddamn child-proof lids. I was really putting my elbow into it, really concentrating, but my mind began to wander anyway. It began to go places I didn't want it to go.

Dark, mildewy places that smelled like blood.

I turned the news back on and flipped desperately through a dozen channels. Cooking shows, cartoons, animals ripping each other apart, commercials for Black Friday specials. Just focus. Pills. Think ahead. Think about where you're going to go.

Just a few more days, just to be on the safe side, the doctor kept telling me, every time she came in to check under the dressings. *And you'll be good to go.*

A few more days in this private Baltimore clinic, and then what? Jesse would get toted off to that island paradise or whatever, and I would go—well, somewhere. Anywhere I damn well wanted. I had options, right? There was my apartment in Los Angeles, a place I'd slept in maybe ten times since signing the lease. And there were my parents, of course. Although the thought of staying with them at this particular era in my life was less than appealing. I could always call on old friends. Yeah. Sure. Wherever they were now.

Total darkness. The sound of tearing skin.

I could move to Switzerland, enroll in hypnotherapy, sustain more blows to the head, whatever it took. I'd put this all behind me and deal with the arm thing. I'd get on with my life. No more cocktail parties. No more Hollows. The end.

Someone knocked on the door. The bottle sprang out of my grip and clattered across the linoleum at my feet.

"Damnit, Jesse!" One button. Most coffee machines have one button. Just one.

I glared over the back of the couch at the opening door, then fought the instinct to look immediately away.

I don't know who was more mortified—me or Ghi. He had one foot in the room, and he appeared ready to turn around on its heel and flee.

"Oh," he said. "Hello."

"Hi."

"I . . . they asked if I could get . . . the agent lady called again and . . ."

"Jesse's out," I said.

"Oh." Ghi didn't move. Apparently, his body had petrified to the door frame. I took the opportunity to look it over, since it had practically been a heap of shattered bones the last time I remembered seeing it.

Last time I'd seen *him*. Corin, Jackson, and Abe had all stopped by the room more than once, and I had gotten a singular glimpse of Khan sprinting past the open door—fleeing, apparently, from an eye exam (during which he'd burnt someone's hand). Only Ghi had not shown his face, not until now.

Which was understandable. He was sort of responsible for frying my arm off, after all.

The first thing I noticed while he stood frozen there was that he looked much . . . *smaller*. Less layers, no sweaters, I realized. He was wearing an ordinary, solitary T-shirt now, and the effect seemed to take off twenty pounds. The shirt also failed to hide what all those sweaters would have easily concealed.

I gawked. Ghi's bare arms were patterned like the topographical map of an island chain.

"Right. Okay. Thanks," he stammered. Having mustered the abilities to speak and move again, he turned and quickly left.

I didn't have time to take my eyes off the closing door, much less digest what I had just seen. Without a second's passing, Ghi burst back into the room, marched directly around the couch, and halted abruptly in front of where I sat, mashing a palm to his forehead in the universal gesture of unease and shame.

"Jordan, I'm—"

Oh, for crying out loud.

"Stop," I cut him off before he could say it. I swear to god if one more person said the word 'sorry' to me I was going to have to kill someone immediately. And I really didn't want it to have to be Ghi. I liked Ghi.

"Please don't say it," I said, my tone more earnest than stern. I wanted him to know I meant it. "Not to me. Not ever. Do you understand?"

He paused. I think he nodded.

"Sit down."

He sat. On the far end of the couch, away from me. We both stared uneasily at the TV for a moment, until, remembering the dropped pills, I bent forward and plucked them off the floor.

"So what did you need to tell Jesse?" I asked, renewing my attempt to get at the sweet pain-killing goodness inside.

"Nothing urgent," he said, and his eyes wandered down to my fumbling hand. Formerly buttery gold in color, those eyes were now a startling 24-karat. "Would you like me to . . ."

"No thanks."

He nodded and looked back to the TV—for my sake, I suppose. That gave me a chance to steal a good look at his arm, just to make sure my retinas hadn't been fooling me before.

They hadn't. Ghi's skin had a muted afterglow to it, not unlike mother-of-pearl; barely perceptible, still pale, still very passable as human. But in stark contrast to this quality was a web of pinkish, slightly puckered marks, spreading out in swirling patterns down half his forearm. Scar tissue.

I didn't get it. If all of Jesse's marks had disappeared, why hadn't Ghi's?

"What happened to you?" I asked frankly. The new amputee in me felt entitled.

Ghi looked at me like a deer caught in headlights, not comprehending the question, so I elaborated:

"Your skin. Why the hell does it look like that now?"

Ghi cleared his throat. "Oh," he said, running a nonchalant finger over a blighted elbow. "They're, um, burn scars, actually. From the other time I should have died." He mimed a gun with his hand, pointing it to his head with a little smile. "Burning building, remember?"

The new amputee in me suddenly felt like a total ass.

Ghi benevolently ignored my discomfort, shrugging. "I don't get it either, why I've still got them. Same with Khan and his tattoos. I mean, you saw Corin's arm, you saw Jesse and me. It's like none of that ever happened.

"But these . . ." He held an arm out, examining the scars for himself. "They've just been a part of me for too long, I guess. So when I came back, so did they. And that's alright with me."

My fingers fiddled absently with the bottle cap and I sank farther into the couch, giving all of that some thought. A bunch of light photons gaining mass, forming into a body, scars and all. I wondered what that had looked like. Probably pretty gross.

"What did it feel like?" I asked, this time in a civil tone. "While you were, you know, not quite yourself?"

I hadn't asked Jesse that question, for two reasons. First, I hadn't really cared to know. I didn't like thinking about him becoming something so violent. Secondly, I doubted he could describe it without giving me a migraine. You should hear him describe a pedicure.

Ghi concentrated on my question, shifting on the cushions so that he was turned toward me, although he wasn't necessarily looking at me. He wasn't looking at anything, really.

"It felt incredible," he said finally. "It felt like I'd been moving through this narrow tunnel my whole life, and all of a sudden—no walls, no tunnel. Only space, in every direction, and speed. I mean, using light is awesome enough, but *being* light? It felt so correct, so much easier. I've always been at odds with my own body, and I always thought it was because I had to get reacquainted with it, after my accident. But now I understand. And I didn't want to come back. None of us did."

Well that was an eye-opener. Far from the pain and terror I had been expecting. I outstretched my arm toward him, holding the pill bottle over his hand.

"So why did you?"

Ghi took the bottle without comment and began twisting at the lid. Instead of answering, he smiled a difficult, bashful sort of smile.

"This is going to sound weird."

"Oh, really?" I smirked, popping the solemn bubble surrounding our conversation. "Because I haven't heard anything weird lately."

Ghi shot me a look which clearly painted me as a smart-ass, and then frowned at the stubborn, unyielding plastic he was wringing between both hands. Told you it was a bitch to open.

"Well, *she* made me come back," he admitted. "I've been hearing her for awhile now, since the dreams started. But when I was light, when I was in that other place, I could hear her as clearly as my own conscience. And she told me to stop, because I wasn't ready. So," he shrugged, and the lid popped off, "I stopped. We all stopped. How many?"

"Two."

He tapped two gigantic blue pills into my open palm. "The thing is, I stopped, but she didn't. And she still hasn't. I can hear her right now, actually."

I blinked. That was, well—weird. Can't say he didn't warn me.

"What does she say?" I asked, before popping the pills into my mouth. One hand, one thing at a time. I grabbed a glass of water from the coffee table and drained them down.

"Nothing, really. I just know that she's here."

The thought filled me with a prickling self-consciousness. I considered the light coming through the blinds, filtering down from the fluorescent bulbs overhead, scrambling across the television screen in fragments of moving color. The air I was breathing. The water I'd just swallowed. All of it alive, seeing, thinking—and apparently speaking.

I wondered if light and water and everything had behaved differently before the sisters had performed their sacrifices. I wondered what they themselves had been like, what they'd looked like.

"What was her name?" I asked.

Ghi looked at me. He beamed.

"She can't remember."

Susan sobbed into the man's arms, speaking with rehearsed and remarkable diction despite her tears. Good old Susan. Good old bewildered, post-coma, pregnant Susan, looking up at that man's glaring cleft chin and telling him that he was the father of the child, that he was the one she loved, that she remembered everything.

"What a load of crap," I yawned.

Ghi snorted. We had been watching the poorly scripted drama unfold for about forty minutes, and by then my body felt halfway fused to the couch cushions. The Luna Latum doesn't fool around with pain medication. They use the good stuff, the stuff that works fast.

"Agreed." Ghi picked up the remote and started changing channels.

I lifted my eyes lazily toward the ceiling, dangerously close to a comatose state myself. "That reminds me, though." I yawned again. "Whatever happened to that head case terrorist? You know, the one supposedly loose in Manhattan?"

Ghi smirked, still clicking away, allowing one channel to stay on just long enough to get mildly interesting before flipping to the next. I guess all men are virtually the same in some regards, even the ones who happen to be gods. He recited his answer laboriously, like he'd been asked to repeat it several hundred times before.

"Ghiyath Ayman had a seizure in New York and lapsed into a second fugue. He was identified by federal agents and deported immediately to Amman where doctors will probably take pictures of his brain and stand around shrugging until he dies."

I nodded. This apparently wasn't newsworthy enough to tear any media attention away from Jesse Cannon, or I'd have heard about it.

I didn't bother asking Ghi why he hadn't opted for a fake death similar to Khan's. He hadn't because dead people don't get notified when someone from their past turns up looking for them. Ghi still wanted to know who he was. Or who he had been.

And how long would he have to figure that out? Not for the first time, it hit me that the Vessel were still left holding an unfinished and gruesomely heavy task. And while I could not help but wonder how soon they would be asked to repeat this nightmare, I did not dare ask my deepest store of intuition whether or not they could actually win round two. Or what would happen if they did.

Because, if everything played out like it was supposed to, if they indeed destroyed Dahrkren next time, would the sisters step in again? Would the results be the same? Or would the Vessel all cease to exist, like the story said they would?

Out in the hallway, an irate and unfamiliar voice exclaimed, "Will someone please tell me why there are coffee grounds in this paper shredder?"

At least I could guarantee myself one thing: I wasn't going to be around next time, that was for damn sure.

With a great deal of sighing, I cleaved my body from the couch and stood up, stretching toward the ceiling. As easy as sleep would have been, all the resting and morbid thinking was wearing on me.

"Sounds like Jesse is somewhere close," I said, "but feel free to wait in here for him, if you want." I began making my sluggish way to the door, and Ghi looked at me with rising alarm.

"Where are you going?"

I turned and shrugged. "I don't know. Just stretching my legs."

Ghi was already tripping over the corner of the couch on his way after me. "I don't think that's such a good idea."

I gave him an amused look and proceeded toward the door, at which point he pasted himself to it.

"Aren't . . . aren't you supposed to stay in here?"

"It's just a little walk." I smiled, charmed by the overreaction. "I lost an arm, not a leg, remember?"

Ghi stared at me with something like terror.

"That was funny," I instructed. "You can laugh."

He didn't laugh. And he didn't get out of my way.

"Ghi." I narrowed my eyes. "Move."

When he didn't, I shook my head, turned the doorknob, and pushed. Ghi allowed himself to fall out into the hallway, where he commenced to panic. Perplexed but nonetheless determined, I stepped around him to get my first look at what I'd been missing, immediately feeling my spirits rise. Five days is a long time.

It turned out I hadn't been missing anything particularly exciting. I already knew that this place was a private facility, a small infirmary, basically, and that's exactly what it looked like. The floor was shiny, the walls were a cheerful mint. There appeared to be a small lounge at the far end of the hallway, dominated by a large but rather bland portrait of a tropical volcano. An odd choice, I guess, but it went well with the walls.

I wondered how cold it was outside, and thought about how heavenly it would feel to simply stand in some fresh air, even if it was the not-so-fresh air of Baltimore. A nearby door opened, and a bored looking man in scrubs stepped out into the hall, carrying a plastic bag full of paper strips and coffee sludge. I recognized him as an orderly who had been in my room almost daily.

"Hi," I said brightly. "Which way to the door?"

The guy noticed me and did not look bored anymore. His attention jumped to Ghi, who was bouncing up and down beside me and practically eating his own fingertips.

"Never mind," I muttered. The less questions I asked in this place, I thought, the better. Picking a direction, I trudged down the hall, acutely aware that Ghi was just behind me, moving with excruciating tediousness. Was everyone back home going to act like this? Like I was made of fucking glass?

The hall opened into the light-flooded lobby. There was no front desk, no soda machine, only a short set of wide marble steps dipping below the gigantic volcano portrait, leading down to the front doors.

I stopped dead.

I stopped because three little green birds—three darling little parrots—flitted across the volcano. Then I frowned.

The portrait's trees moved and rustled in a gentle seaward breeze, the distant water glinted and crested onto a white ribbon of beach, and I gravitated, stupefied, toward what was not a framed photograph, but a spotless pane of glass.

"Ghi," I said gravely, pausing at the top of the steps. "This is not Baltimore."

A solitary white cloud scooted by above the volcano. No, not a volcano, I realized with a wave of nausea, but a building. The most mind-boggling building I had ever seen, perched on the horizon against a dual-blue backdrop of ocean and sky. A creamy golden goliath carved of stone, with five bevelled towers set in an ascending spiral, the highest one capped by a dazzling dome of stained glass. More acreage than the Taj Mahal. More curves than the Sydney Opera House. More helical, ornate beauty than the La Sagrada Familia—on steroids. No one had to tell me what it was.

The Elysium.

I spun and jabbed a finger back toward the window, repeating myself very loudly, and very shrilly. "This is not Baltimore!"

Ghi cringed.

"Jordan, wait," he pleaded, ducking down the steps in front of me, descending them in reverse with his hands held up beseechingly. My ears were too full of static to even hear him, and all I could see in front of me was the image of my own hand, heartily wringing Jesse's neck. I barely registered Ghi tripping, falling ass-backwards down the remaining steps and then sprawling his arms toward the door in some ridiculous attempt to block it.

I jumped over him and exploded into a balmy, tropical garden.

The microscopic shred of hope that I was simply seeing things, that I was suffering some drug-related illusion, vanished instantly in the sweet, floral, seventy-nine degree air. Shock kicked into high gear. Details snapped into focus. I heard the distant lull of ocean waves and the screaming of gulls. I smelled the salt. But I did not see the ocean.

I saw an elaborate brick courtyard spreading out before me, connecting a series of odd, disassociated buildings—a dome of tight mesh, a ceramic-lined crater, a long, isolated tunnel—all surrounded by a dense, tropical forest of waxy palms and bright ferns. The swath of vegetation seemed to stretch all the way to the distant Elysium, which loomed commandingly in its monstrous majesty, sun-bleached and streamlined, like something from an outer space Renaissance.

My scathing inspection then fell upon something much closer. In the center of the immediate courtyard, standing alongside Abe and a pair of men in lab coats, were Jackson and Corin.

They were playing shuffleboard.

"What the hell is going on here?!" I roared. A flock of parakeets took collective flight from a nearby fountain.

Jackson waved excitedly at me with a two-pronged shuffleboard cue, all smiles. "Only the best game *ever!*"

I stormed toward them. Even my shadow looked pissed. "I want to know why no one bothered to tell me *that I'm on a fucking island.*"

Corin had dropped his cue and was rushing to meet me. "We worried it'd upset you—"

"*It does upset me!*" I yelled. "*I am upset!*"

The infirmary door burst open behind me and out came Jesse, clutching at a ceramic carafe, Ghi following on his heels.

"Jordan!" he panted desperately, bounding toward me and shouting generics. "It's okay! Coffee! Look! Let's just settle down, and talk, and—"

I snatched the carafe from him and, gripping the handle fiercely, thrust it at his face.

Jesse ducked. Scalding french roast splashed over Ghi's head, and he howled miserably. I threw the emptied carafe down, and it bounced unsatisfactorily against the brickwork instead of shattering. "You lied to me!"

"I'm sorry!" Jesse wailed.

Not sorry enough. I lunged at him, but didn't get far. Corin looped an arm around me and dragged me backwards, hanging on until it seemed certain that my compulsion toward physical violence had timed itself out.

"I want to go home," I said, after he'd let go of me. "Now. Today."

No one said a word. Jackson had wandered over with Abe, whom I consulted immediately.

"Who do I need to talk to about getting home?" I demanded. "Who's in charge here?"

Abe leaned forward on his crutches, looking at me with sage patience. He didn't sugarcoat it, I'll give him that. "It won't be possible for you to leave, Jordan, not for awhile."

What?

Excuse me?

"Look, I have outstanding health insurance," I stammered, jabbing at the surprise ending of gauze and stitches that was now my left shoulder. "They can take care of this just fine back in Los Angeles, alright? So just tell me who can get me there."

But I already knew it was useless. I knew my arm was not the issue here. I could see where this was going, even before Corin, as he was so prone to doing, appointed himself diplomat.

"Jordan," he said. "You know this whole thing isn't over. The Hollows are still out there, loads of them. The Elysium is just about the only place they won't be able to get to you."

My entire body went pale, turned to lead. In my mind, I saw days, weeks, months . . . all stretching out ahead without a certain ending. My heart started pounding.

"No," I shook my head in total denial. "No, I don't care. I won't. I won't stay here."

"What do you mean, you don't care?" Jackson cut in sharply. "Those things'd hunt you down like starved dogs. It'd be suicide to go anywhere else now."

"Suicide!" I blurted, pointing at Jesse. "Suicide? Keep me here with him, with you freaks, for one more day, and I'll show you suicide! This is a mistake."

And it *was* a mistake. It was a joke, a bad dream. Someone would help me. Someone had to. I looked all around, seeking any other human form, and spotted only the two guys in lab coats, who had gone back to playing shuffleboard as if a hysterical kidnap victim was a daily occurrence on their island.

"I have rights, goddamnit!" I shrieked in their direction. I hope to god it cost one of them a point. "I'm an American!"

Jesse took a very careful step toward me, a sympathetic slant in his eyes. "Honey, this is the best possible outcome, really. Just be glad we stepped in. Stella wanted to send you off to some stuffy mansion where you wouldn't know anybody. Wouldn't you rather be with us? With me?"

There weren't words. There just weren't any.

I backed away from them, turning automatically to face some new commotion, something I hadn't even consciously noticed above my own shouting. A pulsing, dull white noise was beginning to drown out the sounds of chirping birds and crashing waves. Beyond one of the irregular buildings nearby, treetops were thrashing wildly, kicking vivid green debris into the air. And then, like some jet engine angel, a helicopter lifted into view.

Pure animal desperation propelled me forward. Not toward the helicopter itself, but in the direction it seemed to be headed. I sprinted around the infirmary and came to an abrupt ocean overlook, an apparent dead end.

It was neither a fright nor a relief to see Khan there, looking suspiciously in his element against the Pepto-colored sunset, indulging joylessly in a cigarette. A short, wiry woman with blond hair was standing several feet from him, also smoking, also silent. They appeared to be having the kind of interaction two smokers normally have after bumming a light: the non-verbal kind. With equal disinterest, they watched the helicopter glide by overhead, and only after I'd come to a frenzied halt between them did they seem to notice me at all.

"I have to go—" I heaved, "I need to get—"

"You and me both," Stella muttered, flicking her ashes over the wall, where a zig-zag of ramps led down to the beach.

I was at the bottom in another thirty seconds, hurtling across the white sand, waving a frantic, useless hand and pleading in a hoarse, equally useless voice after the retreating helicopter. Its bulk drifted effortlessly above the ocean, fifty yards out, then one hundred, two hundred yards. Higher and higher, further and further, until I couldn't have been more than a speck to the pilots. One very powerless, very exhausted, very pissed off speck.

Knees hit sand. Face hits sand. Ocean hits face. Face begins to sob.

It was a feeling more horrible than anything I could dredge up from the past week. It was like waking up at the end of something co-written by Alfred Hitchcock and M. Night Shyamalan—and there was nothing I could do about it.

"You okay down there?" Jackson shouted from above.

I looked up, feeling at once shameful and furious to see just the five Vessel, standing together on the overlook. Stella had vacated. I didn't blame her.

"Fuck off!" I rose up, rubbing sand off my face. "All of you, I mean it! I will *not* stay here!" For no other reason than to be out of their sight, I began marching down the beach.

"It's an island, Jordan!" Corin called out. "You're not going to get anywhere!"

I darted a choice finger at the sky and kept walking.

The funny thing about walking away in sand is that you can do it neither gracefully nor quickly. Walking closer to the water helps. Two arms for balance is a plus, I guess, but you still don't get anywhere very fast.

So when I turned around again, just to make sure that they weren't going to follow me, I could still make out their faces. They were all looking out at the ocean, watching that same helicopter glide off, and even from a distance, it was unmistakable:

None of them looked happy.

I understood. They were gods. But they were specks, too.

Not that it changed anything. I turned bitterly and trudged on, knowing it was a very small island. Knowing it was only a matter of time before I came right back around to them again.

ACKNOWLEDGMENTS

I owe the existence of *Vessel* to a number of people, not the least of whom being Lindsey Strain, who has been with us since the days when Corin's name was spelled with a 'K' and everyone in my head rode dragons to work. My sister, without your input, your encouragement, and your honest love, this could not have been done. Thank you for never letting me quit. And thank you most of all for the sharing of stories, which makes me happier than anything else in this world. May it never end.

To those who offered their time and talents to the bettering of this book, my deepest gratitude. To Beau Prichard, for his gentle brand of editing and his powerful brand of gusto. To my tireless proofreaders: Bryan Cook, Max Biringer, Erica Clark, and Austin Roberts (to whom I hereby dedicate any and all semicolons). Thank you for putting up with my fragments, and for caring enough to do such tedious and excellent work. You guys are the cat's pajamas.

Special thanks to: Carey Dunn, for his daily enthusiasm at each new chapter—and for his nightly patience as I wrote them under our roof. To Christina Jackson, who stumbled across sample chapters of *Vessel* in the Fall of '09 and wrote just to tell me she loved it. That was the first message from a stranger I ever received, and I never forgot it. Last but not least, to Lady Gaga, who reminded me before it was too late of this vital fact: that I am a tiger in my prime—fabulous, unstoppable, and covered in an armor of flaming sequins. I will thank you in person or die trying.

Endless love and gratitude to my wild and wonderful family, most especially to my parents, who have always pushed me to reach for great heights (even though I often frighten them on my way up). To everyone who has read *Vessel* or shown support—in Poca, Shepherdstown, Seattle, and beyond:

you are too many to name, but please know that you've had an individual part in making this book a reality for me. I thank you all from the bottom of my leopard-printed heart, and I can't wait to do it again.

Love,
Tom

ABOUT THE AUTHOR

Tominda Adkins lives, writes, works, and loves in Seattle, Washington, though she'd like you to know that she is from West Virginia. Tom fears marriage and spiders but not much else. Jesse Cannon is her spirit animal.

Reach Tom at vessel.tom@gmail.com, or read her very inappropriate blog at readvessel.com.

December 2011

VESSEL
BOOK II
THE _____ !?

Name the book.
Win big.

www.readvessel.com

CPSIA information can be obtained at www.ICGtesting.com
Printed in the USA
BVOW041058101011

273166BV00001B/2/P